HERE FOR A GOOD TIME

ALSO BY PYAE MOE THET WAR

I Did Something Bad
You've Changed

HERE FOR A GOOD TIME

A Novel

PYAE MOE THET WAR

ST. MARTIN'S GRIFFIN
NEW YORK

This is a work of fiction. All of the characters, organizations, and events portrayed in this novel are either products of the author's imagination or are used fictitiously.

First published in the United States by St. Martin's Griffin, an imprint of St. Martin's Publishing Group

EU Representative: Macmillan Publishers Ireland Ltd, 1st Floor, The Liffey Trust Centre, 117–126 Sheriff Street Upper, Dublin 1, DO1 YC43

HERE FOR A GOOD TIME. Copyright © 2025 by Moe Thet War. All rights reserved. Printed in the United States of America. For information, address St. Martin's Publishing Group, 120 Broadway, New York, NY 10271.

www.stmartins.com

Designed by Gabriel Guma

The Library of Congress Cataloging-in-Publication Data is available upon request.

ISBN 978-1-250-33055-0 (trade paperback)
ISBN 978-1-250-33057-4 (ebook)

The publisher of this book does not authorize the use or reproduction of any part of this book in any manner for the purpose of training artificial intelligence technologies or systems. The publisher of this book expressly reserves this book from the Text and Data Mining exception in accordance with Article 4(3) of the European Union Digital Single Market Directive 2019/790.

Our books may be purchased in bulk for specialty retail/wholesale, literacy, corporate/premium, educational, and subscription box use. Please contact MacmillanSpecialMarkets@macmillan.com.

First Edition: 2025

10 9 8 7 6 5 4 3 2 1

For S
you are still the only person for whom
I would hike a mountain

HERE FOR A GOOD TIME

ONE

"Are you up?"

A dry, ragged grumble comes out of my phone's speaker before Zwe's empty shell of a voice mumbles, "No."

"Can I come in?"

Another grumble. "It's . . . one forty-seven."

Whirling my chair around, I jump to my feet and, still feeling the buzz from my two post-dinner iced coffees, practically skip out of my office. "I know. But you won't believe what I just did."

"Unless it's *set the kitchen on fire,* I don't—" He pauses. "That better be a masked intruder knocking at my door."

"I'm coming in! Be decent!" I say, hand already turning the doorknob. "And if you're not, get under the covers."

I leave Zwe's bedroom door ajar behind me so that the living room light can stream in. Shirtless, he hauls himself up into a sitting position, both knuckles rubbing at his barely open eyes. "Please tell me you found out that the apocalypse has arrived and you've come to say a final goodbye. Because otherwise—"

I plop myself down at the foot of his bed, facing him. "What are you doing next Friday?"

"Obviously now hosting interviews for a new roommate," he mutters, shoulders hunched. I can just make out the utter contempt that flashes across his eyes. Still grinning, I scoot myself closer across the duvet.

"Well, you're going to have to push those auditions back three weeks, baby, because we're going away!"

"My god, you are *loud* at two A.M."

"That's what all my lovers have told me!" I yell, even louder.

His shoulders vibrate with his chuckle. "Okay, okay, I'm awake. Now, run this by me again? Is this the plot of your next book?"

I shake my head. "No, but it's book-adjacent. I, your best friend on this whole entire planet, in this lifetime and the next, have booked us a two-week-long, all-inclusive trip to—" I scrunch my gaze up at the ceiling, concentrating to make sure I get this right. "—Sertulu. It's this tiny island located near the Philippines, like somewhere to the right." I point to my own right to really solidify my geographical description.

"What—" Zwe scrubs one hand down his face. "—is that? Are you sure that's even a real place? Is this some PR trip Netflix invited you on? Or did you fall for an online scam where this place promised you that, I dunno, Michael B. Jordan regularly holidays there?"

"How dare you, I'm not *that* gullible. And no, it's *very* cool, I promise." I unlock my phone, the contrast between the room's darkness and the suddenly lit screen making me feel like I'm staring into the sun. "You're not ready for this, I swear." When the resort's home page loads, I thrust the phone in front of Zwe's face.

On reflex, he shields his eyes with the back of one hand. "Oh my god, have you never heard of dark mode? What are you, a boomer?"

Through squinted eyes, he takes my phone, and pulls the brightness bar to its lowest before actually reading anything. "Since when did Ms. City Girl want to vacation on a remote island?"

"It's at the sweet junction of 'remote enough to feel peaceful' and 'not *so* remote that we're wiping our asses with leaves we've foraged ourselves in the jungle,'" I explain. "And naturally, I have booked us a suite at the island's most exclusive resort. Well, it's the island's only resort. But it's still the most exclusive! Doesn't it look incredible?"

He's still scrolling through the Cerulean's website. Even when he's 80 percent asleep, Zwe's poker face is inscrutable. He scrolls, clicks, scrolls some more, clicks, clicks, scrolls, clicks, scrolls, scrolls—and finally hands the phone back.

"Poe, it's three in the morning."

I blink. "Yes."

"You booked us a trip to—" He nods at the now-black screen. "There. At three in the morning."

"Yes. I was *inspired*."

"By what? Did you start watching *Lost*?"

I put the phone down and smooth the front of my T-shirt. I'm on a high, and I will not be yanked back to reality by Zwe's quips. "Ironically, by my writer's block." When I glance back up at him, a small smirk is toying with the corners of his lips. "What?"

"Nothing," he says, but as soon as he opens his mouth to speak, the smirk reveals itself.

"What?" I ask, determined to get it out of him.

"You know I love you."

"Mm-hmmm."

"I just . . ." He chuckles and shakes his head. "Over the past four months, I have watched you take up *a lot* of hobbies to, you know, be inspired. Obviously, some of them have been less, um, *logical* than others—"

"Are we still on about the Legos? Because I would say that, to an extent, constructing a quarter of a Taj Mahal did get *some* of the creative juices flowing. I wrote a full two hundred words that first night. It's the most I've written in . . . in . . ." Four months. I don't need to say it out loud, though, because Zwe knows. Because he's *lived* it, right alongside me in our two-and-a-half-bedroom (the half is our converted office space) fourth-floor walk-up.

There were the aforementioned Legos, which came after the violin, but before the cross-stitching. There has also been the ukulele, pottery making, jigsaw puzzles, friendship bracelets, an eight-week planting class that I attended a whopping two times, and birdwatching.

And I know this trip is (arguably) more radical than jigsaws and misshapen "mugs," but at this point, I need radical.

"Maybe we sleep on it," Zwe offers. If you looked up "the voice of reason" in the dictionary, you'd find a picture of him, cleanshaven face with a small mole on his right cheek and all, two dimples tacking up either end of his smile. I press my lips and look down at the comforter. "It's nonrefundable, isn't it?" He sighs.

"Maybe."

"There was a refundable option and you deliberately picked the nonrefundable one, didn't you?"

At that, I look up and hold a finger to stand my ground. "Between flights and accommodation, that would've been close to an extra five hundred dollars. Five. Hundred."

He flicks the tip of my finger. "You realize I know the exact number of your book advance, not to mention your film deal," he counters, but without much conviction. Zwe is the most careful person I know when it comes to anything, including money, and I know that he knows that *I* know he would've had a small aneurysm if I'd paid that much extra for the refundable option.

"We haven't had a best-friend trip in ages!" I point out. Despite his admonishing side spiel, I'm still grinning. "It's going to be, as the kids say, *epic*."

"What kids?" he asks, bemused, and I know he's beginning to tip over to my side.

"The TikTokers."

"When did you say we were leaving?"

"Our flight is next Friday at ten thirty-two p.m."

"And what do we do with the bookstore for—" He glances around as though there's an invisible calendar on his nightstand. "How long did you say the trip was?"

"Two weeks. Well, sixteen days. But basically two weeks."

"The bookstore—"

"Will be fine." I rush to speak first. "I would bet money your parents will agree that you deserve a holiday, and that they can handle the bookstore on their own for two weeks. It *was* theirs first, remember? Last time I checked, it still is."

He glares at me. A real glare, not a sleep-shrouded squinting of the eyes. "You are the worst."

"Oh no, how dare I," I say, flattening my voice. "I'm sorry I booked us on a two-week luxury island getaway with first-class tickets."

"First-class—" He takes in a deep breath, and I bare my teeth in an innocent grimace. "You know first- and business-class tickets are the products of a capitalist, classist system."

"Yes, but it's a nine-hour flight. I would like to be cozy in a horizontal bed for a nine-hour flight. We don't have teenagers' backs anymore, old man." I poke one of his biceps. "These bones be creaking."

A ridge forms between his brows, and I still, knowing he's doing that Zwe thing where he comes at it from angles, making sure he's two—better yet, ideally three—steps ahead of any possible mishap. It's why he's my favorite beta reader—there hasn't been a single plot hole that Zwe Aung Win has missed. That, and the fact that even with my shittiest drafts, he always knows how to deliver criticism with kindness.

I haven't been the best best friend lately, I know this. Between the editorial meetings and Netflix production meetings and publicity meetings and the cumulative meeting-induced panic attacks and the erratic writing schedules and habits and my "weird" hobbies, I haven't been there for Zwe like I need to be. To be honest, if we didn't live together, I don't know how often I'd have seen him over the last few months. He's taken point on all the cleaning and cooking and general keeping-the-apartment-in-a-livable-state-ing, and although Zwe has never been someone who explicitly complains about anything, I know it must be taking a toll. For instance, at one point I realized that his morning jogs were about twenty minutes longer than usual, which was strange because Zwe likes to divide up his daily routine into as specific time increments as possible. When I asked him about it, he'd murmured something along the lines of *Have I? Didn't notice. My stamina must be building up,* which was a lie because I know Zwe runs to de-stress, upping his exercise whenever he needs to *really* work through lingering tension. It stung to know that, by process of elimination, *I* was the thing in his life that was causing him stress.

Hell, I didn't even know his now-ex-girlfriend Julia had broken up with him until I looked up from my laptop one evening last month and found him walking around with a cardboard box in hand to collect her belongings. The memory of that afternoon still hurts, because by the time I'd realized, he'd already gone through the worst of his heartbreak—by himself. My tunnel vision over this next draft has only worsened as I approach my deadline, but this trip will help me become both a better writer and a better friend.

No, scratch that—it will help me go *back* to being a better writer and a better friend.

It *has* to.

"I'm still not—" he begins.

"I need this," I say quickly. And when I meet his eyes, he knows what I mean.

Please, I beg through best-friend telepathy. We *need this*.

"I thought you liked those two chapters you started last week."

"I did, but now I don't," I say, feeling as deflated as I sound. This has happened so many times over the last few months that I'm not even particularly sad about throwing those chapters out into the ether. What's two more chapters anyway? You can't be precious about killing your darlings if you don't have any.

The writer's block started out as any author's routine case of Book Two-induced Writer's Block, but now it's . . . more. It's more prominent, more consuming, has transformed into something that alternates between keeping me up in the middle of the night and giving me nightmares when I do manage to fall asleep. But the harder I try to get over it, the worse it gets, like when you try to remember a dream but the more you concentrate, the faster the picture fades away.

Frankly, as absurd as it sounds, it increasingly feels like a moral failing, like I'm not working hard enough, like I'm being flippant with all the opportunities that have landed right at my doorstep. On my worst days, I view it as proof that I *got lucky* with my first book. That I have only ever had one good book in me, and it's only downhill from here. If I *really* wanted to, I could follow the steps of my anxious spiral even farther down: my book was the "ethnic" card, the big newspapers needed to throw in a "diverse" book into their Hot Books column, and mine just happened to be pitched at the right time, and of course those white reviewers only wrote good reviews because no one wants to be accused of being a racist. I was never good enough, maybe never even good, period.

"How do you always manage to bully me into doing exactly what you want?" Zwe's voice snaps me back to the now.

"Hmmm," I say, swinging my legs on the side of his bed. "By being so funny and charming that you have no choice but to love me. Oh, and by buying this place from our shitty landlord so that we wouldn't have to keep giving him our money."

"Now *you're* my shitty landlord."

"Excuse me," I say and get to my feet. "I'm your shitty land-*lady*."

"Okay, landlady, get some sleep, will ya?" he calls out behind me as I head for the door. "Despite this late-night detour, you still need to be at the store by eleven for the signing! I can't just reschedule a hundred people!"

Without turning around, I hold up a peace sign above my head. "Yes, boss. Anything for my fans."

I return to the office with the sole intention of turning off my laptop (it *is* 3 A.M. at this point), but I'm feeling too giddy to sleep. Giddy and buoyant and possibly inspired.

So instead, I sit down, open a blank Word document, and set a timer on my phone for fifteen minutes and a mental goal of one hundred words. I can write one hundred words in fifteen minutes, no problem.

The island was—

It was what? Bigger than she imagined? Smaller than she imagined? The most beautiful thing she'd ever seen? Something out of her worst nightmare?

It's just a first draft, I remind myself, a mantra that has echoed in my brain so often that by this point, the letters are etched into my brain cells.

The island was massive.

I tap my phone screen to see how much time is left, and then wonder if I'd actually set fifteen minutes because apparently I'm down to nine minutes and fifty-three seconds, and counting. There's no way the only words I wrote in five minutes were "The island was massive." It would be comical if the embarrassment weren't so searing that I felt like I was going to disintegrate into ashes. The cursor taunts me with each blink: *You. Suck. You. Suck.*

I spend the next approximate ten minutes staring at the timer, visualizing an hourglass filled with molasses. Eventually, all four numbers reach zero, the ringing sound goes off, I'm put out of my misery. I don't bother to save the document, instead closing it and dragging it straight into the trash bin icon at the bottom right of my screen where it can join my other ghosts of drafts past.

I've had bouts of writer's block for as long as I've been writing, but it was easier to manage when the stakes were lower and I didn't even have so much as an agent to send it to, let alone an editor. The most infuriating part, though, is that I know what it's like to be on the other side of this mountain, how buzzy and exhilarating it feels when the story comes so naturally as you're typing that the only thing holding you back is the fact that your fingers physically cannot keep up with your brain, that thrill that accompanies the knowledge that you've nailed something *perfectly,* whether that's something as small as the last sentence of a chapter or as big as a central plot twist. The high when you reread something you wrote yesterday and you know it's *good*. Even thinking about it now, I miss it so much that my fingers twitch.

In front of my bathroom mirror, before I wash my face, I remove my necklace, a gold chain holding an oval Georgian intaglio seal pendant set in gold. The red seal features an image of Cupid churning butter, the words PEU A PEU engraved along the top arch of the oval. It had been a present from Zwe when I signed with my literary agent, meant to serve as a reminder of exactly what it said: *Little by little*. As he'd put it, *Good things take time*. Lately, it feels like a taunt. I've been churning away at new drafts and yet none of them resemble anything like a finished product. Ayesha, my agent, keeps telling me to take as much time as I need for my next book, but I know my editors aren't going to wait forever, I know my marketing and publicity teams are hoping that I give them something *soon* so they can strike while the iron's hot. Because at some point, the buzz will die out, and I'll be a has-been.

Last month, another editor at my publishing house contacted Ayesha to ask if she'd pass along an advance copy of a novel coming out at the end of the year by Pim Charoensuk, a "fellow Southeast Asian author." The book was our publisher's lead title this year, and even before Ayesha's email, I'd seen how the hype was already steadily building. It felt like déjà vu—except the last time I'd seen this play out, it had been with *my* book. There are few things publishing loves more than a debut novel by a young, undiscovered talent; I should know.

Objectively, Pim Charoensuk, who, judging by her social media presence, is a funny, insightful, smart person, is not my competition. I know this. Objectively, it's hard enough to be a Brown woman, especially one from a non-Western country, trying to break into traditional publishing without having another author actively trying to compete with you; I also know this. We don't have the same agent or editor, our stories are wildly different, she's a debut, I'm a sophomore. Objectively, I shouldn't be jealous.

And yet, and yet . . .

Why are feelings so funny and illogical? And cruel.

It's far too shameful that I haven't even told Zwe, although I get the feeling that he knows. It must be obvious via the shift in my tone whenever I bring up Pim's book, because every time, *I* can feel my body tense as though I'm preparing myself for battle. It's not like she took "my" lead title spot, because I know I'm not entitled to it, and because I don't have a book this year that could have been in the running for lead title.

But what if? a voice taunts.

But what if I had written faster? What if I'd pushed through all this writer's block nonsense and finished a draft earlier? What if Pim's debut is a hit, and she delivers her second book quicker than I can?

After rubbing cleanser onto my skin, I turn the tap in front of me to full blast to drown out my thoughts.

Lately I've been listening to that Taylor Swift and Phoebe Bridgers song on repeat, wondering if anyone will still want *me* when I'm nothing new. Ten years from now, will I be on some snarky listicle titled *10 Authors Whose Debut Novels Showcased Literary Excellence, But Everything They Wrote Afterward Sucked*?

It's okay, I tell myself as I climb into bed. I just need a change of scenery, new activities to inspire me. I'm only nine days away from inspiration.

As I'm setting my alarms for the morning, a text notification appears at the top of my screen. The name reads *Soraya Mazhary.*

U up?

Soraya lived in the room beside mine during my first year at university. She was studying geography, and even though I didn't know anything about geography and she "didn't give two shits" (her words) about English, it was one of those relationships that, from our first conversation, felt like we were always supposed to have been in each other's lives, it had simply been a matter of time.

We had both signed up for the same Freshers' week club night event, and fell in step at the back of the pack on our way to Neon Bazaar in the chilly October air.

I'm starting to think this won't be worth it, I'd half joked, already regretting wearing a little black dress with no tights.

Wanna ditch it and go get ice cream? Soraya asked.

I laughed. She didn't. *You serious?*

She shrugged, and gave a head tilt at the group, almost all of whom were already drunk. *Most of them sound like proper twats, don't you think?*

I studied them, yelling and whooping down the cobblestones of High Street like they already owned the town. *They do*, I admitted.

And that was it. I've never been one of those people with a core friend group, and it turns out Soraya wasn't either; we liked that hanging out with each other meant hanging out with only each other, only two schedules to sync up, two similar tastes in restaurants and concerts and clothes shops to consider. When everyone was forming their little cliques during Freshers' week, Soraya and I were content being a team of two.

Now, she's got a toddler, and is a professor at the university.

Unfortunately, I type back. Trying to write. What's up?

Why are you writing in the middle of the night?

My thumb hovers above the video button at the top right, but in the end, I stick to texting. If I call Soraya now, I'm going to be up for two more hours, and I can't sleep in tomorrow due to the signing.

Why does any writer forgo sleep to frantically write nonsense in the middle of the night? I write.

Masochism? she offers, which makes me snort.

A contract with a looming deadline and an advance that I've already used, I reply. Anyway, what's up?

My screen fills with a selfie of Soraya flashing a peace sign. From her surroundings, I can see that she's on the tube.

> Not much, in London for the day but heading back to Oxford soon. Just wanted to check in with you. Haven't heard from you in a while. Wanna FaceTime next week?

Soraya is generous to say that she hasn't heard from me in a while when the reality is that I've failed to respond to her last several texts. I want to explain to her that it's not personal and I've gotten terrible at responding to anybody, but that feels a bit cruel because Soraya isn't just anybody. After Zwe, she's my next closest friend. Long-distance friendships are hard, but we're quite good at keeping in touch. Or used to be.

I feel even more guilty as I type my reply:

> Sorry, will be soo busy next week. I'm going away on holiday and need to get work done beforehand. But can FaceTime when I get back? I'll be gone for two weeks.

I swear Soraya replies *before* I press Send. Where? WITH WHOM? she types.

> Fancy island resort getaway. With Zwe.

Oooh. Are you two finally going to rip each other's clothes off and have hot, sexy beach sex?

I let out a "ha!" into the silence of the room. The first time I introduced Soraya and Zwe, she pulled me aside and said, "That man is obsessed with you, and not just in the way *I* am obsessed with you." Over the years, Soraya has gradually let up, but not by a lot; a few Christmases ago, she insisted that she has "a gut feeling for these types of things."

Definitely not, I respond.

Because you're allergic to kind, hot men? Soraya shoots back.

I go to type *Because he's Zwe,* but then delete it. Good night, Soraya, I write instead.

Good night, COWARD, she replies, which makes me laugh. Then, Tell Zwe I say hi. Hope you two have a good trip. Let's talk soon. I miss you.

TWO

I get to the store at 10:52 A.M., and release a sigh of relief when I see the line. Ayesha says that I am now permanently part of the elite club of authors who never again have to worry about nobody showing up to their signings—but that feels presumptuous. As the queen (Beyoncé, not the dead one) instructed, I make it a point to always stay gracious. And although the fact that I accomplished all of this—an accomplishment that, at times, still feels like a delirious dream, like one day I'll blink and my name will be nowhere to be found on all those bestseller list pages that Zwe had framed—with my debut novel means that I was fortunate enough to never have undergone that supposed rite of passage of zero-person signings, I do still remember what it was like before I got published. I remember the literal *years* in the agent query trenches, the high of an agent requesting a full manuscript followed by the devastating low of the email that said some variation of *It's not right for us right now*.

Even after I signed with Ayesha, for years, not a single publishing house wanted the first manuscript we sent out, or the one after that. "Lucky three," Zwe had told me the night before Ayesha was going to submit *Give Me a Reason,* but by that point, "pipe dream" no longer felt sufficient to describe my dream of being a published author; "a fool's errand" or "insanity" seemed more appropriate. It was the terrible, corny, embarrassing adage: I was terrified to keep dreaming, because if you had dreams, that meant they could get crushed. I think of *Give Me a Reason* as my *fuck it* book (not that I'd ever say that in an interview; my publicist would have an aneurysm). I drafted it in a whirlwind—eight weeks, the fastest I've ever drafted any book—and made it exactly the book I wanted to write if it were the last one I'd ever get to write (after reading several blog posts and X threads about other authors who had had multiple books that never sold, I'd gotten it in my head that Ayesha was going to drop me if this one didn't sell, too).

But then one editor made a preempt within twenty-four hours. When Ayesha emailed me, I thought she'd sent it to the wrong client. In fact, I literally responded, "Ha ha, I think you sent this to the wrong person." But she hadn't, she wrote back immediately. This editor was, in her very Ayesha-esque way with words, "shitting her pants" to get this book.

And then another editor had replied saying *they* wanted it.

And then Ayesha had asked how I'd feel about taking it to auction, which could be risky, especially so soon, but this was a *very* good sign and she wanted to capitalize on the momentum.

Sometimes it still feels like it didn't happen. Or at least, like it didn't happen to me. Like I didn't start sobbing when Ayesha called and told me the amount of the winning bid. Like a few months down the line, I didn't get flown out to the Netflix offices because they knew they weren't the only one fighting for film rights. Like everything I had ever wanted since I was approximately nine years old didn't all happen over the course of eighteen months. I wish I'd known back then that the only thing scarier than none of your dreams coming true is having all of them do.

A copy of my own book is waved in front of my face. I follow the hand holding it to a teenage girl, who whispers, "Oh my god, it's actually you!" when we make eye contact.

"Hi, thanks for coming," I say. Then, leaning over to look down the line, I say a little louder while forcing myself to make eye contact with as many more people as I can despite the bubbling anxiety in my stomach, "Thank you all for coming. I'll see you in there! Make sure you stay hydrated in this heat!"

I push open the door to Sar Oat Sin, and although it takes a beat for the cool of the air-con to hit, once it does, a small, satisfied "Mmmm" escapes me, wisps its way out between my lips like the gorgeous lavender scent that's always wafting from the various reeds strategically placed around the space. That, combined with that woodsy book smell, is exactly like coming home. If I could, I would live here and *make* this my home.

"Your Majesty, welcome," Zwe says with a dramatic bow from the metal signing table that he's already unfolded. He's got the setup in its usual space: the corner beside the cash register, which Uncle Arkar is manning today.

"Please, the honor is mine," I say, returning a small curtsy of my own.

Uncle Arkar beams, coming out from behind the desk to give me a hug. "How's my favorite author today?"

"The usual. Anxious," I say with a small laugh. "And I thought Toni Morrison was your favorite author."

He winks. "She was, until you came along."

His words help placate my anxiety. "Where's Auntie Eindra?" I ask.

"Right here." Auntie Eindra paces out of the stockroom in the back with a mug in hand. "And what do you have to be anxious about? We had people lining up before we even opened. But because I knew you *would* be—here."

When she hands me the mug, my face instinctively scrunches up into a smile as my fingers hug the warm ceramic. "Thank you," I say, taking a deep inhale of the peppermint scent to calm my nerves. I had kept a stash of peppermint tea at our apartment as well as the store the whole time I was working on *Give Me a Reason* since they were the only two places where I wrote, and it took me a while to realize that my stash here never ran out because Auntie and Uncle kept refilling it.

"Are you still okay to stay behind afterward and sign the online orders?" Uncle Arkar asks.

"Of course." I take a careful sip of the tea, feeling myself already start to become calmer as the liquid trails down my throat. "I cleared out the whole afternoon for you. Zwe, did you get—"

Zwe holds up a rattan pencil holder with several of the same pens: the quick-drying UNI Jetstream Ballpoint 0.7mm in black. My *favorite* signing pen. "Of course, Your Majesty," he says with another, smaller bow.

I roll my eyes. "Ready?" I ask, and they all nod, and we take our places. I round the signing desk, place my mug down on a coaster, and settle myself into the pink armchair. To my right, Uncle Arkar returns to his spot behind the cash register, and to *his* right, Auntie Eindra sits on the stool next to the carts lined with their bookstore's exclusive edition of *Give Me a Reason,* the pink-and-black spine so familiar to me by now I could point at it even with the lights out. Zwe takes his usual position by the door, ready to guide customers into a neat queue.

"Let's go," he says, pulling both doors and deftly propping them open.

This part never, ever, *ever* gets old. I hate 99 percent of the public-facing aspect of this job, but this is the 1 percent that I enjoy. The girl that I met outside is at the front of the line, and power walks over to me.

"Hi again!" I say.

"Oh my god, hi!" she says as she puts down her copy of the book, along with the slip of white paper that Zwe had handed out beforehand for them to write whatever name they wanted me to make the book out to.

"Are you Chu?" I ask as I sign the title page.

"Yes, oh my god, you know my name," she squeals. "I love this book *so* much. I know you must get it all the time, but this is, like, my favorite book of all time."

"Thank—"

"Is your next book a similar, erm, I'm not sure what the literary term for it is, but *vibe*? I have to be honest, when I saw this shelved in the 'literary fiction' section, I almost walked past it, but it's not every day that you see the words 'number one *New York Times* bestseller' and a Myanmar name on a book cover so I was like, *Okay, fine, I'll check it out*. And it wasn't boring at all! Please tell me the next one is going to be similar to this one!"

I can feel a flush spreading across my face. The cool air isn't anywhere near cold enough anymore; in fact, it feels like there's no air whatsoever circulating in this room. "Well—" I stammer.

"Are Thuzar and Nyunt getting their own story in the next one?

Please, please say yes. I can't imagine what other story you could be writing next!"

I must not have done as good a job as I thought at holding back my grimace, because Chu's eyes widen in apology. "Oh my god, I'm so sorry, that was rude of me. Look at me trying to tell you how to do your job. You must've already turned in your next book." My grimace tightens, not out of anger or even annoyance, but the third A: anxiety. My anxiety, however, simply worsens *her* anxiety over having said the wrong thing, and as I'm unable to reassure her that she didn't actually say anything wrong, she keeps rambling. "I'm sure it's incredible. And I don't know how, but I already know it's going to top this one. Sorry, is that too much pressure? I—"

"Hi, I'm so sorry—" Zwe's hand squeezes my shoulder as he comes to stand beside me. "—but there's a long queue and we need to keep things moving."

"Oh of course!" Chu says, taking back her book. "Well, thank you *so* much for writing this book, is basically what I was trying to say," she says with a nervous laugh, and I will my mouth into a smile. "I can't wait to read your next one."

"Thank you," I whisper up to Zwe as the next reader approaches the desk.

He squeezes my shoulder again, although the familiar pressure barely undoes the knot that is now my whole body. "Anytime, pal," he says before returning to the door.

By the time the sign in the storefront is flipped to "Closed," my wrist aches and my fingers are in what we've dubbed the Pen Claw.

We're spread out amongst the cozy corner seating area, Zwe and I sharing the gray two-seater, Auntie and Uncle on the L-shaped couch opposite.

"So we hear you're taking a holiday together?" Auntie asks.

"Well, I'm trying, but your diligent son here—" I shove Zwe's shoulder with my own. "—says the store would fall apart without him."

"I did not—" Zwe starts.

"Please, *we* need a break from him," Auntie tells me, eyes glinting with mischief. "Thamee, we'll be in *your* debt for giving us a couple of child-free weeks."

"God, how long has it been since we took a *coffee break*"—Uncle makes air quotes—"in the stockroom?"

It takes me a second, but a hacking sound leaps out of me. "Oh my god, you guys!" I scream.

When I turn in his direction, Zwe's face is as pale as the white coffee table in front of us, which is an interesting juxtaposition next to his red ears. "Excuse me while I go drown myself in the toilet," he deadpans.

"And you tried to use your parents as an excuse to get out of this trip," I tell him.

"Two weeks is—"

"Too short if you ask me," Auntie chimes in. When she winks at me, I raise my mug to her. "If it were me, I'd tell you kids to go away for a month. You both have been working so hard lately, and while a good work ethic is important, the last thing we want for either of you is to wake up one day and realize you were too busy working through the good bits of life, too."

"I dunno," Zwe says. "I need to check with my bosses. They can kind of be dicks sometimes."

Without missing a beat, Auntie replies, "Well, I hear they don't say anything about your two-hour lunch breaks, so actually, it sounds like they're pretty tolerant bosses."

Zwe makes a *hmph* sound, but doesn't add anything else. I know he worries about his parents, and it's not wholly unwarranted; Uncle had to have major knee surgery last year, and while he's fully recovered, their age is more apparent now than even, say, five years ago. They move slower, forget more small things. Zwe has taken over almost all the manual tasks such as stocking the shelves and vacuuming at the end of the day. At that, I make a mental note to hire a cleaner to come in at the end of each day while we're gone.

"What did *your* parents say when you told them?" Uncle asks me. "Have you told them?"

I roll my eyes. "What, you think I'd run off to an island with a boy without telling my mom and dad?"

"Nineteen-year-old Poe would've done just that," he shoots back, arched brow daring me to argue, and I laugh in acceptance of the man's point.

"Well, twenty-nine-year-old Poe is much more responsible than her nineteen-year-old counterpart. Yes, I told my parents," I reassure them. "They even asked if we could make a stopover to see them on the way there or back, which, like I told them, we can't, but I promised to visit shortly after we return."

"Good," Uncle says. "Remember, family is important. I know it's not far, but I'm sure your parents miss you very much."

"I know, I know," I say. "Great, now I have *two* sets of parents guilt-tripping me."

My parents had moved to Bangkok last year—a dream that they'd had ever since retirement but couldn't afford. When my Netflix movie came through, I flew all three of us out under the pretense of a holiday and surprised them by introducing them to a real estate agent who helped us pick out an apartment, as well as organizing a meeting with an agency that would arrange their retirement visas. I'm their only child, and although I don't plan on leaving Yangon anytime soon, if ever, this was my opportunity to repay them for everything they'd done for me, particularly all the years they worked multiple jobs to put me through school and university.

"How are they doing? Been a while since I spoke to them," Zwe says like they're old friends with whom he's missed the last couple of catch-up brunches. Then again, he does text them as regularly as I do so I guess they kind of are.

"Good," I say, finishing the last of my tea. "May May went up a level in her Thai language class, and Phay Phay joined this group of aunties who do tai chi in the park at six every morning." At their collective bemused reaction, I hold up a hand. "Don't ask. Apparently he saw them during one of his morning walks and decided to give it a go. Most of them are Thai, but despite the language barrier, they all get along great."

"I miss them," Auntie Eindra says with a soft chuckle.

"You know, you could retire and live that life, too. What do you say, Phay Phay?" Zwe nods over at Uncle. "Feel like doing tai chi in the middle of Bangkok with Uncle Thura every morning?"

Uncle Arkar gets to his feet, and leans over to take the now-empty mugs. "Maybe one day." He looks around the bookstore, gently nodding to himself as he surveys the spines that fill the built-in oak shelves—shelves that he'd made with his own hands in his previous career as a carpenter. He'd literally built this store from the ground up. "I'm not quite ready to walk away from all of this just yet. This is—" He motions, two mugs in each hand.

"Too good," I finish.

He nods at me in a *Nailed it* gesture, an emotion I can't put into words but that I'm familiar with, dancing in his eyes.

Because it is. Too good, I mean. Growing up, this is where Zwe and I would do our homework on the weekends. Where I speed-read all of Jane Austen's novels. Where I held my book launch. Where . . . where Vik proposed to me, right in front of the romance section, and, three months later, where I showed up after closing time, soaked in rainwater and heartbreak, and used my key to open the door and hug Zwe from behind before he could even drop the mop. And yet, even with that memory still looming like a specter that refuses to leave, this place is *so* good. If I owned it, I wouldn't want to retire until I absolutely had to either.

Back at ours, after ten seconds—or maybe thirty—of me trying to put the key in the door, Zwe takes over.

"Blame the Pen Claw. I need a hand massage," I say. "Just from the wrist up. A . . . finger massage?"

"That sounds incredibly inappropriate."

"Sounds like you just have an incredibly dirty mind."

He chuckles. "Thank you for today. You helped bring in a nice chunk of cash. It was a good one," he says, swiftly putting the key in and turning the lock in one go.

"They're always good ones," I reply, meaning it. I might not always have the time or energy to do signings, but when I do, I always love it, especially at Sar Oat Sin. "Oh, Soraya says hi, by the way. I was texting her yesterday about our trip."

"Tell her hi back from me. I feel like it's been ages since I eavesdropped on one of your four-hour-long FaceTime calls," he says, and I try to ignore the acute stab of guilt in my gut from the knowledge that the reason he hasn't eavesdropped on one of our calls in a while is because it's *been* a while since we had one.

After opening the door, Zwe makes a dramatic *You first* gesture with one hand. I roll my eyes and go to take a step when he murmurs a soft "Hey" and his other hand comes to rest on the small of my back, causing my body to lock up. It's not that I feel a spark or a warmth or any of those traditional descriptions, but something more intangible and far more potent that I still can't pinpoint, like the sole millisecond before a candlewick catches on fire.

This happens sometimes. He'll do something inconspicuous that, nonetheless, makes me forget how to *be*.

I've always loved Zwe as a friend, and sometimes, *sometimes*, often in the dead of night following a day where I've had a moment like this, I wonder if I could love him more. Differently. But then I take a step back, recognize that I've had a lifelong habit of dramatizing real life, and ask myself if this is me simply romanticizing our friendship as well (it worked out well that I turned out to be a novelist in the end).

And then there is *the incident*—the still-somewhat-mortifying fact that it's not like Zwe doesn't know how I once felt about him. The summer after our first year in university, when neither of us came home all year long—me from Oxford, him from Brown—because we couldn't afford it, we promised each other dinner on the first night that we were both back in Yangon.

I can remember that night so vividly, like a framed Polaroid that I permanently keep on the shelf at the front of my mind's eye. We had dan pauk that he cooked from his mom's recipe paired with wine that I picked up at the supermarket, and my parents were on a trip to Mandalay so we had the apartment to ourselves.

When I reached the bottom of my second glass, through the lens of nostalgia and love and cheap alcohol, I had thought, *Wait, how have I never noticed how handsome you are?* Because he was. He'd shaved his beard, and he was wearing a yellow T-shirt whose fabric was slightly thinner and tighter than anything he'd have worn in high school when he refused to wear any shirt that might draw attention to his soft, round stomach, and I had thought that this new confidence looked good on him. He loved studying maths, he told me. Statistics, specifically.

Why? I'd asked.

Because with numbers, everything makes sense. It has to.

And instead of asking *How?* or saying *I'm happy you're happy,* I'd leaned in, close enough to smell the scent of his aftershave, two centimeters separating our lips at first, then one, then none, my bottom lip brushing against his, my whole body feeling like an army of Pop Rocks was ricocheting against my insides. *Can I kiss you?* I'd asked, suddenly feeling like I would positively implode if I couldn't.

I'd thought the worst thing he could do was say no. Well, actually, I figured *the* worst thing he could've done was physically recoil backward. But instead, he'd smiled, pushed a lock of hair behind my ear, and then, oh so gently, raised his mouth to kiss my forehead before saying, *We should go to sleep.* And if it weren't for the cushioning that only two glasses of wine can provide, my heart would've shattered right then and there on the tabletop.

The next morning, I did what anyone does with mortification of that kind—I shredded it and set it on fire, never again acknowledging it, even in spite of the small Z-shaped scar that it had scorched into a corner of my heart.

"Hey what?" I ask, still frozen.

"Just . . . I know you were anxious about today, and I'm really proud."

"Thanks. Love you," I say, and step inside so I don't have to look at his reaction, if there is one.

When he drops his hand, I exhale silently, my blood recirculating in the right directions. "You're tired," he calls out from behind. "I'll make us some dinner. What do you want?"

"Try wiped out. I'm not hungry, just going to head to bed," I say, and take the ninety-degree-angle route straight to my bedroom without a backward glance.

A few hours later, while I'm watching the 2005 *Pride and Prejudice* in bed, a piece of paper slips under my door, and a few seconds later, I hear Zwe's bedroom door close down the hall.

Crawling out of bed, I use the light from the TV to read his familiar loopy handwriting on the blue Post-it:

Made chicken penang curry. Left a plate in the microwave. You did great today.

THREE

"I don't know how else to put it: we are not arriving at the airport three hours early. We're just . . . not."

"You're right, we're not. We're arriving two hours and fifty minutes early," Zwe says matter-of-factly, not a trace of sarcasm to be found. When I let out an exasperated "Ugh!" accompanied by an inadvertent stomp of my foot, he simply rolls his eyes in response. "Real mature."

"You know the three hours early rule is extra padding, right? Two, fine. But three is—"

"Taking into account any check-in malfunctions or ridiculous queues at security and/or immigration."

It's the night before we fly out, and we've been talking in circles on this topic for nearly half an hour. It's been years since we flew together, and it wasn't until now that I remember him being this strict then as well. I can now also recall that we had this same argument last time.

"Clearly, we're at a stalemate. Why don't we . . . leave at different times?" I offer. "I'll meet you at the airport."

"No," he says, not even taking a beat to consider it.

"Why not?"

"Because what if you miss the flight? How the hell do I find my way to an island resort where everything is in your name?"

"Wow!" I scoff. "Why are you so certain I'll miss the flight? Just because I want to leave *an hour later* doesn't mean I'm going to miss the whole flight. I'm not a child."

"I don't think you're a child."

I give a dry laugh. "You just think I'm incapable of making an international flight on time."

"It's not you personally, and I know it's just an hour, but a lot can change within an hour. There could be traffic." He starts counting on his fingers. "Immigration and security could take ages. You could have trouble getting a taxi. There could—"

"Fine!" I huff, throwing my arms in the air. Zwe is as stubborn as me, and just like with me, there's always a point in the conversation where you know he's locking down and nothing anyone says or does will change his mind. "You win. We'll leave at *your* time."

"Good," he says, but the atmosphere in the room has become anything but. "Thank you," he adds.

"Sure. I'm going to finish packing," I mumble as I stalk off to my room.

I don't want to start off our big fun best-friend trip like this, especially when it's partially a trip for me to make amends and redeem myself as a good friend, but I can't stand being in the same space as him right now. I know erring on the side of caution is his *thing*, but take a survey of one hundred people and I guarantee the majority of them would agree that my time is the more reasonable one. But that's Zwe for you. By the book, to the extent that at times I want to hit him over the head with it.

It's fine, I remind myself through long, calming breaths as I prepare my toiletries kit. It's one tiny inconvenience.

At the airport the next morning, we're done with check-in, immigration, *and* security in under forty minutes.

"Don't say it," he says when he catches me checking my watch. "Better safe than sorry."

I bite my tongue so that I don't retort with a snarky quip. We want good vibes on this trip. "What now?" I ask. "We have nearly two hours to go." I wouldn't have minded getting to the airport early if we lived in Singapore or Bangkok, but the entirety of Yangon International Airport can be covered in half an hour, and that's if you walk at a snail's pace.

"Head to the lounge?" Picking up on my underlying irritation, he adds, "We could clean them out on finger sandwiches."

"I do like a good finger sandwich. It's like a sandwich, but in one bite."

"There you go." He swings an arm around my shoulders, and I melt. I've never been good at staying mad at Zwe.

After constructing a finger sandwich mountain on our plates, we settle into two large plush sofas facing each other in one corner of the lounge.

"Did you check out that activities brochure?" I ask.

"I did." He looks up from his Kindle, popping an egg sandwich in his mouth. "And *all* of that is free?"

"All-inclusive, baby," I say, pulling up my feet to settle cross-legged into the soft, scratched leather. I know Zwe's right about the airline industry's class system being literally classist, but I could get used to this. "You know what the first thing I'm going to do there is?"

"What?"

"Book a four-hour massage."

He arches one bemused brow. "Can a masseuse even massage for four hours?"

"Okay, fine, I'll split it up into two two-hour massages then. Stop letting logistics get in the way of my dream holiday," I huff.

Zwe's brow raises again, this time pulling the corners of his lip northward as well. "As long as it doesn't cut into your writing time."

"Okay, Dad," I say through a pout, already knowing I'm going to regret making him my human daily word-count tracker. "I'm still allowed to have fun, though."

"You are, as long as it—"

"I will cut into *you*," I hiss, and his mouth opens into a full grin.

"Save some of the sweet talk for the honeymoon, my love."

When we were in university, Zwe and I would regularly email each other our essays to hold the other accountable for upcoming deadlines. When Zwe eventually declared his major and started taking exclusively maths-related classes, I stopped being able to help out, but he'd still offer to read my English essays.

You don't have to pretend to care about Balzac and The Human Comedy *your whole life*, I'd told him once.

I don't *care about Balzac and* The Human Comedy, he'd said. *I care about what you have to say about it.*

I'd studied English because it'd seemed like a safer bet than creative writing; if things didn't work out for me as a writer, my degree would at least help me get a job as an English teacher. I worked hard for my good grades, partly because I loved books, and partly because I knew that if I wanted to be a good writer, I needed to be a good reader first. I was also the first in my family to get a degree from a foreign university—"Oxford!" my mother had gasped when the acceptance email arrived; when I looked up from my computer screen, my father was already crying—so there was that extra pressure.

University had been fun. Growing up, we didn't have enough money to take many foreign holidays, so when I flew out to the UK for my first year, it was the third time in my life that I had ever flown internationally. I cried the whole plane ride, feeling like I was being taken to the first day of kindergarten all over again, except this time I didn't even have my parents beside me to reassure me that everyone would be nice, and yes, I would make friends and soon enough I'd actually come to *enjoy* it. I was certain everyone would be more fun, more attractive, richer, smarter; and a lot of them were one of those, or some combination of the four. I had graduated at the top of our class back in Yangon, but at Oxford, everyone had graduated at the top of their class.

I feel stupid, I'd sobbed on the phone to my mom when I saw the grade on my first essay.

I'd be surprised if you felt smart at Oxford, she'd told me.

What if I don't get better? I said.

Then I'll file a missing person's report, she chuckled. *Because that sure as hell wouldn't be my daughter.*

I know the boring outdated trope is that Asian parents aren't supportive of children who want to go into the arts, but my parents had never tried to dissuade me from becoming a writer, not once. They knew the teaching route was a backup, and that writing was what it'd always been about for me. When it came time, there was never any question about whom I'd dedicate my first book to.

Pangs of love and longing poke at my heart. Uncle Arkar was right—I needed to make time to see my parents soon.

Of course, Mom had turned out to be right (as she always is), and I ended up loving Oxford—both the university and the town—and the community I'd built there so much that I stayed another year to do my MA. Soraya and I got a place off-campus in our final year, and we stayed there until we were both done with our master's degrees.

And through it all, Zwe remained a constant, reading my essays, staying on the phone until the early hours of the morning, he and Soraya vetting my Tinder dates together.

I pick a raisin off of one of the muffins on my plate and throw it at him. "Speaking of love—"

"Oh boy—"

"How's the dating going?"

"How's *your* dating going?"

I give a *Yeah, right* scoff. "I asked first."

He holds my gaze in a cowboy stare-off. Finally, still not breaking eye contact: "I've . . . been texting someone."

I move backward in my seat, clutching the sides for exaggerated effect. "And I'm hearing about this *now*? Who is she? Oooh, is it that Brazilian video producer you brought back the other week? She was *really* pretty. Like, out of your league pretty."

"Okay, first off, that felt unnecessary," he says, face scrunching up with offendedness. "And second, no, she left town the next day."

"So who is it?" I ask in a singsong voice, only jokingly prying—until his features shift, millimeter by millimeter. He begins to look . . . uncomfortable. I sit up, tucking my feet tighter under me. "Oh my god, who is it? Is it, like, a second cousin? I don't care what some people say, I still consider that incest."

"No, it's . . ."

For an inexplicable reason, my gut gets queasy, the five consecutive mini tuna sandwiches I had threatening to come back up. "Yes?" I prompt.

He turns his head away, toward the glass walls with the view of the runway where a plane is currently taking off, another already lined up behind it. "Julia."

Stunned, I watch him watching the second plane. "Julia," I echo at last.

"Julia," he says.

"Zwe."

"What?"

"Is this a . . . different Julia?"

He inhales, *one, two, three,* then exhales, *one, two, three.* When he looks at me once more, his jaw is set, and I know two things: one, it's *not* a different Julia, and two, he's not asking for my opinion.

"Zwe," I say, more softly.

In return, his own tone hardens, like our voices are seesawing. "What?" he repeats.

"Why didn't you tell me you two were back together?"

He shakes his head. "We're not. We're . . . texting."

"Who . . ." I try to pick my words delicately, searching my mental dictionary for the softest, most innocuous ones. ". . . initiated it?"

"Her."

Of course she did, I think, and guilt immediately stabs me right in my carotid. This is why Zwe had been keeping this from me, because he knew this was how I'd react. *You're going on this trip to be a* better *friend,* I scold myself. Besides, what right do I have to be passing judgment on Julia when I haven't talked to her in months?

"What . . . have you been texting about?" I ask. I want him to know that I care and I'm not just being nosy.

He shrugs as he takes a drink of water. "Just stuff. Memes. The news. When we ended, things had been off for a long time. Bad, even. But now it's like we're starting with a blank slate, and I . . . like it. I *really* like it. It's like I'm texting the woman I first fell in love with."

It's not that I hate Julia, or even actively dislike her. Or at least, I didn't until Zwe refused to tell me why they broke up, which is how I know that she did something really shitty. Zwe generally keeps private things private, but if he's keeping something from *me,* then I'm certain whatever happened between them was nothing short of catastrophic. He's not a petty or hateful person, and he won't tell me what went down because he doesn't want me to hate Julia for whatever it is that she did to him, even if (as I said to him at the time) that's Best Friend Code 101. *Thou shalt inherit each other's nemeses and wrongdoing exes.* It still gnaws at me from time to time, though, the fact that I still don't know why they broke up.

"Does *she* want to get back together?" I venture, unsure if this is going to turn out to be a "curiosity killed the cat" situation.

He shrugs again. "We agreed that we'd see how we felt when I got back."

"How long have you two been texting?"

"I dunno, a couple of weeks or so."

I gasp, although inside, I feel more hurt than shocked. This isn't who we are. We don't keep it from each other that we've gotten back in touch with an ex. "Why didn't you tell me?"

He opens his mouth, but then waits for a family with three screaming toddlers—triplets, by the looks of it—who are being shepherded by their frazzled parents as the latter try to frantically divide six tiny hands and two carry-on suitcase handles between the two of them, to pass.

"Because," Zwe says, chuckling to himself as the children's throat-scraping screeches continue down the hall, well away from the lounge's doors. "Like I said, it's just been texting."

"I . . . wish you'd told me. Wouldn't you have wanted to know if I was texting Vik?"

Zwe freezes mid-sip. "Are you?" he asks quietly. His gaze is locked on me, waiting to catch the slightest hint of dishonesty.

"No," I say, and fidget, not because it's a lie, but because of the intensity flashing in his eyes. "It was a hypothetical." I force myself to meet his gaze, and he returns the smallest of nods.

I want to ask more about Julia, but perhaps (definitely) sensing just that, Zwe takes out his book from his backpack, a biography of some famous statistician. Taking the hint, I retrieve my own current read, an early proof of a debut novel that's being edited by my editor. It's called *Not Like This,* and it's a love story between a man and a woman who find themselves seated next to each other on a flight and hit it off, and when the plane goes down over the ocean mid-flight, they're the only survivors and have to figure out how to get back to land.

I'm not a *massive* romance reader, bar the Meg Cabot novels I read growing up, but I'd made an offhand comment to my editor, Tracey, that I was thinking of reading in a new genre to help me with my writer's block. She'd suggested that the pace of the romance genre might help stimulate some ideas, and had insisted that I would love this particular book. She was right. I only started a couple of days ago, but on more than one occasion, I've found myself flipping through with one hand while stirring my coffee with the other. The language is precise, the humor unexpected and cutting, with characters that feel like real people on whose lives you're eavesdropping. It's the kind of book that makes me simultaneously thrilled to read it (especially before the majority of readers), and envious that *I* didn't write it. It's on the longer side for the genre, but I'm already wishing it was longer.

When the two protagonists have their first make-out session on their lifeboat that they built together from spare plane parts, I put a fist over my mouth to muffle my screech.

"You okay there?" I look up, and find Zwe staring at me in bemusement. "Do I need to find a doctor? Your face is so red, you look like you're having trouble breathing."

Only then does it register that my cheeks *are* burning, which makes me flush even harder. "It's this book," I say, gesturing down at the unassuming ring-bound copy in my hands. "I think this might be the best thing I've read all year."

"It's that romance book you were telling me about?" I nod. "Didn't think you were such a big romance fan."

"Me neither," I say, already itching to finish the chapter. "But I'm obsessed. Okay, shush, I have to find out what happens next," I get out in one breath, already mentally clocking out from this conversation. This rush to keep reading feels like when I was fifteen and read *Jane Eyre* (my first-ever favorite book) for the first time, inhaling my dinner so I could excuse myself from the table and get back to where I'd left off. Like when I'd stayed up until 3 A.M. with a flashlight and my copy of *Breaking Dawn,* quickly shoving both under the pillow whenever one of my parents came into my bedroom to check on me.

In my experience, a good book is one of the very few things in life that can be solidly relied upon to speed up time. Because even though it feels like it's only been ten, maybe fifteen minutes, a lounge employee is tapping me on the shoulder to inform us that our flight is starting to board.

Zwe and I make one last bathroom pit stop before heading for our gate. There are a handful of other business-class passengers already in front of us, as well as an elderly couple, both in wheelchairs, in the priority boarding lane, and, seizing the opportunity, I take my book back out.

"You're—" Zwe starts with a laugh.

I halt him with a quick "Ssshhh!," holding up a finger with my free hand. "I have one and a half pages left in this chapter and I've got to know what happens."

Silently, Zwe gives me a small nudge whenever we have to move forward. I finish the chapter right as it's our turn to hand over our boarding passes.

"Have a safe flight!" the agent chirps at us as she scans our passes.

"Uh-huh," I mumble, too stunned by that chapter ending to register her words.

Zwe takes both of our passes from her—I didn't realize she'd been handing me mine and I was staring at it as though she was handing back a bag of dog poop—and says a polite "Thank you."

As we make our way down the slight slope of the boarding bridge, Zwe gently shoulders me. "You look like you saw a ghost."

"Worse," I say to him, shaking my head. "Or better. I can't tell."

"Good chapter?"

"She's an *assassin*. She was on that flight to assassinate someone!" Zwe's cheery expression transforms into shock, and I fling my arms open. "I know!" I exclaim.

"Who was she going to assassinate?"

I wave the book in the air before putting it back into my bag. "We're going to find out in the next chapter. I hope." I clutch Zwe's shoulder as an epiphany strikes me. "Oh my god, what if it's—"

"Him!" Zwe says. Without meaning to, my hand curls into a fist and I punch him in the arm.

"Sorry, sorry," I say when he gives me a *What the fuck* expression. "That was an excited punch. Exactly! What if it's him?"

We press pause on our conversation while we hand the smiling flight attendants our boarding passes and settle into seats 3A and 3C. As always, I take the aisle seat because I have a persistent fear that after takeoff, I'll suddenly develop a medical condition in which my bladder shrinks to a quarter of its current size and I'll have to pee every twenty minutes.

"That book sounds ridiculous," Zwe says as I peruse the little free toiletry-packed pouches that were waiting for us at our seats (again, I could get used to this life). "In a good way, I mean. It sounds so . . . fun. I mean, a plane-crash romance with a trained assassin? It sounds like it wouldn't work, but—"

"But it does!" I say with a loud, satisfied sigh. Despite my clear enthusiasm, I still feel like I'm not doing the book enough justice. If I could, I'd shove a copy into the hands of every single passenger on this plane, babies included. "You're right that the plot is ridiculous, but it's *so* fun, Zwe. I'm already sad about finishing! I wish *I'd* written this thing!"

"Huh," he chuckles.

"What?"

He gives a tentative shrug. "What if . . . you *did* write it? Or something like that? Or just tried?"

"What? Romance?"

"Yeah. Something . . . fun. And ridiculous. Maybe that's what you need to get past this writer's block. A genre switch."

I give him a *Yeah, right* look. "Sure, my agent and publisher will absolutely go for me pivoting to romance out of the blue. Afterward, what, I try my hand at sci-fi for the next one?"

Zwe's smile doesn't reach his eyes. The dimples aren't there. "Why not? Is it written in your contract that you can't?"

"Well, no, but under a two-book contract, it's generally assumed that you'll stick to the same genre. They're expecting something . . . *not* romance. I can't turn in a book about assassins and plane crashes and inevitable hot lifeboat sex. Besides—" I pause, unsure if I want to say this for fear of sounding like a total loser. But it comes out anyway, and it is precisely as sad as it was in my head. "I'm not exactly the best person to write a love story. What do I even know about love anyway? Any romance novel I write would just end on a bitter tone with the scorned main character, I dunno, moving to the rainforest to become a celibate hermit."

He laughs under his breath. "I think you need to give yourself more credit. You can be pretty romantic when you want to be. Look at this trip you booked for us."

"Alternatively, look at the fiancé who broke up with me three months after we got engaged," I say without thinking. Immediately, I want to take it back. But it hangs there now: the ghost of fucking Vik. "I just . . . don't think I have what it takes to be a romance writer." *It'd be ironic if I did, though, since writing* was *the reason my romance ended.* But I don't say the second part out loud.

Zwe puts up his hands in surrender. "Sorry, I don't want to

be that guy who tells you how to do your job. Last thing I'll say is that I haven't seen you this excited about books, *any* book, in a long time. Maybe this is a genre you didn't realize you could love this much, and maybe it's the solution to your writer's block. There. Oh, and he-who-I-refuse-to-name sucks. That's it, promise, *actual* last thing I'll say." To prove it, he makes a zipper motion across his mouth.

An attendant stops by before I have to respond, and hands us two warm towels. By the time we finish wiping our hands and have picked from another attendant's silver tray of drinks—I get sparkling water, Zwe gets orange juice—it's silently agreed that the conversation has ended.

The flight to Singapore is approximately three hours long. I read a couple more chapters before deciding that I want to savor this book like precious wine while lounging on a chaise bed with the ocean breeze messing up my hair. So, I re-watch *Knives Out* because Chris Evans in a cable-knit sweater is always a good idea. When I glance over, Zwe's screen is still playing *Everything Everywhere All At Once,* but he's asleep, head slumped against the closed window shade. We've barely said a word throughout this flight, traces of the Julia conversation and the book conversation and the Vik cameo still lingering in the air. It's not that the mood is bad or awkward, it's just slightly *off.*

By the time we land, though, things are normal again between us; we've reset, silently agreed the little things are too little to ruin the present moment. I've never had that with anyone else, not even Vik—that ability for the atmosphere between myself and someone else to fall back into comfort without either of us actively trying. Our layover is four hours long, so we repeat the same sequence of events as in Yangon: snacks in the lounge, light reading, and another quick bathroom dash before we're boarding our final five-and-a-half-hour flight.

"What else did you have your eye on? In the activities brochure?" Zwe asks, dragging another warm towel across his neck as we make ourselves comfortable in our new set of seats.

"We could go snorkeling—"

"You're terrified of fish touching you."

"No," I correct him. "Everyday Poe is terrified of fish touching her. Island Poe might be a regular Ariel. Maybe I'll make a little fish friend who I visit every day, like in that documentary."

"You mean the one where the guy becomes friends with an octopus?" Zwe's smirk is gleeful. He starts making wavy movements with his hands. "You're going to make friends with an octopus? With its eight slimy tentacles and the tiny suckers that will latch onto your arm and—"

I slap a hand across his mouth, just the mental image of what he described making my body want to break out into hives. "Okay, maybe a new fish best friend is out of the picture. But we can still go snorkeling!" Zwe's blank stare screams *Be serious*. "I *am* being serious!" I say. "The whole point of this trip is that I'm going to find new inspiration for my book, and I can't be inspired if I'm only doing the same things I do at home. Look, maybe I'll hate snorkeling, but even then, *that* could be inspiration for a character who has to overcome a lifetime fear of snorkeling."

"I suppose that's fair." He exhales. "What else did you have in mind? Any land-based activities? Maybe some more pottery?"

Too lazy to locate the email with the brochure PDF, I try to remember off of the top of my head. "I think a cooking class could be fun. They offer Thai, Filipino, and Malaysian cuisines."

"I'd be down for that."

"There are some guided hikes and rainforest tours that I wouldn't mind trying—" At Zwe's reaction, I quickly add, "Yes, I know it's exercise out in the wilderness, but this is what Island Poe does, okay?"

"The lady doth protest a little too much," Zwe notes.

"We could take a helicopter tour of the neighboring islands," I continue, but not without first flipping him off. "See the wildlife and the ocean from a different perspective?" Zwe wrinkles his nose, which surprises me because out of all the activities I've just listed, *I* would've wrinkled my nose at the humid rainforest hike, not the fancy helicopter ride. "What?" I ask.

"Aren't those terrible for the environment? It feels, I dunno, *icky* to be in a helicopter that's emitting all that pollution over the same wildlife we're trying to admire. There's the noise pollution as well."

"Okay, Steve Irwin. When did you become such a big expert on aircraft pollution and wilderness conservation?"

"I've been reading up on it lately."

"You have?" I ask, surprised.

"Yeah, actually. There's some really interesting literature that's been published over the past few years. It's kind of . . . all I've been reading lately." He gestures at the book shoved into the seat pocket in front of him. "I actually got the memoir to break it up a bit."

There's no judgment in his voice, but there's the guilt again, striking me once more when I least expected it. Now that I think about it, I do remember two books—although maybe there have been more—lying around on the coffee table or on Zwe's bedside table that were titled something like *Wasteland,* or at least had "waste" in the title. But why hadn't this registered in my brain earlier? In fact, now that I'm really thinking, when *was* the last time I asked Zwe about what book he was currently reading?

"You're right, we'll nix the helicopter," I say, swallowing the lump in my throat. *Note to self: talk to Zwe about* his *current reading list.*

"But hiking and cooking, I think, would both be great. I also saw they have some muay Thai classes—maybe we could check those out one morning?"

"Mm-hmm," I reply, wondering if *that's* another new Zwe hobby that's just gone over my Worst Best Friend Alive head.

It's okay, I reassure myself. *We're making up for all of that.*

We'll just reset.

FOUR

Antonio had been waiting for us with a sign with our names on it and the resort's logo in the top-right corner, but had *not* noticed that the sign was held upside down, probably because he was finishing off what looked like a cornetto. When we'd walked up to him, necks craned at an angle because we wanted to make sure those were indeed our names, he stuffed the whole remaining bottom quarter of the cone in his mouth like he'd been caught with drugs and didn't know how else to get rid of them. The professionalism of his resort-branded navy polo shirt was offset by his neon pink shorts and green flip-flops.

He waved and said something that got lost in between vanilla ice cream and chocolate waffle cone. When we cocked our heads in confusion, he held up a finger, and the three of us stood there, waiting for him to finish chewing. "Hi," he said on his last swallow. "I'm Antonio." He put out his hand, but right when I was going to take it, retrieved it. "Actually, maybe not. It's a bit sticky with ice cream," he said and laughed. When he glanced down and realized that he'd been holding the sign upside down the whole time, he laughed again, not a trace of embarrassment to be found. I got the sense that Antonio wasn't the type of person who got embarrassed easily, if at all.

Now, after exchanging names and confirming our identification and hotel booking, he takes our suitcases. He doesn't move, however, instead tilting his head and studying our faces.

"Is everything okay?" I ask.

"No offense, but you two look terrible." He gestures with a finger at my upper face. "Ms. Poe, as soon as we get to the resort, I'm going to book you in for a facial to get rid of those bags under your eyes."

Zwe lets out a snicker when Antonio turns his attention to him. Making a cutting motion with two fingers, he gestures at Zwe's hair. "Mr. Zwe, you should've gotten a haircut months ago. Not to worry, we have a barber at the resort as well. And not just any barber, I guarantee you it'll be the best haircut you've had in your *life*."

"I—" Zwe begins.

But Antonio removes his white cap and musses up his hair, turning his head left, right, and down to give us the full 360. "See? He cut my hair just a few weeks ago. It helped me get a date the same night." He grins, perhaps waiting for one of us to say something like *I don't doubt you, tiger*.

Zwe's mouth opens and contorts into a dozen different positions before he finally lets out a succinct "Oh."

I try to come up with a better, actual compliment for fear that we've hurt Antonio's feelings, but before I can think of one, he's getting on with business, wheeling our two suitcases toward the airport exit. Flashing an unfaltering grin at the throng of people that fill up the arrivals hall, Antonio snakes his way through as he yells out, "Excuse me! Thank you!" while Zwe and I power walk to keep up with him.

"Did the first staff member we just met insult us to our faces?" Zwe asks. Despite our pace, we're struggling to keep up, and Antonio doesn't so much as glance backward to check.

"I like to think of it more as helpful criticism," I reply. "Look, you're getting a free haircut out of it." I tiptoe so I can ruffle his hair, which is tough given our power-walking situation, but I just about manage it.

Zwe glares down at me. "Since when don't you like my hair?"

"I didn't say I don't like your hair. If it makes you feel better, I can get a haircut, too."

"Why would you do that?" His brows pinch. "Your hair looks great. Apart from that time you tried bangs. Let's not take another ride on that roller coaster."

"Fuck you," I say, tucking my hair behind my ears, one side of my mouth still ticking up into an involuntary half smile.

Before we've even left the airport grounds, we learn that Antonio basically grew up at the resort. He's twenty-four now, but he's been there since he was a kid. Both of his parents were employees before retiring—they now live in Java—but his grandfather still works there as the person in charge of the on-site organic garden. Another fun fact we find out is that he is an avid bird-watcher. During the thirty-minute Jeep ride to the harbor, he provides a name and fun fact for every bird he sees, already jumping to the next one before we can ask any follow-up questions. I realize that the first human to come up with the term "wacky" probably did so after encountering their own Antonio.

When we reach our destination, I get out of the car and stretch my arms as high as they'll go, basking in the glorious sunshine after a cumulative eight and a half hours in a metal tube in the sky. I'm a city girl at heart, but even I have to admit that the wind, water, earth all seem different here—they smell better, *feel* purer, like this is how nature is supposed to be. Already, I can sense all of my muscles start to relax, the human equivalent to when a dog shakes out their whole body. This is exactly what I wanted. What I needed.

The boat is about a foot lower than the harbor's edge, and there's only a thin wooden plank connecting the two that Antonio promises is secure, despite its general very not-secure appearance. Zwe offers to help with loading the luggage onto the boat, but Antonio smirks and shakes his head. "No offense, Mr. Zwe, but you're a city man. The last time a city man tried to help me put his suitcase on the boat, I ended up having to fish *him* out of the water."

"We are *so* tipping him well," I whisper as Antonio balances along the plank while carrying my yellow case with an effortlessness that makes you think, *That doesn't look* that *difficult*.

"I want to adopt him as my little brother," Zwe whispers back. "I don't think Nyan will mind us having a third brother."

We're instructed to put on life jackets before we're even allowed on the plank. Zwe goes first, then me.

It's a wooden cabin cruiser, which is apparently the usual favorite boat among guests thanks to its large open cockpit, but to be honest, it's precisely the large open cockpit that's making my palms sweaty in spite of the cool, fast wind. Even before we set off, I can tell that Antonio is the kind of person who takes advantage of the fact that there are no speed limits out on the water (I turn out to be right).

"Wanna try steering?" he shouts over, beckoning at the wheel.

"No thanks!" I reply. I can feel the blood draining from my knuckles as I grab tighter onto the edge of my seat.

"I'm good!" Zwe adds.

Antonio chuckles and shakes his head. "City people!" he yells, and throws in a wink to soften the insult.

I sit in the covered part of the boat on the cushioned bench on one side of the wheel while Zwe is taking in the breeze down the far end of the opposite bench, head tilted back, eyes closed, ocean air tousling his black strands. The top two buttons of his sand-colored linen shirt are undone, and his chest hair peeks through. This is one of those moments where I think, *Where did the time go?* I've known this boy since he was ten, and it's like I blinked and now we're almost thirty and he has fucking chest hair and we live in our own apartment and we pay bills and occasionally unclog our toilet and do other Very Adult things. Everything has changed, and also nothing has. I still love books and he still loves numbers (I always know when he's wrapped up the month's accounting for the bookstore because he comes home looking like a kid who just came back from meeting his favorite star athlete) and if I'm going to be on a secluded island for two weeks, there's no one else I'd rather drag along with me.

"How long have you two been together?" Antonio's yell startles me.

I look to see if Zwe heard him, even though between the wind and the water, *I* barely heard him. "We're not together!" I yell back.

"Are you sure?!"

"Pretty sure!"

Antonio smirks a smirk that is best described as "devilish" before yelling, "So then why were you looking at him like that?"

There is a surge of heat in my cheeks that spreads across my face, as though the wind has punched a hole in the roof and there's no longer anything between me and the sun's rays. "I–"

"Don't worry!" Antonio cuts in. Another cheeky wink. "I won't say anything!"

Zwe and I take a few photos on the boat, including a selfie where, in the background, Antonio's turned around to smile at the camera—a move that had me yelling, "Antonio! The wheel!" to which he'd chuckled and yelled back, "It's okay, Ms. Poe! I know this boat better than I know my own body!" which doesn't seem like an actual phrase, but maybe it's an "island person" saying that I, a city person, has never heard of.

We slow down as the resort comes into view, three staff members already awaiting our arrival on the long bamboo bridge that juts out from the beach.

"Do you think they're all this . . . eccentric?" I mumble to Zwe as Antonio steers us toward a long piece of rope that will, presumably, tether us to the bridge.

"God, I hope so," Zwe replies.

Antonio and the man who was waiting help us off the boat.

"Mr. Zwe, Ms. Poe," says a woman wearing a white linen pantsuit. She takes one step forward with the confidence of someone who is single-handedly in charge of a five-star island resort. "Welcome to the island of Sertulu, and on behalf of all of us, welcome to the Cerulean. My name is Sandra, I'm the manager of the resort. I hope you had a good journey here?"

"It was great!" I beam, now self-conscious about my eye bags with every new person I meet. I'd thought of getting my sunglasses out on the boat but didn't want to risk them flying off of my face. I make a mental note to book that spa the second we're checked in.

"Antonio took good care of us," Zwe says. Upon hearing his name, Antonio grins and holds out a fist, which Zwe bumps.

"Antonio," Sandra says through a weary sigh, but he interrupts her first.

"It's chill, they're not the snobby kind," he says, still with that grin, the kind that could melt a Popsicle in the dead of winter. "We've had some *real* snobby ones," he explains.

"Okay, that's enough, Antonio," Sandra says, sounding like a mom politely ushering her moderately behaved child to his bedroom. "Why don't you go ahead and send those suitcases to the villa while I give Mr. Zwe and Ms. Poe their tour?"

Antonio makes a small saluting motion. "Come on, dude," he says to the other man, but then stops in his tracks. "Oh, where are my manners? Mr. Zwe, Ms. Poe, this is my boy Eka." I suppress a giggle at Antonio calling Eka his "boy" when the latter is clearly several years older than him and closer in age to me and Zwe.

Eka, who is less *animated* than Antonio, smiles and bows his head slightly. "Pleasure to meet you. I will be your assigned porter during your stay."

"Nice to meet you, Eka," I say.

As the two men walk away, Sandra gestures at the young woman standing next to her. "This is Leila. She will be your personal villa host while you stay with us."

"Hello, Ms. Poe, Mr. Zwe." Stepping forward, Leila offers us the silver tray she's been holding. The constant "Ms." and "Mr." is already making me squirm, and I make a note to brainstorm with Zwe as to how we can politely ask everyone to stop. "Would you like to try our welcome drinks? We mixed them according to the online questionnaires you emailed us," she says, referencing the "flavor questionnaire" we'd been sent a few days after I made our booking. "Mr. Zwe, for you, we've mixed honey syrup, fresh lime juice, mango purée, and a splash of ginger beer. Ms. Poe, yours has lychee, lime juice, club soda, and some honey-ginger syrup. All of the fruits are grown on our very own organic farm, and the honey is sourced from a local aviary on the mainland. Please, enjoy."

Zwe and I take sips from each of our glasses at the same time, and let out matching *mmmm*s, also at the same time.

"This is the best thing I've ever drank," Zwe says. "And not just today. I mean, in my life."

"I'm so happy to hear that," Leila says with a light laugh. "The recipe cards for both are in your minibar, and we would be happy to provide the ingredients as well if you'd like to do some in-room bartending. Of course, we're also happy to mix it ourselves at our own bar whenever you'd like a glass."

"Shall we walk while you enjoy your drinks?" Sandra offers. She squints up at the sun. "I don't think heatstroke on your first day would be an ideal start to your holiday."

"No, it would not," I reply, and we walk in pairs, me and Sandra in front, and Zwe and Leila behind.

"If you're not too tired," Leila says, "I'd like to take you for a quick buggy tour around the resort. But please don't feel pressured to say yes. If you'd rather go to your villa immediately and relax for a bit, we can schedule the tour for another time. Whatever suits your needs."

I've never been anywhere that was close to this level of fancy, and although I know this is part of their service, to be honest, this much attention to solely *our* needs feels uncomfortable. Then again, I read all the reviews and intentionally booked *this* resort because everyone had said that the steep price was worth it given the highly personalized experience you get.

"A tour sounds fun. I just got a second wind," I say, looking back at Zwe. "You?"

Zwe holds up his glass, which is already half-empty. "As long as I can have another one of these waiting for me at the end of the tour."

Leila grins. "Deal," she says, already taking out her phone and typing a discreet text.

We make our way across the sand and onto the paved walkway that divides the resort from the beach. Two white four-seat buggies are already parked. While Leila puts the silver tray and our glasses into a small basket that's secured on the back of one of them, Sandra reaches into her pocket for her wallet.

"This is my number," she says, handing us each a business card. "If for whatever reason you run into a problem, please don't hesitate to reach out. You can also inform any staff member that you'd like to speak to me, and they'll find a way to put me in touch with you. We're *so* thrilled to have you with us, and I do hope you'll have a beautiful and nourishing stay here."

"Oh . . . my god . . . that is . . . so nice of you. Thank you so much," I say, increasingly stunned at the level of customer service here.

After saying our goodbyes, Sandra hops into the other buggy and drives off.

With Leila behind the wheel, Zwe and I get into the back seat, jolting a bit when the vehicle starts.

"You two okay back there?" Leila asks as she steers the vehicle up the curved ascending pathway toward the actual resort.

"Couldn't be better," I reply half-distractedly.

I had been stunned by the photos when I was perusing the website, but I am *gobsmacked* seeing it in person. In contrast to the sticky air that awaited us when we stepped out of the airport, this seems like the kind of place where the sun, moon, and clouds work in tandem to ensure that the temperature is consistently perfect, and that if there *is* ever, say, a thunderstorm, it a) only happens late at night when everyone is already indoors, and b) is the kind of picturesque thunderstorm—strong, but not terrifying—that movie studios employ CGI to re-create. Basically, it feels like an island you'd see in a Disney movie.

With short pauses in front of each stop so that Leila can talk us through the facilities, we see the organic garden where Antonio happens to be chatting with his grandfather (they both wave), the open-air reception area with the glamorous marble fountain in the middle, the cliffside bar and adjacent pool, the beachfront barbecue "shack," the main all-day restaurant, the main infinity pool framed by towering palm trees that is separate from the "lap pool," and their Vero Spa, whose multiple certified masseuses and aestheticians exclusively use organic, high-quality ingredients across their carefully curated treatment menu.

"I apologize for the mess, but I promise you won't hear any of it from your room. They're also ordered to wrap up by four P.M.," Leila says as we pass by a section of the resort that's currently under construction. Nothing's been built yet, but there are several tractors digging up the land while men in hard hats direct them from the ground. "We're working on expanding the resort."

"You're going to make it even *bigger* than this?" I open my arms to gesture at the sprawling land around us.

"Believe it or not, yes," Leila laughs.

"What are you building? What more could this resort possibly need? An aquarium?"

"A museum? Indoor go-karting track?" Zwe muses.

"Last I heard, they're still trying to decide on what exactly it'll be." She tosses a nod over her shoulder at Zwe. "But that indoor go-karting has my vote."

I can't tell if she's flirting or simply continuing to be welcoming. By the way Zwe is smiling, though, I can tell which one *he* hopes it is.

"Don't take this the wrong way," he says once we've left the site behind, "but I haven't clocked any other guests here. Are they off doing activities around the island or . . . ?"

Over her shoulder, Leila widens her eyes at us in a secretive *You didn't hear this from me* way. "We had a glitch with our booking system that no one was aware of," she explains. "We only realized recently that the rates had been displaying online at four times the actual price. Because of our location and exclusivity, it's rare for us to ever be at full capacity, or even close." *Read: we're too expensive for the majority of people.* "We just assumed we hadn't been getting the normal number of bookings due to a mixture of bad weather on the mainland and the fact that this is the region's annual low season. It wasn't until a routine technical check that someone noticed the glitch."

"Oh, that explains the email," I say, snapping my fingers.

"Email?" Zwe asks.

"I got an email the other day apologizing for some pricing discrepancy and a notice they'd be refunding a chunk of the payment," I explain.

"That would be why," Leila confirms. "As soon as we found out, management temporarily closed our bookings while they fixed the system to ensure that something like that doesn't happen again. Everything's running as normal now, and I promise we *do* typically have guests."

"Eh, I think it's kind of cool—" Zwe shrugs. "I've always wondered how it'd feel to be a millionaire with my own private island."

"Well, lucky you," Leila says. "Here we are." She slows down and parks in front of a bungalow with a thatched roof and bamboo exterior. We get out and follow her to the door. "This—" A tap of a card on the unassuming black box by the door, a flash of green light, a beep. "—is your home for the next two weeks," she says, pushing open the door.

The villa is perched on the edge of a cliff with uninterrupted panoramic views of the Indian Ocean. Outside, there's a small private infinity swimming pool with a hot-tub section. The entrance opens right into the living room, whose two large accordion glass doors leading to the exterior are currently pulled open, allowing the breeze to circulate through the whole place. The room is decorated with hardwood furniture and neutral-toned linen fabrics that give off a crisp, minimalist vibe.

Leila takes us to the bedroom, where a plush king-sized bed faces the water. On this side of the glass doors that lead out to the balcony, there are two large rattan one-seaters that face each other, a marble coffee table separating them. In the bathroom, there are two separate marble sinks, a spacious rainfall shower in one corner, and (my personal favorite) a stand-alone claw tub by the window so you can take a bath with a view.

"Holy shit," Zwe breathes, jaw practically on the hardwood floor as we circle back to the living room.

"This is literally the most gorgeous place I've ever stepped foot in," I say, unable to process it all even though I was the one who booked this. It's like we've stepped foot in one of those celebrity *Architectural Digest* videos.

We stand in a row at the edge of the pool, stunned by the sand, sea, and sky. "Breathtaking, isn't it?" Leila says. She closes her eyes and takes in a deep inhale. "My family has lived on this island for generations. When I was growing up, resorts like this were things we only saw on TV. Sometimes I can't believe I work at a place like this now. In fact—" She points down to a spot on the beach. "—that's where my parents got married. Of course, none of this is in their wedding photos. All you'll see in the background is, well, jungle."

"Does your family still live on the island?" I ask.

With a small smile, Leila looks back, over the villa and toward the mountains in the distance. Zwe and I follow her gaze, but all I see is the looming silhouettes of nature. "Only a few at this point. Most of my aunts and uncles moved to the Philippines, which is the closest mainland country, and the rest have gone a little farther down south to Indonesia. None of my cousins actually grew up here, although we visit each other regularly, which is how we've remained so close. The older members have stayed, though, like my grandparents and their siblings. They've relocated up there to the mountains in the woods. Less to worry about when a storm comes in," she explains.

"So in a sense, this"—I make a wide sweeping motion with one hand—"is your hometown?"

She lets out a sweet laugh. "I suppose in a sense it is." Stepping back toward the room, she walks over to the large wooden desk in the corner where there's a welcome basket with an assortment of snacks. "Your key cards are over there. They'll give you access to the gym and sauna as well. There's also a book of all the activities we can arrange for you, complimentary of course. And if you need anything at all, my number is here—" She picks up the small business card (printed in the same style as Sandra's) sitting at the front of the basket. "Whether you want me to book you in for the spa or one of our activities—snorkeling is popular amongst our guests—or you require an extra set of towels, please don't hesitate to text or call me. I'm on duty twenty-four hours." My face scrunches at that, because surely she can't be on call *24/7*. As though reading my mind, she adds politely, "It's my job."

"Thank you *so* much," I say. "By the way, I was trying to recover from sea legs earlier so I didn't get to tip Antonio and Eka, but if you three—" I'm reaching for my wallet in my bag but Leila raises a hand.

"We don't accept gratuities here," she says. I open my mouth to insist, but she insists first. "Management ensures that all employees are paid fair wages. I truly appreciate it, Ms. Poe, but any money you give me will simply be transferred to bar and dining credits for your stay."

"Are you sure?" I ask after a pause. "I don't—"

"Like I said, it is *genuinely* appreciated," Leila assures me, smile still bright. "But I cannot accept it."

"Okay, well, if there's anything I *can* do to show *my* appreciation, you'll let me know?"

She nods. "Deal." The sound of the doorbell travels down the corridor, and Zwe and I turn to each other, confused. Leila, though, is already heading for the door like she expects just this. "Oh, and speaking of deals—" she calls out while accepting something from the person on the other side. When she turns around, she's carrying a small tray with a familiar light orange drink. She walks straight to Zwe and hands him the glass. "You didn't think I forgot, did you?"

He grins, taking the drink. "Not a chance."

It's not on purpose, but I can't *not* notice his fingers grazing hers during the few seconds where both of their hands are wrapped on either side of the tall, thin, translucent glass. He's smiling that big Zwe smile, dimples imprinted, cheeks reddening like someone swiped on the lightest layer of blush. This time, they're *both* definitely flirting.

"By the way, will the bed—" Leila clears her throat, trying to pose the question tactfully. "—situation be . . . okay?" She gestures over at the bedroom, and it takes me a few beats to realize she's referring to the fact that there's only one bed. "This room has always been reserved by couples and we assumed since there were two names on the booking . . . but we could set up another villa," she adds quickly.

In retrospect, I should've asked Zwe if he was cool with having to share a bed, especially because now it feels weird since he and Julia are in contact again. But none of the villas had an option for twin beds, and unless one of us took the couch (or worse, the floor) or forked out the money for an entire separate villa, this was the only solution. Besides, we've shared beds before in hostels and group trip scenarios, and given that it's a massive bed, I'd assumed he would've been fine with it. It's never been a big deal. If needs be, I figured we could sleep with our heads on either end.

Now, I'm scared that I've screwed up something so basic.

"Just so you're aware, this one does have the best view out of all our rooms." Leila indicates out the window at the magnificent view in question. "But we could arrange one nearby so you've got a similar view, that is, if you don't mind giving us a couple of hours and the additional payment."

"We don't need another villa," Zwe says quickly at the mention of more money being spent. "We don't want to trouble you. This place is more than big enough for two people."

"In that case, if you'd like, we can set up some sort of extra sleeping arrangement here. Maybe in the living room if you'd prefer?"

Leila looks expectantly between the two of us. "I could swap out the sofa for a twin bed?"

"Do you—" I start.

"I'm good if—" he begins.

We shift in an awkward dance.

Finally, Zwe ventures, "I'm cool with it if you are?" I meet his gaze, nod, and then nod at Leila to double confirm. "It'll be like we're back in that hostel in Paris that only had one bunk bed left," he adds with a lighthearted laugh.

"Ah yes, the one where the rat got into the lockers and chewed through my underwear," I say.

Leila raises one hand solemnly. "I promise there aren't any underwear-chewing rats here," she says, and we all laugh, and the weirdness in the air seems to blow back out with the breeze.

After she leaves, I plop down on the edge of the bed. Zwe sits beside me, but doesn't lie down on account of the drink in his hand.

"You liiiike her—" I singsong.

"What?" Our eyes meet, and he raises one brow. "Who?"

I raise both of mine in return. "Who do you think? You have a little crush on our villa host."

"I do not—"

"Hey, I get it, she's gorgeous." And Leila is. Even swept into a bun, you can tell her hair has those natural beach waves that take me three to five separate hair products to re-create. She's tall, with toned calves and arms. "Also, her boobs are *amazing*."

At that, Zwe coughs on his drink. "She was wearing a polo shirt, you perv."

"Please, you can totally tell that the boobs underneath are amazing. Don't act like you weren't thinking the same."

"You're a menace," he grumbles, looking away as though his reaction might confirm what I already know to be true.

We sit in silence for a bit longer, the travel exhaustion finally catching up to us. Outside, the sun is starting to set, and like with everything else on this island, it looks magnificent. A warm-toned, cotton-candy dream.

"Do you want to go to the restaurant, or get room service for dinner?" I ask.

"To be honest, I'm kind of beat," he says as he chews on shaved ice. "I vote room service."

"Are you sure? What if Leila's unwinding with a drink at the bar tonight?"

He snorts, then nods over at the desk. "I've got her number, remember?"

I point a finger gun at him. "Smooth."

After long, warm showers, and bundling up in luxurious cotton bathrobes on the sofa that's bigger than any I've ever owned, we watch an episode of *MasterChef* with our room service. When Zwe gets up and carries the tray to leave outside the villa, the low murmur of dread that had been present throughout dinner gets louder.

"So," Zwe says when he returns. He lingers in the hallway, and by the way he clears his throat, it's obvious we're both thinking the same thing.

"This is only weird if we make it weird," I say.

"I have no idea what you're talking about," he teases, but the uneasiness in the room is tangible.

"Look, it's fine." I sit up on my knees and pat the couch cushions. "I'm smaller, I can take the sofa."

"If you don't want to sleep in the same—"

"I didn't say I didn't want to sleep in—"

"But then why did you just offer to take the—"

"Because clearly you feel uncomfortable about—"

"I only feel uncomfortable because you've been side-eyeing the bed all night!" Zwe says, flinging his arms wide. The action slightly tugs open the crisscrossed fabric on his chest, exposing bare flesh underneath, and my breath catches. He looks down, and as though reading my mind, he pulls the robe close and tightens the belt.

Everything feels different here. *We* feel different here. With no other guests around and the staff doing their best to be invisible, it feels like it's just us. Part of me wishes it was, and that the whole island was ours for the taking, forever and ever. I imagine us spending the rest of time galloping around in our swimsuits, napping under a tree at two in the afternoon, lying in the clear water, our backs wet, faces squinting up at the sun. And if not forever, at least until I was ready to return to all the scary, messy things I've temporarily left behind. Two weeks with Zwe on this island isn't going to be nearly enough time, I can already tell.

"Look, we can draw straws or something for the bed," I tell Zwe. "But I genuinely don't mind taking the sofa. I'm sure I'll enjoy it as much as the bed."

His eyes narrow, calling my bluff. In my defense, it's a gorgeous bed, with a mattress and sheets that probably have a cumulative four-figure cost. And although we've shared a bed before, every nook and cranny of this setting oozes romance. Clearly, this is a villa where people come to fuck. I bet some couples barely even make it out of that king-sized, Egyptian cotton–draped bed during their entire stay.

"I'm okay sharing the bed," he says after a long pause. "It's . . . really big. We'll probably not even touch each other at all."

With a snort, I burst out laughing. Which makes Zwe laugh, and we're both shaking our heads at the absurdity of this situation. "Damn right we won't. At least, not until after you buy me dinner," I say.

"You know what I mean," he groans, covering his face with one hand, and it's so cute I want to go over and give him a hug. "Why are we being like this?"

"It's the air." I wrinkle my nose. "I'm telling you, all this nature isn't good for the human body. Makes our brains do weird things like . . . turn sharing a bed with your best friend into this awkward situation."

"Even though it's not," Zwe says. "Awkward, I mean. You take your side of the bed—" He gestures at the left side, and I don't linger too long on why the knowledge that he still knows which side of the bed I prefer pricks at a tender spot in my heart. "And I'll take the right side."

"There we go!" I say. And as though to prove it, I jump off of the couch, march over to the left side of the bed, sit down on top of the duvet, and pat the spot beside me for him to join. Here we are, just two friends sitting on the same bed, looking out of a set of glass doors at the Indian Ocean in the distance. "It's so beautiful here," I murmur, my body relaxing as I focus on the roar of the waves hitting the cliffs, which is audible even with the doors closed. Ariel had always been my favorite Disney princess, and when I was a kid, I'd beg my parents to move to the beach so I could try to befriend a mermaid.

"It is," Zwe says. I swear I feel his gaze on me, and it takes everything in me to not turn in his direction and check.

After prepping for bed, we get under the covers with our books, settling in as we angle the pages under our individual overhead reading lights. At one point, I stretch out my legs and my left foot presses into Zwe's calf.

"Sorry," I mutter, retracting my foot across our invisible dividing line.

"It's fine," he says with a low chuckle. Without warning, his foot glides over and grazes mine, the sudden, intimate contact tripping up my neurons.

It lasts for only a second, so short that I can't decide if it's weirder to comment on it or to not. When I chance a glance at Zwe, he's still fully focused on his book, nothing new on his face. He must've just been stretching, too.

Zwe turns in first. An unintentional smile comes to my lips when he starts lightly snoring. Even with the space between us, I can feel his body heat emanating from him under the sheets and tempering the cool of the air conditioner outside them; then again, that's Zwe for you—radiating warmth even when he doesn't mean to. For all of my talk about us becoming adults who do adult things, in this moment, I'm a kid again, buzzing at getting to have a sleepover with my best friend and already looking forward to the morning.

I read a couple more chapters, and, not feeling drowsy in the slightest, I carefully slip out of bed. There are few things I love more than writing late at night; it feels like I don't have to worry if I write the worst one thousand words anyone has ever written since the dawn of time, because every single person in the world is asleep and so who will read any of it anyway?

Taking my laptop out onto the deck, I open a new blank document, trying to embrace rather than be scared off by the extreme whiteness of the page.

I tell myself that we're starting over, that the dozen or so failed first drafts sitting in the virtual trash bin don't exist. Here, we're writing a new story. A *good* story. A new, good story with a *big* idea, like . . . time travel. Okay, I can work with that. Time travel. That's a big idea.

Beside my laptop, my phone lights up with a text from Soraya.

> How's the trip so far? Have you had hot hammock sex yet?

It makes me laugh out loud, and I promise myself to reply to her once I'm done writing for the night, or at least definitely in the morning.

I write for half an hour—a completely new story, one about a young woman who accidentally trips into a time-traveling manhole that takes her into the future for twenty-four hours. Unhappy with how her life turns out, she becomes obsessed with making changes in the present day followed by a trip to the manhole to see how it's affected her own future.

It's a story with potential. I can already foresee some plot holes off the bat, but that's what editing is for. On the whole, though, it's the kind of book that, if someone pitched me the premise, I'd add to my To Be Read pile.

But it's not . . . fun. Writing it isn't fun. Frankly, writing it feels like work. But then again, that's what this is now. Guilt spirals through me as I realize that, lo and behold, I'm again complaining about having the exact job that I've wanted my whole life, that I'm complaining about having to *write*. This is normal, though. Every professional writer has had days where stringing together three coherent sentences has felt like pulling teeth; I just have to remember that it won't be this way forever.

Like the boogeyman jumping out from around the corner,

Vik's face pops up in my head. It wasn't that he was ever mean about me wanting to be a writer, or even that he didn't believe I could do it. I'd been used to people doubting that I'd become a published author, but that wasn't the case with Vik. He always thought I was a good writer, but that was also what made it a new, particular kind of heartbreak, a pointed cruelty: he thought I was good, just not good *enough*. Of course I'd sell a couple of books and they would do okay—but that's all they would be. Okay. I would make an "okay" amount of money, but not enough for me to do this and just this alone. I would have an "okay" readership size, but not actual fans who would be actively wanting my next book. Okay, good even, but not *great*. And with every day that passes where I can't write this second book, the notion that maybe he was right becomes just that little more plausible.

I'll revisit this tomorrow, I think, shutting my laptop.

I lean back in the chair and stare out once more at the waves beating toward and away from the shore. Two weeks here. If this doesn't inspire me to write another bestselling book, nothing will.

FIVE

"What the fuck is that?" I moan.

"It's the alarm that I'd be able to turn off if I wasn't in your death grip," replies Zwe's voice from somewhere above me.

My ramble comes out muffled, but I'm too sleepy to lift my head. "What death grip? What are you talking about?" The high-pitched ringing sound vibrates through every fold of my brain. I push my face deeper into the soft pillow in an attempt to drown it out, and kick my feet under the covers like a petulant toddler being woken up for school. "Make it stop! Why must you torture me so? Just use Siri to turn it off!"

"Oh, right," Zwe mumbles. As he shouts over at his phone to turn off the alarm, I blink awake through the slight sheen of sleep and eye crust. The right corner of my mouth is dry, which means I must've been drooling in my sleep. Instead of the view of the sofa that I'd fallen asleep to, however, I come face-to-face with soft white fabric that feels warm and smells so . . . familiar. I inch back, tilt my gaze up—and see Zwe's chin.

"Oh my god!" I yell when I'm finally able to take stock of the whole scene. I'd moved around in my sleep into a position where I have my face pressed into Zwe's chest, one bent leg thrown over both of his (which, given the length of my legs, has resulted in my foot just dangling in the air) and the other foot resting on *his* other foot so that he's essentially sandwiched from the waist down. From the neck up, I have him in a half headlock, one of my hands having somehow slipped under his neck and the other linked around both of his forearms. When I scramble to sit up and scoot several feet away, there is a giant mortifying drool spot on the front of his shirt where my mouth had been resting.

Zwe laughs at my horrified expression. "You've thrown up on my shoes before. I can handle a bit of drool. By the way—" His face shifts to teasing, and I brace myself for the situation to get even more horrifying. "Were you having . . . *intimate* dreams, by any chance?"

I want to fling myself off of the balcony.

"No?" I squeak out. I'm almost certain I wasn't.

"Really?" Zwe's nose wrinkles. "Because you were kinda—" Sitting up himself, he pulls back the covers and makes a thrusting motion. "—grinding my thigh. A lot. And you were moaning about . . ."

I'm already picturing myself swimming to the bottom of the ocean and never resurfacing. "About what?" The words sound jagged.

"An Eric? Like Prince Eric? I'm assuming the one from *The Little Mermaid*?"

I can physically feel my soul, along with my will to live, leave my body. *The Little Mermaid*. Zwe's flowy white shirt. Surely I didn't—

"You're kidding," I sputter, face burning so hot it feels like I got sunburnt.

Zwe erupts into a fit of laughter. I'm still so buried under a cloud of shame that it takes me a beat to realize why he's laughing. "You fucking dick!" I scream, and whack him with a pillow.

He protects his head with his hands as he gasps for air. "Can we acknowledge that this confirms that you having a sex dream about Prince Eric is totally within the realms of possibility?" he cackles. "I know you used to think he was hot, but a—" He stops to wheeze.

"Sex dream?"

"I'm tired! And I didn't think I'd be gaslit first thing in the morning!"

"Was it—" He takes in a huge gulp of air, barely able to finish the question. "—better down where it's wetter?"

"You're dead to me!" I screech, and start whacking him repeatedly with more force.

Zwe jumps out of the bed, and holds open both palms. "Truce! Truce!"

"I am never going to forgive you for this," I say. "*Ever.*"

He gives me a playful wink. "Whatever you say, Princess Ariel."

Shrieking, I hurl the pillow at him, he catches it, throws it back at me, and I duck. "I hate you," I pant each word.

"Love you more," Zwe calls out over his shoulder as he makes his way to the bathroom.

Once I process and move past my mortification, I can't help but chuckle while surveying the now mess of a bed, pillows strewn about, a third of the sheets falling to the floor. And here we thought it was going to be awkward.

"Gooood morning!" Leila greets us at the restaurant entrance. "How'd you two sleep?"

"Like a baby seal on a beach," I say. "At least, I assume baby seals sleep well on the beach? We had a great sleep, is the answer."

She, Zwe, and the restaurant's formal host, whose name tag reads Jay, all laugh. "Was the, um, bed situation okay? Do you want me to add that extra bed after all?" she asks, eyes darting between me and Zwe.

I feel Zwe's attention transfer onto me, and it takes more effort than it should for us to make eye contact. It's like we're tuned in to two radio channels that are just one frequency off. I can't tell if he's asking me *Should we?* or *I think we're fine, right?*

I take the plunge. "I think we're good?" I say slowly, my uncertainty inadvertently drawing up the end of the sentence into a question. I tilt my head at Zwe to communicate *Right?*, and this he understands because he responds with a smile and a nod.

"Yeah, thanks. It's perfect how it is. The view in the bedroom is—" He swallows, almost tripping over the next word. "Incredible. I wouldn't change a thing," he says, and my stomach does something it's never done before. Immediately, I think of that blink-and-you-miss-it moment last night where his foot had brushed mine. Fuck, the air here really is different.

"That's wonderful!" Leila says, breaking my one-sided tension. "If you change your mind, you know how to reach me."

I expected us to be the only guests in the restaurant, but I did *not* expect the near-mile-long L-shaped buffet table that takes up two walls. From a quick sweep, I clock a multicolored fresh fruit selection, enough baskets of pastries to fill the display at a medium-sized bakery, a cereal bar, an assortment of cold cuts and cheeses, closed stainless steel silver domes with small placards in the front that denote a variety of hot foods, and a separate vegetarian section. That's in addition to the five small "freshly made" stations where there's a small stove and smiling chef waiting to cook us congee, eggs, noodles, crêpes and/or waffles, except at the last station where there is no stove because that's where you can get freshly cut and rolled sushi. For drinks, there are several clear glass jugs of fresh juices made from more fruits than I've ever simultaneously had in my fridge at one time.

"Is there a small wedding you're expecting?" I ask Leila.

Leila laughs and shakes her head. "This is our usual breakfast spread. We wanted to make sure you filled up. Not to sound like a parent, but it *is* the most important meal of the day. Besides, you'll need all that energy to last you until lunchtime. Speaking of—" She pulls out my seat for me. "What do you feel like doing today? You can take the active route and do some water activities. Some of our most popular options are kayaking, paddleboarding, and snorkeling, and I can check the weather to see if windsurfing is a possibility. There's also mountain biking if you want to stay out of the water. Alternatively, if you want to kick-start your time here with some relaxing, our spa menu is incredible. I'd be happy to book you in for a day of pampering. What do you two think?"

"Definitely spa," I say at the same time that Zwe answers, "I've always wanted to go windsurfing." There's a pause, then we all laugh.

"As you can see, we have two very different definitions of holidaying," I tell Leila.

She waves a hand. "No need to explain. That's why we make sure to cover all our bases in terms of activities. How about after breakfast, I drop you off at the spa where one of our masseuses will help put together the best treatment plan for you, and then"—she turns to Zwe—"we can make our way to the beach?" She peers out toward the deck. "Again, I need to double-check for safety reasons, but the weather looks perfect for a windsurfing session in my opinion."

Zwe pumps a fist in the air. "Do you think we could also do some kayaking afterward?"

"Sure, I can hook you up with a kayak!" Leila says.

"Me?" Zwe crosses his arms, the move infusing his words with a flirtatious subtext. "Don't tell me you're not joining me. What, are you chicken I'll beat you in a kayaking race?"

Leila grins through her scoff. "I don't think Sandra will be too happy that I'm taking advantage of the resort's—"

"But it's what I want," Zwe says. "As a guest. I'd assume Sandra would want you to go the extra mile to keep a guest happy, right? Isn't that this whole place's *thing*?"

Leila's smile is so wide, the corners of her pink glossy lips are hooked onto her cheekbones. Meanwhile, I'm wondering when Zwe got so smooth with his flirting. This is the same guy who panicked before his first kiss and excused himself to the bathroom where he texted me that he was eating ten mints in one go, and then threw them all up on his date's shoes.

I don't recognize this version of Zwe, and it scares me that I can't tell if it's this new setting that's making him different, bolder, more willing to ask for what he wants, or if this is yet another new side to him that I've overlooked: Zwe flirts now. Not just that, he's *good* at flirting.

"I don't want to intrude on your guys' trip, though." Leila's voice breaks my train of thought. She's looking at me with an uneasy expression. "If you're going to be kayaking with someone, then surely it should be Poe."

I'm about to say *Yeah, actually, that massage will feel much more satisfying after a day out on the water,* but Zwe interrupts with "Poe hates water sports. In fact, she kind of hates all sports."

"I do not!" I kick his shin under the table. "I like—"

"Mario Kart?" Zwe supplies.

I kick him again, even if his answer makes me giggle. "It's a sport! It requires both strategy and skill!"

"Which is why you're the reigning champion of our apartment," Zwe says. "But you hate water sports. Look, if you really want to join me today, then of course I think it would be fun. Your call. We *do* have two whole weeks here, though. Plenty of time."

"You guys could also do separate things in the morning and something together in the evening," Leila offers.

"I have to work in the evening," I explain, hating how clichéd I sound. I don't want to be the person who's glued to her laptop during a trip, but I also can't afford to not write for two weeks. I throw Zwe an apologetic smile, and he nods in understanding.

Two things stop me from insisting I'll join Zwe and Leila this morning: one, I *do* hate water sports. And two, I'd effectively be cockblocking Zwe if I tagged along. I'd be lying though if I said the framing of me being the person who's "tagging along" didn't make me feel a bit left out. This was supposed to be *our* trip where *we* bonded over fun activities.

"How about we go snorkeling tomorrow?" I suggest. "That spa is *really* calling to me today."

"It's a date," Zwe says.

After the fit-for-an-army breakfast we had, we agree to skip lunch and regroup for dinner. At the spa, the masseuse hands me a questionnaire where I can pick my desired level of pressure, and, using a figure drawing of a body, circle any sections where I'd like extra attention. I circle my back, shoulders, and hands.

"Do you spend a lot of time on a computer?" she asks with a knowing smile.

"A bit," I say, suddenly embarrassed that I must be living up to the hunched-over-a-computer city-person stereotype they get here all the time.

After my first two-hour four-hands massage, I'm led out to the spa's deck where someone brings out a flask of iced tea and a bowl of artfully cut and displayed fruit as soon as I sit down on a cream chaise lounge. I have an unobstructed view of the beach, including of Leila and Zwe out in the water. They look like they're having the time of their lives, any sound they're making drowned out by that of the Jet Skis they're maneuvering.

Happy. Zwe looks so happy, which makes *me* happy that I was the one who brought him here. It's cheesy, but sometimes I watch him at the bookstore, juggling everything from stock take to the cash register to making sure his parents eat lunch at a reasonable hour, and I'm overwhelmed by what a good person he is, down to his bones. I was never going to bring anyone else here. It was always going to be him, or nobody.

Remembering that I never responded to Soraya last night, I pull out my phone and call her. It's early morning in the UK, but according to Soraya, the concept of sleep is a faraway dream now.

"You're up," I say when she answers.

"Do you mind if we stick to audio?" Soraya's British accent comes through. She sounds like she's at the level of exhausted where you don't give a crap about niceties like *Hello* and *How are you?* "I have to hold this kid with one hand and push my tit into his mouth with the other, so I'm all out of free hands. I can turn on my video if you want, but you'd be staring at the ceiling with me occasionally flashing you."

"You have great tits, I'd be honored," I say. I smile when that gets a tired laugh from her. "I'm sorry I've been so shitty with texting back."

"It's okay, I get it, you're a big-time author now. Hollywood is begging you to write more books that they can adapt."

Now *I'm* glad we're sticking to audio and she can't see the inadvertent grimace I just made. "How are you? How's the family?"

"Don't ever have kids. They'll suck at the teat of your will to live." I laugh, she gives a weary sigh. "I don't want to think about diapers and sore nipples. Distract me. How's your tropical getaway?"

"Good," I say. "It's so gorgeous here, I keep looking around and being like, *This has to be some sort of simulation.*"

"Mm-hmm. And Zwe?"

I take a sip of iced tea and pop a triangle of dragonfruit in my mouth. "What about Zwe?"

"Oh come on, don't play dumb, you're one of the smartest people I know. You know what I'm asking."

"I keep telling you it's not like that," I say. She snorts, and I swear she can somehow see me rolling my eyes. "Besides, he's talking to his ex again."

"So? People talk to people all the time," Soraya counters. "Last week, I was talking to Jeremy Strong at the Oxford Union. Does that mean we're riding off into the sunset together? Unfortunately, no," she answers herself.

"I heard that!" yells a male voice, presumably her husband, Alex.

"He'd be a midlife crisis. You know I'd come crawling back to you after a whirlwind month-long fling. *You're* the love of my life, sweetheart!" Soraya shouts.

"The chances of me being with Zwe are as high as the chances of you being with Jeremy Strong," I say.

Soraya goes silent, the only sound coming from my speaker that of her baby gurgling. "Fine, fine, I won't push it," she says. "How's everything else? How's your book? Are you inspired and shit?"

"I don't know about inspired, but it's definitely shit," I say with a self-effacing laugh. "Do you ever have moments where you're, like, *What the fuck am I doing?*"

"Oh, all the time. At work, with this baby, with the garden we're remodeling."

"What happened to us?" I sigh. "We used to be so cocky. The world was our oyster."

"Because we were young. We had all the time in the world."

"The good old days," I muse. "Sometimes I wish we could go back to that."

"I dunno," Soraya says. "I kinda like the present days. I mean, yeah, I'm older and jaded and it feels like I pull a new muscle every morning, and sure, at least once a day I think about leaving all of this behind and fleeing to some island in the Bahamas to become a surf instructor, but then I take a deep breath, and it's like, actually, I've wanted this life for a very long time. I worked really hard for a really long time to get it."

That tugs at something between my ribs, and I smile. When we were teenagers, I would dream about becoming a bestselling author, and Soraya, of being the first Asian woman to lead an Oxford college's geography department.

"You get what I mean, right?" Soraya asks. "Poe . . . you *are* happy, right?"

"I think—" I pause, inhale, know that Soraya will detect even the smallest of fibs. "I think I'm too stressed to be happy right now. I'm just so . . ." I exhale as I fall back into the plush seat cushion. "Tired." As though on cue, the sound of a wailing child pierces the speaker. "I think that was your son's way of reminding me that I am in no position to tell his mother about 'being tired.'"

"I will tell both my son and you that you have every right to be tired. Look, try not to think about your book for a bit. You're on holiday. *Be* on holiday." Soraya's in what we call her "Mom Mode," which was a thing way before she became an actual mother. "Have Zwe change your laptop password. If I can go on maternity leave for ten months, you can put your book away for two weeks. It will still be there at the end of the trip. I want to live vicariously through you, and I can't do that if you're sitting there in paradise just as bloody tired as I am."

"I know, I know," I huff.

"I—fuck, sorry, I got to go. This stupid son of mine just sucked me dry and then threw all of my milk back up on me and . . . fuck, that's going to stain. Hey, you're not in the market to buy a baby, are you? Because I might have one going."

"I don't think you're legally allowed to say that," I say. "Go take care of your child. And remember that you love him."

"Yeah, yeah," she says, a glimmer in her voice. Before I can press the red button, I hear her call out, "Alex! Come take your offspring!"

I think about Soraya's question, turning the words like they're lines in a Rubik's Cube. Of course I'm happy. The problem isn't that I'm unhappy; like Soraya, *I* have my dream life now, too. The problem is that if I want to *stay* happy, I have to write this book.

Zwe's still not back by the time I'm showered. Still floating on a cloud of facial treatments and massages, I decide I want to dress up a bit tonight, and pick out the one "fancy" outfit I packed: a sleeveless red lace jumpsuit with a low-cut neckline. I put my hair up in a messy bun, put on gold hoops, and for the final touch, swipe on a rich layer of Elson 4 by Pat McGrath, the vivid red a perfect match to my outfit's fabric. I've spent the last few months in an exclusive rotation of the unofficial work-from-home writer's outfit of slouchy jeans and baggy sweatpants; tonight, I look hot. It's nice to remember that I have boobs and a waistline.

I decide to head to the restaurant early with my laptop and get some writing done before dinner. Taking a seat outdoors—it would feel like a disservice to this view and weather to sit indoors—I order a yuzu cocktail, put on my headphones, and start writing. I've powered through approximately five hundred words (not great, but not *awful*) when my peripheral vision clocks a figure walking in my direction.

Zwe is wearing a light pink button-up shirt tucked into black trousers, the outfit finished off with a navy blazer and sneakers—all of it a far cry from the T-shirt, shorts, and flip-flops he was wearing this morning.

One side of his mouth tips up into a lopsided smile when I stand, his head also cocking ever so slightly as though a random thought just popped into it.

"You look fancy," I say as I pull him in for a hug.

"I saw the tissues with the red lipstick in the bin," he tells me. I don't mean to smell him, but I inhale while we're mid-embrace, and his cologne smells so good that I almost let out a small *Mmmm* (almost, but I don't). "I knew I couldn't show up looking like a slob while you look like—" He steps back, works his jaw with one hand while gesturing at me with the other. I blush, a fizzing sensation inciting in my stomach. "—this. You look . . . incredible."

"Don't get used to it, I packed one nice outfit and five pairs of ripped denim shorts."

"You look incredible in ripped denim shorts, too," he says, and I'm blushing again. "Although the state of some of those shorts really begs the question of when something goes from 'intentionally ripped' to 'piece of denim vaguely strung together by various pieces of thread,'" he adds.

He laughs when I strike his hand with the menu. "It's *fashion*, okay?" I argue.

"I don't get why you won't let me sew them," he says with a shake of his head. He's been on this particular crusade for a while now. "That one pair doesn't even have a hem! It's just a tangle of white threads! I can't believe brands are getting away with charging the exact amount for a *full* pair of shorts while using a third of the fabric."

"You know that at this point, I'm stopping you from sewing them more out of principle than anything. I will not let a man police what I wear."

He rolls his eyes. "I'm going to make an honest woman out of you yet."

"What are you implying?" I throw my hands in the air. "Can't a girl wear shorts that have half her ass hanging out without being called a 'whore' anymore?" I exclaim.

"Good evening!" I don't know how long our server has been nearby, but I wish he'd made his presence known *before* I'd proudly declared myself a whore. By the look on Zwe's face, he absolutely saw the staff approaching us from behind my back. I shoot him a death glare, and he widens his grin. "My name's Brandon. Can I start you off with some drinks?" Brandon asks.

"I'll have another of this yuzu drink," I say, gesturing at my empty glass.

"And I'll have a beer," Zwe says. "Bartender's choice."

"Of course, I'll be back with both of those. And please let me know if you have any questions about the food."

"Zwe Aung Win," I say, cocking a suspicious brow. "When was the last time you drank on a weekday?" Zwe barely even drinks on weekends because he's almost always the one opening up the bookstore.

"Probably when I was in my early twenties?" He laughs, like he can't believe it. "You're going to have to keep an eye on me tonight. Make sure I don't do something stupid."

"Oh yeah? Like what?"

He bites his bottom lip as though to stop himself from answering. "You tell me," he says.

"Like . . . ask Leila to join you for a drink? I don't think that'd be stupid, for the record." Zwe gives a halfhearted chuckle at that.

Brandon returns with our drinks. "Are you sure *you* don't want to ask out Leila?" Zwe asks as we clink our glasses.

"A writer's block–inspired awakening of my sexuality?" I shrug. "I suppose I've had costlier crises. But alas, no. Still just into good dick, I'm afraid. I only brought up Leila because I saw you two out there earlier. You looked like you were having a good time."

"We were. I was." There's a pause where I don't know if I'm supposed to respond with something. "How was the spa?" he asks.

I shake out both of my arms. "Amazing. I'm as loose as a noodle. Nary a knot to be found in *this* body," I say, and gesture dramatically at myself.

Zwe smirks, his eyes following where my hands are directing him, down my neck and shoulders, right to my chest. His gaze briefly lingers, and it's enough to stop time, even if only for a second.

I cough and gesture down at the menu, shaking both of us out of whatever sunset-induced daze this place keeps pulling us into. "Do you know what you want?"

Zwe murmurs a "Yes," and like last night, I could almost swear I feel him still staring at me. And just like last night, something stops me from checking, instead locking my gaze onto the piece of paper in my hands.

Leila stops by as we're halfway through our second round of drinks. "How was your meal? I heard you got the salmon and steak? Those would've been my recommendations, too. They were both flown in fresh from Japan just this morning."

I do a double take, certain I must be drunk and misheard her. "Did you say you imported the salmon and beef from Japan? Today? But it's just us here—" I swivel my head around, having to check. "Right? Did a new party check in?"

"Nope, still just you two," Leila says, gliding past the first question like it doesn't even warrant addressing.

"It was a great meal," Zwe says. "Easily top five across my lifetime."

"Do you want another round?" Leila gestures at our empty glasses.

Zwe shoots me a glance, and knowing him, he's on the verge of saying no (two beers have become his limit, even on holiday, but maybe I could nudge him into a third). Before he can reply, I stretch and fake a large yawn. "I'm going to turn in, but Zwe, you should stay."

I'm expecting him to throw me a sarcastic *That was subtle* expression, but instead, he tilts his head, his dark brows furrowing like he's confused. "I . . . will . . . head back, too," he says slowly. I frown at him to telepathically ask *What the hell are you doing?* but he either doesn't catch it, or ignores it altogether. "Today wiped me out," he tells Leila.

"That's fair," she says. She cracks her knuckles and then her neck. "You two need to rest up for snorkeling tomorrow anyway."

"You sure you don't wanna stay out? Don't feel like you have to come back on account of me," I offer. "I'm not *so* drunk that I can't make my way back on my own."

"I can call a buggy for you if you'd like?" Leila asks.

I'm about to take her up on that if it will put Zwe's mind at ease while he stays behind, but he beats me to a response. "I think the exercise and fresh air from walking back will do us good."

The way the night ended is still nagging me even by the time we're in bed, and at last, I decide I'm not going to be able to fall asleep if I don't ask. "Hey, why didn't you stay behind with Leila? She sounded like she was down to hang out with you."

We're sleeping with our backs to each other, so I can't see his reaction. "Why are you so obsessed with me hooking up with Leila?" Zwe asks.

"I'm not *obsessed*," I scoff. "I just . . . want you to be happy."

There's a soft laugh from his side of the bed, followed by a long, elastic silence, the kind that could be filled with any interpretation of your choosing. "Poe" is all he finally says, alcohol and sleepiness smoothing out the edges of his words.

"What?" I ask when he doesn't say anything else.

"I'm on what is probably *the* most beautiful island on this planet, and more importantly, I'm here with my best friend. I *am* happy."

SIX

"So I have to put my *whole* face in the water?"

"Yes." Zwe's hand makes a circular motion in front of his own face. "The whole thing."

I eye the snorkeling mask in my hand. "But what if I accidentally breathe in water?"

"Well . . . don't."

I glare at him. Behind me, Antonio and Leila let out inadvertent snorts that they scramble to cough away. "Yeah, yeah, laugh it up. City girl isn't born to be the next Moana—shocker." I wave my mask around at all three of them. Antonio and Leila grin, and I'm glad they feel comfortable enough around us now to toe that line between "friend" and "guest." Pointing out that there were literally *no other guests* at the resort, Zwe and I had convinced them to join us at snorkeling, partly because we would've felt *so* awkward knowing they were sitting on the shore just waiting for us, and partly because I feel much safer knowing there'll be three other people in the water around me at all times should I find myself in some freak snorkeling accident, like a sudden attack by a school of jellyfish.

"Ms. Poe, how about this?" Antonio pushes the snorkeling mask hanging around his neck to the back so that the pipe bit is behind him. "If you're comfortable with it, I can hold you from underneath while you paddle out. You can practice breathing until your body relaxes and gets used to it, and I'll be right beside you if something goes wrong."

I consider it. "Only if you stop calling me *Ms.* Poe."

He chuckles. "Deal, Poe."

"And you'll carry me and run if a shark approaches me?" I ask.

Antonio puts a palm on his heart. "With my bare hands. I *am* your porter after all. Carrying is literally my job."

Since he was the one who mentioned them, I take this opportunity to check out his bare, muscular, strong, large hands, tracing them up to his equally muscular, strong, large biceps and shoulders. He smiles when we make eye contact. Suddenly, my turquoise bikini set feels too skimpy and exposing, my own bare skin warming up like the sun's been dialed up a few notches.

"*I* can hold you while you get used to breathing with the mask," Zwe offers out of the blue.

I frown at him. Zwe has a protective nature, but I thought if anything, he'd be thrilled that Antonio has offered to look after me so that he can go off on his own with Leila. "I'll . . . be okay," I say. I nod at Antonio. "I'm certain I'll be in good hands."

"You sure?" Zwe doesn't so much look at Antonio as he does survey him, like he doesn't think Antonio *would* be able to save me in the event of an emergency. If this were anyone else, I'd almost swear it looks like jealousy. Almost.

"I'm sure," I say. "You two kids go have fun." I make a shooing motion at him and Leila. "Don't let me hold you back. I'll come join you and your new fish friends in a bit."

"Okay," Zwe says, but doesn't move.

I roll my eyes and give him a push. "Go, I mean it. I'll be too self-conscious if I know all three of you are watching me."

Still with that dubious expression, Zwe finally nods, and he and Leila jog off into the water while pulling on their masks. I watch his figure slowly disappear into the water, his sunscreen-covered skin gleaming in the sunshine, and I can't help but think once more how young and free he looks while splashing around in the ocean, droplets of water jumping into the air with every bouncy step his blue rubber fins take. After I watch the two of them go underwater, I turn to Antonio.

"I apologize in advance if I freak out," I tell him.

He shakes his head. "No apologies necessary. Although I think you should cut yourself some slack. You're a smart and fit woman—I have no doubt you'll pick it up in no time."

I almost ask *Are you flirting with me?* but stop myself, because even if he is—which I'm pretty certain is the case—I don't think official employee rules would allow him to admit it. Which is just as well; it's been nearly a full year since I last went on a date, and to be honest, I don't really remember how to flirt with an actual man that I'm attracted to. Which leads to the realization that this attractive, muscular man is about to make skin-to-skin contact with my torso, and oh god what if my body forgets how a body is supposed to act and reacts in a weird, definitely not sexy manner? What if I cough and spit water in his face? What if a wave crashes into us and my top slips down and my boobs pop out (also in a definitely not sexy manner)?

"You ready?" Antonio raises his forearms into a ninety-degree angle, biceps flexing in the process. His slightly confused smile must mean that in the midst of my panic, my face began doing something weird.

To hide it, I pull my very sexy plastic mask on and give two thumbs up. "As ready as I'll ever be."

Not to toot my own horn, but I pick it up way more quickly than I thought I would. There were some abrupt starts and stops at the beginning, but that was solely because I got in my own head; otherwise, there was no inhaling or spitting of sea water, which is a major win. Once I managed to go several minutes without stopping, Antonio even began teaching me breathing control techniques: shallow inhales and full exhales will make your body less buoyant and let you sink deeper into the water, while full inhales and shallow exhales will keep you floating closer to the surface.

"Look who's joined us! Ariel herself!" Zwe says after I snorkel on my own to demonstrate my newfound ability, the three of them watching like a trio of proud parents. It would've easily sounded like sarcasm coming from anyone else, but not Zwe.

We stick close together at first underwater, one person waving and gesticulating at a cool fish and the others giving thumbs-ups to acknowledge them; eventually, though, we drift off on separate paths, close enough to keep each other in our peripheral vision, but far enough that we're doing our own thing. And for the first time in a long time, I realize the typically frantic part of my brain has . . . stopped.

As great as the spa day was yesterday, lying on a massage bed in a quiet room while other people worked through a menu of massages and facials left me with nothing to do but think. Despite my fervent pleas to my mind to *relax* and *do nothing,* it did what it always does, whether that's on a commute or while queuing at the supermarket—plot, fidget, wonder, worry. I once tried explaining to Zwe that it feels like I'm a video game character running through my own book, repeatedly running into dead ends or down plot holes that I don't know how to overcome on the next try.

Not today, though. Today, the physical activity keeps my brain distracted. I'm not worrying that my next pitch for Ayesha won't be exciting enough, because I'm too busy worrying about breathing correctly and staying alive.

When I look around, I see crystal-clear turquoise waters and iridescent fish and coral reefs and Zwe taking photos with his waterproof disposable camera. The water is cool but not freezing, and I'm awestruck by the way the sunlight breaks through the surface and makes the seabed shimmer. Ironically, here—in the middle of the Indian Ocean with a piece of plastic shoved into my mouth—is the first time in months that I've felt like I can breathe. Right now, life feels manageable, and being happy, really *truly* happy, seems like such an easy and achievable goal.

I'm cured! I think, and immediately chuckle, making a couple of bubbles float up in front of my face. Noticing, Zwe makes a questioning *Okay?* gesture with his fingers, and I nod and return it. I've never been more okay in my life. If snorkeling turns out to have been the solution to my problems all along, I'm going to sell our apartment and move us to a shack on the beach.

"Do you think we should move here?" I ask Zwe as I pop another cheese cube in my mouth. Antonio and Leila had arranged a post-snorkeling picnic for us, but even with our most fervent pleas, refused to join us for this part. So now it's just the two of us, sitting on a blanket, enjoying a substantial cheese and fruit platter served with two pitchers of our signature drinks. It's the beginning of yet another perfect cotton-candy sunset, a pattern that would seem improbable if you wrote it into a movie.

"What would we do with our place?" Zwe asks.

"Your brother can take it. Or we can sell it."

Zwe chuckles. "I wish we could move here," he says. "But it'd be a logistical nightmare." Even when we're fantasizing, he's realistic. "I'm glad we're here right now, though. Thanks again. For"—he gestures around with a hand—"paying for everything."

"Don't even mention it, what else would I do with my advance?" I say, waving a sand-specked hand. "You know, Vik and I used to say that we would go on a big, fancy holiday whenever I sold my first book. He wanted to climb Everest—"

Zwe interrupts me with a snort. "You would not have survived thirty minutes on Everest."

I throw a grape at him even though we both know he's right. "But *this* was the kind of trip *I* always envisioned," I admit. "Where we just sat around and . . . talked. Wherever we went, though, for me, the most important part was that *I* paid for it."

"Why couldn't he pay for it? The man was the poster child for finance bros."

"It was an ego thing."

"Yours or his? Because I distinctly remember the latter being big enough to make your relationship a throuple."

I roll my eyes. "Mine, in this case. I wanted to show him I could do it, you know? Buy us nice things. That my books would one day be worth . . . something."

Zwe's eyes are unreadable behind his sunglasses. I can't even tell if they're open or closed as he lies on his back, face tilted right up at the sun. "If there's anyone who doesn't need to prove themselves to anybody, it's you," he finally says, delivering a gut punch of a reply.

"How did you do it?" I ask.

"Do what?"

"Always believe in me. Believe that one day my books would lead to—" I throw my arms open. "—this. You're the most level-headed person in the world. How did you keep on believing that I'd actually do it when all the evidence was pointing to the contrary? When even my own fiancé eventually viewed it as a pipe dream?"

Between the two of us, I'm the dreamer, the one who believes in Manifestation with a capital *M,* who grew up blindly pointing at my bookshelf and declaring *I'm going to have copies of my own book one day.* In contrast, Zwe has always, always been a numbers guy, had become an accountant because he didn't trust anyone else to look after his parents' money. I've always thought it was more than slightly unfair that his younger brother got to move to Hong Kong to try to become a fine dining chef there while Zwe was stuck looking after the family business and their parents, but Zwe's never given any indication that he dreams of a life more similar to his brother's. I don't know how much of it is because he's genuinely happy where he is, and how much is because he feels that it's his eldest son duty.

"Who the fuck cares what Vik thought?" Zwe props himself up on his elbow, and I'm startled by the way his tone has stretched, like my last sentence has left him a millimeter away from snapping. Seeing my expression, he raises a hand to apologize. I forgive him, because I know how he feels about Vik. "It wasn't difficult to believe in you, Poe," Zwe says. He pushes his sunglasses on top of his head, as though he wants me to see in his eyes that he's telling the truth.

"I read your drafts. Of course it was always going to happen. It was just a matter of time," he says as he leans forward and reaches for my pendant, swiping one thumb across the words. The back of his hand makes contact with my chest, and on instinct I look down at where his hand is resting between the turquoise triangle cups of my bikini top. Zwe nudges my chin back up with his thumb but doesn't move his hand, and when I raise my head again, I'm looking straight into his brown eyes. Most of his hair is dry now, but the roots are still slightly damp, making him look like he's just been done up for a swimsuit photo shoot. There's some sand stuck to his right shoulder that I wonder if I should brush off.

"You did great today," he says. "Maybe we can graduate to paddleboarding tomorrow."

"Baby steps," I say. "I'm glad you came on this trip with me."

"Would you have done it with anyone else?" He retracts his hand, and my skin burns where his had made contact. I tell myself that I should've put on more sunscreen.

"No," I answer truthfully. "It was you or no one else."

Without saying anything else, he smiles, as though that's exactly the answer he was hoping for.

―――――

After dinner that night, we make our way to the cliffside bar, and I text Leila to ask if she, Antonio, and Eka can join us. Almost instantly, three dots appear.

"What'd they say?" Zwe asks.

"She says they'll sit this one out. I think they feel weird about getting a drink with us."

"You know, I get it, but it also makes me feel . . ." Zwe looks around at the warmly lit open space.

"Uncomfortable?" I offer.

He nods. "I'd like to think we're friends by now. Or at least pals."

"Eh, we'll rope them into more activities tomorrow. Oooh, maybe we can go paragliding."

Zwe raises his Moscow mule at me. "Now there's a plan."

Silence settles into the air between us, inserting itself into the crevices between the sound of the waves below. Smooth jazz is playing on low via the speakers near the bar, and there's a random clinking of glass whenever the bartender shifts bottles around. Neither of us says a word until we've finished our drinks and order a second round.

"It's like another world out here," I murmur over my glass. "It feels like . . . anything's possible."

"What do you mean?" Zwe's voice is also low, as though there's an unspoken rule that we can't be louder than the sea.

"It feels like . . . none of the messes we have waiting for us back home ever existed."

"Like what?"

I swallow, guilt pulling at a tender nerve as I ruefully think, *Here she goes again*; it's a broken record by this point, but I can't make it stop. I sound like that friend who won't quit moaning about her breakup, but when you *are* the person who's going through the breakup, it feels like your lens has shrunk into this tiny pinhole and it's the only thing through which you can process the world. "Like my next book. Like . . . like the fact that I read an early copy of Pim Charoensuk's book, and it's *good*."

It's the first time I've said it out loud. Every single emotion I've been trying to keep at bay washes over me as soon as the words leave my mouth: anger, jealousy, shame, fear.

"I didn't know you'd read it," Zwe says quietly.

"I was asked if I'd consider blurbing it." My chuckle makes the line sound menacing, as though this whole time, I've been plotting to sneak a bad blurb onto Pim Charoensuk's cover.

"Are you?"

"I . . . don't know," I tell him honestly. I don't tell him that it's not a matter of whether or not I like the book, because I actually love it; I don't tell him that I'm still not sure because of more terrible, selfish reasons. "I'm still considering it."

"That's good," he says.

I wrinkle my nose, confused. "*Good?* What do you mean 'good'?"

Zwe smiles at me, the alcohol already painting his cheekbones the lightest shade of pink. When I catch myself thinking *How does every single color look so good on you?*, I know the liquor has entered my bloodstream, too. "I mean that I know you don't *have to* blurb it, and that a part of you doesn't want to." My lips have parted a mere millimeter when he reaches out, his forefinger already hushing my protest of a white lie. "It's okay that you don't want to. Competing for survival is a human instinct. But the fact that you didn't outright refuse is proof that somewhere deep down, she's still there."

His finger, still on my lips, smushes my words together as I ask, "That who's still there?"

With zero warning, Zwe's finger slides down the middle of my chin, my neck, makes a sharp left turn on my chest, stopping at the spot between my collarbone and where my breast technically starts. When he presses the skin there, it's as though he's pressed right into the center of my heart, causing my body to stand to attention, the cool metal of the stool's back pressing into my own.

"That little book nerd I became friends with."

I let out a nervous laugh, wondering if he can feel the rate at which my heart is thumping right now. It feels like it's asking for something new with every beat: *Stay. Yes. More. Please. You. What. If?*

Which is all so ridiculous. Zwe and I fit, but not like this. He's numbers and logic, I'm all emotions, the kind of person who cries at YouTube videos of senior dogs getting adopted. He's always held a steady job, and I want to be an artist even if it means I don't know when or where my next paycheck will come from. He arrives at the bookstore at 8 A.M. sharp every morning and leaves at 7 P.M., seven days a week; I book spontaneous island getaways.

It's not that I think I'm not good enough for him, but that if you merged our five-year plans, there would be very little overlap. We would be "quirky" together. But quirky can't be sustained for a lifetime, and I don't *want* to be his—or anyone's—quirky ex. We've built a life that's good and solid, and Zwe would be the first person to say that it's not worth risking destroying something good and solid for something new and exciting that has a high likelihood of ultimately failing. One of us would need to find a new place to live, I wouldn't be able to come to the bookstore anymore, our families would feel weird about staying in contact with one another.

And the thing is, even if I could convince myself that those are all things we could overcome, there's also the embarrassing fact that if Zwe wanted to ask me out on a date, he would have by now. Because he knows. He knows how I feel, or at least felt. There's a reason he never brought up my failed attempt at kissing him, that he never asked me out even after Vik and I ended. Maybe sometimes he wonders about all of these things too, but clearly, he's reached the same practical conclusion I have.

Maybe in another lifetime, we make sense. Maybe in another lifetime, I'm as pragmatic as him and we meet in an accounting class, or he's also an artist, a painter or a screenwriter. In that lifetime, people remark that they've never met two people who were so perfectly made for each other. In that lifetime, our biggest point of conflict is that I want a dog and he wants a cat, or we can't agree on what color to paint our living room.

It's the alcohol, I remind myself. Take alcohol and remote island paradise and a very long dry spell of the coital nature, and ta-da: you get horny Poe who very easily could've had a sex dream about Prince Eric.

"Is 'little book nerd' a compliment?" I ask.

"Of course it is," Zwe says. "I'm really proud of you, you know."

"For what? Not trying to sabotage my new literary nemesis?"

A shadow falls across his face, and it's not from the lamplight. "You know, you're . . . wrong. There's no way Pim is your literary nemesis."

"Feels like it."

"You—" His finger pushes into my skin again, and again I trip over my breath, my body forgetting how to do anything on instinct. In this moment, Zwe *is* the instinct. "—are unmatchable. No one can be your nemesis because no one comes close. You're just so . . ."

"So what?" I ask.

"So . . . you."

For a fleeting moment, I wonder what would happen if I shot my shot a second time and leaned over, tried again. But even with the cushion of intoxication, I remember how deep that rejection cut the first time, the hairline fracture it created never having fully healed.

The way he's looking at me now could almost convince me that he's asking me to try again. Almost.

A needy part of me whispers that it doesn't have to be anything serious, that it could only be for tonight, and then all of it—the good and the bad—will be erased in the blue light of dawn. But it feels terribly like cannonballing into the ocean from a cliff's edge: a thrilling story if it works out the way you envision, an irreversible tragedy if it doesn't.

Silly. Silly girl with her silly thoughts.

We're both tipsy bordering on drunk right now, and I've never quite figured out if the things people say and do when they're inebriated are what they truly want, or their biggest mistakes.

"What are you thinking?" Zwe asks, face illuminated by the soft yellow glow of the small table lamp.

Everything.

Too many things.

"Nothing," the coward lies.

SEVEN

Zwe is a light sleeper. I am not. I don't wake up until he clamps a hand tightly on my mouth and whispers "It's me, don't scream" so close into my ear that each syllable is a hiss of air directly into my eardrum. My first instinct is to scream, because what else are you supposed to do when you wake up in the middle of the night with a large male palm pressed against your mouth (and not in a sexy way)?

I move just my eyes to make sure that it *is* him, although it's hard to do when my eyes haven't adjusted to the dark yet, and the only light source in the room is moonlight that's being filtered through a gauze curtain. But I can smell him, can sense that it *is* him, and so I nod slowly. I try to open my mouth to ask a question, but feeling the movement, he shakes his head at me, then motions with his gaze outside.

"Gunshots," he whispers, his mouth pressed right up against my ear.

It takes several long seconds for me to understand the singular word. The moment it hits, though, I feel a rush of blood to my head that's so quick, I would need to lie down if I weren't already doing so. That can't be correct. He has to be carrying out some weird prank. Or hallucinating. Maybe his drink was stronger than he thought. Or night terrors. Yes, maybe he *dreamt* he heard gunshots, but that's all it is . . . right?

"Gunshots?" I mumble into Zwe's palm. I'm about to ask a garbled *Are you sure?* right as another shot goes off. One that *I* hear, too.

"Do. Not. Panic," he says, and I widen my eyes at the glass walls at the foot of our bed, walls that suddenly seem like a *terrible* idea on the architect's part. "I'm not going to remove my hand until you promise me you won't make a sound." A pause. "So, promise?"

I nod.

"*Promise* promise?"

I nod again. Like he's backing away from a grizzly bear who's promised not to lunge toward him, Zwe cautiously removes his hand.

My mouth is dry, and I have no feeling in my fingertips even though my hands are visibly shaking. In fact, I can't really feel any of my limbs. "Maybe it's the security staff shooting a wild bear that's wandered into the resort?" I propose.

"I think the receptionist would've called us to let us know if that was the case. Instead—" He points at the landline on the table by his side of the bed. "The phone is dead. There's no dial tone."

"What do we do?" I whisper.

"We need to get help." I'm about to reach over for my phone when Zwe adds, "The Wi-Fi is down. They must've cut that, too."

"Fuck," I exhale. I fight the urge to pull the covers over my head and go back to sleep with the belief that this will all turn out to be a misunderstanding by the time I'm awake again. "There's no cell service anywhere. Someone must've called for help already, right? Every resort has security—*they* must have satellite phones . . . right?"

My eyes have adjusted to the darkness, and I can see the groove between Zwe's brows. Not one to lie, even to give me much-desired false hope, all he replies is "Hopefully."

"What do you think they want?"

"I don't know."

"How did they get here?"

"I don't—"

"Do you think they've gathered all of the resort staff? How many of them do you think there are?"

"Poe." Zwe pinches the skin between his brows. "How would I know the answer to any of those questions? I have access to the same amount of information surrounding the situation as you do."

I scoff. "Really? Attitude? Right now?"

"Why would you think I'd know what they want?"

I throw up my hands, straining to keep my voice within whisper territory. "Because you were awake before me! Maybe you heard something!"

"You think there were gunmen stationed outside our room conveniently laying out the whole plan for me to overhear?"

"Don't be a dick," I sneer. "I—"

Two more gunshots. Shots that are closer.

"Fuck," I say, right as Zwe commands, "Get dressed."

"What's wrong with my pajamas?" I ask.

He pulls back the covers in one swoop and points at my matching plaid set. "You get cold easily as it is. That's not going to keep you warm in the woods."

"The w—" In a moment of distraction, I raise my voice, and Zwe's palm swiftly slaps my lips. "Ow!" I mumble.

"We have to go to the woods," he says, leaning in and dropping his voice as though demonstrating to a kindergartener the importance of using our Inside Voices.

"Why"—I push his hand away—"do we have to go to the woods?"

"Because we need to find a way to reach the authorities. And remember what Leila said?" I try to remember through my brain fog, but Zwe answers his own question. "She said her family lives in the mountains. Which must mean there's at least a village there, and *they* must have a way to communicate with the mainland. We also can't just hide here like sitting ducks. Whoever these people are, I'm sure they're already starting to make their way around the resort, and it's only a matter of time until they reach us. So before they do, we leave, make our way to the village, we ask for help, and we shelter in place there until the help arrives. Now let's get dressed."

"How have you already planned out all of this?" I ask.

"Remember that small business security course I took a few years back?"

"Vaguely," I say as I try to recall. He had wanted me to join him, but it would've involved giving up my weekends for an entire month. Besides, it wasn't like we worked at a jewelry store. *What kind of foolish robbers would want to rob an independent bookstore?* I'd asked.

"We were taught that if someone is in the back room while robbers come in, that person's primary focus should be on getting help, either by escaping or trying to get the attention of your neighbors. You should *not* try to be the hero and free everybody," Zwe is saying. "The closest source of help right now is Leila's family."

"Leila said her family lives in the *mountains*," I remind him, taking the first sweatshirt and pair of jeans at the top of my suitcase. "How the fuck are we going to know *which* mountain they're on? There are, like, fifty of them!"

We've got our backs to each other, but I can hear Zwe changing out of his pajamas, too. "There aren't *fifty*," he says sarcastically. "And I imagine there's a way for *them* to access the resort too, which means there must be a path somewhere, probably out in the back. There was a map of hiking paths here somewhere—" He trails off, and I first take a tentative peek over my shoulder to make sure he's dressed. He is, in jeans and a long-sleeved henley. Making his way over to the desk, he quietly checks the drawers until he locates what he's looking for: a rectangular sheet of paper that's been folded multiple times (the map, I'm presuming).

I sit down on the bed with rolled socks in one hand, my sneakers in the other. "You seriously think we can make our way through this massive resort, toward the hiking trail, climb up a whole-ass mountain, and locate a group of people we've never met? And in the cold dark of the night? Do we even know *which* hiking trail is the correct one?"

"Do you have a better plan?" Zwe says as he forcefully tugs his own shoelaces tight. He's sitting on the floor, backpack by his side, map folded into a smaller rectangle that's already tucked into his pocket.

"I never said I did. I just am asking if yours is . . . the best."

"No plan." He gets to his feet and slings on the backpack. "No input."

I open my bag with the intention of unloading any items I might not need, but almost instantly talk myself into believing that I *might* need a pen or mints or wet wipes at some point. And I certainly can't leave my water bottle and wallet behind, and you always, *always* pack a book with you. In the end, I remove my mini floss and Tide pen.

"Passport?" Zwe asks.

"Yes, Dad," I say, although I feel for the rectangular bump within the inside zip compartment, just to be sure. Reaching across him, I unplug my laptop from its charger and am putting it inside my bag's padded laptop compartment when a hand stops on top of mine.

"What are you doing?" His expression is one of utter bafflement.

"What does it look like?" I zip the bag shut, laptop secured. "I'm getting ready to go hike a mountain. We're going to need to ration the granola bars, by the way. I only have two."

"You're not bringing your laptop."

I blink to make sure I've heard him right. "I'm not *not* bringing my laptop."

"Poe, you're going to struggle enough as is to hike a mountain—"

I rear back. "Hey! I can hike—"

"Ssshhh!" he hisses, eyes widening.

Sorry, I mouth. Then, whispering this time, "I can hike! You think I'm leaving my laptop behind in a hotel room that we're never going to return to? My manuscript is on there!"

"Seriously? *That's* what you're concerned about right now? Your *manuscript?*" he hisses out the last word.

"Yes, because I've been working really hard, and—"

"You don't even have a manuscript, though! You hate everything you've been writing! They're all in your trash folder!"

I know he doesn't mean it as an insult. It's a fact, one that he heard from my own lips: I *have* hated every word I've been writing.

But still. Even in this particular moment, to hear it said out loud by somebody else—it feels like I accidentally touched a lit candle. The hurt isn't massive, but it *does* still hurt.

On his part, Zwe immediately looks apologetic. "I'm—" he starts.

"I started a new one last night—" I cut in. "And I think it's got real potential, and I haven't connected to the Wi-Fi so I can't email it to myself. Zwe, call me insane or inefficient or stupid, or whatever you want, but I'm not leaving my laptop behind."

"I would never think any of those things," he says. "But a laptop is not a priority right now."

"It's coming with me," I state matter-of-factly.

We engage in a staring contest that might've gone on for much longer were it not for a new sudden explosion of gunshots.

"Fine, but if you need a break, we're switching bags," Zwe says resolutely.

I roll my eyes. "Ugh, we get it, you're a gym bro, you can hike a mountain carrying *two* backpacks."

His smirk lasts for a few seconds before he settles back into Serious Zwe. "All of the trails start at the same point," he explains. "From the reception area, we have to walk approximately half a mile east. Now, the trails all take you to different viewpoints around the island, but I'm guessing the longest one will take you to the *highest* mountain. That's the one that also has a lunch break factored into the overall round-trip time, and I'm assuming we'd be having lunch at the village. That's the trail we want."

"Are you certain it's the longest one? Counterpoint: What if it's the shortest one?" I'm trying to lighten the situation with some terrible humor, but Zwe's reaction (or lack thereof) makes it clear that nothing is going to make him laugh right now.

"It's the longest trail," he states blankly. He's about to push down on the door handle but pauses, and turns back to me. "Ready?"

This is when it hits me.

"No," I answer honestly. I reach out and steady myself against the wall, although what I actually want to do is sit down and cry, ideally for a few hours. The adrenaline is still pumping through me, but the gravity of the situation is starting to settle in.

He nods, like he knew already. "I know," he says. His voice is soft but steady, a far contrast from my own shaking physique. "This is all fucking terrifying. *I'm* scared as fuck right now. But Poe . . . I need you to be. Ready, I mean."

A small sniffle escapes me. "You really don't know how to lie, do you? Not even some light sugarcoating? No sweet coaxing to get me out the door?"

He gives me a half smile, but even that is visibly weighed down by fear. He *is* scared, too, I realize.

"Those people have guns," I say.

"I know."

"Do you think they've—" I swallow. "—shot anyone?"

"I don't know."

"Do you think they'll shoot at . . . us?"

He lifts one shoulder. "I don't know."

"I don't want to die," I whisper. Despite my incessant blinking, the prickling in my eyes doesn't abate. I can feel the wetness trailing down my cheeks, my chest getting tighter with each word. "I don't want to die, not here, not like this. I want to die when I'm seventy-five, and ideally in a nice little cottage on a cliff overlooking the Mediterranean Sea, and you're sitting beside my bed and singing me Taylor Swift covers while playing your ukulele."

"When did I learn to play the ukulele?" he snorts.

"When I vetoed the guitar because we had no space in our living room. Do you know how small cottages are?"

"We're still living together when we're seventy-five?"

I recoil in pretend shock. "Of course we're still living together when we're seventy-five. Do you know what a hassle it'd be to find a new roommate I'll vibe with? And it's not like I'm going to get tall enough to change the light bulbs myself."

"How are you cracking jokes right now?" he asks with an incredulous laugh.

"Is the fact that I use humor to deal with uncomfortable situations news to you?" I ask.

He shakes his head. "Then you're going to have a whole stand-up routine by the time we're done with all of this. Now—" He tilts his head at the door. "Shall we?"

"I don't know if I can." My voice is a croak, the terror constricting my throat and my chest so that I can't breathe. My knees are trembling, and my heart is beating so fast, I'm convinced it's going to give out any second now. This cannot be happening to me. This happens in movies, or to strangers that you read about in a news article that makes you go, *That poor woman, thank god that wasn't me.* "What if we just waited?" I offer, desperately clutching at straws. "Why can't we do that? Why can't we just lock ourselves in here and wait for someone to come help us? Even if they find us, I bet they'd take pity on us. I bet they'd look at us and be like, *Yeah, those two aren't going to give us any trouble. The small one just keeps yelling, 'Tell Taylor Swift I love her!'*"

That makes Zwe laugh again. He lets go of the door handle, takes the two strides to close the gap between us, lifts one of my hands in each of his, and gives them a good squeeze. I shut my eyes, focusing on the weighty feeling of his fingertips pushing into my palms. "Because we will be sitting ducks, and they *will* find us, and we won't have a shot at getting away."

I sniff in a disgusting trail of snot. He snatches a tissue off the table and hands it to me. "I hate hiking," I hiccup out.

"I'm aware," he replies instantly. "But we have to do this. And we have to do this now."

I try to blow my nose as quietly as possible, which results in a drawn-out low-pitched *eeeee* sound that makes Zwe want to laugh so hard he has to bury his face in his arm. "Is my pain providing humorous relief for you?" I ask.

Rolling in his lips, all he does is nod.

I shake out my shoulders, and take a deep breath. "All right, let's do this. You lead, I'll follow."

He gives a small salute, and this time, opens the door in one swoop. We both freeze for a few seconds, as though waiting for two gunmen who were idling outside this whole time to reveal themselves. Instead, we're met with the cold, still air. It feels like a sickening joke opening your door to paradise when you're about to run for your lives. Zwe points at himself, then out the door, and I give a thumbs-up.

There are two paths from our villa to the reception area: the massive open-air stairs that run directly through the middle of the resort, and the longer winding vehicle path that spirals around the side. As we make our way forward, I realize that Zwe is picking the latter, probably because while the stairs are much quicker, we'd have nowhere to hide if someone spotted us.

Every time we hear a noise, we duck behind a tree or a bush. We're approximately halfway up the path when I tap Zwe on the shoulder, and make a time-out motion with my hands. There's an ever-increasing pain in the side of my gut, and my lungs and calves are both on fire.

A water bottle appears in front of my face. While I was hunched over and leaning on a tree, trying to take deep breaths without making any noise, Zwe unzipped his bag and opened his water bottle.

Thank you, I mouth. Aware that we have to conserve as much water as possible, I try to take the smallest of sips. The moment the cool liquid hits the back of my throat, though, my body screams for more. Instinct overrides guilt, and I put the metal opening to my lips once more, and take a second drink.

You good? Zwe mouths when I hand back the bottle.

I nod. *Thanks,* I say.

I see the way he hesitates before he takes a tiny swig as well, his brain doing some sort of calculation that involves the amount of water we have left, the number of miles we have to go, and how much longer our two bottles need to last us.

We resume the uphill climb, him in front. He's going slower than he would if he were on his own, and, feeling guilty again about being the one holding us back, I try my best to keep the panting to a minimum. We're one step away from rounding the next set of sharp corners when we both see it: two bright yellow headlights, four speeding wheels. A buggy.

I'm about to be a literal deer in headlights but before I can process it, Zwe's strong arms close around my waist and yank me to the side, the suddenness of the movement propelling an "Oomph" out of me.

"Ssshhh," he whispers into my ear. Not trusting myself, I clamp my own hand over my mouth this time.

He's pulled both of us into the shrubbery, half a second before one of the resort buggies drives by. They're so close that if even an inch of the top of our heads were peeking out, we'd have been made. And although it's only for a moment, I catch two masked people inside: one at the wheel, the other in the passenger seat, the latter with two rifles in hand.

I don't even exhale for fear of a rogue sob escaping.

When I'm at last certain that the coast is clear, I finally, *finally* breathe in, and then out. "Oh my god," I whisper.

"They must be rounding up anyone left," Zwe says.

"They know we're here. We're the only guests, it can't be difficult to go on the computers and find out which room we're in. Oh my god, they're going to our room and we're not going to be there and . . . and . . ." My tongue stops working. My brain stops working. All of my senses begin distorting my surroundings. The sound of the ocean suddenly becomes loud in my ears, like I'm right at the shore. I can even smell the sweet woodiness of sea salt.

"Hey." Zwe gives my shoulders a rough shake, and it sort of works. I return to my body, although it doesn't feel like it'll take much for me to drift away again. "We're still good. By the time they find us, we'll be in the woods. Let's keep going."

"But—"

"We're going to keep going," he states, refusing to hear my spiral. Which is for the best. I gesture at him to start walking, and I keep my eyes down on the ground, my mind occupied with stepping in the exact same spots that he does. It works so well that I'm startled when he stops walking. When I look up, we've made it, and are standing just a few feet away from the brightly lit reception area. Zwe points at a giant tree a few paces away, and we rush on our tiptoes until we can hunker down behind it.

Once we're both hidden, I motion that I'm going to peek. Craning my head as far as I can, I try to take stock of the scene. It looks like all of the staff members—or *nearly* all of them, depending on how many there are—are gathered in a circle in the middle, hands tied behind their backs. I spot Antonio and Leila and Sandra and Eka. There are two armed guards around them, and two more stationed at the front steps that connect the reception area to the rest of the resort.

I return to the safety of our giant tree. "Women," I whisper, frowning as I try to recall something.

"What?" Zwe asks.

"They're all . . . women," I say slowly. "Or at least . . . most of them are."

"How do you know? Can you see their faces?"

"No, they're wearing masks," I relay. "But it's their hair. The ones with long hair at least have their hair braided. And also their . . . general physique. I think . . ."

"What?"

"I think . . . the people in the buggy were women, too."

"Are you sure?" he asks.

I gasp. "The perfume." *That's* what I smelled.

"What perfume?"

But I'm already thinking aloud. "It's Jo Malone. Wood sage and sea salt. I thought I was smelling the ocean but it was their perfume."

"That's both weird and impressive," he says, one brow arching up. "Weird that they're all women, impressive that you can pinpoint a perfume on a passing buggy."

"The definition of 'superpowers' isn't limited to just 'flying' and 'teleportation,'" I say sagely.

He rolls his eyes. "Well, woman, man, nonbinary, it doesn't matter because they're still armed and trying to find us. Can we cross over to the other side without them noticing?"

"There are four of them so we'll have to be quiet," I say. I look around, willing a field of tall, unkempt grass to magically appear, but all I see is a row of pruned trees. Damn these perfectly kept gardens. "We need a distraction."

"What kind of distraction?"

"The kind that will confuse them long enough for us to make a run for it behind the trees."

"Like what? We don't have anything."

"I don't know!" I huff. "Let me take another look." I stretch out my neck again and am scanning around for something, maybe a vase I could throw a shoe at, or—I freeze when I make eye contact with Antonio.

He widens his eyes, and I can't tell if he's saying *Help us* or *Get the fuck out of here*.

I motion over at the woods behind the reception area, hoping that he puts two and two together.

His face scrunches up as he looks back and forth between me and the general direction in which I'm gesturing, but then he sits up straight and I know he's got it.

"Are you ready?" I whisper at Zwe without taking my eyes off Antonio, who nods.

"For what?" Zwe asks.

"To run."

"Wha—"

"Three," I say and hold up three fingers so that Antonio can see as I count us down. "Two. One."

That boy should absolutely consider an acting career, because he lets out a bloodcurdling scream so realistic that for a second, I'm worried he got shot. But so does everyone else, and the two guards who were manning the steps rush over. In a moment, everyone's crowded around him.

"Run," I say, grabbing Zwe's hand.

We bolt. I'm trying to make as little noise as possible, and the thudding of my heart in my ears is so loud that I can barely make out what's happening a few feet away.

"Something's wrong!" Antonio is screaming. "I can't feel my legs! And my heart is beating too fast! Is it a heart attack? I think I'm having a heart attack!"

"Shut up! You're not having a heart attack!" one of the guards barks. Definitely a woman.

"How would you know? Do you have any idea how stressed I am right now?"

"Listen, little boy," she snarls. I don't know what she's doing, but everyone's gone very silent.

A mental image of her putting her rifle to Antonio's temple pops up. Before the image can get any worse, I squeeze my eyes shut and shake my head like an Etch A Sketch.

I don't know why I thought shutting my eyes as I charge through a grove of trees at the fastest speed I ever have during my twenty-nine years on this earth would be a good idea, because it instantaneously turns out to be *not*.

I trip, my speed making it impossible for me to catch myself. My left ankle makes a popping sound that ankles are not supposed to make. It feels like someone's set off a flash grenade *inside* my foot as heat threads itself through my veins and muscles. I clench my teeth together so I don't so much as yelp, but it doesn't matter. My fall has made enough noise that someone yells "Who's there?", and I know there's no hope.

"Go!" I yell at Zwe, who's stopped several paces in front of me. He shakes his head, and I cry again, "Go! Just go!"

"It's them!" comes a female voice, followed by the sound of quick footsteps.

Cold metal presses into the nape of my neck. On reflex, I pivot around and onto my ass, coming face-to-face with a pair of calves. By the time my gaze rises up to her masked face, I feel like I'm on the precipice of fainting. Before I can think twice, my body acts on a primal urge to survive, and I start violently thrashing about. My right foot lands on the woman's jaw, causing her mask to fly off.

She's around our age, dark brown skin, hazel eyes. When she reaches up to rub her cheek, I notice a tattoo on her left wrist of an opaque black blob. For a distracted second, I try to make out if the tattoo is maybe an animal? A country?

My kick has left her dazed enough that although she doesn't drop her rifle, she does fall to her knees. Her eyes glaze over as she tries to recenter herself, but when they meet mine, a chill spirals up my spine.

Angry. This woman looks *so* angry, although I suppose getting kicked in the face will do that to you. At my continued staring, her eyes flatten into a sharp glare that makes me suddenly understand where the phrase "shoot daggers" came from.

Before I can take note of any other features, however, I feel two arms lifting me up from under my armpits.

"All you have to do is not let go," says Zwe's voice. "Do not. Let go."

"Wh—"

His hand claws into mine, fingernails digging so deep I would cry out in pain if it weren't for the context of our current situation.

And then he runs. He runs like we're trying to outrun a fire, and I'm tripping over my feet with unsteady knees and I want to tell him to slow down but I know that is the exact opposite of what we need to be doing right now so I let him keep dragging me through the trees and bushes and jumble of roots.

We duck when we hear gunshots, but we don't stop. Part of me is expecting to feel a bullet penetrate my back, and I morbidly wonder if it'd be lodged inside or if it'd be a clean through-and-through.

"Signs!" I manage to say and simultaneously gulp for air.

Zwe looks at where I'm pointing: a pole with arrows pointing in different directions, each one with a trail name written on them.

"Ko. Mo. Do. Trail," Zwe wheezes.

"What?" I ask.

Despite being in very good shape, running while dragging a one-hundred-and-ninety-pound human being has taken a toll on him too, and I can just make out each word that he huffs out. "Komodo. Trail. We want. To go."

"There," I say, feeling somewhat useful when I clock the green letters that say KOMODO TRAIL.

"Where. Is. There," Zwe croaks out.

"Two. O'clock," I reply.

Somehow, once he spots the sign, he starts to run even faster.

And maybe it's because I hear more gunshots and running and shouting behind me, but somehow, *somefuckinghow,* I keep up.

I'd blocked out that we would be running into the actual woods, but it's undeniable almost as soon as the trail starts. Even in the darkness, it's clear that there are no more picturesque fruit trees or grass that's mowed on a daily basis.

The first thing I notice are the frogs and the cicadas. I don't see them, but croaks and buzzes echo all around us in spite of it being an open space, and I try not to linger too long on the question of *What if I accidentally step on a frog?* The air smells different, too.

There are a lot of a few kinds of trees, or a few of many trees, I'm not quite sure. They're all so tall, though, the kinds of trees where you have to tilt your neck up to an uncomfortable angle in order to see the tops. It's like I was plucked and transported into a whole new world, one whose scents and sounds and little oddities my brain can't decipher due to lack of context.

After what feels like miles upon miles, we slow down and eventually stop altogether; we don't need to talk to know that it's a mutual decision based less on a sense of safety, and more on the fact that our bodies physically cannot take another step.

I sit down on the dirt, my throat pleading for hydration, my fingers too shaky to even unzip my backpack, let alone open a bottle of water. No matter how deep of a breath I take, it feels like there isn't enough oxygen to satisfy my lungs. "Safe?" I ask on an exhale.

Next to me, Zwe has his knees up, his head sandwiched between them. "Think. So," he replies, head still down.

"I saw her," I say.

"I know."

My brain has been racing over and over this one thought this entire time, like a treadmill that I can't get off of. "They're not going to let me escape now that I've seen her."

"I know," Zwe says, and the fact that he doesn't add any logical, levelheaded piece of advice to calm me down is how I know that we're royally screwed.

He lifts his head at last, and we hold each other's gaze, still panting, still trying to catch our breath.

A voice in my head screams, *Well? We're here! What do we do now? Tell me what to do now!*

But if he knew what to do, he'd have told me. The next thought

I have is *I want my mom,* and I want to laugh out loud because look at me, with all of this big talk about being an adult who pays for big holidays on her own, and at the end of the day, when I'm scared, all I want is my mom. My mom, whom I've kept putting off calling since we got here. I pull the cord on that train of thought because all it's doing is keeping my heart rate up. It's too early for fatalism. I'm going to talk to my mom again soon. I have to.

EIGHT

I groan at the sunlight that attacks my eyes as soon as I stir awake. "Zwe," I mumble. "Why didn't you close the—"

And then the night's events all come rushing back to me like a movie that someone's played on fast-forward.

I dislodge the sleep crumbs from my eyelids. "Are we dead?" I ask, groaning with pain this time as I sit up. "My back feels like I slept on a boulder. Is this what death feels like?"

"Like you'd be able to stay on top of a boulder through the night with the way you flail about in your sleep," Zwe says, already awake. "You slept slumped against the trunk of this majestic banyan tree."

"Is that why I just heard my spine crack?" I ask, wincing as I try to stretch upward.

"No, *that's* because of the whole precipice-of-entering-your-thirties thing. We're not teenagers anymore. Things crack when we wake up now."

"I'm still in my twenties, you dick. How'd you sleep?"

"Terrible. You?"

"Like a baby who popped a Xanax."

He tosses a pebble at my calf. "I really think that's a medical condition that you need checked out. It is alarming that if I hadn't been there, you would've slept through a group of armed intruders taking over an entire resort."

"Yeah but thankfully you *were* there to give me all of these lovely scrapes and bruises," I say, pulling up my sleeves. My arms are covered in long red scratches, some of them barely scabbed over. I look like I was tossed into a cage of rabid cats.

"You're welcome. You know, for keeping you alive," he retorts.

But I can't respond to him, because the sight of my arms brings the previous night to the front of my mind, the red marks on my flesh making it all real and not just a terrible nightmare I can laugh about.

"That really happened," I whisper, rolling my arms left and right to take in the full extent of my injuries.

"It did." Zwe's voice has sobered, too.

We fall into a silence that feels eerie. Weird. Scary.

"What should we do now?" I ask.

"Stay hydrated," Zwe says matter-of-factly.

As he pulls out my water bottle, I'm temporarily impressed that we both managed to escape with our backpacks still intact.

I'd mentioned it last night as we were trying to find a safe, dry spot to sleep. *We would have been fucked without our bags,* he'd said. *We'd have a better chance of surviving by turning ourselves in.*

"Afterward?" I ask before taking a gulp of water.

"Probably split one of your protein bars. We need sustenance."

I put my water bottle back in my bag and take out one of the two granola bars that I always carry with me in case I forget to eat while caught up in a writing spree. "We should eat as we walk." I tear the paper wrapper and break the bar in half, giving him a piece. "We don't want to waste time."

He considers it for a minute, bar in hand. "I don't think that's a good idea," he says. I was just gathering the energy to get up, but pause. "Eating might distract us. We don't want to be distracted, or running around in circles. We'll solidify our plan before we leave."

I take a deep breath to calm down the part of me that wants to snap at him. "I think we can handle eating while we walk. Not exactly rocket science now, is it?" I ask, trying to sugarcoat my sarcasm. Why isn't he panicking over the general fuckery of this all? Why isn't he moving so we can get out of this whole thing as soon as possible?

"Multitasking means we'll be giving half our attention to two different tasks," Zwe replies, not the least bit bothered by my quip. "I'd rather we sit here for an extra ten minutes and give a hundred percent of our attention to each task. Look, I'll double-check the map while we eat, so as soon as we're done, we can be on our way."

I want to remind him that he already double-checked it last night using the last of his phone's battery to turn on the flashlight, but for Zwe, "double-checking" actually means "quadruple-checking."

"Fine," I mumble, and take my annoyance out on my half of the protein bar by chomping down hard on it. If I weren't indebted to Zwe for saving my life, I'd put up more of a fight; but I am, so I don't. Ten minutes won't make a *world* of difference.

"Hey, who do you think those people are?" I ask. We're barely above whispering, but our voices boom here. "The ones with the guns. What do you think they want?"

"Not sure," he mutters half-distractedly. Pen in hand, he's retracing the same line he drew yesterday. Once he's satisfied, he gives himself a small nod, and stashes away the pen.

"It's weird, right?"

"Maybe, but it also kind of makes sense," he says with a shrug. "If you want to pull off a big robbery, where's better than a remote island with a ludicrously expensive resort that only rich people can afford?"

"You think they're just after the money?" I ask. "I dunno, it feels like a lot to be risking for money."

He gives another shrug as he takes a bite out of his bar. "Money's a good motivator. And like I said, if you've got a proper plan in place, a heist here"—he gestures at the space around us—"is a hell of a lot easier to get away with than somewhere like a bank."

When he looks at me properly for the first time all morning, I see the dark bags under his eyes, and a speck of dirt on his chin. I reach over and wipe it away. "Dirt," I explain.

"Thanks," he says. "You don't buy it?"

"Buy what?"

"That they're here for the money?"

I tilt my head side to side. "It's not that I don't buy it, it's just that it all still feels so bizarre. I kept thinking yesterday that this is the kind of thing you read about in the news, you know? Like, how is this actually happening to us?"

He gives a rueful smile. "I know what you mean."

We'd picked a spot far enough away from the trail that no one would be able to find us. After we've both finished our food, Zwe points back toward the direction of the main path. "So, we have a clearly marked trail. Obviously, we're not operating at a hundred, but still, it shouldn't take us more than a few hours. Absolute worst-case scenario, we'll be at the village by sunset."

He makes it sound so simple and systematic, like it's just a matter of going on a long hike, and by this time tomorrow, help will be here and we'll have a plan on how we're going to get home.

"They're going to come looking for us," I point out.

"I know. That's why we'll walk in the grass alongside the path. No sneaker prints."

"My ankle still hurts," I say. Instinctively, I try to turn it, but grimace with pain. We determined last night that it was thankfully not broken, but it's definitely swollen and I slept with it elevated on my backpack. "I'm going to slow us down."

Scooting closer to me, he gives my shoulder a reassuring squeeze. "That was part of my absolute-worst-case-scenario calculation."

"I feel disgusting." I gesture at myself. "My body is caked in a medically unhealthy amount of debris."

I'm wondering if I could somehow wash out the faint bloodstains at least with my hand sanitizer, but Zwe produces a neatly rolled T-shirt from his bag.

"You packed an extra shirt?" I ask, snatching it from him.

"I packed two. In case *we* fell into a river or—"

"Glad to see you had so much faith in my physical prowess." I'm caught off guard when I unroll the T-shirt. It's not just *any* T-shirt; it's my favorite one of his. The summer after my Oxford graduation, we'd splurged on a two-week holiday in London. One day, there was a freak rainstorm that left us drenched. The closest open shop was a novelty T-shirt stall in Camden Market, and the only shirt they had in his size was a plain white tee that said BIG DICK ENERGY LEADS TO BIG DICK INJURY in bold black letters on the front.

"I love this shirt," I say. "I want to be buried in this shirt."

"I know," he says, rolling his eyes. "Every time I put it in a donation bag, it somehow ends up back in my closet."

I clutch my chest. "That's an act of divine intervention if ever I saw one." Grinning, I take off my top. "What?" I ask at Zwe's reaction, which can really only be described as *lingering*. "You've seen me in a sports bra," I say, trying to ignore the goose bumps that have popped up on the back of my neck.

He nods and swallows, although the motions are stilted, like for a moment there, his body had forgotten how to carry them out. I think I feel my cheeks blush, but that could also be the heat. *Adrenaline,* I remind myself. We still have adrenaline shooting through our bloodstreams.

We relieve ourselves behind some trees, and get ready to hit the road. Zwe offers to take my backpack because of my ankle, but I refuse because it's actually not that bad once I start walking slowly.

Zwe lets me set the pace as we start off, and although I try my best to go as quickly as possible, I don't do great. Eventually, I tell him to go ahead, and he reluctantly does so, making sure to never be more than a couple of feet in front. And although I also try my best to keep the complaining to a minimum, my fear and general stress keep mounting in the back of my mind, compounded by my frustration over my own slow pace.

"How are—" I pant between every few words. "—things with Julia?" I wanted to reconnect with my friend, and what better opportunity than right now, right?

I try to read his body language, but there's nothing that I can discern from back here. "We don't need to talk about Julia right now."

"I know we don't need to. But I'd like to."

"I'd . . . rather not. Don't want to jinx anything," he adds.

"Oh. Right. Gotcha," I say, not used to Zwe keeping things from me. I try a different route. "Hey, do you think your parents will ever retire? Sell the store?"

"The day they do, I'll know they've officially lost it," he says, sounding like he's smiling.

"Would *you*?"

"Would I what?"

I make an effort to keep inhaling and exhaling through my nose instead of my mouth. "Sell the store? If it were up to you?"

Zwe doesn't answer for a long while, keeping his focus down and on the grass. "It doesn't matter," he finally says. "The store isn't mine. What would I do if I sold it, anyway? That bookstore's all I've ever really known," he adds with a dry chuckle. "I'm happy as long as they're happy."

I could immediately list ten things for him to do if he sold the store, but instead I bite my tongue. Zwe's happy if his parents are happy, and *I'm* happy if he's happy.

We keep going in silence until I have to pause to take a breather.

"You okay?" Zwe asks as soon as his hearing clocks that I've stopped moving. He immediately turns around and walks over.

"I'm okay, just tired."

"Hi, okay, just tired," he retorts.

"Don't test me right now, Zwe Aung Win. I swear to god, I will impale you with a branch."

He chuckles under his breath. "Come on, we have to keep going. We can't stop yet, we've only been walking for—" He checks his watch. "—thirty-one minutes."

"You're lying."

"Hand on heart," he says, placing his palm on his left chest.

"Uggggghh! I hate nature!" Although I try to keep my groan quiet, there's a rustling commotion as two birds fly out from the branches of the tree next to me. "Sorry, no offense!" I whisper-call after them. "Great, now I'm apologizing to birds. Maybe the dehydration and exhaustion are already getting to me. Whoever said nature was relaxing was a bold-faced liar."

"You know, if I were a dick, I would point out that *you* booked this trip because *you* thought all of this nature would be rejuvenating." I go to punch his arm, but he laughs and hops out of the way. "However"—he lifts a quieting finger—"I'm going to be nice and *not* point that out. Come on, let's distract your brain. Tell me about . . . this newest draft of yours. It must be good if you risked your life to save it. What happens?"

Despite its innocuousness, I'm taken aback by this specific subject change. I *hate* talking about my work in progress. It puts too much pressure on me, forces me to talk about an idea that might or might not even turn out to be a real book as though it already *is* one. Generally, Zwe knows this, too, and the rule is that we don't talk about my new project unless *I* bring it up. But then again, we're kind of short on conversation topics right now, and I *was* the one who made a big deal about bringing my laptop with me in a life-or-death situation because I couldn't bear to leave my precious manuscript behind. So I guess I had this one coming.

"It's . . . time travel," I try to explain. The words come out slowly, because the truth is that I don't actually yet know what does happen in this book. "This woman discovers a time-traveling manhole and she becomes obsessed with changing parts of her present-day life and then traveling forward in time to see how the changes have impacted her future."

"Time travel, that's fun," Zwe muses. "How does it end?"

This is how I write: I know how a book starts and how it ends.

"She dies," I say.

He laughs out loud, then clasps his hand over his mouth because we're not supposed to be making any distinctly loud sounds. "Sorry," he says. "I didn't expect that. That's funny, though."

I stop in my tracks. "What's the joke?"

He turns around, confused once he sees that I've stopped walking. "That she dies." He's drawing out each word as he gauges the situation. When I fold my arms, he adds, "Right?"

"Why's that funny?"

"Wait," he says with a small snort that makes me grind my teeth in response. "You're not joking? She actually dies?"

"Well . . . yeah."

"Okay, fair enough." He shakes his head. "Why?"

I shift my weight to my other foot, remember that that's my *bad* foot, and promptly re-shift to my original foot. "Because it's supposed to be a dark ironic ending. She spends all this time tweaking her present-day life bit by bit so that she forgets to actually live in the present, but after she makes the final tweak that will give her her dream life in ten years, she . . . dies."

Wordlessly, he scrutinizes me in that way that makes me feel like I've been shoved under a magnifying glass. "I see" is all he says at last.

"What?" I demand.

"Nothing. It . . . sounds like an intriguing story."

"Just say what you're really thinking," I snap, surprising myself. Zwe flinches, not having expected that reaction either.

"Okay, fine, you want the truth?" he asks, eyeing me like he doesn't think I can handle it. I nod, but my shoulder muscles pull back, readying myself for whatever his truth is. "It . . . feels like it could be more fleshed out. A person who exploits their newfound time-traveling powers? It feels . . . clichéd."

The word feels like a kick, the exact kind that I delivered yesterday to that woman: forceful, out of left field, hitting me dead center.

"But this is a first draft," he backtracks as soon as I react. "None of your first drafts are fleshed out. Sorry, I shouldn't have said clichéd. That was shitty of me."

"Yeah, it was."

He scrubs his face in frustration. "I'm sorry. I didn't sleep well last night. I kept having nightmares where you tripped and . . ." He cuts himself off and turns toward the sea, the angle of the sun not letting me make out his expression from just his profile. "I'm sorry," he repeats. "I don't know what I'm saying. Look, can we make a deal that we can't hold the other person accountable for whatever they say in the next forty-eight hours, give or take? I think you were onto something back there about the exhaustion and dehydration already getting to us."

My anger all but melts the moment he turns back to me with his patented puppy face. He's right. We're both cranky. I can't think too hard about how badly I want a shower because I'm positive that, best-case scenario, I'll start crying on the spot, and worst-case scenario, the delirium will make me take off all my clothing and run down to the beach so I can skinny-dip in the ocean. "Deal," I say, holding out my hand.

His demeanor visibly relaxing, he strides over and shakes it.

For a few seconds, we stay grinning at each other.

Reset.

I move to drop my hand, but Zwe doesn't let go. Or maybe I don't let go. I don't know, but we're just . . . holding hands now. And it feels . . . nice. Comforting. He is the closest thing to home I have right now, and I wish we could call it for the day and sit down and read our books and try again tomorrow.

"I'm tired," I say, restating the obvious.

I expect him to say *I know* or *Me too* or *It's just a couple more hours.* But instead, he closes the gap between us and, one hand still laced with mine, moves the other under my hair so he can rub the back of my neck. It feels so good, his skin on mine. I close my eyes and try to sync my breathing to the up-and-down motion of his hand. I'm so focused on the movement that I don't notice him letting go of my fingers until he's pulling me into him for a hug, arms completely enveloping me around my shoulders, his chin lightly resting atop my head as I bury my face in his chest.

"We're going to be okay," he tells me.

"You are not allowed to try to convince me to go on any more hikes for the rest of our lives," I mumble into his shirt. "I get an indefinite number of plays with this card."

He laughs, the action causing friction between my face and his chest. "That sounds fair. Now come on, let's get you to that village so we can get some lunch."

I smile but don't move. Neither does he. "Do you think they'll have cake?" I ask.

"No," he says. "But I'll phone my parents once we get cell service, and I'll make sure they have a cake waiting for us when we get home. I'll even tell them to write a message on it. Something like—"

"WE'RE HAPPY YOU'RE NOT DEAD?"

"HOPE YOU HAD A GOOD HOLIDAY," he says.

I snort. "They would do that. Ugh, they're going to give us a proper Asian-parent scolding for this, aren't they?"

"'You wanted to run away to a remote island? Was that remote enough for you?'" Zwe asks in a dead-on imitation of his mom. "'Or should I drive you out to another forest and leave you *there* overnight? I'll only charge half of what that resort charged you.'"

I snort again, my voice still muffled by his shirt. "They are never ever going to let us live this down."

"Never," he agrees.

I take a long inhale and pull back. "Right. Shall we—"

At first, I don't place the footsteps as footsteps. At first, for some inexplicable reason, I think it's a rabbit who's hopping rapidly through the grass as rabbits do in cartoons. "Do you hear—"

"Someone's coming," Zwe confirms, his embrace suddenly rigid as it transforms from affection to protection.

My brain tries to decide between fight or flight. "We have to hide," I say.

He points at a tree that's just close enough that I can sprint to it if I don't think *too* much about my ankle. Before I can even nod, he snatches my hand and starts dragging me in its direction.

"Ow, ow, ow," I mutter through gritted teeth as we navigate the underbrush. I place too much weight on my bad ankle on one particularly forceful step, and heat shoots up my leg like the ball in a pinball machine, ricocheting against every pain nerve. The tree now seems like it's a mile away, and there aren't any others closer by that could hide both of us, and there are too many roots and uneven patches for me to be able to move quicker.

The footsteps get closer and louder, enough to make out that the person is not walking quickly, but *running*.

"I can't make it," I say, shaking my head, the pain so acute I'm tearing up.

"You have to—"

"Poe? Zwe?" yells a female voice.

A female voice that . . . we recognize.

"Is that—" Zwe begins.

"Leila?" I finish.

Another, younger voice also calls out, "Mr. Zwe! Ms. Poe!" A male voice.

"Antonio?" Zwe asks.

As the footsteps near, Zwe crouches even lower, and I get as low on my knees as my ankle can handle. "What if this is poison ivy?" I look around with a newfound suspicion at the various shades and sizes of green in which we're immersing ourselves.

"It's not poison ivy," Zwe replies.

"How do you know?"

"I don't. Wishful thinking."

"Zwe!" I hiss.

"Even if it is, we won't die from poison ivy. We *will* die from armed women who are pretending to be people we know in order to lure us out into the open, so ssshhh!"

They're still shouting our names, getting closer and closer until the sources of the two voices come into view. It *is* Leila and Antonio. Better yet, it's *just* them, and there are no strange, masked people forcing them to call out for us at gunpoint.

They pause in approximately the same spot Zwe and I had stood in while we were hugging. "Are you sure it was this trail?" Leila huffs. Antonio gives her a sheepish look. "Oh my god!" she exclaims, shoving his shoulder.

"I'm ninety percent sure!" he retorts. "It was dark, I couldn't see *exactly* where they ran!"

"We haven't seen any shoe prints for hours!"

"The wind could've covered them up with debris," Antonio says, then points at the forest. "Or maybe they pivoted to a different path from here. If that's the case, then that's not my fault they went off track."

"I knew I shouldn't have let you come with me," Leila shoots back.

"*Let* me?" Antonio scoffs. "Need I remind you—"

"Antonio?" Zwe asks. I'd been so engrossed in their conversation that I hadn't noticed Zwe standing up to reveal himself. He waves, and Leila and Antonio break out into relieved grins the second they spot him.

"Mr. Zwe!" Antonio's already bounding over. "See, I told you this was the right path," he adds over his shoulder to Leila, who rolls her eyes.

"Just go and help them," she orders.

Zwe helps me stand back up, and as soon as I'm on my feet, Antonio throws his arms around me. "Ms. Poe! We thought you were dead! Well, at least *I* did. You didn't really look like the hiking type when you arrived, but—" He gestures at me from head to toe. "—I was mistaken. My apologies." *This fucking kid,* I think, too overcome with joy to be offended.

"You weren't too far off, to be fair," Zwe mutters. I give his ribs a sharp elbow.

"I'm so happy to see you two." I can feel how big my grin is. "How did you guys escape?"

"Leila managed to cut through her zip tie," Antonio says, jerking a thumb at her.

"I had a small knife on me," she explains. "We have several emergency kits around the resort. I managed to get to the one at the bar before they found me. I also picked this one up—" She dangles a small square red bag that she'd been holding on to this whole time. "—at the start of the trail." She nods at me. "I saw you take that nasty tumble yesterday. Thought maybe you'd need it. I'm not just a pretty face, you know."

"Clearly," Zwe says. All three of us whip our heads in his direction. His eyes widen and his cheeks redden in keeping with the symptoms of someone who accidentally said a thought out loud.

Leila blushes right back. "Thanks," she says, and, to my even bigger surprise, lightly shoves his shoulder with her own. Zwe looks down at his bicep as though the spot where her bare arm touched him might've left some sort of tattoo, like a cursive *Leila was here*. There's a spasm in my chest. I look over at Antonio, who waggles his brows up and down at me.

"Can you walk?" Leila asks, turning to me and trying to get a better look at my foot.

"Yeah. Can't, like, climb up a tree in case of danger, but I can walk at a more-than-leisurely pace."

She offers me her arm. "Come on, let's get you back on the path. You can sit down and I'll wrap a bandage around that ankle to keep the swelling down. We need to bring you back in one piece, after all. We should also generally stay out of the grass. You know there are snakes in here."

"I am trying very hard to *not* know that," I say. Then, remembering, I hobble-turn to Antonio. "Speaking of yesterday, thank you for providing that distraction. We owe you our lives."

He waves us away. "You know what they say about teamwork."

"What *do* they say about teamwork?" Zwe asks, a curious lilt to his voice.

"If you take out the 'team' in 'teamwork,' it's just work, and who wants that?" Antonio answers, looking proud. I can't tell if that's a joke, or if he genuinely thinks that's a saying that people throw around.

"They *do* say that," Zwe says earnestly, throwing me an *I love this kid* expression behind Antonio's head as we make our way out of the bush.

Zwe and Antonio help me sit down on the side of the path. I wince as Leila removes my sneaker. "Is it broken?"

With gentle motions, she lifts and examines it. "Pretty sure it's not, but it *is* injured. The bandage will help in the meantime," she says, already getting started on the procedure.

"I'm so glad you guys escaped," I say. "But Leila, how did you hide the knife from them? Didn't they search you before tying you up?"

"When I heard the gunshots, I slipped it into my shoe right before they caught me."

"Smart," Zwe and I both say at the same time. I slide him a smirk that he pretends not to see.

"How's this pressure?" Leila asks me.

I try wiggling my foot. "Good," I say. "It's not too tight."

"Great, let me just tape this up." Holding the bandage with one hand, she deftly takes out a roll of tape with the other, and Antonio helps cut off a piece. "There we go. Perfect. I'm going to hold on to this knife, but ditch the bag. And now—" She stands up, tucks the knife into her back pocket, and indicates in a random direction. "I'm so sorry to be blunt about this, but, um, I have to go pee. Be right back."

"How about you?" I ask Antonio after she's left. "How'd you get free?"

"Pfft, easy," he says. He holds his fists out side by side, palms facing down. "When they ask you to put your hands together, you give them your hands like this because it makes your wrists bigger." He aligns his fists so that all eight knuckles form a straight line. "Then after they tied me, when they weren't looking, I just turned my fists so they were facing inward—" He rotates his hands to demonstrate, his thumbs now facing upward. "It takes a bit of time, but as soon as you get the first thumb out, the rest is pretty easy."

Zwe and I look at each other, speechless. "How the hell do you know that?" I ask.

Antonio shrugs. "Don't remember. I know a lot of things. *I'm not just a pretty face either, you know.*"

"Did you help Leila get free?" I ask.

"Nah, we kinda managed it at the same time. There weren't any guards around so it was pretty easy to sneak away, too. Actually, I think they were scattered because they were trying to find you two. Anyway, I was already close to freeing my right thumb when Leila took off her shoe and retrieved her knife."

"Why didn't you two free everyone else?"

At that, his generally peppy face droops, making him look like a toddler who got told off in front of the entire class. "We didn't have time. They told us to leave and get help. I promised my grandpa I'd come back and save him."

Above his head, Zwe and I exchange pained expressions. "Hey, we will," Zwe says, clapping Antonio's shoulder.

"Thanks, friends," he mumbles through a faint, hopeful smile.

"Do you think—" I swallow. "Did it seem like they wanted to hurt anyone? The bad guys, I mean. Any information you can give us is useful."

Antonio's brows pull together in concentration. "I don't know," he says at last. "They always went off to the side to talk, and they kept their voices down. They'd take us to the bathroom if we wanted to use it, and they passed out water and sandwiches and fruit that they collected from the kitchen."

"That's good," Zwe says.

"But they were also so . . ." He gazes off into the distance, as though attempting to recall what he saw.

"So what?" I prompt.

"Angry," he says. "They would break things."

"Break things?" Zwe asks.

Antonio nods. "Throw vases over the hill and laugh. Smash the computers. They were destroying . . . everything. Like, *everything*."

Zwe and I exchange a *That's not good* look behind his head. Every time I close my eyes, I see that woman's face, the unfiltered fury in her eyes, how her jaw clenched like she wanted to rip me apart with her bare hands.

"I know the clock is ticking, and we don't know what their *final* plan is, but the fact that they're looking after everyone in the meantime is good," Zwe says in his best attempt at a reassuring voice. "It means we might be able to negotiate with them, and they might not actually want to hurt anybody."

"Is everyone there?" I ask. "Sandra and Eka too?"

Antonio nods. "Everybody."

"I'm back!" Leila's voice catches our collective attention. She raises her open palms. "Don't worry, I washed my hands in a creek. Anyway, should we get going? What was the plan?"

"You know, it's a good thing that *you* of all people were the one who escaped," Zwe says. Once he's on his feet, I lift my arms to ask for help, and he reaches under each of my armpits to gently get me up, too. "We were going to go to your family."

Leila's face pinches with puzzlement. "My . . . family?"

Zwe points up in the general direction of a mountain. "You said your family still lives here on the island, right? We figured they must have *some* way to contact the mainland. And out of all the hiking trails, this was the longest one and the only one that included a lunch break, so we took a wild guess that this trail led to the village."

"It does! Holy shit, that's brilliant!" Antonio punches Zwe's arm. "Well, well, well, look at us, a quartet of pretty *and* smart faces."

"They do have phones, right?" I ask Leila, who looks confused.

"Your family, I mean. They have a phone, right? Maybe a satellite phone?"

"Oh, yes, of course." Chuckling, she rolls her eyes and points to her head. "Sorry, I'm *really* tired and sort of thirsty. My brain isn't working quite right."

"Here, take a sip," Zwe says, already unzipping his bag.

"No, you guys need it for your—" Leila argues.

"We *all* need to," Zwe cuts in. When she opens her mouth to argue again, he reaches over, opens one of her hands, puts the body of the bottle against her palm, closes her fingers around it, and closes *his* fingers on top of hers. "I insist."

"Well," she says with a playful smirk, "if the guest *insists*," she adds as they hold their gaze.

"Right!" I say, a little forcefully. I am *very* happy for Zwe, but this is not the time nor place for a little flirtatious exchange. "Shall we head for the village? Preferably before the bad guys catch us? Zwe, do you want to check the map?"

Leila shakes her head. "That map might not be much good. Sorry, we shouldn't have left that in your room, our hiking options are quite limited right now. Management has been drawing up plans to expand into the forest as well, and they've built some new paths and dug up certain places so they're not accessible anymore. They want to build a helipad."

"A helipad? That's honestly a shame, this place is beautiful," I say, taking in the surroundings.

"I know," Antonio says. "They also want to build a new glamping experience or something."

"I sort of know a new shortcut, though," Leila offers. "I've only used it once, and it'll take us off the trail, so bear with me—" She cuts off after seeing my expression. "Don't worry, even if we get lost, we'll be okay," she laughs, and places a soothing hand on my shoulder. "I'd know my way around these woods blindfolded."

"Okay," I squeak out.

The four of us start walking, Leila and Zwe leading.

"I can't wait to take a bath," Antonio says. He could easily walk alongside the other two, but I appreciate that he's slowed down to a leisurely stroll so he can be beside me. "A nice bubble bath, with candles and everything."

"That's nice," I mutter absentmindedly. As I watch Zwe and Leila having a lively conversation up ahead, I can't help but feel like one of those discarded elderly pets.

What a show-off, a small voice in my head huffs. I crack my neck to shut it up. Leila is being nice. Efficient. Helpful. It's great that she's taking the lead and it's no longer entirely on Zwe to formulate a plan that'll get us out of here, that she can pitch in where I can't. That's a *good* thing.

NINE

"I think we took a wrong turn somewhere." It's approximately the tenth time that Antonio's said that, but I'm beginning to take his side. While we may have started out buoyant and optimistic, our batteries are drained and no one has said a word for the last hour, not even Antonio.

"No, we couldn't have," Leila says, still as adamant as she was the first time he made the observation. "Just give me a bit more time to gather my bearings."

"The old trail usually takes us what, four? Five hours? But that sun"—he extends his arm toward the horizon where the former blue sky has been replaced by a soft blend of oranges and purples—"is setting. We've been out here for *way* longer than five hours. And I'm pretty sure we're going around in circles, because I've seen these trees before."

"We're not going around in circles!" Leila snaps. "You have no idea if you've seen these trees before! I told you from the start that this is a new path, so you need to bear—"

"But we don't even know if we're any closer!" Antonio huffs. "Admit that you've got us lost!"

"I haven't gotten us lost! Maybe if we cut through these trees—" Leila stomps off the path, then freezes.

"Leila? Are you okay?" Zwe calls to her back. We trade wary glances as she bends over. My first thought is that she's spotted a snake.

"Leils—" Antonio starts, pausing when she stands back up and turns around. With a red emergency kit in her hand. The kit we'd left behind after patching up my ankle. My heart drops in my stomach, and I feel like I'm about to faint.

"Oh my god," Leila whispers, staring at the bag in disbelief. When she looks back at us, her eyes are glazed with tears. "We *are* going around in circles. I'm so sorry. I thought—" She has to pause to hiccup.

"Hey, it's okay." Antonio's already jogging over and pulls her in for a hug. "None of us know what we're doing," he says as he guides her back toward us.

I push past the tightening in my own chest to reassure her by rubbing one of her shoulders. "Yeah, you don't have to—"

"I think we should break for dinner," Zwe suggests.

"Dinner?" I whip my head around, uncertain if I misheard. Zwe nods. "Surely dinner can wait. I think we should focus on getting on the right path while there's still light. Isn't it better to get our route sorted before we rest?"

"But we're all tired, and being hungry is only slowing us down," Zwe replies. "We haven't eaten since this morning."

"We also haven't made any progress since this morning. Which isn't anyone's fault," I quickly add. "But resting now seems . . . counterproductive. Let's just push on."

"Come on, Poe, we could all do with some food."

"That sounds like a good idea," Leila responds before I can. She shoots him a tired smile. "Food will help us recharge, get our brains working again."

"Exactly," Zwe says.

I look at Antonio for backup, but he's taken a newfound interest in some moss on a nearby rock. "If you're that hungry, you can have my remaining granola bar," I offer, irritated by what's happening. Zwe isn't even considering my proposal.

"A single granola bar split between the four of us isn't going to do anything," he says in a near-sarcastic manner. "We'll all feel less cranky once we get some proper food—"

"We don't *have* any proper food," I say, pointing out the obvious.

"I'm sure we can find *something* to eat," Leila says. "I love camping. I know how to hunt for dinner. We're not talking about shooting a deer or anything, but I can scrounge together enough for one meal."

Zwe throws his arms open. "Exactly! We're surrounded by plants and animals! We just have to start a fire, which will be easier to do while there's still sun—"

"You want us to, what, forage for mushrooms?" I decide that I don't like this alpha male Zwe who dismisses my suggestions without any further discussion, and seems very much like he's trying to show off in front of his new crush. And while Leila might be used to hunting for her food, I know for a fact that city boy Zwe is definitively not. "We're not fucking Bear Grylls, Zwe!"

"Like I said, we can take care of that." Leila gestures at her and Antonio. "We're used to these woods."

"We're going to have to find *something* to cook our food with, though, not to mention keep us warm," Zwe muses. "We almost froze to death last night, and that was while you—" He raises his brows at me in a pointed manner, and I want to slap them right off of his face. "—were wearing a sweatshirt. You're in only a T-shirt now."

"A fire *is* the best course of action moving forward," Leila puts in.

I grit my teeth before I say something I'll regret. What the hell are they doing, tag teaming right now?

"How are we even going to start a fire?" I ask, fixing my stare on Zwe. "And what happens when the people with the guns who are looking for us see the smoke from your fire?"

His jaw hardens as though he wasn't expecting me to make a valid point.

"Oh, that's easy," Leila's breezy voice comes. *Of course* it's easy for her. "Fire pit."

"What's a fire pit?" Zwe and I ask at the same time.

"It's what it sounds like," Antonio says, rolling his eyes like *Duh*. "It's a pit that you dig into the ground so you can start a fire underground. It produces minimal smoke so unless you're really looking for it in the sky, which will be even harder to do with no sunlight, there's almost no way you'll spot it."

"The fire also burns hotter because it's contained within the pit," Leila explains. "And it's easier to start even when it's windy, which it will be by nightfall. Do either of you have a pair of reading glasses, by any chance?"

"I do," Zwe says.

"But we've never built a fire above ground, let alone *under* it," I point out. "What if—"

"Oh, that's okay, I've done them plenty of times!" Leila says with a casual wave. "My grandparents taught me. Come on, let's find a place to settle for the night, and leave the fire to me and Antonio. It's the least I can do, seeing as how the shortcut was my idea."

"The shortcut that doesn't exist," Antonio mumbles.

"One more word"—she points a sharp, manicured finger at him—"and I will chop you up and use your limbs for kindling."

Antonio sticks out his tongue. "Stupid, you'd be smelling burnt flesh the whole night."

"I won't mind if it's *your* flesh."

My gag reflex starts to act up at the increasing mention of burnt human flesh. "In that case," I interrupt, "how can Zwe and I help?" I want to be a team player, and I suppose giving my ankle a rest wouldn't be the worst idea.

"Hmmm, do you want to find food?" Leila offers. "We can set up close to the river. There's fish in there. I can clean it if you can catch it." I can't stop my face from grimacing, and Zwe must do the same, because Leila laughs and adds, "Or we could stick to fruits and vegetables? Although maybe we stay away from the mushroom foraging tonight, just in case. Let's stick to stuff that we know for a fact won't kill us in our sleep."

"Let's do that," Zwe says. He grins at her as though they've exchanged some inside joke, even though they . . . haven't. "But Poe, you should rest," he says to me. "I can find the food."

"No, I can help," I insist.

Zwe glances down at my foot and shakes his head. "We need you to be better tomorrow. Keep that ankle elevated and take it easy for the rest of the night. The three of us have got this."

I don't want to feel like a useless loser while the three of them set about on their specific tasks, but my pain *has* been gradually spiking over the last half hour. "Okay," I relent. Then, so as not to be rude, add, "But if any of you *do* need me at any point, you'll let me know?"

"Promise. But for now, you rest," Leila says, and guilt gives me a sharp slap in the face. Of course Zwe likes her—she's sweet and funny and can build a *fire pit* with her bare hands. Silently, I vow to be less irritable going forward.

Once we've settled on a spot, and because it's a) starting to get too dark to do much else and b) one of the few things I actually have *to* do, I take out my laptop and pull up my draft.

"I thought you were joking about bringing your laptop," Antonio laughs. I'd mentioned it to him earlier.

"I'm an author," I explain. "My latest book draft is on here. I didn't have a chance to connect to the Wi-Fi and email it to myself."

At that, Antonio's expression changes, and he lets out an impressed whistle. "Oh shit, that's fucking cool. I've never met an author before. Hey, are you going to put us in the acknowledgments section of this book?"

"Absolutely," I say, meaning it.

"Okay, kid, let's find some of this kindling before it's too dark." Leila jerks a thumb over her shoulder and into the woods. "And just so you know, Sandra might be okay with you blabbering on beside her, but I like to work in silence."

"Is that because you're concentrating really hard on not letting it bother you?" Antonio asks.

"Letting what bother me?"

"The stick up your ass," Antonio says coolly. Leila gives his shin a swift kick. "Ow! That hurt!"

"Good! That'll teach you to perpetuate the misogynistic joke that a woman in charge who likes things done efficiently has a stick up her ass."

"Are you two always like this?" Zwe asks.

"Yep," Antonio responds with a proud grin. "Leila's the uptight big sister I never had. I'm the funny one, she's the smart one."

Leila rolls her eyes, but a smile dances at the corners of her lips. Despite their bickering, it's clear she cares about him. "No need for flattery, let's get this pit built."

The two of them head out in one direction, and Zwe in the other.

Leaving me alone for the first time in twenty-four hours. If I were in better spirits, I'd almost view it as peaceful and tranquil.

My screen opens to the page with the 12-point font, but every time I try to type a sentence, my vision goes blurry. The only thought going through my head is terrible and macabre and makes me want to curl up into the fetal position: *What if this is my last night alive?*

I stare at my laptop, suddenly wanting to laugh at myself for thinking I'd be able to work on a book while hiding in the forest. I know it'd have killed me to just leave it behind, but right now all it's doing is making me feel stupid and more useless. Once again, I can't do anything right.

The thought pops up before I can usher it away: *Should I write a goodbye letter to my parents?*

As though the words could jump out and attack me, I slam my laptop shut, not even worrying about the screen.

It's been in the back of my mind this whole time: What will happen to my parents if something happens to me? Thankfully, I don't mean in a financial sense, but mentally. Emotionally. Besides Zwe and Soraya, my mom is my best friend. And I promised my dad that next time I was in Bangkok, we would go see this Green Day tribute act he's obsessed with. And we were all going to go visit my cousins and aunts and uncles in Mandalay next Thingyan. The realization that I might not be able to do any of that would bring me to my knees if I weren't sitting down already.

I wipe away a stray tear from my cheek.

Positive thoughts. Manifesting an escape safe and unharmed.

I put my laptop to the side, and because this is the only other thing I can do besides write, I take the book I was reading, flip to my earmarked page, and pick up where I left off.

"How was writing?"

"Jesus," I exhale. "You scared me. And I . . . wrapped up writing for the day. It was fine."

"Uh-huh," Zwe says, his tone hinting at suspicion. "How's the book? Do you know who she was sent to assassinate yet?"

"What?"

"Your book." He gestures at the book I'm holding. "The main character. Who was her target?" he asks, confused that he's having to explain the plot of the book *I* was reading *to* me. "Do we know yet?"

"Oh. No, not yet," I say, recomposing myself. "It's hinting that it was the main guy, the love interest. But I dunno, it feels like too obvious of a plot twist."

Zwe sits down, and I notice that both of the reusable shopping bags that I'd dug out from my backpack and gave him are full. "Good job," I say, nodding down at them. "Leila would be proud."

It's not meant as a dig, although I'm not sure if I mean it as a compliment either. But he smiles as though it *is* a compliment, and says, "Thanks, it actually wasn't as difficult as I was worried it would be." Then, "Who would *you* make it?"

"Huh?"

"If you were writing that book, who would *you* have her assigned to assassinate? What would be a good plot twist in your opinion?"

"I'd change the whole plot," I say immediately, because I've been pondering this exact question for the last few chapters. Zwe's face morphs with surprise, and he nods at me to explain. "They're rival assassins from rival organizations, and they don't realize that they've both been assigned to kill the same target until they see each other on the plane. And their mutual target is this big deal in their industry, and they each want to be the person to kill him, so they also keep preventing the *other* one from killing him."

Zwe nods slowly as he considers it. "Would yours still be a romance? Where's the romance plot?"

"They have history. They went to the same assassin training program where they used to date or were best friends who—" I pause to swallow, my eyes instinctively flitting away for a beat. "—had a whole *will they, won't they* thing. But they had a huge falling-out and eventually got recruited by different organizations. And they've spent the last few years circling in and out of each other's orbits."

"Does the whole book take place on the plane?" He tilts his head up, squints like he's playing it out like a movie in his head. "That's a small setting. How would you maintain enough action in such a confined space?" This is why I love talking to Zwe about my writing, because he always keeps pushing, keeps asking *How?* and *Why?* and *What next?* and forces me to expand the story. It's like having a second editor. It *is* having a second editor.

"That's a good point." I chew on my bottom lip as I consider. "It could open at the airport. The check-in counter. The narration is from the main character's point of view, so she spots the other assassin first, quickly works out why he's on this plane as well, and then maybe pulls some strings so they're seated near each other so she can keep an eye on him. And the majority of the book *would* be on the plane, but I think that'd be good for me."

"In what way?"

"It'd push me. Like, as a writer. But I could also insert flashback chapters to when they were in the training program together to break things up a bit."

Like I've aced a test I didn't realize I was taking, Zwe leans forward at my answer, smile stretched, dimples deep. "Has it worked?"

I blink. "Has what worked?"

"Have I distracted you from whatever catastrophic thought you were having when I found you? After all, nothing distracts you like a good book, right?"

His words are a stun gun right to the center of my heart. "Thank you," I say, now wanting to cry for a new reason.

"Anytime. But also, I think you should write a romance novel. You're clearly great at it."

I barely register that this is the second time he's made this same ridiculous suggestion. His face is so close to mine that I can see the specks of dirt on his cheeks and nose, probably from his food foraging. For a few minutes there, I forgot that we were stranded in the middle of nowhere with no food, water, or shelter; instead, it felt like we were back home, me tossing out a plot, him asking the questions that will help round out the story so I can see it better. That's the thing—we've done this *so* many times, and yet, right now, *this* time, it feels different. For various reasons.

You make everything better, I think. *Whenever there is a terrible, awful, shitty situation, you are the person I want to get through it with.*

"I think you're trying to project your real-life horniness onto my books," I finally say, but not without having to swallow past a star that's become lodged in my throat.

Zwe shifts back, like he accidentally got zapped by an invisible electric fence. "I'm sorry? You think I'm horny right now?" he asks, but I note how he diverts his gaze.

"I think—" I raise my brows up and down in the general direction where Leila and Antonio went. "—the feeling's mutual."

Zwe follows my gaze, looks back at me, back at the woods, at me, and finally barks out laughing. Except I know his laugh. And this isn't a genuine *You are so off base, it's hilarious* laugh. This is his defensive laugh. The one that he'd used to laugh around the kids at our high school who made "friendly" jokes about his weight.

"Leila?" he asks, but not without glancing around to make sure that he didn't accidentally summon her.

"Leila," I confirm. "Promise me something?"

"No," he says.

"Promise me that if you two are going to do it tonight, you'll go off somewhere far away so that Antonio and I won't be awakened in the middle of the night and be scarred for life."

"I'm not going to do *it* with Leila tonight."

"Ah," I say, lifting my head in understanding. "Building up the tension so that you can have celebratory sex when we're rescued? I get it. Make her wait for it, tiger."

With just the last rays of sun illuminating him from behind, I can't discern the contours of his face as well as I'd like to, but I think I catch the flexing of his jaw, or at the least, a slight tightening of his muscles. The dimples are gone. "Fine, you wanna play this game? I'll play." His reply takes me by surprise. "Would it be the worst thing in the world if I *did* have a, let's say, *crush,* on Leila?"

The star in my throat pushes deeper, its edges even sharper than I initially thought. "If you *did*," I say, and clear my throat to get rid of the hoarseness. "No, it wouldn't. I would be very happy for you. Because she's great, and you deserve someone who's as hot and smart as you are."

"At least I'm not texting Julia anymore," he remarks.

"That is a very good point."

"What's a good point?" Antonio asks.

"Noth—" Zwe starts.

"We were talking about dating," I jump in. Zwe throws me a glare, and I give him a subtle *I've got this* nod.

"What about dating?" Antonio asks. "And how does that relate to a good point?"

"Before we came here, Zwe was in this on-off relationship with his ex," I say. "But now they're very much *off*, which was the 'good point' I was referring to."

"What happened?" Leila asks.

Zwe does not like talking about his personal life. Even his parents never got the full story about him and Julia. In fact, I don't think anyone in his life—apart from me, and that's only because we live together—would know if he was in a serious relationship until the day he announced his engagement.

"We made sense until—" Zwe shrugs. "—we just . . . didn't. We had . . . different perspectives on things."

Leila starts digging the pit, but I notice that she's not showing us her face, and I would bet my last granola bar that it's deliberate. After all, who among us hasn't busied ourselves with a fire pit in order to hold back our unbridled interest in our new crush's last relationship?

"Like what?" I ask, partly to ease Leila's itching curiosity, and partly because this is news to me. As far as I was aware, Julia and Zwe had the same views on all the big things in life. They both liked having a stable nine-to-five, disliked traveling, wanted to live in the same city as their parents, and—to my utter shock—kept spreadsheets of their monthly expenses.

Zwe doesn't answer, instead buying himself time by going over to help Antonio and Leila dump all the leaves and twigs they gathered into the pit. If he's hoping we'll take his silence as a hint, though, we're absolutely not. In fact, after a few more seconds, Antonio urges, "Oh, come on, Mr. Zwe. We might be the last people you ever talk to." He presses down on a pile of leaves. "What's the point of secrets?"

"Look, I need something to keep me entertained out here," Leila says. "Consider this piece of gossip your contribution for the night. Or at least a thank-you to me for building us this fire pit."

"You accept compensation in gossip?" he asks.

She waves a twig around. "Desperate times."

"She wanted to move in together, buy a house, settle down. I said we were moving too fast, and she left because she felt like we were moving too slowly."

He says it all in one breath, so quickly that it takes my brain, which wasn't ready for this specific stream of words, several moments to process it. I try to catch his eye to make sure he's telling the truth, but he's deliberately avoiding me, focusing down at the pit as his hands fall into a repetitive motion. Collect, dump, pack, repeat.

Leila is the first to speak. "Not wanting to live together does sound like a solid deal breaker," she says, awkwardness straining her voice.

"I didn't know you guys were looking at houses," I blurt out, hurt distorting my own. Why wouldn't Zwe tell me about such a big move?

"We weren't," he says. "*She* was. That was kinda the point."

"You didn't tell me."

Finally, *finally*, he meets my gaze. "You were busy with work," he says. It's the shrug that makes me feel sick. "And it wasn't a massive deal. There wasn't anything more to that conversation."

Why didn't you want to move into a house with her? I want to ask, because I know for a fact that he's always wanted the backyard life, one big enough so that the shelter dog he eventually adopts can run around in it.

The other, more pressing "why" that's balancing right at the tip of my tongue, though, is, *Why didn't you tell me?*

If we were alone back at ours, I would press and pry until he spilled. But we're not alone and we're not back at ours, and right now I can see how tired he is, even if he's done a good job of masquerading it. Sweat sticks his shirt to his skin, his hair is greasy and ruffled by both the wind and his own hand raking through it throughout the day, and as he helps build this fire pit, he's not moving as quickly as he typically would.

So I let it go, deciding that, actually, *not* making him talk about the worst heartache I've seen him go through in front of strangers while we try to survive a night in the wilderness, is an easy grace I can and should give him.

"Just in time," Leila exhales once they've packed it all tightly within the pit. "Zwe, glasses?"

He complies, passing along his navy-rimmed pair.

"Hopefully we have *just* enough sunlight left to—" Holding up a medium-sized stick in one hand, she angles the sun through Zwe's glasses, shifting the latter a few degrees down and then to the right. The rest of us stay silent while she works. Biting her bottom lip, she continues to adjust the angles and mutter, "Come on, please, please, work, please."

There's a quiet sizzling sound before orange embers start dancing atop the kindling.

"There we go," Leila breathes out as she carefully places the tinder at the top of the pit. We exhale a collective breath when the fire spreads, its delightful shadows already dancing across our faces.

She wipes the concentration-induced sweat off her forehead and returns Zwe's glasses.

"You are amazing," Zwe laughs out. He looks like the personification of the heart-eyes emoji. "You just built a fucking fire in the ground. Using a stick and a pair of glasses!"

"Like I said," she says with a playful toss of her hair. "Not just a pretty face."

We get started on dinner soon after, and surprisingly, it's not *the* worst meal I've ever had. He hadn't found any vegetables that could be eaten raw, but Zwe ended up gathering a variety of berries, guava, water apples, star fruit, and three large ripe mangoes.

"Not bad, city boy," Antonio tells him.

"So this ex of yours, was that your worst breakup?" Leila asks Zwe.

"No," he says. "My worst breakup was a girl in high school who, it turned out, was dating me because she had a crush on my brother and kept coming over to the house because she wanted to hang out with him. What about you? What was *your* worst breakup?"

"Oh my, let me count the ways." She swallows a chunk of water apple, and begins counting on her fingers. "There was the guy who left me because I wasn't *adventurous* enough after I refused to sail the open sea with him for a year. There was the one who dumped me mid-flight at the start of our Iceland holiday. Oh, and I took the last one to a family wedding where he broke into the bride's hotel room before the ceremony and stole all the jewelry that she and the bridesmaids were supposed to wear."

"No!" I gasp.

"Yep," Leila says dryly. "They were all my cousins, too. The bridesmaids, I mean. My family has now ordered me to run background checks on all future partners before bringing them to any big event, and you know what, I don't blame them."

"Did you ever find him?" Zwe asks.

Leila nods. "Oh, of course. Nobody gets away with pissing off the Chen cousins. But anyway, that's my baggage. How about you, Poe?"

"Me?" I stammer, not expecting to be tagged into this conversation.

"What's your worst breakup?"

I intuitively look over at Zwe, who gives me a half smile, one that says, *You can lie if you want. I won't tell.*

"I was actually . . . engaged." I say each syllable slowly, hesitantly, like I don't quite believe I'm talking about it in the past tense. A teeny, tiny part of me still kind of can't. Not because I'm still in love with him, but because now I absolutely can't fathom a life where we were going to spend our future together. "And then he . . . broke up with me. He got tired of me for not *getting a real job*," I say. I force myself to look up and make eye contact at that last part. Even now, I can hear Vik's voice in my head saying that exact phrase, his frustration cloaking every word. "I spent over two years working on my first book, but it got rejected by every publisher we submitted it to. When it came time to send out my second book, things weren't looking much better. When Vik and I first got together, he was *so* supportive, thought it was *so* cool that I was an author. But I didn't want to get a corporate job because I knew that would eat into my writing time, so instead I worked shifts at Zwe's parents' bookstore. And Vik, that was his name, by the way," I clarify, "would get increasingly agitated, pointing out that we were never going to be able to afford a wedding, let alone a house this way."

My vision blurs as I stare at the flames, the yellow and orange coalescing into a new, bright, unnamed, untamed color.

At first he'd suggested I pick up more shifts at the bookstore. Then it was sending me random job postings that vaguely related to writing, like technical writing for a software startup or content writing at an agency. But it wasn't like we were *struggling*; we just couldn't afford to go on holidays with his friends or his parents, at least not without him paying for the majority of the trip.

We have to prioritize our future together, he'd said. But I didn't see why I had to choose, why our future together couldn't have both us *and* my writing. I knew I would've been miserable in a corporate job, and more importantly, if I didn't give my books my all, then I knew, I *knew*, I would've spent my whole life regretting it. Part of me knew he was being sensible, but another part of me also kept wondering why, as my partner, his support for me drastically waned over time. Why, if he was as proud of me and believed in me as much as he claimed to, he couldn't be okay with sacrificing a ski trip to Japan with his brothers so I could give my dream my best shot.

When my agent and I decided to shelve my second book, that had been the breaking point.

I can't build a future with someone who wants to pursue a hobby her whole life, he'd said.

When I realize I'm struggling to breathe, I reach into the front zip of my bag for a tissue. They all divert their eyes when I blow my nose and dab at my eyes. "That relationship really screwed me up, in case you can't tell," I laugh. "Joke's on him though, because guess who has a Netflix movie deal now?"

"What a shitty human being," Leila scoffs.

Antonio shakes his head. "Yeah, Ms. Poe, what a fucking loser," he says, lips curled. He seems genuinely pissed off, which warms my heart.

"Thanks, guys. Oh, the *best* part—" I sniffle, throwing Zwe a knowing smirk. Zwe rolls his eyes in disgust. "—is that when the book I eventually published made the *New York Times* bestseller list, he texted me out of nowhere 'I was always rooting for you.'"

"Oh no, that's not the *best* part," Zwe interrupts. "The best part is that when the movie deal got announced, including that it would be Tyler Tun's directorial debut, he texted Poe to ask if he could get two tickets to the premiere for him and his niece."

"Okay, fine, maybe *that* was the best part," I say.

Leila's mouth drops open. "What did you respond?"

"Nothing. Blocked him."

"I told her to send a selfie with her and Tyler and *then* block him, but she wasn't petty enough for it," Zwe tells her.

Leila nods at him. "I would've totally done that. But also wait, you have a selfie with Tyler Tun?"

"Yeah," I say, feeling like I'm name-dropping, but also how do you casually say you're friends with a Hollywood megastar like Tyler Tun *without* name-dropping? "He's *really* nice."

"He just got married, right?"

"Yep," I say. "I met his wife, Khin. She's a journalist, and *so* cool, probably actually cooler than him. You didn't hear this from me, but when we talked, she was saying that Tyler's been itching to start working again, so maybe if this movie goes well, he might be doing more? Dunno. But I'm getting sidetracked." I turn to Antonio. "You're the only one left. What's *your* worst breakup?"

"Try 'every single breakup he's ever had,'" Leila answers. "Antonio is what we call 'a dick.'"

"I prefer 'wild stallion,'" Antonio says.

"Ew, don't tell me you're one of those," I say, wrinkling my nose. "You need to do better."

"Zwe, maybe you can teach him how to be a real man. *Please?*" When Leila simultaneously juts out her bottom lip and widens her eyes, she looks like one of those adorable cartoon meerkat mascots that could convince you that purchasing car insurance is a good choice even if you don't have a car right now.

"Nah, you have it backward—" Antonio shakes his head, and makes a show of puffing his chest. "Now that I know he's single, once we get back to the mainland, *I'm* going to show *Mr. Zwe* how to be a real Casanova. And think of the story we'll have to tell! We had to hide in the jungle because masked gunmen were chasing us?" He lets out a low whistle. "The girls will lap it up."

"Women," I correct.

"Sorry. The *women* will lap it up."

I wave a hand. "No, I meant they're not masked gunmen, they're gun*women*. All of them. Or at least, they're female-presenting. What *is* the procedure for asking your kidnappers their preferred pronouns?"

"Wait," Leila says, leaning forward. "How do you know they're *all* women? I'd assumed they were the same gang who robbed the Second Heaven Resort the other month—"

My jaw drops. "Wait, this has happened before? Where is this other resort?"

"I didn't hear anything about that," Antonio says.

"It's in the other direction from the mainland," Leila says. "It happened in the middle of the night. They held the receptionists who were on duty that night at gunpoint and made them transfer all the money into an offshore account. Thankfully nobody was hurt so management kept it really tight-lipped. I only know because their manager warned Sandra, who warned me. But—" She returns her attention to me. "—that gang was definitely a mix of men and women, according to the Second Heaven team. How do you know *these* people are all women?"

"They passed us in a buggy after we left our room," I explain. "It might not be anything, but it's *interesting*, at the very least. A horde of armed women taking over an island resort? You don't see *that* in the movies."

"Yay, feminism," Zwe says, and gives the air a weak punch.

"Are you sure?" Leila chews on her lip. "I'm pretty sure the two that got me at least were men."

"Really?" I'm not doubting her, but I know what I saw. "Zwe, you saw them, and you thought they were all women too, right?"

"Well, the one whose mask you kicked off definitely was," he says. "But other than that . . . it was dark, and we were rushing, and we don't even know if we saw *all* of them."

"Antonio?" I ask him. "What do you think? All women or not?"

He shrugs. "To be honest, I'm not sure. They didn't do a lot of talking, and they had different body builds so I can't tell for certain. I was also more distracted with making sure my grandpa was okay." His face falls again at the mention of his grandfather. "Do you . . . do you think they'll hurt him?"

"No," Zwe says firmly. He puts an arm around Antonio. "You said it yourself, they seem to be taking good care of everyone so far. If they wanted to hurt you, they would have already. And if they *are* the same group that robbed the other resort, that means they're only after the money, which is good. It also means they should be leaving soon, if they haven't already. I know it's hard, but let's try not to preemptively worry. Why don't we get some sleep?" he says when Antonio yawns.

"Not going to fight you on that," Antonio replies.

We'd agreed earlier that we would take shifts so one person would always stand watch. Zwe volunteers to go first.

"What are you going to do?" I ask as I settle into a pile of leaves to the best of my abilities, my backpack doubling as a pillow.

"Read, probably," he says. He brandishes the hiking map from his back pocket. "Or study this map. I know the routes are incorrect, but the better we understand this island's geography, the better our chances of survival are."

"You can take a night off from being Protective Dad Zwe, you know," I say, cocking a brow. "Do some yoga or meditate."

He rolls his eyes. "Go to sleep."

"Yes, Dad." I give a two-finger salute. "You'll wake me if you need something? Like if you get cold and want your hoodie back?"

He smiles and tucks the shoulders of his hoodie tighter around my figure. His body heat feels nice when he leans over me, nicer than even the fire. "I promise. Now go to sleep."

"I can't wait to be home," I mumble as I close my eyes.

He squeezes my arm. "Me, too."

I had initially thought I'd be too freaked out about sleeping yet another night in the jungle, but having Leila and Antonio in our group now makes me feel safer. Beside me, the crackling fire and the rhythmic sound of Zwe flipping pages combine into an unexpectedly reassuring lullaby.

Zwe. Books, I think right before I doze off. *Home.*

TEN

Despite my protests that the last thing I want is to be treated like an injured Bambi, the other three agree that I need the longest amount of uninterrupted rest, and so they give me the last watch shift.

After swapping with Leila, I sit in the same spot for a long time, hunched over on my knees, blinking incessantly to make myself stay awake. I consider going for a short walk, but the whole point of this is that I'm watching over the group. There's also the small but aching fact that my ankle needs all the recuperation it can get.

A task. I need something that will keep my brain busy, but not my body.

You want a task? I'll give you a task! my brain seems to taunt with a smirk. Various hypothetical scenes involving my parents begin to flash through my mind like one of those old View-Master toys.

Them getting a call with some random police officer telling them that their only child is dead. Them and Zwe's parents opening the door to our apartment and my mom breaking down before she's even crossed the threshold. Them having to plan their own daughter's goddamn funeral.

I take a deep breath, willing my lungs to expand and take in more air.

Recognizing that I'm spiraling and catastrophizing, I scramble to redirect my active imagination toward something else.

Plot. I can plot out a new story. Zwe said it best: nothing distracts me like a good book.

I shake out my shoulders as I open a blank document.

An excruciating four hours later, and after going over my two pages of single-spaced 12-point font enough times to make sure I haven't missed anything, I wake everyone up at our agreed time, although I've been wanting to wake them for a solid hour and a half by this point.

"It doesn't make sense," I say as Zwe crawls into a sitting position.

"What doesn't make sense? Mornings? Sunrises?" He yawns and wipes the sleep from his eyes. "I know they're a relatively new concept to you, but believe it or not, they've been around for a while. Some might even say since the dawn of time."

"I knew I should've lured a family of bears to eat just you—" I scowl. "No, this." I plop my laptop down on his lap.

He rubs his eyes, squints, blinks, and at last gestures at the device. "I'm going to need some more context here."

"I plotted it out, and it doesn't make sense."

"You plotted what out?" Antonio asks. He takes a swig of water (river water, which he *swears* is drinkable although I still have my doubts), gargles, then spits into the pit.

Leila makes a gagging noise. "Ew! What is wrong with you?"

"What? We have to put it out anyway," he says defensively. "You want to hang out with my morning breath all day long?"

"We wouldn't have to if you kept your mouth shut—"

"Which we all know I'm not going to," he says, beating her to it. "But what did you plot out, Ms. Poe? A new book? How many are you working on right now?"

"No, I plotted all of this." I wave around, trying to encompass the whole island in one gesture. "I plotted what happened. What's *happening*. I took everything we talked about yesterday into account, and it doesn't make sense. There are too many holes. It's not adding up."

"I'm still lost," Zwe says.

I talk as rapidly as I scroll, highlighting the key points. "Why hasn't anyone found us? It feels like no one's even *tried*. Yeah, it's a big island, but there's, what, eight of them? At least? You don't need eight people to guard a group of resort staff in one spot. These people have guns and buggies. We should've heard something."

"We're pretty deep in the forest," Leila says, looking around as though to really emphasize her point. "People who aren't familiar with the wilderness don't typically stray from marked paths. Even if you have guns and buggies."

"That's the other big thing," I say. I throw my arms open again. "*Who* are these people? *Are* they familiar with this place? Why did a group of people take over a remote island resort? A villain needs a motive. What's their motive? What do they want?"

"Didn't we agree that it was money?" Zwe offers. "You know, like they did at the other resort."

"That's what I thought at first." I refer back to my plot. "Money" was the first thing I'd plugged in, too, but that led to a dead end. "But what money? What, they're going around and looting all the designer furniture in the rooms? The organic spa products? Breaking into the cash registers at the bar and restaurant? Which also doesn't make sense because it's a resort, and the majority of people are going to have the charges billed back to their room. Rooms are paid by card. If they want the hotel to transfer their money, they're going to need internet. They shut down the Wi-Fi, and there's no regular cell service here."

"Maybe they turned the Wi-Fi back on? While we were out?" Antonio offers.

"Maybe," I say. "But why gather everyone then? Why didn't they repeat what they did at the other resort and just quietly hold one person at gunpoint to transfer the money? Why go through the trouble of rounding up every individual person? I don't think it's the same group."

"Well—" Leila starts.

But I need them to hear the whole thing first.

"My second thought was 'What if they wanted to rob the *guests* at gunpoint?' That makes sense. The people who can afford a place like this are people with money. But then that leads to the next plot hole." I open a palm at myself, then at Zwe. "*We're* the only guests here. So either they didn't know about the resort's booking glitch and assumed it would be packed with multimillionaires, but *that* also doesn't add up because a job this big, surely they'd have planned every detail beforehand, *or* they *did* know about the glitch and that there were no guests currently here, but they still came anyway because the guests' money isn't what they're after.

"Another thing—the only two ways onto this island are by water or air. We would've heard them if they came in a helicopter, but we didn't, so it must've been a boat. There are security cameras on the pier. There are security guards patrolling the grounds.

Unless they rowed in on a dingy little rowboat, someone should've seen them approaching. How did they get in undetected? Too! Many! Holes!"

I'm out of breath by the time I finish, and the three of them stare at me like I've entered full Mad Scientist Mode. Even Zwe, who *has* seen me turn into this version of myself when I'm neck-deep in plotting and replotting a book, looks concerned, as though he's worried I'm suffering heatstroke or tripped and hit my head on a very large rock while they were all asleep.

"So what," Leila asks slowly, "*are* they after?"

"That's my question!" I say. My fingers curl with a shot of adrenaline and she rears back slightly. Upon realizing that I look like I'm about to strangle her, I give an apologetic grimace and place my hands down in my lap. "It's too many inconsistencies. You know what the three biggest motivations in a plot are?" I'm on a roll now, but I'm buoyed by the fact that none of them have been able to tell me I'm wrong. My delivery might be unhinged, but the content stands up. "Money, power, and love. 'Power' makes no sense because it's not like they want to take over running the place. So it's either 'money'—"

"Or love," Zwe finishes. There's a deep groove between his brows as he looks up, as he thinks, turns it over in his head. My favorite beta reader. Not a single plot hole that Zwe Aung Win has missed.

"Or love," I echo.

"You figured all of this out on your laptop?" Antonio asks. For the first time since we met, he's speechless.

"Like I said, I plotted."

"This is all very impressive," Leila starts. "And I don't want to be dismissive of what you're saying in any way whatsoever. But . . .

I don't really see what the point of all of this is. Our priority should still be how we get off of this island. And then we can pass on all of this information to the authorities. They can get in touch with the staff at Second Heaven and see if there are any overlaps between the two cases."

"But don't you think we'd have a better chance of escaping if we figured out why they're here? Then we'd know *who* they are and what they want, and that in turn would give us a better sense of how their minds work," I counter, pushing past the feeling that I'm being dismissed. "Because if these people aren't the same ones who robbed the other resort, then—" I swallow, chancing a glance at Antonio. "—we don't know how dangerous they are, and what they're capable of. Shouldn't our new priority be to free everybody else? If this group isn't after money, then that changes everything."

"I . . . don't know," Leila muses. The three of them have the same unconvinced look. "It feels like we're wasting time with every second we're not moving."

"Yeah, Mr. Zwe said yesterday that it's a good sign that they're taking care of everyone," Antonio points out. "As long as they're doing that, then *we* should focus on getting help. Besides, what if we make them mad by going back and trying to free everybody?"

"But we don't know what the stakes are," I press. It's basic character development. Who is your protagonist? What do they want? What's standing in the way of them getting what they want? What'll happen if they *don't* get what they want?

"Stakes?" Leila asks.

"You need major stakes to propel an entire novel forward. And no one shows up armed and angry on a remote island unless there are *big* stakes at play. What did they come for, and what's going to happen if they don't get it? If we figure that out, then worst-case scenario and we get recaptured, maybe we can come up with some sort of compromise so they still get what they want, and all of us, including the rest of the staff, get to go home."

"What are you saying? That we go back to the people who kidnapped us and ask them, 'What do you want'?" Leila's tone is speckled with condescension, and she sounds like she's holding back from laughing at me.

"Well, no," I say, embarrassed because I didn't really think through my next step quite yet. "But I just . . . something's wrong." I can't help but motion back at my laptop. "The pieces aren't fitting. We need to know more about who we're dealing with here."

Leila studies me, clearly gauging whether or not to say what she actually wants to say. In the end, she decides to say it. "Poe, this isn't a novel."

"I know this isn't a novel." This time, I don't try to temper my irritation.

"Then we can't treat this like it's a novel." I'm so startled by Zwe's interruption that I turn around to make sure it was him that said it and that I didn't just hallucinate his voice. "You can't seriously be suggesting we go back to the resort right now. We'll all get captured, too. We're sticking with our original plan, which is to either call for help, or get off of this island somehow and go get help ourselves."

"But I'm right. You know I'm right," I stammer.

"I know this will all be really useful information for the police," Leila replies, keeping her cool. "For now, though, Zwe's right, we have to figure out how the hell we're going to escape. I fucked up yesterday with the trail, and I'm so sorry about that." Her voice goes wobbly, and Zwe puts a hand on her shoulder.

"You were under a lot of stress," he says. Leila's buried her face in her hands, and Zwe gives her shoulder a squeeze. "Between that and the adrenaline, anyone would've gotten confused, too. It was super dark. It's okay, there's daylight now, and we're all rested and recharged. We'll make it there today. We have to."

I know I shouldn't be making this all about me, but what Zwe's doing right now feels like a twisting of the knife he stuck in my back just a few minutes ago. I get a condescending *Then we can't treat this like a novel* and she gets *You were under a lot of stress?*

"I can try leading the way today," Antonio suggests. "I know these woods pretty well, too."

Leila's head pops up, and her gaze drifts toward the ocean. "Unless there's a quicker way for us to get help." There's a glimmer of hope in her voice. "Hey, what day is it today?"

"Um—" I press on a random key to turn my laptop screen on. "Friday."

Leila and Antonio share a wordless look, and he punches the air. "Supply day!" he shouts.

"What?" I ask.

"Supply day," he says with a new burst of energy. "Every Friday morning, our food suppliers make their delivery from the mainland. They'll be at the pier in a few hours."

"Exactly what I was thinking," Leila confirms. She sounds like she already has a plan. "When I was a kid, you know what my parents taught me would always be a constant if I ever got lost?"

"What?" Zwe asks.

"The sea," she says, pointing across at the horizon. "In case I ever got lost in the jungle, they told me to head down to the water, and that they'd meet me there. You can get lost in the jungle, but not on the shore of an island."

Zwe peers over even though from where we are, we can't actually see the sand. "Won't we be sitting ducks out in the open?" he asks. "At least here, we can hide."

"Not if we hide out close to the water until the boat arrives," Antonio says.

"And they're not going to know about the supply boat," Leila points out. "So it's not like there'll be a group of them waiting at the pier. My guess is one, *maybe* two, and that's mainly to guard the boat *they* arrived in. Assuming they've moved their boat to the pier. We just have to take them out before they can alert anyone that there are people approaching."

Right then, I feel a small drop of water on my forearm. Then another. We all look up. Small, feathery raindrops brush our skin.

"Does the supply boat come even if it's raining?" Zwe asks. "Leila, weren't you saying when we first arrived that there's bad weather on the mainland?"

"Fuck." Antonio's whole face scrunches up on the word.

"I forgot," Leila groans.

"Forgot what?" I ask.

"Storm's arriving tonight," Antonio mumbles.

My stomach flips. "A storm? Like with . . . rain and wind?" Already, I feel like I need to sit down. "Great. If this were a novel, I'd say that it's a bit in the face to foreshadow gloom and doom with an approaching storm."

"It wasn't a problem yesterday because I thought we'd be safe by nighttime," Leila says. "But now it does put a timer on everything."

"But it's okay," Zwe says. When I meet his eyes, he gives me a nod. An *I know you're spiraling, but I promise you it'll be okay* nod. "Because by the time it gets here, we'll have already left on the supply boat."

"But what if it arrives sooner?" I ask, panic jacking my voice up several octaves. "The storm, I mean. Or what if the supply boat decides not to come because there's a storm on the way? Or what if the bad guys *told* the supply boat not to come?"

"My grandfather is the only one who talks to the suppliers," Antonio cuts in. "There's no record in the computers or anything. He writes it all down in a notebook. Old-fashioned like that."

"And the supplies always come," Leila reassures us. "The storm won't land until the evening. Trust me, it's part of my job." When I look at her quizzically, she explains, "I need to know what the weather's going to be so I can advise guests on which activities they can book. Can't exactly arrange a parasailing session for the weekend a storm blows in. And some guests get real pissy if, god forbid, their parasailing afternoon gets canceled."

"Those guests sound like real assholes," Zwe says.

"You don't know the half of it," she replies, rolling her eyes. "But this—" She stretches out an open palm, and a couple of small drops land on her skin. "—is just light rain. It'll stop in a bit."

Stretching, Zwe twists his waist to one side, then the other. "Okay, then, all the more reason to hurry back down. Should be a quicker trip since it's downhill."

"Everyone ready?" Antonio asks.

I clear my throat. "I . . . I think we should still try to free everyone first," I say quickly. I can't stop worrying about Sandra and Antonio's grandfather and everyone else. I can't leave them behind here when we don't know what this group's motive is. "Strength in numbers, right? We know where they are, so we're not going in blind, and we have the two knives from the emergency kits that Leila kept. On the other hand, we don't know what they'll do to everyone else if they catch us escaping on the supply boat. *That* might cause them to panic. This new supply boat plan has too many variables." I look at Zwe as I say "variables" because if there's one thing Zwe Aung Win hates, it's variables.

He chews the inside of his cheeks, running through all the scenarios in his head, and even though I want to reiterate my point, I know that the best thing to do right now is to let him come to the safest, most logical conclusion himself.

"Do you really think they'll hurt my grandpa?" Antonio asks.

For all of his charm and bravado, in this moment, he can't pretend to be anything other than what he is: young and scared. "No," Zwe rushes to answer, throwing me a stern look. "No one's hurting anybody. Your grandfather will be fine."

"The supply boat is a certainty, too," Leila says.

"It's—" I try.

"Leila's right. They've never missed a delivery, Ms. Poe," Antonio says with a sheepish shrug.

"But the moment they fire a single bullet, that boat is going to turn right around," I say, standing my ground. "And then we'll be right back here, only from the starting point and without even the advantage of surprise. Right now, they don't know where we are. There's a good chance that we can take them."

"It's too risky," Leila says. "Strength in numbers only works if we do manage to free everyone, but what if we don't? There's only four of us currently, and we don't know how many of them are guarding the reception area. They've most definitely already upped their surveillance once they realized two of us escaped. Plus, we're not in the best shape either. We barely found enough to eat yesterday, and the exhaustion is already catching up to us. They *will* capture us."

"Aren't you worried about your friends?" I snap.

At that, Leila's expression changes. "Of course I'm worried

about my friends," she says, barely holding on to her last traces of politeness. Her cheery persona has slipped. "Which is precisely why I want to get the hell off of this island, and get help so they can be freed."

I fold my arms, and hope that the posture makes me look authoritative and not like a sulky child. Leila doesn't say anything else, but her posture is just as rigid as mine. There's no compromise here, not unless we split up. If she's not backing down, then neither am I.

Zwe's voice loosens the tautness between us, a referee stepping in the middle of an unmoving game of tug-of-war. "Why don't we take a vote?"

I'm about to say *Yes, why don't we* with smug triumph until I look at Zwe—and find him staring at me, lips flattened into a tight line, brows marginally sloped inward. My sense of triumph morphs into searing embarrassment as I realize, actually, Zwe *isn't* on my side.

I know I'm not as outwardly brave or as great at Being a Leader as him and Leila, but I thought my plan and reasoning were pretty solid. Suddenly, however, I feel two inches tall.

"You know what, it's fine, we'd be wasting time," I hear myself say, wishing I'd kept my embarrassing mouth shut in the first place.

"Poe—" Zwe starts.

"No, you're right, we're in no shape to take on a group of people with guns," I say with a wave. "Let's go to the beach. I'm just going to, erm, take a quick bathroom break."

"Want me to come with?" Leila asks. She points at my ankle. "In case you need help . . . squatting?" She gives a small smile—a gesture of truce.

"I'm good," I say. "I can go on my own. I'll be right back."

"I'll come with you," Zwe says.

"I said I'll be fine on my own."

"Good for you, but you're not the only one who has a right to pee around here," he replies calmly. If he had a reaction to my snippiness, he's not showing it.

I take a long, deep inhale, locking my anger away into a box that I then shove to the side. I will get mad at him later, probably on the plane home, or maybe even while we're waiting at the airport boarding gate—but not right now.

"What's going on?" he asks as soon as we're out of earshot.

"Nothing," I reply, aware what a blatant lie it sounds like.

"Why are you mad at me?"

"I'm not mad at you," I say, while thinking that he surely can't be this obtuse. "I'm taking this bush."

He snorts. "Excuse me?"

I walk behind a bush that comes up to about my waist, then gesture at him with two fingers to avert his eyes. "This is my bush. You go find yourself your own pee bush."

"Good news is, I don't need a bush to pee." As I'm pulling down my pants and crouching, I hear the scratch of his zipper also being pulled down. "Haven't you heard? Perks of having a penis."

"Which you seem to be using a lot today," I mutter.

"What does that mean?" he asks.

Shit, I didn't think he'd hear me. "Nothing!" I insist from the security of my bush. Great, now I'm too riled up to pee. I take deep breaths, willing my body to relax and . . . unclench.

"What's going on?" Zwe's voice comes again.

My lower body does an unintentional Kegel, and I groan with frustration. "If I promise to tell you afterward, will you shut up right now? I can't argue with you *and* use the bathroom at the same time!"

"Fine!"

"Fine!"

I do my business, get dressed again, step out from behind the bush, and offer Zwe my hand sanitizer. "Thanks," he mumbles when I squeeze a dollop into his palm. I pivot away from him, but his ridiculously long legs allow him to block my path in a matter of one step. "You promised. Now, what's wrong?"

"You're not taking my side," I say, cognizant that I sound like a kid who's mad that their best friend has a new friend. A new friend who doesn't like me.

Zwe's face creases. "Taking your side on . . . what?"

"Earlier, when I was explaining everything that I'd worked out overnight. And also on whether we should try to escape or free everybody."

His head tilts, like he's leaning forward to make sure he's heard me correctly. "You mean when you . . . compared our lives to a novel? *Then?*"

I could strangle him. "You took her side!"

"Whose? Leila's?" he asks at the same time that I blurt out, "Leila's!"

"I didn't—" he begins, stunned.

I'm one of those people who inadvertently cry when they're angry. "You know I was making sense but instead you took her side and dismissed me." I try to keep my voice stable even if my sight is already blurring over.

"Poe!" Zwe laughs out my name. "I can't side with her over you, because we're all on the same side! Look—" I watch his nostrils flare as he takes a deep breath. Unlike me, Zwe knows how to stop his emotions before he erupts. No stinging eyes and hot cheeks for him. "I'm sorry it sounded like I was dismissing your earlier point. You *were* making sense. But Leila was also making sense when she insisted that our priority should be getting off of this island first. I know you're worried that they might get angry and hurt the others if they catch us leaving, but they'll *definitely* be angry and are even more likely to hurt them if they catch us trying to free them. Your plan was the result of a vague book plot that you drafted overnight, it wasn't even a plan!"

"That's not fair! I thought mine through a hell of a lot longer than Leila did."

"But the supply boat is coming for sure. What do we have to free everyone with, apart from two small emergency knives?" The center of his words is soft, but the edges are hard and determined. "I'm not taking Leila's side, but she knows this place the best. She knows what she's talking about better than any of us. *Your* plan has too many variables. Remember what I told you about that security course I took? You're not supposed to try to be the hero."

I can feel myself reverting back to being a toddler, with not enough words to encapsulate my anger. "You're not even giving it a chance!"

"Because this isn't a book! We don't get to play out several scenarios until we find one that works. If we screw up, you get hurt!"

I scoff. "What does that mean? That *I'm* the most useless one so *I'm* the one who's going to get captured while the rest of you escape?"

Zwe stills, looks at me with an inscrutable expression. "No, Poe," he finally says on a dark chuckle, as though I missed the joke. "What that means is that while I care about Leila and Antonio,

I . . . I don't know what I'd do if *you* got hurt and I couldn't protect you."

"Oh," I say, startled into silence.

"I weighed the situations, and at least if we fail with the boat, we can make a run for the woods again and try to still hide. If they catch us at the reception area, then we're cornered," he sighs. "Once we're talking to the police, I *promise,* we'll sit down together and run them through everything you said."

He holds out a fist, and reluctantly, I bump it.

Reset.

I'm still annoyed, but I don't want to be fighting with Zwe right now.

"Shall we go back to your girlfriend?" I ask.

"She's not my girlfriend."

"Yet," I mean to say, but my intonation makes it sound more like "Yet?"

Zwe simply smiles and shakes his head.

ELEVEN

"Ms. Poe," Antonio says, watching as I dig around in my backpack. "Why do you have a pair of binoculars in your bag?"

"I was going to go bird-watching," I reply as I produce the item.

"Since when do you bird-watch?" Zwe asks.

I shoot him a glare. "I was going to start here. Try a new hobby, get the creative juices flowing, remember? Maybe the main character in my new book is a bird-watcher."

"A time-traveling, bird-watching protagonist?" he asks.

"Whatever," I sneer, the best retort I can come up with on the spot. "Do you want to use the binoculars or not?"

"Yes, please," Leila says, and I hand them over to her.

Too tired to produce any meaningful conversation, and still somewhat irked, I mainly stayed silent during our walk down to the beach; in contrast, Leila and Zwe talked. A lot. The whole way. In some ways, it was like they were on a date. An acute, sharp sensation poked at my solar plexus from behind the whole time, something that felt a lot like, frankly, jealousy. But that was ridiculous, because what did I have to be jealous about? Zwe and I had made up. And Leila is really, really great, the kind of girl who, if you met her in a club bathroom, would slide you an extra tampon from under the stall divider while giving you a pep talk about why you absolutely should *not* text your terrible ex. All *I* was doing was being possessive, like a child who's been forced to share her favorite toy with the new kid in class.

I tried to make small talk with Antonio, who turns out to be a great person to make small talk with when you don't really want to talk because all you have to do is throw out a question like *I wonder how many different types of berries are growing in this forest?* and he'll take care of the rest. And while typically I'd be exhausted by a man who took over the majority of the conversation, in this case, that was precisely what I wanted until our trek reached level ground.

Now, we're huddled against the wall of one of the beachfront villas, trying to get a gauge of the exact manpower we're up against.

"There are two of them," Leila says, binoculars pressed against her eyes. "They're only patrolling up and down the pier." Her head moves a few degrees to the left. "The resort boats are all still there."

"They must be keeping them for their getaway," I say.

"My babies," Antonio murmurs. "No one will lay a hand on any of you, I promise."

"Are they armed?" Zwe asks.

"Yes," Leila says. "But I think we could take them."

"How?" I ask.

She lowers the binoculars, a small smile on her lips indicating that she's already got a plan. "With a little help from—" Reaching into her back pocket, she takes out two long pieces of metallic silver. "—my trusty friends," she says, the sun reflecting off of the knives. "Poe, I'm assuming you have a spare hair tie in that Swiss Army knife of a backpack? Preferably two?"

"Naturally." I dig into the front zip pocket and retrieve two black ties.

"On an island, do you know what people's number-one fear is? Because there's nowhere to hide or run, apart from right in the ocean?" Her smirk tells me it's a rhetorical question.

"What?" I ask.

"Fire."

"I don't know if this is going to work," I mutter.

Zwe exhales, fingers folded into such tight fists that his knuckles are beginning to turn white. "Positive thinking," he nonetheless replies.

"We're about to find out," Antonio says.

We managed to hop four bungalows over so that we're as close as possible to the pier without being found.

From beside the next bungalow, the one directly facing the pier, Leila gives us a thumbs-up. I watch her straighten from her crouched position, smoothing out her polo and tightening her ponytail as she gets ready. She takes one step, pauses, and peeks into each of her long sleeves, where she's tied the knives to her wrists with the hair ties. When she's satisfied, she slowly pushes her hands down in the air in front of her, as though reminding herself to remain calm. Then—

"Fire! Fire! You have to help me, there's a fire!" Arms flailing, she rushes out into the open.

The intruders, who had had their masks attached to their elbows (assumedly because of the heat), scramble to put them back on. "Put your hands up!" one of them orders.

Leila obeys, and her run also slows down to a brisk walk. "I'm not armed!"

"Stop walking or I'll shoot!" the other one barks.

"There's a fire in the forest!" Leila screams, waving behind her. "Please! You have to put it out or it's not going to matter if you shoot because we're all going to die! You can take me hostage afterward, I don't care! But there's a fire!"

They're still too far away for her to execute her plan. "There's no smoke," one of them says.

Leila groans, gesturing to imply that they can go see for themselves. "By the time you see the smoke, it'll be too late. Do you have any idea how quickly wildfire spreads? Please, we have to get the fire extinguishers!"

Still flailing and shouting, she stumbles around, at one point pretending to almost trip backward on her own foot.

"Now," Zwe says when the intruders have shifted enough that they're both facing the ocean, their backs turned toward us.

We leave our shoes and bags behind, moving as briskly yet quietly as we can. On the plus side, the sand automatically mutes our movement, and the sound of the waves helps cover whatever other small noises we might make. The disadvantage is that having to power walk through sand is a real fucker.

My body freezes when I realize that the next step I take is *the* step—the point of no return. The step where, if even one of the masked people slightly pivots around, I'll have nowhere to hide, no bush or bungalow steps to duck behind.

"I can't," I whisper to Zwe.

Pressure on the small of my back. A hand that has held mine through hundreds of terrifying scenarios.

"Just walk," he whispers back. "Pretend it's just us."

I nod, and, gulping in air, will myself to pace forward and stay in step with the two of them.

The woman with a short pixie cut steps closer to Leila. Leila reacts appropriately, continuing to shift between acting scared and standing her ground. Perfect. Now to just get the other—

We all hear the engine at the same time. It's unmistakable: blades slicing through water. A boat.

"Fuck! They're early," Antonio mutters as the vessel obliviously charges toward the pier.

He's too distracted to notice his newfound attention. Having turned to locate the source of the noise, the two intruders have inevitably discovered us. "Hey! Don't take another step!" Pixie Cut yells.

We raise our hands, Zwe yelling out, "Don't shoot! We're not armed!"

That doesn't stop Pixie Cut from going to raise her rifle—but then she stops.

Leila's removed the knives and has them pointed into the back of their necks. When she nods at us to signal that she's got a handle on the situation, we approach.

"One word, one stray shot," Leila warns. "Give me a reason to slice your neck, I dare you. Now, slowly, give your guns to my friends here." When they start lifting their weapons, Leila increases the pressure, digging the sharp metal tips deeper into their flesh. Both of them flinch, but don't say anything. "I mean it, try something funny, and you'll be fish food before anyone can find you."

After they've removed and handed over their guns to me and Zwe, Leila directs them toward the pier. Now that they've taken off their masks and I see that they're around our age, just like the first women who tackled us, I'm more convinced than ever that they're *all* women, and that Leila mistakenly identified the two that captured her. I make a note of one distinguishing feature each: Pixie Cut has a nose ring, and the other has freckles and roughly shoulder-length bleached hair (creatively, I've named her Bleached Hair). They're both Southeast Asian, too, although I can't quite place their accents. Bleached Hair has her light hair up in a ponytail, and when she turns around, I'm now close enough to see the same blob tattoo on the back of her neck; this time, I mentally trace it so that I can draw it later on. Maybe it's some sort of gang symbol that the police will be able to identify.

This whole time, the supply boat has been getting closer, close enough that I can make out people on it. Unable to control my joy, I shoot up my hand and give large, frantic waves. The person behind the wheel waves back, and I could *cry* at the mere sight of this stranger acknowledging that they see me.

This is it. We're going home. I—

I know it's not actually possible, but I swear the shot makes the whole pier vibrate.

"They spotted us!" Zwe yells as another shot leaves from the top of the resort and toward the boat. It doesn't hit the boat, but the vessel makes such a sharp swerve that it nearly topples over. More fired shots hit the three resort boats that were tied to the pier, and the air is filled with the sounds of glass breaking and bullets ricocheting off of wood and metal.

"No!" I scream. "No, come back!" I go to run for the edge of the pier, already having decided that I'd rather jump into the ocean and try to swim to safety than spend another hour on this fucking island, but Zwe's arm captures my waist. "Let me go!" I screech, hitting his forearm. "I'll swim! They're so close! No! Come back! Please! Please don't leave us here! One of you, do something!"

By the time I turn around, every inch of the picture has changed. It all happens in a literal blink of an eye, and I don't even know it's happened until I hear Leila yell, "They're getting away! One of you shoot!"

Antonio now has his hands up, and both women are using him as a human shield as they slowly walk backward. "You shoot, and your friend here loses his pretty little head," Bleached Hair tells us, the knife that was previously pushed into her skin now pressed deep into the back of Antonio's neck, her other arm braced tightly across his chest. Pixie Cut is holding the second knife, the sharp tip aimed at us.

"What the fuck happened?" I scream at Leila, although now I notice that there's blood dripping down one of her elbows.

"I got distracted by the shots! I'm sorry! Let him go!" she yells.

She tries to take one step forward, but Antonio yelps as Bleached Hair shoves the blade deeper into his skin. "One more step, and you'll have to watch him bleed out on this beach," she says, lips twining into a sneer.

"Shoot them!" Leila tells us.

"We can't shoot them!" I say, watching in horror as Antonio's figure moves farther away. "What if we miss? We could hit him!"

"You have to do something!"

"Please! Help me!" Antonio cries. I'm crying, too, and I'm shaking so much that I don't actually trust myself to hold a loaded weapon, but I'm also too frozen to put it down.

I look at Zwe, and although he's still got a solid grip on his gun, his finger is nowhere near the trigger. There's no way he's firing a shot either, clear or not. We never talked about whether we'd actually shoot them, because this hadn't been part of the plan.

"We have to run. Try to zigzag," Zwe commands, dragging me away from the water and back toward the trees. "Keep your head down," he orders, and I try my best, the three of us trying not to stumble as we rush across the sand while shots still ring out from every side. I try to turn around at one point, and catch one last sight of Antonio's figure being forced toward the resort.

Our pace picks up once we're on solid ground, the adrenaline keeping the pain in my ankle at bay. We round the corner of the farthest bungalow, and, in the safety of its shadow, stop, leaning against the wall as we gasp for air.

It isn't until Zwe yells "Fuck!" that my senses rush back, like at last someone's unmuted the TV.

"He's gone," I mumble. I don't sit so much as fall to my ass, warm sand scattering around my thighs. "They took him."

"I'm sorry," Leila says, falling down beside me. "I'm so, so sorry. I wasn't expecting the shots. Or . . . I thought we'd be closer to the boat by the time anyone spotted us, or that the people on the boat would've helped us or . . ." She takes in a shaky breath. "I don't know. I don't know what I was thinking. Antonio—" She stops on a hiccup.

Zwe is the last one to join us on the soft ground. "What do we do now?" he asks.

"I—" I start, but nothing else comes out. "I don't know," I whisper. Part of me wants to laugh because this is it, isn't it? We're screwed, and there's no way out, and what do you do in situations like this except laugh at the universe?

"Me neither," Leila says.

"Do we . . . wait?" Zwe asks.

"For what?" I say, giving in and letting out a dark laugh. "Death?"

"The silver lining is that they saw us." I peer at him, confused. "The supply boat," he explains, gesturing with the rifle at the water. Then, as though realizing that he's still holding a death weapon, he gently lays it down and continues gesticulating with his hands. "They saw us, and now they're going to get help."

"But what if—" I swallow, not wanting to say it out loud, as though we're not all thinking the same thing. "What if help doesn't arrive before *they* find us?"

"Then we make sure they don't find us."

"We can't stay here, though," Leila says. She points up at the sky where the clouds have multiplied and gotten more opaque. "That storm's definitely arriving tonight," she says, also pointing to the shore. "The water's already coming up. We need to get to higher ground. The woods will become dangerous when the storm hits. Maybe we can sneak into another building in the resort and wait out the storm there."

In fight-or-flight situations, I am very solidly a "flight" individual. If I were on my own right now, I'd take the ostrich route and bury my head in the metaphorical sand and wait for an act of divine intervention that would end this whole thing. Deus ex machina me, baby.

But I have adrenaline and fear pumping through my system, and as soon as Leila suggests we *get to higher ground,* anger coils its way up my spine. "Another building in the resort?" It's the first time in days that I can be loud, because at this point every fucking one knows where we are and what we're trying to do so what's the point in being quiet—and boy, do I take advantage of it. "You mean like the reception hall? The one I suggested earlier that *you* wrote off?"

"That's not fair," she says. She grinds her molars, the action making her sharp cheeks even more angular. Seeing *her* angry causes my own previous anger to evolve into unfiltered, stinging infuriation. *She's* mad at *me* right now? "We all agreed to go for the supply boat."

"No, *you* said that's what we should do. *I* said we should free everyone first, and that the supply boat plan sounded too risky. *You* were the one—"

"No, we said we would vote on it and *you* said—"

"Will you both shut the fuck up?!" Zwe roars, stunning both of us into silence. "Who the fuck cares? Antonio is gone! They know we're still here and we're trying to escape! They know the supply boat spotted that something was wrong! They're going to be coming after us even more quickly than before, and we need to get moving now. And I for one refuse to babysit grown adults who have suddenly regressed to being toddlers, so whatever stupid, petty rivalry is brewing between the two of you right now, both of you need to squash it immediately. Jesus, who needs armed enemies when the two of you are ready to push each other off of this island yourselves?"

I've been mad at Zwe before, but I've never felt whatever I'm feeling right now toward him, like I'm this human pinball machine of emotions. I march several feet away, deeper amongst the trees, because I refuse to let either of them see me cry. The thing is, I *feel* like a toddler. I'm angry and sad and I just want to go home to my bed and hug my mom and dad. And I want my best friend.

As though he read my thoughts loud and clear, Zwe appears beside me.

"Go away," I say, my tears placing my words on shaky stilts.

"We need to get going, Poe. I know you're scared right now, but Leila says it's not—"

I whip my head around so violently that my tears streak down my cheeks. "Don't you patronize me."

He flinches, like I turned and slapped him. "I'm not *patronizing* you."

"I don't care what fucking Leila says. Did she send you over to placate me? Because I'm the injured, whiny little kid who won't stop crying about wanting to go home?"

"Nobody thinks that," he says with a scoff that makes me want to push him into the water. "And if *you* think we're thinking that, then that's just you projecting your own insecurities."

I open my mouth, stopping myself in time for a voice to step in and ask if I really want to say it. I decide I do. "You're just like him. You don't think I can do *anything*, do you? That whatever ideas I throw out are just stupid, half-baked ones that aren't actually practical."

A wrinkle forms between his thick brows as he deciphers my words, and I watch in real time as they land. "Vik," he says, my silence all the confirmation he needs. "You think I'm *just like Vik* because I'm calling you out on your unfounded and frankly bordering-on-misogynistic—"

"Misogynistic?!" I yell.

"—contempt toward Leila?"

"You think I'm not capable of anything!"

He throws his hands in the air. "When have I said that?! Tell me one point in all of this when I've told you that you couldn't do something!"

"That's why you didn't move in with Julia, right? Because you don't think I can survive living on my own? And you didn't *tell* me that you broke up with Julia, or *why* you broke up, because then I'd realize you're still living with me even though you don't want to and I'd feel guilty over it, and you thought I couldn't handle that either!"

It's the thought bubble that's been hanging over my head ever since I found out the reason for their breakup earlier. Still, even *I'm* not prepared for the gut punch it is, for both of us.

He considers me with an emotion whose resemblance to hatred frightens me. "That's not even remotely close," he says at last, voice so still it takes on an eeriness. "I didn't tell you about my breakup because you were so goddamn preoccupied with your own crap that I knew you wouldn't care. But you already knew that. That's why you booked this trip, right? Because you know what a shitty, self-absorbed friend you've been lately?"

If my words were a punch to the gut, his are a stab to the jugular.

Because he's right.

Because I'm not mad at him.

Because I'm mad at myself.

I'm mad at myself for tripping and injuring myself and slowing us all down. For booking this trip at all and being the reason we're in this mess in the first place. I can't stop pulling at the thread now that I've started. I'm mad that while Vik was wrong that I was never going to be a published author, being a one-hit wonder doesn't exactly put *me* in the right either. I'm mad that I might have to go back to a life of selling books that other people have written, only this time, it'll be with the knowledge that I let it all slip from the palm of my hand. And I am *so* mad that I can't write another book, that by the looks of it, I will *never* write another book, and all of this is *because* I couldn't write one more fucking book.

But none of that even fucking matters, I realize. Because it really, truly doesn't.

The thing I'm most mad about, as Zwe just pointed out, is that I'd become so engrossed in my own writer's block—which, in the grand scheme of things, isn't even a real problem—that I didn't even know my best friend had been looking at buying a house, or that he'd gotten his heart broken. *That's* the thing that's going to keep me up at night for the rest of my life.

"I'm sorry," I whisper.

"Save it," he says, and even though I should've been aware of this beforehand, for the first time, I register how cutting my words had been. Zwe doesn't really hate people, but he *hates* Vik, and I knew what I was doing when I compared the two of them. He begins heading back toward the bungalow, and I fall in step behind him.

When we reach her, Leila looks at me, at Zwe, at me, back at Zwe, then away at some vague point on the horizon. "I'm sorry to make things awkward, but we need to get moving," she says slowly. She points up at the sky, which has become the shade of dark that, if you didn't have access to a working watch or phone (which we don't), would leave you uncertain as to whether it was afternoon or evening. "If they don't catch us first, the storm will. Add all of that water to all of that mud, and the ground turns dangerous real fast."

"We need to weather the storm," Zwe says.

"Literally," Leila says with a small chuckle, but Zwe's face remains as unmoving as the stone statues by the reception hall.

"Where?" I ask.

"One of the villas?" Zwe suggests.

"They might have access to the security system," Leila says. "All the rooms and villas have security cameras outside. There's a tower on the other side of the island." She makes a half-circle gesture to her right. "It's where guests can go zip-lining. It's a bit of a walk, but it's not as long as the hiking path, and it's all on flat ground. If we hurry, we'll make it right before the storm hits." As though proving to all of us that she knows what she's talking about, a huge wave hits the shore right after her last word.

"The tide's already risen some more," Zwe notes.

"Do you think help will come before the storm arrives?" I ask.

She shrugs. "I don't know. Communicating via radio channels is tricky around here at the best of times. With the way the weather is right now, the supply boat's comms system might be glitching and they might not be able to talk to anyone until they reach land. By the time the boat gets back to the mainland and notifies the authorities, who assemble their own rescue operations, they *might* decide that it's safer to wait until the storm's over. Either way, we need to shelter in place until then. We might have a view of the pier from the tower, so we could keep an eye out."

"Then we should get going," Zwe says, and, without so much as a glance at me, starts in the direction that Leila indicated.

I stay behind, watching him and Leila walk side by side. Their mouths are moving but the wind has become louder, making them look like two actors in a silent movie I can only watch from my seat. She says something, he replies, she says something else, and he smiles. I had never been popular in school, but I'd also never cared because I never had to do anything—group projects, lunch, school dances—alone, because I'd always had Zwe. This is the first time I'm seeing him from this perspective, up ahead with somebody else without even turning around to check that I'm still there.

I can only think of one time when we had a big blowout. It was right after we'd moved into our current place—back when we were still renting—and, because it only came partly furnished, we went couch shopping. After we sat and bounced on literally every single couch in the store, I voted for a smallish teal L-shape number. It wasn't *the* most comfortable one we'd tried and the quality wasn't great, so I knew those cushions were going to sink in approximately six months, but I liked the color, and, as I pointed out to Zwe, the moderate price tag meant we wouldn't have to feel too bad about eventually throwing it out.

He, however, wanted a larger brown one, the one that, admittedly, had been our collective favorite as soon as we sat down. It was made with the kind of high-quality smooth, supple leather that would only look better over time, its accumulating creases and scratches adding to the overall character and evidence that this was a sofa that was loved.

It's too expensive, I said.

We spend half of our time watching TV, reading, or writing on the couch, he'd said. *It's an investment,* and *it's in our budget.*

Just barely. And think of the hassle when one of us moves. What are we going to do, saw it in half? I pointed out, thinking about Vik and Julia, both of whom we'd been dating long enough to know that these were partners we could see ourselves with for the long haul.

Anger laced through Zwe's features, and he told me that he didn't want a shitty couch to be the centerpiece of our living room, and I said that it wasn't *shitty*. Neither of us are yellers so it's not exactly that we got into a full-on screaming match, but we *did* start arguing right there, surrounded by couches and other customers who steered clear of our particular aisle. I asked him why he was being so dramatic over a fucking couch and he said that it was *his* home too and we both had equal say, and round and round in circles we went.

In the end, we drew straws and ended up with the leather couch—the plush, criminally comfortable one that I write from every day to this day. Sometimes I fall asleep mid-writing with my laptop still open, and when I wake up, my laptop is closed and on the coffee table, and I'm tucked under our pink knit throw, the brown leather so soft it feels like I'm sleeping on a cloud. It's the couch I was depressed and crying on when I got the idea for *Give Me a Reason,* and later, the one I was sitting on when my book auction closed, the one I was eating popcorn on when the Netflix offer came through.

I pointed it out to Zwe once—how almost every big milestone of my life has taken place while I've sat on that couch.

So it was a good investment? he said with a chuckle, the closest he's *ever* come to saying "I told you so."

I've never thought that our friendship would sever, but that afternoon, in a corner of Sofa, So Good, it stretched to an extent that I didn't think it ever would. In those twenty minutes, I saw an alternative version of us where we didn't *get* each other the way we did and always had, and I thought, *My god, what a terrible life that would be.*

This time, though, it feels like I single-handedly overstretched us and now there's a rip right in the middle of the fabric, the kind that you can patch up with time and patience and the right tools, but will leave behind a permanent stitch, a reminder that at one point, I tore it.

This trip was supposed to make us close again, and yet here we are, unable to even stomach walking alongside each other.

Way to go, Poe.

I add "pick a holiday" to the increasingly long list of things that should be easy for an adult, but, it turns out, I have no fucking clue how to do, right there under "be a half-decent friend."

TWELVE

"So Poe, what book are you working on now? Or do you not want to talk about it?" Leila adds quickly.

It's the first time either of them has directly addressed me, but I suspect that for her, it's more because she's worried she'll accidentally say the wrong thing. We're weaving through the trees on the coastline, and every now and then, I look around and continue to be stunned by the picturesqueness of this place. It seems wrong to feel so miserable here.

"No, I don't mind," I say. I can't tell if she's genuinely interested or making small talk, but I don't look at her, staring down at the path as I have for the past however many minutes. I don't want to trip over something again, and more importantly, I don't have to worry about accidentally making eye contact with Zwe. "It's about time travel."

"No way!" Leila gasps. "That sounds incredible!"

She sounds so sincerely excited that I break my own "no looking up" rule. Leila's face is split into a grin, and she begins gesticulating with her hands to prompt me to tell her more.

"Thanks," I laugh. Fleetingly, I'm annoyed that she's one of those people that you can never stay mad at for too long.

"What's the plot? Sell me this book."

Automatically, I look back down. It's humiliating, but I'm worried that if I maintain eye contact while I tell her, she'll see it written in 12-point font across my face that I don't actually know how to "sell" this half-baked "plot."

"It's about this manhole that allows the main character to time travel. She becomes obsessed with it and keeps making changes in her present-day life and then travels to the future to see that's brought her closer to curating her perfect life," I say, almost by rote at this point.

"How does she discover the manhole?"

"Oh, um, she was just . . . walking one day. To . . . work." Which sounded like a *fine* idea when I wrote it, but now that I say it out loud, it's embarrassingly clear that I need a more exciting inciting incident. Which is something that I should know. It's something that I *do* know.

"Where does she time travel to first?" Leila continues. "Does she arrive at, like, whatever point in time she's thinking about? How does she get back to the present?"

It's not that Leila's done anything wrong. In fact, being earnestly excited about their latest work in progress is one of the greatest gifts you can give a writer. However, in a matter of seconds, I'm transported back to my last signing at Sar Oat Sin where that girl—what was her name? Cho? Chu?—asked me about my next book with the same enthusiasm, and I really, really wished she hadn't.

I also don't want to talk about my book right now. In fact, I don't want to talk about anything with anybody. But I don't want Zwe to think that I'm brushing off Leila, so I force myself to hold the conversation.

"I'm . . . still working out the details," I mumble.

"How did you come up with the idea?" she asks.

This, I can answer. "I tried to think of the kind of plot and themes my readers would like and arrived at this. I mean, time travel is always fun, right?"

"It sounds really interesting," she says. "I'm even more sorry now that we had to leave your backpack behind. Did you already have a lot written?"

"Nah, just a couple of chapters. Like I said, I'm still figuring out the details, it's all a mess. Honestly, they weren't even that good." I mean it as a semi-ha-ha self-deprecatory statement, but the edges feel too raw on my tongue.

She gives me a cursory "I'm sure that's not true," to which I return a polite nod and tight smile.

"Have *you* read any of it?" she asks Zwe.

"No," he replies instantly. Without realizing, I wait for him to elaborate; my stomach pinches when he doesn't.

Because with Zwe, it's typically *No, but*.

No, but I've been pestering her for ages to let me.

No, but only because I haven't successfully hacked into her laptop yet.

No, but I already know it's going to blow everyone's minds.

"I see," is all Leila says.

We resume walking in quiet until Zwe asks, "Hey, do you think your family heard the shots? Earlier?"

"Not sure," Leila says. "Even if they did, they might just assume it's some new resort activity. Guests ask for the weirdest things sometimes."

"Oh yeah? What's the weirdest request you've ever received?"

She blubbers air through her lips. "Off the top of my head?" After considering for a bit, she says, "Oh shit, how could I forget? We were once asked to host a, wait for it, *dog wedding*. As in, two dogs got married."

A shocked, hearty laugh comes out of Zwe. "You're kidding. Did you guys actually do it?"

She shrugs and rolls her lips in a *What can ya do* expression. "Here at the Cerulean, our job is to curate your perfect getaway."

Zwe waves both hands, and then makes a time-out signal. "Walk me through this. Did you know this dog wedding was happening beforehand, or was it a case of guests bringing their dogs and springing it on you last minute that they wanted to marry their dogs? Was it two different guests, or did both dogs belong to the same guest? Were there other dogs in attendance? I have to know everything."

Leila explains that yes, they *did* know in advance, because the whole event had a wedding planner behind it, and yes, there were other dogs in attendance, all of whom belonged to the betrothed dogs' owners' friends and "carpooled" across two private jets. The two dog newlyweds belonged to a couple of human newlyweds who, on their honeymoon, had the brilliant idea that their canines should also be joined in holy matrimony.

"Do I want to know how much all of that cost?" Zwe asks.

Leila's grimace speaks for itself. "There was a wagyu wedding cake. The 'guests' could pick between salmon and lamb chops. Oh, and some of the dogs in attendance, naturally, had food intolerances, so we had to prepare special plates for them. Our head chef has worked in multiple Michelin-starred kitchens, and this was the closest I've ever seen to her almost quitting."

"Your job is turning out to be both the weirdest and most interesting role I've ever encountered," Zwe says. "Do you like it?"

I've inconspicuously put myself behind the two of them again, and from my angle, I notice a slight straightening of Leila's spine. Her gait slows, like she's *really* thinking about this. "If I answer honestly, do you promise not to report it back to Sandra?" she asks at last.

"Promise," Zwe says.

She gives a dark chuckle. "It depends on the week. I mainly took the job to stay close to my family, and the majority of the guests we get are great, but every once in a while, you get some real pieces of work. But it pays well, and my parents rely on me for most of their money, so—" She finishes on another *What can ya do* shrug.

Zwe nods. "That's really admirable of you." His tone shifts with concern. "Wait, what if your family goes down to the pier? Like, to get to the mainland—"

She shakes her head. "I appreciate the concern, but it's okay, they don't use the pier. They're not allowed on resort property, so they have their own makeshift dock. It's closer to the trail that connects the village to the beach. Or at least, it was. That's a whole thing we're having to sort out. But they'll be okay, they always are."

"Okay, that's good," he says on a sigh of relief, and she shoots him a grateful smile.

"You work at your parents' bookstore, right?" she asks. "What do you think you'd do if they didn't own that store? Or sold it? Do you think you'd still be selling books?"

Without taking a beat, he replies, "I'd do a PhD," and the speed at which he says it makes me jerk back.

Since when has Zwe wanted to do a PhD? Sure, sometimes we've joked that his dream job would just be "Statistics," but I didn't think he was serious about it.

"Oh, yeah?" Leila's asking. "In what?"

"Statistics. It's what I did my undergrad in."

"Ew, you want to do math?" she says, wrinkling her nose. "You were giving off hot nerd vibes, but I didn't realize the *nerd* part of your whole schtick was that strong."

"Hey, stats isn't *just* math!" Zwe shoots back. He's grinning like a teenager on a first date, and I feel the overwhelming need to climb up a tree and give them some privacy. "It . . . makes sense. It *helps* everything, anything, make sense. But ideally, I'd do a PhD and become a teacher. I know it's corny, but I'd love to show kids how exciting math is."

"That's not corny. Do your parents know you want to go back to college and get into teaching? What did they say?"

He slaps a mosquito that landed on his arm. "They don't know. If they did, they'd make me go, but I wouldn't feel good about leaving them on their own. Especially now that they're older."

"Family, right?" she says quietly. He nods, and when they look at each other, there's a silent exchange of understanding that makes me return to staring at the ground. It was one thing to feel the emotional distance increase between me and Zwe. But to feel that *and* see him actively get closer to somebody else? I feel like I'm going to be sick. "And how did you two meet?"

I look up right as Zwe glances back at me. Something jolts me from the inside when our eyes meet, because it's like I'm looking at someone I don't know. Because I don't know this Zwe. I've met so many versions of him over the years, but never this one. He still looks so . . . angry? No, that's not it.

Passive.

He looks passive, like I'm another guest at the resort he just met today. Like he forgot I was even walking two feet behind him this whole time.

"School," I say. "Elementary."

"Aaawww, so since you were babies!" Leila gushes. "Who approached whom?"

"I wanted to check out one more book than the library allowed and started crying because the librarian wouldn't let me," I say. Despite myself, I smile and steal another peek at Zwe. The knot in my stomach loosens ever so slightly when I catch a flash of dimples. "So Zwe came over and offered to borrow it under his name."

"Stop!" As if commanding herself, Leila stops in her tracks, and puts a hand to her chest. "That is the fucking cutest thing I've ever heard!"

"It was a Betty and Veronica comic," Zwe says.

Now it's *my* turn to come to an abrupt halt. "You remember?" The words fly out before I can consider that Zwe still loathes me.

He stops walking too, completing our awkward triangle. "Of course I remember," he says.

Oh, I think.

Because I thought I was the only one who remembered.

One Christmas when I was shopping for Zwe's present, I tried to track down a copy of that exact comic. I found one approximately a month later, too, thanks to my eBay alert. I didn't buy it, though. I put it in my cart, went to check out, and then thought, *What the fuck, Poe, this isn't a present that Zwe would like.* Because he's not the nostalgic type. I am. Because he would open it and wonder what the punchline was but be too polite to ask outright.

But he remembered, I silently think as I study the dirt under my feet.

Without warning, the backs of my eyes start to prickle at the thought that we might die on this fucking island and I will never get to go Christmas shopping for him again. And at the thought that even if we do get out alive, I might have so irreparably damaged our friendship that even *if* that comic was still available in Dominik from Budapest's store, there would be no point in getting it now.

"And you've been friends ever since?" Leila asks.

Unthinkably, that sounds like such a loaded question. I look back at Zwe, and find that his brown eyes are still fixed on me. It feels like there are so many things bubbling under the surface all at once, but I'm too scared to dive down and look.

Are we still friends? I ask, searching his face for the truth while praying that the truth is what I want it to be, what I need it to be.

"Yeah," Zwe says, looking away on the hoarse word as though he knows what I was up to, and is doing me the favor of not letting me find what I was looking for.

In a scene right out of a movie, the first droplets start to fall right as we reach the zip-lining tower's base. It's a high but pretty bare setup: wooden stairs that make a zigzag pattern to the platform at the top, which, thankfully, has a roof.

"So, not to be *that* person," I say with my most apologetic smile, "but is there a toilet nearby?"

Leila laughs and points at a narrow, unmarked path winding away from the tower. "It's not far, just a few feet away," she says.

"Believe it or not, you're not the first person to need to use the bathroom after seeing this tower."

I thank her and power walk, almost bursting with relief when the wooden shack comes into view. I was preparing myself for a hole-in-the-ground situation, but to my surprise, there's a proper toilet inside, and even a small window with mosquito netting above the door for ventilation.

When I come back, I'm half expecting Leila and Zwe to have already started climbing, but they're still waiting where I left them.

"Since we might be here a while, I might as well go, too. Do you want to go first or should I?" she asks Zwe.

He gestures at the path with an open palm. "Ladies first."

After anywhere from five seconds to five minutes of torturous silence, my *flight* response kicks in, and I begin to craft some pathetic statement like "Maybe I should get started on the climb first, so I'm not holding you two back."

"We were saying that we should take off our socks and shoes when we reach the top. So that we don't get trench foot," Zwe says first. It's the "we" that catches me off guard. They're a "we" now?

"I don't hate her, you know."

He pivots his attention from some faraway treetop to my face, and as much as I want to turn away from his sudden scrutiny, I force myself to maintain eye contact.

"Don't lie to me. Genuine question, why do you dislike her so much?" he asks, sounding like he's done with all of this.

"No, I actually *really* like her," I protest, aware that that's exactly what you say when you dislike someone. "I think she's funny and smart and thanks to her, we're not getting trench foot."

"So then what is it? What—" He tugs at his hair in frustration. "What is your complaint about her?"

I wonder how honest of an answer he's asking for. How honest of an answer *I'm* willing to give him. "I think—"

"Because all she's done so far is keep us alive. Hell, she was even asking questions about your stupid fucking book!"

It comes out of left field, almost knocking me out. "What does that mean?" I ask, feeling my defenses raise. Turns out I'm not as solidly a *flight* person as I thought. Turns out that sometimes, I pick *fight*.

"Nothing," he says quickly. His expression is one of regret, but it's not because he regrets what he said. It's that he regrets saying it to *me*.

"No, what did you mean by my—"

In yet another act of great fucking timing, the universe intervenes and sends Leila back at this precise moment.

Judging by the fact that she loudly clears her throat from far away, it's obvious that she heard us arguing. "All yours," she says to Zwe, who gives a curt nod before marching away.

"So, um, do you think the rain will get worse?" I mumble. I hold out an open palm, but my hand stays dry. "Oh, it's stopped?"

Leila imitates my gesture. "Seems like it. But that's the weather on this island. Likes to tease."

"Is there a chance the storm won't come either?"

She grimaces at my obvious hopefulness. Instead of answering, she indicates upward as though to say, *Look for yourself, what would you say?*

I let out an embarrassed laugh when I see that the dark clouds that rolled in while we were on the beach are still there, and still very dark. "Actually, never mind."

"We'll be okay, though," she says. She knocks on one of the wooden beams. "This thing was built to withstand anything."

"Even, like—" I search my brain for an objectively-ridiculous-yet-at-this-point-possible scenario. "A raccoon attack?"

"There aren't raccoons around here," she snorts.

"Here as in in this area—" I make a circling motion with one finger. "—or on this island? Because if it's the former, hey, maybe they know it's anarchy now and they've decided to strike."

Leila shakes her head and laughs. "On this island," she says. "You make it sound like we've been transported into *Jumanji*. This place is my home, and trust me when I tell you I've never seen a raccoon on these shores. Now, a few dozen varieties of snakes, on the other hand—"

"Stop!" I say as I reflexively break out into a shiver. "Please tell me you're kidding."

"Hey, this is what you wanted, right?" She winks. "The full remote island experience? Think you'll sign up for it again?"

"Sign up for what?" Zwe asks.

"The rugged remote island experience," Leila says, to which Zwe gives a short, amused *Hmph*. "Maybe this can be inspiration for Poe's *next* book?"

The air goes still around us. My face burns hot. Zwe mutters, "Let's get going." If Leila realizes she misspoke, she plays it off. We revert back to silent mode as we climb the steps, me sandwiched between Leila at the front and Zwe in the back, all three of us making sure to crouch and stay low the whole way up.

"Hey, silly question, but do we run the risk of being struck by lightning at this height?" I ask.

Leila shoots me a reassuring smile over her shoulder. "The trees are still taller, and there's also a lightning rod at the top, so we're good," she says, and I give her a thumbs-up.

"Now what do we do?" I ask through my wheezing pants when we arrive at the top.

Of course, the two of *them* are breathing as regularly as though we took a leisurely sunset stroll along the beach.

"Guess we sit and wait," Leila says. There are several small wooden stools lined up along one wall, and she drags three of them toward the center. She takes a seat, and gestures at us to join her. Zwe and I angle our bodies so that we're not directly facing each other. "Did Zwe tell you about trench foot?" she asks as she takes off her sneakers and socks. "I apologize in advance for my odors."

"I don't think any of us have a right to complain about anyone's odors," Zwe says as he removes his own footwear.

"How are we going to run if we're barefoot?" I ask, trying not to gag as I remove one sock. No amount of detergent is going to save these babies.

Leila leans over and peers down at the ground. "If they corner us up here, I don't think 'running' is going to be a viable escape plan."

"Fair," I say.

"Are you guys hungry?" Barefoot, she walks over to a small plain cabinet in one corner and reaches inside. "We don't have the breakfast buffet spread, I'm afraid, but we do have—" She waves three rectangular pieces of foil with a triumphant look as she makes her way back to us. "—the finest granola bars this side of the island. We've got mixed berry, coconut macadamia, and vanilla almond. Any preferences?"

I make eye contact with Zwe, who gives a nod. "Ladies first."

"Coconut macadamia, please," I say.

"Excellent choice," Leila says. "Zwe?"

"Like I said, ladies first."

"Vanilla almond for you, it is," she says as she hands it over.

Open granola bar in hand, Zwe takes out a folded piece of paper from his back pocket and places it on the floor beside him.

"Is that the map?" Leila nods over at it. "You kept it?"

He unfolds the small rectangles until the whole map is laid out. "Yeah, I know it's outdated now, but I figured it was better than nothing. It'll still be a good backup if we need to figure out where to go next."

"What should we do to pass the time slash distract ourselves from the fact that our feet smell like a bucket of rotten fish?" I ask.

"We could . . . play a game?" Leila suggests.

"Like what?" I ask. "I Spy?"

"Truth or Dare?" she asks.

I look around the completely empty space. "What could we possibly dare each other to do?"

Leila bites her bottom lip as she considers. "To . . . tell the truth?"

"So, like, Truth or Truth?"

She flashes a smile. "Why not? I'll go first."

"Leila—" I lean back and stretch out my legs, shifting my weight onto the heels of my hands. I didn't realize how sore I was until this moment, but my calves are burning with relief. As though finally relaxing, my bandaged ankle begins to slightly throb. I want to keep on sitting for an hour or five. "Truth or truth?"

"Truth," she answers immediately, eyes glinting as she looks back and forth between me and Zwe.

"Who . . . is your least favorite coworker?" I ask.

"That's not fair! You're going to tell on me afterward!"

I hold up my right pinkie. "I won't, promise." She opens her mouth, and I quickly remind her, "It has to be the truth, though."

She works her jaw as she thinks. Finally, hands raised, she answers, "I don't have one."

"Lies!" I gasp.

"It's the truth! I genuinely love everyone I work with. Now, management on the other hand . . ." She verbally trails off, but her face tells a different story.

"You don't like the management?" Zwe asks.

Her shrug is weary. "Frankly, I think they're out of touch about a lot of things. They come once a year and point out all the things we could be improving on, and all the ways they're going to make this place *bigger*. Meanwhile, they're not hiring any more staff because surprisingly, it's very hard to recruit for a role that involves you living on a remote island for the whole year, barring three weeks. But that just means that it's up to the staff who *are* here to go to even more ridiculous lengths to keep the increasing number of guests happy, and it's not like we get the most easygoing guests either. No one comes all the way out here and spends this much money to just happily sit on the beach with a cocktail in hand. No, they want unique, personally tailored experiences for a once-in-a-lifetime trip, but it's also like, how many once-in-a-lifetime trips can a single team of hotel staff create?"

Judging by the way she has to sit up to replenish all of that oxygen she just used, I don't think even *she* was aware that she was about to go on a rant.

Zwe lets out a half snort, half chuckle. "So that's a 'no' then? To liking management?"

"Ugh, you're going to make me say it out loud, aren't you? Fine, I would say 'no.' Okay, my turn." She points at me. "Poe, truth or truth?"

"Truth."

"What . . . is your . . . biggest regret?"

I blink. "What?"

"I know it's kind of morbid, but if this were an end-of-the-world situation, what would be your biggest regret? Like, the thing that when you think of it, you go, *God, I wish I had twenty-four more hours?*"

Even without looking at him, I can sense Zwe's gaze on me, anticipating my answer.

I know what it would've been if she'd asked me just forty-eight hours ago: *I only published one book.*

But now I pause, picking through the note cards in my mind, each holding an equally plausible answer.

I wish I'd seen more of the world.

I wish I'd gotten matching tattoos with my mom like we'd always joked we would.

I wish I'd made the time to fly to Oxford and meet Soraya's kid in person.

"I'm not sure," I muse. "Probably something clichéd and cheesy. Like . . . I . . . wish I'd found true love before I died. As you might have pieced together earlier, my last relationship wasn't exactly the pinnacle of unconditional love, to say the least," I say.

"Yeah, sorry, that sucks," Leila says quietly.

I cast a glance at Zwe. Something ticks in his jaw, and he looks like he's trying to figure out if I'm lying.

"Oh wait, I got it," I say as one card finds its way to the top of the pile.

"I wish I'd gone on a girls' trip with my mom." My voice turns hoarse, and the back of my eyes begins to sting. "We didn't have a lot of money growing up and she didn't have the time because of her work, and when I *did* make a lot of money with my writing and my parents retired, *I* became too busy. We wanted to go somewhere like Greece, because we both loved *Mamma Mia*—" I give a wet laugh, remembering how we sang along in the cinema to the utter annoyance of everyone else. When Meryl Streep sang "Slipping Through My Fingers" to Amanda Seyfried, my mom laced her hand in mine and gave it a tight squeeze, saying, *I understand what she means.* "If I could go back, I'd book us two first-class tickets to Santorini, and we'd go island-hopping and eat seafood until we couldn't look at another piece of calamari."

Leila gives me a kind smile. "I'm sure you'll get to do that once all of this is over."

"Thanks," I reply.

There's a short pause before I realize it's my turn. "Zwe," I say, darting the shortest of looks in his direction. "Truth or truth?"

"Truth."

"Oooh, good choice," Leila says, rubbing her hands. "Poe, do you have any ideas about—"

"Do you like my book?" Typically, I wouldn't have asked it outright without any buildup. But typically, Zwe wouldn't have said to my face that he hated my book. Anger and hurt and confusion and Leila's voice contextualizing *If this were an end-of-the-world situation* have all swirled together inside me and congealed into a nauseating sensation, one that I can only get rid of by asking a question I am 99 percent certain I don't want to know the answer to. When Zwe doesn't reply instantly, that 1 percent of hopeful, delusional doubt flickers out.

He yanks back in surprise. "What? Of course. You know I do. It's my favorite book."

But his answer is stilted, each word pricking me like the tip of a very, very sharp pin.

"No." My voice cracks on the word. "Not *Give Me a Reason*. My new one. Do you like it?"

"I . . . haven't read a single word of it."

I have a flashback to university, of me insisting to Zwe that I didn't want to send him the last chapter I'd written for my work in progress because it was stupid and probably not even that good, him telling me that that was impossible. Blind faith, which was so very un-Zwe that I knew what a privilege it was.

"But do you like it? Do you think it's good? Or that it *will* be a good book?" I ask.

At this, the fold between his brows slowly disappears from view. "What are you doing?"

"Answer the question."

"I don't know," he finally says.

"You don't know," I repeat, hot tears distorting my voice.

"I don't—"

"You can't lie, Zwe. That's the rule."

I can see it happening in slow motion, like when you knock over a glass of water and watch every single preceding second in horror, as certain in your knowledge of what's going to happen (a smashing of shards that fly everywhere) as in your ability to stop it (nonexistent).

As I watch him sit up, shoulders squaring, lips pulling into a taut line, I realize, *this* is it. This is when and where and how Zwe Aung Win sucker punches my heart the way only your best friend can.

"No," he says calmly.

"Have you liked *any* of the drafts I've shown you?"

"No," he repeats without any prompting this time.

"You think I'm a bad writer," I say, unsure whether my response to this is fight or flight. "You think I'll only ever write one good book."

"Honestly? At this rate? Maybe," he scoffs, running a frustrated hand down his face. Each word is a fresh blow to my chest.

"I thought you were my friend!" My voice has raised several octaves, but I can't give a single fuck about anyone hearing me.

"You know what your problem is?" he snaps. "You're so obsessed with writing a book that your agent and editors and reviewers and readers will love that you've given up on writing a book *you'll* love. No, I don't think your book with a time-traveling manhole will be good. Frankly, it makes no sense and sounds boring, and *you* sound bored when you talk about it. You know why your first book was as fucking good as it was? Because you didn't give a shit if anyone hated it. All that mattered was that *you* loved it.

"And now, now you're too busy making up imaginary competitions with authors you've never even met! You don't make time for your parents or Soraya or me or anybody that's not you. Hell, even right now, you're thinking about your book, as though there's *nothing* else that could be more important. And sorry to break it to you, but your problems aren't that important in the grand scheme of things. Poor you, with only *one* internationally bestselling book. It would sound like a joke if that wasn't exactly the sob story you've been spinning. I don't recognize you at all anymore. You make having to go back to working at the bookstore sound like hell on earth, when newsflash, that's what *I* do! I have tried to be understanding and patient, but it's clear now that I'm waiting around for a version of you that's long gone."

Reset, I scream in my head. *Reset, reset, reset.*

But we can't.

The glass has shattered.

"At least I've done something with my life," I spit out, not reacting in the slightest when he recoils. We're throwing barbs, aiming at each other's weakest, most tender spots. "At least I've become an author. How dare you stand there and act like *you* love doing the same thing you did when you were a teenager and running your parents' bookstore, when the truth is that you don't have the guts to pursue what *you* want to do and change terrifies you. You're a coward, Zwe. You stick to what you know and you're scared to go out on a limb for anything or tell people how you actually feel, whether that's doing a PhD or moving in with the love of your life. If this trip sounded like such a bad idea from the start, why didn't you say no? And if I've been a terrible friend for so long, then why didn't you tell me earlier? Why *did* you just keep living in the same apartment as me?"

"Why do you think I've been talking to Julia again?"

"Good!" I jump to my feet. "I hope you and Julia will be very happy in your new home where everything is perfect and nothing ever changes and the taxes always get filed on time."

"Where the hell are you going?" he sighs.

"Away," I reply, tugging my damp socks back on.

"You can't—"

"I'm not staying here with you. Clearly, you don't need me." I fling an arm in the direction of Leila, who is sitting so still I had forgotten that she was present. "You have your island girlfriend in the meantime before you can go back to Julia. *I* never want to see you again."

"I get that you're mad at me, but you can't leave now," Zwe's saying, but I'm using more concentration than an adult should as I try to tie my shoelaces. My fingers are too shaky, so I settle for scrunching the laces together into misshapen knots.

"Watch me," I say, marching over to the stairs. The wind has picked up, and even though it's not the smartest idea right now, I grab the rail and get ready to storm off.

"Poe, if you leave," Zwe says, following me, "you know I'm going to have to come after you."

"Actually, Zwe—" I stop on the second-to-last step before the first landing, although I regret it because when I whirl around, I come face-to-face with Zwe and Leila's feet. I look up at them, endeavoring to look as wrathful as possible from five feet down. Leila's also stood up and comes closer, although she's still leaving enough space between her and Zwe, like we're two feral lions who might pounce on each other at any moment. "If you want to show me how to be a good friend, since clearly I have no clue myself, then why don't you start by demonstrating the importance of giving your friend space when they ask for it?"

I hear Zwe's frustrated sigh, but if he says anything else, it's a whisper into the ether because all of my senses have zoomed in on something else, something that makes everything around me fade to black.

If I had blinked just two milliseconds later, I would've missed it. It's low down on the inside of her bare right ankle, low enough that it was covered by her sock.

Opaque black. A blob. Permanent ink.

"Zwe—" I say, my grip on the rail tightening.

"Look, come back here and we'll talk it out, okay?" Zwe takes two cautious steps forward. "I'm sorry I—"

I miss the rest of *this* sentence as well. I should be fleeing, but instead I'm . . . freezing. I *can't* flee. I can't leave Zwe behind.

"How about we . . . talk in private?" I say, willing the corners of my mouth to turn upward.

Zwe's expression morphs, confused by my sudden 180. "What?" he asks, sounding suspicious.

"Yeah, look, why don't we go for a short walk and talk?" I lean sideways and force my smile wider at Leila. "No offense, I think some privacy would be good for us."

She doesn't smile back.

"I think we should stay up here," Zwe says.

"I agree," Leila says, and I can't tell if I'm imagining a new, sinister undertone to her voice, or if it's always been there.

"No, I think a walk will be good," I insist, trying not to make any sudden movements. "Endorphins and all that."

"It's too dangerous," Leila says. She moves forward, and that's when I make the error. I look down at her foot, and when my eyes dart back upward, she's staring at me. I know. She knows. The only one who doesn't know is—

"Zwe—" I start.

"Oh my god, Zwe!" At her cry, Zwe turns around before I can say anything or yank him toward me. She gives a short shrug. "Sorry." Before he can even open his mouth, she knocks him over the head with one of the stools, and he topples over.

My instinct to not leave Zwe overpowers my instinct to run—and Leila knows it, too. "Come up here," she says, nothing subtle about the malice in her voice now. She beckons me with one finger like an adult calling a kid over to dole out punishment. Zwe's unconscious body is limp on the floor, and when I hesitate, she nudges his shoulder with one foot. "Come here, or I will hurt him in ways even *you* couldn't make up in one of your little books."

I obey, willing my leaden feet to climb back up. I'm staring at Zwe as I move, and my eyes stray to the map that's still lying open a few feet away.

The blob.

It's the island.

But wh—

"Now turn around and close your eyes," Leila says, halting me mid-thought. "And believe me when I say that I *am* sorry I couldn't do this in a less painful way" is the last thing I hear before there's a dull thud against the back of my head and my brain shuts off.

THIRTEEN

It feels as though I blinked and woke up in a new place. As I slowly reenter the world of the conscious, my only recurring thought is that the strange throbbing in my head is starting to amplify by the second.

When I remember what happened, I try to gather my bearings despite the hazy state I'm still in. I blink several times as my vision comes into focus. Zwe's several feet away, tied to a chair facing me.

"Leila," I say, not recognizing my hoarse voice, unsure if I'm whispering or yelling. "Tattoo."

His mouth moves in a "What?" but it sounds mumbled, like he's talking underwater.

"Wait," I mumble, and take a deep breath. I close my eyes, and immediately realize it's a bad idea because I want to drift back off. I reopen my eyes and blink rapidly, willing myself to stay awake.

We're in one of the resort's rooms, one that's smaller than our suite, and, I presume, much closer to the reception area where everyone's still gathered. Even though the lights are off, there's enough moonlight and artificial light from outside streaming in that I can see the whole room and our general states of being.

"We're so stupid," I say. "Of course it was a trap the whole time."

"You know what they say about twenty-twenty hindsight," Zwe says. "I can't believe we didn't see it. She was . . . convincing."

"Leila has the tattoo."

He cocks his head. "What tattoo?"

"*The* tattoo. Their tattoo," I say tiredly.

Confusion etches ridges onto his forehead. "You're concussed, aren't you?" he asks, although it's more of a statement.

"No," I say, then consider. "Maybe. Probably. But I'm making sense. The tattoo. They all have the same tattoo. I noticed it on two of them before. But Leila's was hidden on her ankle. I only saw it because she was barefoot and I was eye level with it when I—" I stop, unable to finish the sentence.

The unspoken words make Zwe shift in his chair.

"I'm sorry," I sigh.

At the same time, he says quietly, "I didn't mean what I said."

I don't know if this new, sharp pang in my right temple is a reverberating remnant of getting hit in the head, or because my body physically cannot take reliving that conversation. "Thanks," I say, and he nods.

"We'll be okay," he says. He smiles at me, and even though I don't fully believe him, the sight of those dimples eases my queasiness a little, like someone's spread a very thin layer of Tiger Balm over the knot in my neck—not enough to undo it completely, but enough that exhaling becomes easier.

"What do we—"

"What was the tattoo?" he asks.

"It was the island," I say, the island's silhouette on his map coming back to me.

"The . . . island?" he asks. The way his face is scrunched, I can tell he's wondering again just how concussed I am.

"I'm not concussed. Or it's not the concussion talking," I say briskly. When his mouth quirks in amusement, I can't help but smile back, even if the act of doing so sets off a short stab in my cheeks. "You had the map laid out on the floor. That was it. That was the tattoo. It's the island."

"Why does Leila have a tattoo of the island?"

"Because it's her home," I say. "That must be it."

He nods. "That tracks. But what about the rest of them? Why do *they*—"

"Because it's . . . their home, too." I gasp as it dawns on me. "Remember when we came this close to getting '101' tattooed after I bought the apartment? To commemorate our first place? *Together?*"

"Um, yeah? But what does that—"

"That's why they all have that tattoo! They all have a connection to the island. They know each other. Clearly, she's an inside man. Sorry, woman."

"Ohhh-kayyyy," Zwe says slowly. "But I'm . . . still not seeing the whole picture."

"It's right there," I say. "We have all the puzzle pieces." Mentally, I take each metaphorical piece, turning it this way and that to figure out how they slot together.

"You're plotting."

"What?" I look up to find Zwe with an amused expression. "Why are you smiling?"

He shrugs. "Is it cheesy if I say that I was smiling because you're plotting? You've got your plotting face."

I arch a puzzled brow. "What's my plotting face?"

"This," he says, and he turns sideways to stare at a spot on the wall. The muscles in his face relax as he zones out like he's going on a shrooms trip. "And then when you've thought of something very specific, you do this." His brows scrunch together, and his front teeth bite into his bottom lip. I snort, and he turns back to me, returning to his normal state.

"That's my plotting face?" I ask, unable to stop giggling.

"Yep."

"Oh my god, I write in public all the time," I say, equal parts mockingly and genuinely mortified. "You let me make that face in public? People must have thought I was seeing a ghost. Or on drugs in the middle of the day. Or both."

"Oh, absolutely. You've scared more than one customer while you were sneaking in some writing behind the cash register," he says. "You can tell because they immediately scan the store for an employee who *doesn't* look like the drugs just kicked in and it's a particularly bad trip."

"If we were closer, I'd kick you."

"I know."

Reset.

And just like that, it feels like we're us again. There's a small voice in the back of my head saying we're not, that even if Zwe *says* he didn't mean everything he said, we both know he did, at least a little. That our relationship will never be able to go back to how it was. That the conversation we're going to have "later" will traverse new grounds that we haven't covered before.

But that's all later.

For now, it's us. Him and me.

"What did you figure out?" he asks.

"I think . . . okay, so this might be a bit bonkers—"

"Poe, look around." He makes a circular motion with his head. "All of this is bonkers."

I make a finger gun, only to remember that he can't see it. "Good point," I say. "So I think Leila and those women are . . . friends? Maybe they've been plotting this whole attack for a long time, and the last missing piece was an inside person. Enter Leila."

"But the tattoos. You don't get matching tattoos with a random accomplice."

We've been keeping our voices down in case someone is stationed out the door, but I unintentionally yell it once the light bulb goes off. "They're her cousins!"

Zwe goes silent. "Her . . . cousins," he says, stretching each syllable.

"Holy shit, it's been in front of us all along." I race through my thoughts, more pieces sliding into place, the puzzle's vague patches of color turning into real scenes. "Of course they have matching tattoos of the island. It's their home. They're family."

A roller coaster of emotions plays out on Zwe's face. His "Fuck" is drawn out on a breath.

I can't believe we didn't see this earlier. "She's been talking about her cousins this whole time. What was it she said about that wedding? Nobody gets away with pissing off her and her cousins."

"So who pissed her off? The resort management? But she said she got a good salary."

"Maybe it's someone she works with?" I venture. "She's been talking a lot about guests being rude. Maybe there was a guest who was really shitty to her and her bosses didn't back her up."

"Fuck, and the thing with Antonio earlier."

My insides feel like there's an avalanche happening. "That's why she volunteered to be the distraction first. She must've whispered something to them while her back was to us, and then when the supply boat came—"

"Which her cousins would've known was coming because *she'd* have given them a heads-up—"

"And while we were distracted by the boat, she made it look like she lost control of the situation and basically handed Antonio over."

Zwe's shaking his head, as furious as I am that we didn't figure this out before. "The trail," he says hoarsely. "She intentionally made us go in circles."

We need to bring you back in one piece, she had said.

"She *was* right when she said she knows those trails blindfolded. Knows them so well in fact that she can lead us as far away as possible even in the dark," I say. "And she brought up the supply boat so she could make us do a U-turn. She was never going to let us get to that village."

"The zip-line tower was a trap." Zwe scoffs in disbelief, looking like he could kill someone. "This whole time. Even if you hadn't seen her ankle, we were trapped up there. Her cousins must've been on their way. You just figured it out before they arrived."

"She shut me down when I was trying to figure it out earlier," I say. Heat coils through me to the point where I'm on the verge of tears. "She gaslit me. I wouldn't have made sense of it all perfectly, but if we'd kept talking about it, maybe I could've worked out *some* of the parts."

"You were right. Fuck, you were right, and I—" He lets out a bitter laugh. "I should've believed you."

Zwe's figure starts to get blurry, and unable to covertly wipe them away, I blink off the tears. "You should've," I say, not realizing until now that I've been carrying around the sting of that moment like a sharp splinter in the sole of my foot.

He opens his mouth, closes it without a sound. The air in the room somehow gets colder, goose bumps bristling the hairs on my arms and legs.

"I'm sorry," he says.

"I know," I tell him, my voice cracking as the full weight of the situation hits, an icy lake finally giving way. "Zwe . . . what if this is it? What if there's no way out of this? Like, what if we're all out of lives?"

"It's not," he says firmly, but I see the way he swallows an invisible lump.

"I want to see my parents again." It sounds like a hollow prayer. "I want to go home and see my parents, and I want you to go home and see your parents, too. And . . ." I weigh whether or not to say it. Will uttering it be taken as a peace offering, a sign that we're good, or stir the pot further? "And Julia," I finish so softly that part of me is hoping he misses it.

I can't tell if he catches it, because all he replies is, "We will."

"You're my best friend," I say. As fucked up as all of this is, I suppose it's a privilege to know in advance if you're going to die, because at least then you can say your piece, every single thing you were ever afraid to say. Or almost every single thing. "I love you, and you're my best friend, and I don't want us to die with a weird argument hanging over our heads. I know I've been a terrible friend these past few months, and I know I don't deserve—"

"Stop." I sniffle, but do stop. "We're going to get the hell out of this place, because, if nothing else, I refuse to accept that this is how it all ends, with you dying in a shirt that says BIG DICK ENERGY LEADS TO BIG DICK INJURY."

I let out a loud, snotty, disgusting laugh at that, and now I don't know if I'm crying out of fear, or because I can't stop thinking about how lucky I am to have *him* as my best friend.

"I love you," I repeat, feeling the words more acutely than I ever have any time I've said them.

"You know I love you, too," he says. "We're going to be okay. Here, and after."

"How?" I ask.

"Because we just happen to have the most creative, perceptive, astounding writer of our generation in the room with us."

It's cheesy to the point of clichéd, but it still elicits an equally cheesy grin out of me. "Thank you. But I don't think my job as a person who professionally makes up tough scenarios with incredibly raised stakes that imaginary people have to get out of by dealing with both internal and external obstacles is going to be quite the thing that gets us out of this predicament. Again, truly appreciate your unwavering support. But if this whole time you're a secret spy or trained assassin, or I dunno, have been taking bodyguard lessons, now would be a great time to reveal that."

"Sorry, I was shortlisted for the 'trained assassin' role but in the end they decided to go with someone else."

"Darn tootin'," I say with a huff. We stare at each other for a beat before bursting into laughter. "I see we are absolutely not using humor as a coping mechanism when stressed. Our therapists will be glad to hear that."

"Darn tootin' right they will," Zwe replies. I aim to look affronted, but my laugh betrays me. "I meant what I said. I know I dismissed it when you said it earlier, and I will forever be so unbelievably sorry for that—" He pauses, and I give him a short nod to acknowledge both that he *should* be sorry and that I appreciate his apology. "But you *were* close to figuring all of this out, and it was because you sat down and plotted. Do that again. Plot."

"You make it sound so important," I laugh. "Anyone could've done it."

"*I* couldn't do it," he says softly. "And you're selling yourself short by saying that anyone could."

Hundreds of past moments like this one flash through my mind. Moments where not a single person in the world, including myself, still believed in this author "thing"—except for Zwe. Zwe, who replenished my steady stream of teas, texted me YouTube links to stretches and wrist exercises for writers, who left a proper laptop stand with a giant red bow tied to it on the dining table one morning with a note that said *Now can we please put our board game stack back in its rightful place?*

Except, it's different this time. Because this time, I still remember how he'd agreed with Leila when she dismissed me before. There's a gnawing voice in my head that keeps whispering, *You're a bad writer and he thinks so, too.*

"This feels stupid," I say, not admitting the rest of it. "This is such a stupid way to try to get out of a mess. This is real life, it's not a novel. In spite of my current feelings toward her, Leila was right when she said that I can't treat this like a novel."

Zwe's face crumbles at that. "Ignore anything Leila said. Hell, ignore anything I said! You were the only one who knew something was up. Please, just try it again? For me?"

He knows I would do anything for him.

I'm not the most intricate of plotters, but whenever I've gotten stuck in the middle of a draft, I step back, look at the bigger picture outside of that specific scene or chapter, and see if there was something in the past that can be brought back up to propel the story forward. Because that's the key of any story: always moving forward.

"I don't think we're going to figure out *why* they came here, so let's focus on *how*. They arrived to this resort somehow," I say. "They didn't fly or swim here."

"What if they were already at the village? Before *we* got here?" Zwe asks.

I shake my head. "Maybe, but even then, I doubt their plan is to stick around after they do whatever it is they're planning on doing. They destroyed all of the resort boats by shooting at them, but they'd never strand themselves. Which means—"

When I meet Zwe's eyes, I can tell that he's caught up. "They have a boat somewhere."

"Somewhere far enough away from the resort that there are no cameras. Maybe on the other side, so even patrolling security wouldn't see them. Or Leila gave them the patrol schedules and routes so they could arrive undetected."

"So we get to the boat," he says. "We get out of these ropes, get to the boat, and go get help."

I scoff. "You make it sound so easy."

"I know it's not easy, but also . . ." He hesitates, and the tightness in my throat returns.

"What?" I prompt.

"It . . . is. It's always easy with you, Poe."

Oh. "If this is about earlier . . ." My voice is a dim rasp. "Let's save it for later."

To my surprise, Zwe shakes his head. "You know what? No. I've been thinking about it and . . . and I'm done saving things for later. You were . . . right," he says, laughing on the last word. "You know what one of my favorite things about you is?"

"What?"

"You have these huge dreams, and I know everyone does, but unlike most people, you actually go for your dreams. You achieve one thing, and then you get a glimpse of something else around the corner and you decide you want it, and you work hard at it until you have it. I *am* a coward. I *do* stick to what I know because I'm scared of what comes next if I do something new."

New goose bumps rake down my skin as my words from before come back to slap me in the face. "I didn't mean any—"

"I love you."

A weird chuckle-esque sound escapes me. I'd been bracing for something scathing. "I . . . love you too?"

He drops his head back, letting out a groan at the ceiling. "No, stupid, I *love* you."

And when he looks at me again, I feel the core memory form deep in my bones, like your first kiss or the first time you ride a bike with no training wheels. Just as scary, just as thrilling. That sensation of *I want to remember this for the rest of my life*.

"I love you so much it scares me. Julia and I didn't break up because I didn't want to move in with her. We broke up because I didn't want to move out of our home," he says, looking like he doesn't know whether to cry or laugh. "I've spent so much time pretending I didn't feel any of this, but when she asked me, even though it was the next logical step in our relationship . . . I couldn't do it. Which made no sense to me because as you just said, I am naturally a logical person. It wasn't that I thought *you* wouldn't be able to survive living on your own, Poe. It was, and brace yourself for the corniness, that I knew *I* wouldn't be able to without you."

"Wh—" I don't know if I want to ask *what* or *why*.

What are you saying?

Why are you saying this right now?
Why didn't you tell me before?
What next?

I'm breathing hard but it's not enough. "You never told me," I finally say.

His mouth slacks. "I didn't know how."

"But y-you were talking to Julia again," I sputter, tripping over my metaphorical two feet. "And you were flirting with Leila."

"Because I knew I needed to move on." He laughs like it's an obvious joke. "I almost told you so many times, but there was college, and then there was Vik, and also Julia, and then you got engaged, and then your engagement was called off, and then you had all those book rejections, and then you *sold* a book, *the* book even, and then *I* had a breakup, but then you were in the middle of this great, amazing book whirlwind and in the middle of a movie deal, and then you started working on your second book and were trying to get through this writer's block, and it was just . . . never the right time."

"We live together!" I don't expect my voice to be ragged as it is. "You could've told me *any* time. Over coffee, while doing the dishes, while folding the laundry. I spend more hours in a day with you than with anybody else!"

"But I also didn't want to be that guy! Because I hate that guy!"

"What guy?!"

The way his shoulders jerk, I can tell he forgot where we were and was going to spread his arms. "That guy who sticks around pining for the girl, hoping that one day she'll wake up and realize she's been in love with her best friend this whole time, too, and then they'll have a big romantic moment in the rain and that'll be it.

"But every morning, I wake up and walk into the kitchen and that girl is sitting at the table, brows furrowed, fingers clacking away on her keyboard as she writes the literary world's next big thing, and I have to stop and take a breather. I see you, and I think, *Good god, how lucky am I that I get to be in your life?* I've watched all of these people fall in love with your words and that ridiculous, perceptive brain of yours, and in my head, I'm the snob that's going, *Well actually, I was a fan before she became 'cool.'"* I snort, and he smiles, and my heart flutters.

"And it's so stupid and clichéd in the movies, because you think, *Grow up, dude, stop making excuses and just fucking tell her.* But I get it now, that reasoning of *I would rather have you as a friend for the rest of my life than try to enter new territory and risk losing you forever.* Before, I *was* angry when you accused me of taking Leila's side, because how could you ever, *ever* think that I'd take anyone else's side over yours? All I was trying to do was keep you safe. If it came to it, I would give myself up to keep you safe, you have to know that." After a long silence, he says, "Please say something."

I reenter my body, feeling for the first time the wet trails cutting down my cheeks. Someone's flipped the earth on its axis and rearranged every frame of reference I've ever held—and I'm meant to make sense of this new worldview while tied to a chair in an empty hotel room.

"What are you thinking?" Zwe prompts gently.

"I—" My head is spinning, and that near-passing-out sensation returns. "I don't know," I answer honestly. "This wasn't—"

The lock makes a familiar click, and the door swings open. Leila slides the key card in her back pocket, a saccharine smile plastered on her face. "Hi, friends," she says, taking long strides toward us. "How are we feeling? Still in the mood for a little adventure?"

FOURTEEN

"I know they're your cousins," I blurt out. The rest follows like word vomit. "You didn't have the knife on you. That wasn't even part of the plan, was it? They slipped it to you and you pretended to escape so you could come after us. But Antonio messed it all up." Immediately, I regret it. I hadn't considered if we were supposed to hold our cards close, or threaten her with what we've figured out so far.

Leila pauses mid-step, evidently jostled. "Let me guess," she says, rolling her eyes. "You *plotted* your way to that conclusion? God, don't you ever get annoyed with that nonsense?" she asks Zwe.

"You're not getting away with this," he says.

At this, she puts a hand to her chest and laughs. "Jesus Christ, you sound like a character in a clichéd action movie." She turns to me. "Couldn't you have written him some vaguely original dialogue? Your book was *much* better than this."

"You read my book?" I ask.

She flicks a hand. "Yes, I read it. And yes—" She crosses her arms and straightens her stance. "I also already knew about your Netflix deal. I know how much you're worth."

"So this is about . . . me?" I shake my head, a chill spreading down to my toes. "You did all of this for—"

"For you?" she cuts in with a snicker. "Please, don't be flattered. I googled you, not orchestrated a complex multi-person operation to specifically hold you hostage. If I wanted to do that, I could've just snatched you on my own. You don't really put up much of a fight."

I'm so relieved that I can't even be offended. "So let us go," I say. "Let all of us go. Whatever you and your cousins want, none of us can give it to you."

"See, the thing is," she says, and clicks her tongue, "that *was* the plan. But then you had to go ahead and snatch off Nita's mask. And *then* you had to figure out we were all cousins, so—" She shrugs. "Really, it's *your* fault that you're not getting out of this alive, Poe."

"We won't tell anyone," Zwe pleads. "No one else saw your cousin's face. No one else knows you all are related. I don't know if *you've* told them, but if you haven't, we won't even tell anyone *you* were a part of all of this. Please just let us go. We all have families."

"And we don't?" she spits out.

"I . . . never said you didn't," Zwe says. We both tense at the change in her demeanor. She went from haughty to angry in a second, as though we accidentally flipped a switch.

Maybe that's the key. Judging by her reaction, this has to be about her family somehow. Her cousins, their family, the resort. I'm both so close and so far from solving everything.

"So what *is* it that you want?" I ask.

There's a knock on the door. "Come in!" she calls out, and then to us, "Well, right now I want you to say hi to my cousins."

Two women walk in, both removing their masks with one hand as they cross the threshold, while clutching a large rifle in the other.

"What took you so long?" Leila huffs. When she twists around to address them, I see the gun tucked into the back of her jeans pocket. I glance over at Zwe, who nods to confirm that he's clocked it, too.

"Bathroom break," one of them says. Then, plastering on a big, bright grin, she says, "Hi, I'm Nita," facing Zwe before locking onto me, her equally saccharine cadence and facial expression multiplying the eeriness of the situation tenfold. "Hi, Poe, was it? *So* happy to meet you officially. Although—" She gives a pout. "—what you did back there wasn't nice, the whole kicking me in the face and everything." She points at a spot on her right cheekbone that's black and blue. "I don't like this. At all."

The other one, aka Pixie Cut, says, "And I'm Garima. I gotta give it to you, you guys gave us a little run for our money. Out on the beach there, I was worried for a minute that you might actually shoot at me. But Leila here"—she cocks her head in Leila's direction—"assured us you were far too sensitive to do anything like that." She chuckles as she scans me up and down. "She was so right. You could've ended all of this right then and there but alas—" She sighs.

"I was literally begging you to shoot and you still couldn't. What a couple of babies," Leila says with a snicker. "Anyway, enough chit-chat." She snaps her fingers, and Nita and Garima hand over their rifles before heading toward us. "That storm should be coming in—" She looks out the windows. "Right on time. So here's what's going to happen. We're going to take you down to the reception hall, and neither of you are going to try to pull off whatever harebrained scheme you've *plotted*—" She makes air quotes with one hand. "—like this is one of your silly little books. I promise you, unlike the two of you, none of *us* will hesitate to pull a trigger." To prove her point, she lifts and aims both weapons at me and Zwe.

Nita comes behind me, while Garima stands behind Zwe. Working at the same time, they start to untie us as we sit there motionless, hesitant to even cough.

"One move," Nita says nonetheless, her breath spreading across the nape of my neck, "and your pretty boyfriend will have a perfect bullet hole in the back of his pretty head."

"We've got a small problem, by the way," Garima says as she works on Zwe's rope.

"Let me guess." Leila lets out a tired groan. "Andrea's piped up. Again."

Garima shrugs. "She still thinks we should take them with us."

"I fucking swear, all of that bleach has seeped into that girl's brain," Leila mutters. "And what happens once we reach the mainland? Should we also arrange cars to the airport and flights for everyone as well?"

"Don't shoot the messenger, dude."

"We're already letting them go. She wants us to *chauffeur* them too?" Leila runs her fingers through her hair and grabs the crown. "I told you she was too soft for this. We should've left her at home with her computers."

"She's worried the beach won't be enough of a barrier—"

Pinching the top of her nose, Leila says, "Well, if she wants to give up her spot on the boat, then she's free to do so. I'll have a talk with her later." She shakes her head. "Fucking kids."

"Get up," Nita orders. Too absorbed in the other conversation, I don't hear her immediately, and she gets my attention by elbowing my shoulder.

"Ow!" I yell.

"Oh shut up, it wasn't even that hard. Now get up. Slowly."

I raise my hands as I get up off the chair, but then almost immediately have to bend over and steady myself against the back of it once I'm on my feet. "I said no funny business!" Nita barks.

"I need a minute," I snap under my breath. "Your cousin knocked me unconscious with a stool. I'm not exactly in tip-top physical shape, now, am I?"

Out of the corner of my eye, I see Nita take a step forward, stopping when Zwe's rough growl comes from the other side. "You touch her, and I will drown you in the sea myself, I swear," he murmurs.

"Oh, how cute," Nita coos. "Your boyfriend is trying to stand up for you even when you're both hours away from your grisly, untimely demise."

Gathering myself, I straighten and raise my hands again while trying to relocate my center of gravity. "Ow!" I yell when she yanks my hands down and behind me again.

"I said—" Zwe starts.

"Yeah, yeah, not a single strand of hair, I heard you," Nita tells him. "But look around, sweetheart, you're not exactly the one calling the shots here. Now, put your hands behind your backs again."

"And remember," Garima says, already reworking the rope around Zwe's wrists. "There are two of you, and three of us."

After they've retied us, Leila walks over and hands them their guns. With more speed (and glee) than I'm comfortable with, Nita and Garima shove the barrels between our shoulder blades.

Leila opens the door, steps aside, and makes a big, sweeping gesture. "After you, my esteemed guests," she says with a mock bow.

The room is right next to the elevator, whose doors open as soon as Leila presses the down button, as though they, too, have been waiting this whole time—another cog in her well-oiled machine. We're seven floors up, and as the five of us descend, I can't help but feel something like I'm going down to the gates of hell; the feeling is made even eerier by all the mirrors around us, trapping us in a seven-by-seven fun house.

When I catch Zwe's eyes in the mirror, he narrows them just slightly, and I get the sense that he's still trying to reassure me that we'll be okay even if all the current evidence is pointing to the contrary. Still, it *is* reassuring to know that he's here. I take a deep breath to try to calm myself down, and, beneath the smell of sweat and dirt and rain, locate his scent.

White tea and sage cologne, a birthday present I first got him six years ago, the only present he's ever asked for every year since. A series of flashbacks is set off in my brain, like someone's put the last coin into the pinball machine.

Zwe, me, our parents and his brother at our high school graduation.

Zwe video-calling me from Rhode Island, me answering in Oxford, our outfits and the glimpses of scenery outside our windows changing throughout the seasons.

Zwe when I first asked him if we should rent a place together.

Zwe behind the cash register when I emerged from the stockroom after a call, *the* call, with Ayesha. How he crushed me into his chest when I said, "I think I have an agent."

Zwe popping open the champagne after I bought our apartment.

Zwe, Zwe, Zwe.

But there's one piece of the puzzle that doesn't fit, no matter how I flip it, where I try to place it. He said that "college" had been one of the things that got in the way of him telling me, but that can't be true. I graze my teeth over my bottom lip in that spot where his once brushed it. The spot that I only let myself remember in my least sober moments, like a trinket locked away that I only take out and examine when I'm certain no one will catch me.

He hadn't even wanted to *kiss* me. No way he could've been in love with me then. There's just . . . no way.

There's a ding, the doors slide open, and the cool metal that's been pressed into the nape of my neck this whole time digs in. "Move," Nita orders, although I already am.

As we make our way down the lobby's hardwood floors toward the reception hall, I'm surprised by how quiet everything is. I can hear the frogs and cicadas and pattering raindrops that signal the beginning of a storm, but there are no human voices. When we round the corner into the open reception area, I learn why: there *are* no humans.

Leila marches ahead, rearranging two chairs so that they're both facing the ocean. "Take a seat," she orders, patting each cushion. "The view's great from here."

Very conscious of the guns still pressed to us, Zwe and I slowly sit down.

After passing the guns to Leila, Nita and Garima once again go through the motions of untying us only to retie our hands on the backs of the chairs.

When I go to put my hands behind my back, some instinct propels Antonio's voice to the front of my brain. I try to follow along as best as my hazy, injured, dehydrated memory will let me.

Makes your wrists bigger, his voice instructs, and I line up my knuckles to form a line.

Nita's making sure my rope is *tight,* and at this point I can only pray that Antonio's hack will still work.

"Where have you two been?" Leila calls out to the sudden

footsteps that echo around us. On instinct, I turn to see who they belong to, but Nita shoves her shoulder into mine.

"What the fuck!" I cry.

"Eyes forward," she retorts.

"Bathroom break," a new female voice says.

Leila rolls her eyes. "What is with you all today? Have you been helping yourselves to the bar?"

"We've been drinking a lot of water. Sorry we didn't want to pass out from dehydration," the voice replies flatly.

"But the bar's a good shout. We should've thought of that earlier," another new voice adds.

Leila purses her lips. "Do you also want to run a hot bath while you're at it? Check out one of the suites? Take a dip in the infinity pool?"

The voices belong to two new cousins, who come to flank her on either side.

My heart skips several beats when I clock the four red gasoline cans they're carrying. Judging by their posture when they place them on the floor, those cans are all full.

"Sure, if you're offering," one woman says. She's got a buzz cut and is the largest out of the five of them, her tank top and leggings highlighting some serious muscles.

"Fuck me, Faith," Leila sighs. "We're so close to the end. Can you please stay focused?"

I recognize the other one's bleached hair, and, remembering the earlier conversation, place her as Andrea. "Yes, I agree, can we get this over with?" Andrea nudges one of the cans with her toe. "The smell is starting to make me sick. Wha—" Her expression turns to confusion when her gaze lands on me and Zwe. "Wait, what's going on? Leils, why are they being tied up?"

"Because we're going to put on a show for them." Garima flashes a sarcastic smile. "Why do you think?"

Andrea's brown eyes widen until she looks like a cartoon character. Blindsided, she stutters out, "No, that wasn't part of the plan."

"Plan's changed," Leila says.

"And you're all okay with this? We said no one would get hurt." Andrea looks around at her other three cousins, who all glance in different directions to refuse eye contact. Nita gives my rope a final tight yank, and, satisfied, starts backing away.

Leila's the only one who talks. "They know what we look like," she says, gesturing at each of them.

"But—"

"They know you're my cousins," she adds. At that, Andrea shuts up. "If we let them go, all of *us* go to jail. Think of Raj. You guys *just* got engaged."

Andrea's throat bobs as she gulps. "But we can't *kill* them," she says.

"*We* won't," Leila says. "The fire will."

I don't hear anything after the word "fire."

This whole time, I had been turning my fists inward like Antonio had demonstrated and trying to free my right thumb, but as soon as I hear the *f*-word, it's as though someone's injected a paralytic drug into my veins. A fog settles over my skin and seeps under it, turning my muscles ice cold. I look over at Zwe, whose eyes have also glazed over.

Fire. Fire. Fire. It's echoing in my head in Leila's exact inflection.

Another puzzle piece slots into place.

There's nowhere to hide or run, apart from right in the ocean.

She had told us their plan. Right to our faces. There was always going to be a fire.

"Why are you doing this?" Everyone's heads whip in my direction. I blink, barely registering the tear that rolls down my cheek. "We didn't do anything! Please let us go!" I yell, moving from denial to anger to bargaining in the span of five seconds.

Leila doesn't even flinch. "You just have bad luck, I guess." She hands two cans to Nita and Garima. "Start pouring."

They take one each, walk to opposite corners of the reception area, and begin pouring gasoline all over the floor. The smell takes a second to hit, but once it does, it overpowers everything else.

"Leila, please, don't do this. Let us go, please," Zwe also begs.

But Leila acts as though he hasn't said a word. She picks up the third can and hands it to Andrea.

Andrea.

"Andrea, you don't want to do this," I say, straining my neck so I can make eye contact. She squirms at my using her name, and when she *does* look at me, she looks terrified. Maybe even remorseful. "Please, our parents are waiting for us at home. *We* have cousins and siblings, too. They'll all be wondering what happened. Andrea—"

"Andrea." Leila steps right in my line of vision, eyes narrowed into slits, jaw hardened, furious that I've addressed Andrea directly. When I strain my neck to try to see Andrea again, Leila swiftly shifts the gasoline can still in her hand so the spout is pointed in our direction. "Say my cousin's name one more time, and I will douse both of you. I dare you to test me."

I'm so desperate that I *want* to test her, but then I look at Zwe, and remember that I'm not the only one at risk here. So instead, I lower my gaze to the floor and helplessly watch a small trail of gasoline from one corner of the room snake its way parallel to my feet.

"Go to the boat, Drea," Leila is saying. "Have it ready. We'll join you soon."

"You said . . ." Andrea says softly, not finishing the sentence.

"They've seen our faces," Nita reminds her. "You have to choose between them or us."

Andrea doesn't reply, the gasoline-saturated air going still. "I need to get my laptop from the security office" comes her answer at last. "I'll be back in ten." I hear her sneakers squeaking away from us.

So this is it. This is how it ends.

With immeasurable effort, I lift my head, watching, as if in a dream, Leila covers the reception desk and couches in gasoline while Faith takes the last can.

My eyes land on Zwe. What I wouldn't give right now to feel the steady weight of his palm on my shoulder.

I'll miss you, I think.

I am going to miss it all. So, so much, I think, and begin soundlessly crying.

A loud crack of thunder, so close it sounds like it struck right in the middle of this room, makes us all jump. "Right on cue," Leila says.

"You really didn't want to hurt anyone." At this point, I've disassociated so much that I barely recognize the raspy voice as my own. But a part of me that's realized something pushes on in one last attempt, past the fear and compelling desire to give up. "That's why you wouldn't let us return to the reception area and free everyone, right? Because you were worried the staff might get caught in the crossfire. There's a difference between burning a hotel and murdering people. Please. You can still let us go." I don't know where everybody else is, but they're like Leila's second family, and I know she wouldn't hurt them. If they're still in the same building as us, then—

"You're right, I do care about the staff, and I can promise you that they're all fine," Leila says. "You two, on the other hand, are strangers to me."

"Why?" I don't know why I ask it, but I suppose it's true what they say: desperate people do desperate things. "What did we do? This isn't fair."

Leila cocks her head, studying me for so long and with such intensity that I stop crying, stop moving altogether, like prey futilely hoping that they haven't been spotted when they clearly have. She doesn't look like she has a threatening quip on the tip of her tongue. My stomach flops as I watch her anger steadily accelerate. Even her cousins have gone quiet. I've obviously said something wrong, something that's turned me into her sole target.

"Not fair?" Still firmly staring me down, she points behind her, at the beach. "Do you think it's *fair* that my parents were told they couldn't renew their vows at the spot where they got married? Is it *fair* that some billionaire swooped in and suddenly my whole family was forced to relocate to the top of the mountains, like sheep herded away? From the home that they'd been in for generations?"

Nita loudly clears her throat. "That's enough, Leils. We said we wouldn't—"

But Leila's so far from the line that she can't even see it anymore. "Who cares? They're not going to make it out alive," she says with a menacing smile. "Is it fair that my grandparents, who used to walk along the shore every evening, can only touch the water a handful of times a year because the hike is too treacherous for them? And the fact that you believed me when I said it was *their* choice to move goes to prove that you're just the same as every rich, entitled, oblivious asshole that stays here. And now this place is *expanding*? Those rich fucks are spending more money than I'll ever see in a lifetime to bring over bulldozers and destroy even more of our home. All while marketing themselves as a resort that *helps guests reconnect with the natural beauty of Sertulu*?" She shakes her head with a disgusted scoff.

"Why are you punishing *us*?" Zwe asks, as stunned as I am.

"To be fair, it *was* bad luck on your part. Kind of. You weren't supposed to see any of our faces, so that's entirely on you," she tells me. "But you weren't supposed to be here in the first place either. Andrea hacked her way into the booking system, and she was working on shutting it down completely. Before she could do that, though, she first jacked up the prices to such exorbitant numbers that no one in their right mind would book a holiday, especially given that it's storm season. And yet, right before we managed to turn off the system, one person with shiny new book money looked at the number and thought, *That sounds like a perfectly reasonable price to me.*" She cocks her head, giving me a pitiful look. "I guess it's true what they say about people with more money than sense."

"So your plan is to burn this whole place down?" I ask.

Leila purses her lips to one side like she's casually considering it. She looks left, then right, then shrugs. "Sounds good to me. They destroyed our home, I think it's only fair we destroy their toy."

"But what about your family? The fire will spread."

"You ever see a *real* storm? It'll take care of the fire, no problem," she says with another dark smile that confirms she's thought of everything. "We would never harm our family. We've got precautions in place. I was annoyed, you know, because the storm was a day late, but that gave me time to come and find you two and get you back here, so I'd say it all worked out in the end. Of course, there were a few hiccups, like Antonio escaping, the brat. And the supply boat spotting the guns. But we're tuned in to the radios, and safe to say—" She unhooks her radio from her belt, and waves it in the air. "—no one's coming now in this storm."

"What about you?" I ask.

"What about me?"

"You're the only staff member unaccounted for. Everyone's going to know you were in on it."

"Oh, you see—" She juts out her bottom lip. "—unlike you two, *I* managed to escape the scary intruders, and because I know the woods so well, I knew how to hide until the fire went out and help arrived."

"What will your family say when they find out what you guys did?" I ask, desperate to find a hole in her plan.

But she's three steps ahead. They all are.

The four cousins exchange eyebrow raises. "They'll never know, obviously," Faith says.

"But they'll be happy when this damn company leaves, that's for sure," Nita agrees.

"They'll just rebuild it," I say.

At that, Leila starts laughing. "Are you kidding? Look at this place." She opens her arms. "Do you know how much it costs to build a resort on a remote island? Garima has an MBA." She jerks a thumb at her cousin. "She's crunched the numbers, and it will cost way more to clear out the damage and rebuild it than just cut their losses and leave. All those shits care about is profit. Our island will be ours again."

I'd said earlier that almost all character motivations came down to love, money, or power. I had been right.

They're burning it all down. This sprawling, picture-perfect, extravagant resort—and they want to literally burn it to the ground. For love.

"What about everyone else?" Zwe asks. "The people who work here are innocent."

Garima gives a *Duh* scoff. "We agree. They'll be okay. Cold, but okay. Like Leila said, we never planned on hurting any of them."

"What the hell does that mean?" Zwe yells. "You said it yourself, they can't escape a fire! You're really going to kill all of those innocent people? How does that make you a better, more responsible person than the ones who own this resort?"

The beach. A barrier. Andrea had worried they weren't going to be safe, but Leila said the beach would be a barrier.

"They're on the beach," I say. "The sand will stop the fire from spreading."

Leila gives me an impressed look. "Well done, Little Miss Plotter."

"Fuck, she's smart, I'll give her that," Nita says.

Footsteps quickly stride toward us, and for a moment, I'm thinking it's the police sneaking in to ambush them. But instead, Andrea's voice comes. "Got my laptop. The rest of the cans are already lined up outside. Let's finish here before the rain picks up?"

They file out, Leila last. Before she's fully out of our line of sight, she swivels around, and we get one final look at the last person we'll ever see. Her expression is almost remorseful. Almost. "We'd have let you stay lost in the woods, you know, if only you hadn't tripped and kicked off Nita's mask—" She sighs, giving a pointed look at my ankle.

"Please don't do this," I beg, although even to myself, I sound like someone who's given up. "Our parents still need us. They'll never get over this. Imagine if something like this happened to one of your cousins. Think of what that would do to your family. You know *we're* not the ones you want to punish. Leila, please."

She stops mid-pivot, turning her head so that she can look at us over her shoulder. I see her bite her lip as though in hesitation, and a thin string of hope tugs at my heart. She opens her mouth, closes it, thinking, studying us.

Zwe picks up on it, too. "I get why you're angry, Leila," he says. "I would be, too. If someone hurt my family the way these people have hurt yours, if someone pushed *my* parents out of their home, I'd be so mad there wouldn't be any limit to what I'd do for justice. But you're a good person. You made sure your cousins looked after everyone, I know that was all you."

I see her forehead creasing as she thinks.

Finally, she shakes her head. "If it's any consolation, I'm pretty sure it'll be over fairly quickly. And hey, at least you'll have each other."

It's the last thing she says to us.

The squeaking of her sneakers along the gasoline trails is the most ominous sound I've ever heard. They're gone, and all we can hear is the brewing storm.

I'm too worn out to try to come up with an escape plan. And after a long silence, I think, *Fuck it. We're going to die within minutes.*

"You didn't want to kiss me." I squeeze my eyes shut as the words leave my mouth. It feels exactly as good as I'd always imagined it would to address it, this albatross of a memory that's been weighing me down for over a decade. When I gather the courage to face Zwe, he's looking at me like he doesn't know if I was addressing some invisible person behind him.

"What are you talking about?" he asks.

"That night. At dinner. The summer after freshman year," I say, suddenly realizing that maybe he has no idea what I'm talking about, either because he was too drunk to remember it, or because . . . it meant nothing to him at all. I hadn't considered that this one moment in time that I've replayed throughout the years, like a botched pass in slow motion, didn't leave so much as a thumbprint on *his* timeline of our friendship—and now I have a worse, more embarrassing fear. "You know what, it's okay, you probably don't remem—" I try to laugh it off.

"My mom's dan pauk and your terrible cheap wine," he interrupts. "How could I not remember? You had on this sugar lip balm that tasted so sweet."

"And you didn't want to kiss me."

"Because you were tipsy, and we had three years of college on different continents ahead of us. And as much as I wanted to, and believe me, I wanted to, I had to remind myself, *Not like this. Not with these odds.*"

"It wasn't because . . . you didn't want me? Like that?"

His eyes are glistening as he laughs. "Not want you?" he asks, sounding incredulous. As he speaks, hope flounders inside of me, like a determined animal with a broken leg. "Of course I wanted to kiss you," he says, voice raspy. "Kissing you, being with you, is all I've ever wanted. *You* have always been all I ever wanted. But I kept thinking that if we were going to do this, we were going to do it right. And then fucking Vik." He shakes his head.

"What . . . about Vik?"

"You were so in love with him. I never thought he was good enough for you, but then again, I never thought anyone would be good enough for you, not the way I would be. Cocky, I know," he says. He's trying to play it off with a rueful smile, but I see how difficult this is for him. Zwe Aung Win doesn't put his heart on display.

"You could've brought it up again. After we broke up."

"I thought—" He stops himself.

I frown at his hesitation. "Thought what?"

"That you weren't over him." My jaw drops at the statement. "You still kept bringing him up," Zwe explains. "About how he didn't think you could do this or that, how you wished he could see you now. I was scared that you were still in love with him, and that even if we did get together, I'd always be the rebound or the . . . second option. The guy you settled for because you couldn't get the one you actually wanted."

"You're an idiot," I say without thinking, and Zwe laughs in surprise. "You are!" I repeat. "Settle? You think *you'd* be the second option? *He* was the second option! *He* was the one I would've settled for."

Now it's Zwe's turn to look astonished. "Really?" he asks, sounding the most vulnerable I've ever heard him.

"Really," I say. "The reason I keep bringing him up is because there's a part of me that is still stuck on how little he thought of me, how little he believed in me. And yeah, that's clearly something I need to work on in therapy. But how could you—" I swallow, unable to believe that this is what's been going through his head this whole time. "When Vik broke up with me and told me I was never going to become an author, I was heartbroken and I felt so small, but I also thought, *I hope Zwe doesn't secretly think this too*. But you always showed me that you didn't, and that's what kept me going. That *you* believed that I could."

I smile, and he smiles back, and my god, the way my heart pinches in on itself. "That's why it hurt so much that you tore my book apart," I say. "Yours is the only opinion that ever matters to me."

He shakes his head at himself. "I'm sorry. I was angry. I'm so, so sorry."

"I'm sorry, too," I say. Because this is our love: love that knows when to bend and bow in humility so it doesn't break.

I can't tell if the buzzing in my skull is from the adrenaline or the sensation of overwhelming love, the kind that would make you, I dunno, write about it.

"I want to write a romance novel," I blurt out.

Zwe looks like he can't tell if that's the setup for a joke. "Okay?"

"If we're admitting things," I say, somewhat embarrassed, "I . . . I *do* want to write a romance novel. You're right. A time-traveling manhole is *so* stupid."

"It really is."

"Okay, you don't have to rub it in." He meets my scowl with a chuckle. "It . . . it turns out I already knew more about love than I *thought* I did."

"Yeah?"

"Yeah," I say, a fresh wave of tears blurring my vision. "It turns out everything I needed to know about love was sleeping on the other side of the wall every night. God, that's cheesy, isn't it? It's all right, I'll work on it."

"I think love is built on a solid foundation of cheese," he says with a wink.

"But . . . what if my agent hates it? What if my publisher hates it? What if no one takes me as a *serious* writer anymore?"

"Fuck all that. You do what you did before. What you're doing now."

"Which is?"

He smiles, and I already know that that's all the encouragement I'm going to need. "You keep going. No matter what. No matter how long it takes, you keep going like you always do."

"Little by little. Because good things take time," I whisper.

A good book.

A good love.

When his gaze drops to the pendant around my neck, it's like he's set every inch of my skin ablaze. "They do," he says.

"I love you," he says. "You have no idea what you do to me."

"And I love you," I say. Because of course I do.

And this, this is the moment that snaps me out of it. This is the thought that drills through all of the rubble.

I am not going to die without having kissed you.

"No," I say.

"No?" Zwe asks. I've already begun stretching my right thumb again, gritting my teeth at the hot friction between the jute and my flesh, too focused to reply to him. It's not until he says tentatively, "No, you don't mean it, or . . ." that I realize he's waiting for an answer.

"What?" I shake my head. "No, of course not. No, fuck, not no like that." I pause to take a deep breath. "Yes, of course I meant *it*. I'm saying no, we're not dying like this."

"We're . . . not?"

"No, we're not," I confirm. "Because we still have a lot to do. We have a ton of sex to have and several fights to get into and makeup sex to have and a wedding to plan and a movie to produce. And did I mention we still need to have sex?" Zwe snorts, but I'm on a roll. I can see it all now: the most breathtaking, beautiful story I could ever come up with. In fact, it's better than any story I could've come up with. "And birthdays to celebrate and dogs to adopt and family holidays to go on together. And every morning, we're going to sit down for coffee and look at each other and just think, *Look at this beautiful life we've built together*. We can't die right now, because

I want a whole life with you." I swallow past the golf ball in my throat. "Okay?"

Zwe's eyes are shining with tears, and despite the shittiness of it all, he's grinning so hard that his joy radiates from the inside out.

He looks like a man in love.

A man in love with me.

A love so big and consistent and unconditional that it knocks the wind out of me.

"Okay," he says.

"Now, maybe it's a long shot, but when they were tying us up, did you remember Antonio's—"

"Yes."

Same wavelength. Always. "How's your thumb?" I ask.

"In a lot of pain," he says. He starts wriggling his shoulder more rapidly, no longer needing to hide what he's doing. I'm doing the same. "Do you think this will work?" he asks.

"Yes," I say, biting down on my lip as I'm pretty sure I feel flesh tear.

"How do you know?"

I shoot him a smirk. "Because, sir, I believe you owe me a kiss."

His mouth curves to match mine. "That's all the motivation I need."

FIFTEEN

Antonio lied when he said this was, and I quote, *Pfft, easy.*

"How the fuck did Antonio do this?" I yell. My skin feels raw to the point of numbness.

This is one of those situations where it *feels* like we've been at this for a solid twenty to thirty minutes, but the clock above the reception desk tells us that we've actually been alone for a whopping two minutes and fifteen seconds.

"I don't know how much gasoline they poured outside," I huff as another trail of sweat seeps down the side of my face. The wind has significantly picked up, almost getting strong enough to knock over the lamps on the tables, and I assume the rain isn't far behind. "But if they're going to start the fire before the storm arrives . . ." I can't finish the sentence. My determination from earlier is waning with every passing second. An image of my body on fire pops into my head, and I start hyperventilating.

"Poe! Poe! Hey! Breathe!" Zwe's voice clangs through the room. His upper body lifts as he takes a deep breath, and he nods, telling me to follow along. When he exhales, so do I. "Don't give up on me now," he says. "We can do this. It's so easy. We know what we have to do."

I want to argue that it would be even easier to give up now. I'm emotionally and physically drained, and my brain wants to shut down and go to sleep. If Zwe weren't also here, I'd have thrown in the towel by now.

I test working both thumbs at the same time, but that's making me only able to give 50 percent to each hand, so I return to only focusing on the right one. The air is pungent with the smell of gasoline. It's slowly seeping into the lines between the hardwood paneling, which gives the whole floor a glossy sheen.

"I cannot believe—" I stop myself mid-sentence when one particular motion makes the rope dig into a soft part of flesh and sets off a flash of pain. Aware that I don't have too much time to spare, however, I immediately start working again, wincing through the rest of it. "This whole time, you thought—" The stray hairs scrape along the side of my forefinger, but I'm getting close. The rain is starting to pelt, so I begin shouting, "I! Loved! Vik!"

Zwe's panting makes his laugh ragged. "I dunno, the guy—" He grunts. "—had a lot of money!"

I laugh, and am going to return a quip when my nostrils react to something. Zwe's already looking around, but we can't spot anything. At last, we make eye contact. We're both thinking it, and we both *know* we're thinking it, and yet we're delusional enough to hope that if we don't say it, it won't be true.

I bite the bullet. "That's smoke, right?"

"Yes," is all Zwe says.

"Faster," I say.

"Save it for the bed," he says, and I make a sound that would be best described as a guffaw. "Maybe the rain will put out the fire before it gets to us," he offers.

"Given how thoroughly they've planned this out—" I now know for a fact that I'm bleeding, because I can feel the blood dripping down my wrist. Still, I wriggle my fingers more rapidly. "—I highly doubt that. They most likely started it right outside the building to minimize the chances of it spreading to the village before the storm puts it out. The fact that we can smell smoke means that it's really close."

"God, I hate smart women," he mutters, then throws me a wink. I roll my eyes.

We're working so furiously that we can't even talk anymore. I attempt to contort my thumb in a way that thumbs are not supposed to contort. In an agony-induced daze, I momentarily wonder if the pain of breaking my thumb would be either less than or equal to what I'm doing right now.

"I'm going to throw up!" I get out. I'm falling apart. I'm actually falling apart.

"You didn't think blood, snot, and tears were sexy enough?" Zwe yells. "Going to throw some bile into the mix?"

I want to laugh, but I hold it in on account of my fear that *that* will be the thing that makes me vomit. "You know what they say, the wetter the better."

Black spots start speckling my vision, and I close my eyes, diverting all of my attention to my breathing.

One thumb, I plead with myself. *Antonio said that was all it took. One thumb. You can free one thumb.*

"How's it coming—" Zwe begins.

"Shut up," I reply. Then, eyes still scrunched shut, I huff out each word, "Sorry. Can't. Talk. Tired. Pain."

"Okay," he says.

One. Thumb. I recite it one syllable at a time, a steady metronome to remind me of the only thing I need to focus on right now. The only thing that will—

The tension around my entire right wrist goes slack. I fling my eyes open, half expecting to find that the reason my hand is free is because I died and am now a ghost.

But no, I'm still here, right alongside the trees that are thrashing in the storm, the smell of smoke and gasoline still the only scents permeating my lungs, several feet away from Zwe, who looks like he's on the verge of passing out. I'm right where I was before—but with one big difference.

"I did it." In my head, I exclaim it with unbridled glee. But by the way Zwe simply frowns at me, I'm guessing it came out significantly weaker. "I did it!" I yell as loudly as I can.

He blinks several times, like I've said the words in a language that he technically knows but is not in a current state to process. At last, he says, "Really?"

Again, I *mean* to pump my fist in triumph like you see in the movies. Instead, I barely manage to sling my right hand over onto my lap, the whole limb dangling like a dog chew toy that should've been thrown out ages ago.

"How about you?" I ask, wiggling my left hand free, too.

"I think I'm close, but I might need your help," he says. We exchange the faintest smile to acknowledge that in any other case, that would've been a great *That's what she said* line.

I bend over to untie the rope around my ankles—although I don't necessarily bend so much as flop, and consequently topple onto the hard floor.

"Are you okay?" Zwe calls out.

I'm lying sideways on a gasoline-soaked floor with blood-caked wrists, so "okay" seems like an exaggeration. "Never been better," I reply.

"Poe!" Zwe yells. "Wake up!"

My eyelids fling open. I was on the brink of passing out, woozier than I thought.

Despite now having two free hands, being on my side on the slippery floor makes it trickier for me to undo the rope around my feet, although I attribute a large part of that to the fact that it's tied in the kind of knot that would impress even the most veteran of sailors.

While I'm fumbling to untie the knot, my throat begins itching and closing up. I try to cough, but it's like all of the oxygen is being suctioned out of the room. It's only then that I look up and see the thin black fog that's rolling in. Still no flames, but smoke means they can't be far behind.

"Faster!" Zwe shouts.

I gulp, a new rush of adrenaline coursing through all ten of my mangled fingers. I undo one knot, and then another, then another—but it doesn't seem to end. Now, in addition to the air getting harder to breathe, the whole room is getting hotter. I feel like I'm in a sauna room that's made of metal and has been cranked up to the max.

Wiping sweat off of my forehead, I look at the jumble of rope still binding my legs together. The knots have to end *somewhere*.

"Fuck! This! Fucking!" I gasp for oxygen with each word. "Stupid! Place!"

On the last word, the rope falls to my feet, and I flail about to kick it fully off. I know I have to get up, but I feel like a crumpled piece of paper.

"Run!" Zwe shouts. "Poe, go! Run!"

"You dummy," I pant. Rolling myself over and onto my palms and knees, I crawl toward Zwe, wheezing with each movement. "I make a big, grand speech, and you think—" I gulp in some desperate oxygen. "—I'm going to just leave you here?"

"Don't be stupid!"

"*You* don't be stupid!" I retort, still crawling. I glare at him through my blurry, still-speckled vision, then remember I shouldn't be getting angry because I need to save my energy, then get even *angrier* at him for making me angry in the first place. "Shut. Up. Just shut the hell up."

When I reach him, I begin working on the rope around his feet while he continues to work on his hands.

We go at it in tandem, each focused on our own tasks while the wind swirls leaves and bits of foliage in dramatic movements around us.

After several long moments, Zwe exclaims, "Got it!" He wriggles his shoulders a bit, and then his hands are working on top of, next to, underneath mine as we try to free his feet.

"Maybe you can crawl," I suggest. I don't want to bring it to his attention, but I'm certain he can see how trembly my fingers are. So trembly that I don't think they could even hold a cup, let alone untie a series of complex knots.

He doesn't respond immediately. And when he does, it's not with words.

I'm attempting to pull out a particular loop when both of Zwe's hands close around mine. "What?" I snap. I'm about to scold him for stopping when he gives me a soft smile, and my stomach twists. "No," I say.

"Go," he says.

"No!" I repeat.

"It's okay. It'll be okay."

If I had the energy, I swear I would reach up and slap him. "It's obvious that the smoke has gotten to your brain," I say. "We'll get that checked out when we make it to the hospital."

I go to push his hands away, but he firms his grip. "You're not—"

"No, *you're* not."

Aware of the timer, my mind starts scrambling. I wonder if I can pick up this chair like mothers who suddenly find the strength to lift a tractor off of their child, but it's one of those large traditional Chinese antique rosewood chairs that require several people to move in the best of circumstances.

I straighten myself from my prior hunched position, and although we're not quite at eye level, with him bent over, I *can* lean into his face. Which I do. Despite our proximity, the rain and wind have picked up so much that I still have to yell. I turn my back on the storm outside and lean in closer. "You are out of your fucking mind if you think I'm leaving you!"

"And you're out of *your* fucking mind if you think I'm going to take you down with me!" Zwe shouts back. "What is the point of *both* of us dying here?"

"The *point*—" While he's distracted, I forcefully shove his stupid wide palms away and resume working. "Is that I don't want to go home without you! I'm not going to! You really think you love me more than I love you, don't you?"

"I do!" he shouts through tears.

"Well, that's fucking arrogant of you!" Why won't this damn knot untie? Why, dear God, why? "You are the most infuriating person—"

Warm, rough skin presses into each of my cheeks, and Zwe lifts my face, places his forehead against mine. I can smell the sweat and saltiness coating his face.

"*You* are the most infuriating person," he says with a smile. When he leans in further, I shake my head.

"If you're thinking of kissing me right now, mister—" I warn. He cocks an amused brow at "mister." "It's not happening."

"Why not?"

"Because it's really damn morbid. Think of all the therapy I'm going to have to have to work through the PTSD. And I won't even be able to bill you for it!"

His laugh is rough. "You have *so* many books left to write. *So* much art left to share with the world. Your mom is waiting to hug you. You need to go. I'll be okay."

"I don't care about any of that!" I try to sound firm, but I can't hide what I am: scared. "None of that means anything without you! Please, please, please don't give up now. I don't know what I'd do without you. I don't want to find out. Please, Zwe, please don't make me find out. None of it would make sense without you. I would spend every miserable day seeing you everywhere. *Everywhere.*"

Zwe swipes at my cheeks with both thumbs. "I think it's my turn to ask if I can kiss you now."

I nestle my face into his palm. "I can't say 'yes.' This isn't how our story ends."

"I'm sorry," he says. "I wish—"

As though being sucked into a wind tunnel, I'm yanked backward, up and away from an equally shocked Zwe.

SIXTEEN

Instantly, and despite being a non-religious person, my first thought is, *God?*

My wobbly legs give in, but I don't fall. Instead, each of my arms are hung around two different figures on either side.

"Hold tight, we have to go," Garima says. She's soaked, her T-shirt sticking to her body like it was spray-painted on. The same goes for Faith, who's propping me up on the right. Garima is at least a foot taller than Faith, which puts *me* in a somewhat lopsided stance, but I'm not going to complain.

"What—" I blink rapidly to make sure I'm not hallucinating them. "You're . . . What are you doing here?" Fear grips me as I think that maybe they came back to shoot us and make sure we died.

"What does it look like? We're saving you," Garima says.

The smell of gasoline and flames has still got me groggy, and I'm not certain I heard her right. "You . . . are?" I ask.

She gestures down at the fact that she's propping me up. "What else does it look like we're doing?" she asks, then nods over to the side.

When I look at Zwe, two other figures—also drenched—are knelt down in front of him, one with a pair of green garden shears. On instinct, I want to reach over and shield him, my mind jumping to the worst conclusion. I breathe when I see that they're using them on the rope, not on him.

"You're doing it wrong!" Leila yells.

"How the fuck would you know, you haven't even given me a chance to start!" Nita shoots back.

"Are those shears even sharp enough?" Leila asks.

Nita widens her eyes. "They were the only ones left out in the garden! What did you want me to do, locate the toolbox in the shed and examine each gardening tool first before deciding on the optimal—"

"Oh my god!" Faith yells. "You have a whole boat ride for arguing! Can you please just free him so we can get out of this alive?!"

I'm giving myself whiplash by the speed at which I'm looking around, trying to keep track of who's talking. Part of me is still doubtful that they're really here to save us and that they don't have a much more sinister plan up their sleeves, but I don't have any choice but to trust them right now.

"Who the hell tied this?" Leila yells, then, remembering the answer is right in front of her, she glares up at Garima. "How did you even know how to do this? Was it in a TikTok?"

"Just cut him out!" Garima barks.

It's an oddly endearing scene, all the more so given the life-or-death stakes. This kind of bickering is the exact sort of situation you get when you put me, Zwe, his brother, and all of our cousins in the same room at Thingyan or any other stressful holiday. You only get this level of multi-conversational yelling when you know you have a family who will always have your back.

"What if we lift him and carry him out?" Garima suggests.

Silently, we all eye Zwe, gauging if that's a realistic possibility.

Faith shakes her head. "Probably, if it were only him, and all five of us could pitch in." She lifts the shoulder that's propping up my underarm. "But we need to get Poe, too."

"What if we take her outside, somewhere far enough that she's safe, and then come back for him?" Garima asks.

"We don't have that much time," Leila says after another beat of consideration. "The fire is right on our heels. We barely have enough time now, which is why it would be great if *we could set off the sprinkler system*," she finishes with loud, unbridled sarcasm.

"Hey, sis, if you want to take over, be my guest," comes the reply, and for the first time, I realize Andrea's in the room, too. She'd straightened the chair I'd been tied to so she can place her laptop on it, and is crouched on her knees, face mere inches away from the screen.

They *all* came back.

"I don't get why it was so easy to turn it off in the first place—" Leila gestures upward. I look to where she's pointing, and for the first time, notice several water sprinklers hanging from the ceiling. "—but it's taking a lifetime to turn it back on."

"Because, my brilliant cousin," Andrea yells, "would you believe that people have found out there's *something* going on here? And would you also believe that those same people have probably alerted the resort management and security teams, who, having realized that their system was hacked, have since placed numerous obstacles to significantly strengthen said system? I'm working as quickly as I can." Sparing one second, she looks up and widens her eyes around the room. "Surely there must be other things in this room that can help cut through rope, or, I dunno, create some sort of trolley to wheel him out on," she points out before gluing her eyes back to the screen. "I'm going to get this, I just need some peace and quiet."

"We could drag him?" Leila offers.

"I don't know about you all—" Nita huffs between every couple of words. The shears are either the dullest shears on the planet, or the rope is too thick. She's changed her techniques so that instead of cutting into them, she's making a seesawing motion with just the top blade to saw through. "—but I don't have the energy to drag out a fully grown adult man. Especially when the building is on fire."

"You came back," I blurt out, still stunned.

Faith, Leila, and Garima all fix me with dumbfounded expressions, as though to say, *What nap did* you *just wake up from?*

"We did," Garima says. "We were already three-quarters of the way to the boat, too."

"You have Andrea to thank." Leila nods in her cousin's direction, who, without lifting her eyes from the computer, holds up a peace sign. "She wouldn't let it go. She's good at that, you know."

"What, having a moral compass?" Andrea asks.

"Being annoying, like a puppy who won't stop asking for your food," Leila answers loudly. "Yapping on and on about how this wasn't the plan, and we were never supposed to hurt anyone, and you two seemed like good people, and how could we insist that we were in the right if we had this on our conscience for the rest of our lives."

"And which wonderful, brilliant, kind cousin of mine taught me the importance of treating people with kindness?" Andrea shoots back.

Leila rolls her eyes, but I see a soft smile.

Then, she looks us straight in the eye. "I'm sorry. To be frank, I hated you guys before you even arrived because I thought you were just like every other rich fuck we've had. But you're actually nice people." She tilts her head at her cousins. "I have to protect them, you know. I'm the oldest, that's my job."

"We're all sorry," Nita says with a sigh. "I was so scared you were going to escape and describe my face to a sketch artist."

"We really didn't want to hurt anyone," Garima tells me, looking as sheepish as the rest of them. "We specifically came when there were no guests *because* we didn't want to hurt anyone."

Leila gets to her feet. Despite their apologies, my instinct is to back away, but I physically can't.

"Don't blame them. I know you're going to go to the police, but when you do, please . . . say that it was me." Beside me, Soraya and Garima gasp and start to protest, but Leila gives a firm shake of her head, pressing on before they can interject. "It *was* me who came up with this plan. I was just so angry, watching these rich assholes take more and more from our family, our land. Watching guests traipse around our island without a single ounce of respect for it. This stupid pile of imported wood and marble—" With a scoff, she gestures at the mess around us. "—kept getting bigger and bigger, pushing my family out of *our homes*. But *I* was the one who told my cousins what to do, including to tie you and leave you here. Please tell the police you have no idea who the other people were, and that all you know is that *I* was the inside man who orchestrated the entire thing."

"I—"

A dancing amalgamation of light catches the corner of my eye.

The three of them and Zwe follow my gaze, Nita and Andrea still too preoccupied with freeing Zwe to recognize what's happening.

"Fire," Faith whispers.

As though on cue, there's a small explosion of flames. "Shit!" Nita curses, moving the blade even quicker. "It's not cutting through!"

As if a collective switch has been flipped, everyone starts yelling at the same time, making half a movement in one direction only to stop and consider going in the opposite one, like our brains are both not working and also overworking.

"Just go!" Zwe is shouting. "Take Poe and go!"

"What do we do?" Garima yells across my face and at Nita.

"I don't know! Do we go?" Nita replies, helplessly looking around at her cousins. "We can't leave them here!"

"No, we're not going anywhere!" yells a voice that sounds like mine after it's been scraped across rocks.

Leila is on her knees again beside Nita, tugging at the bottom of the rope.

"Move! I might cut your finger!" Nita yells.

"I don't care!" Leila cries. "We need to free him!"

"Let's just drag him out!" Nita says, gripping and sawing the shears with so much force that her fingertips are red. "You and me, let's just drag him out sideways if we need to."

"We'll have to jump through the flames at this point," Leila points out. "There's no way to drag him out."

I start thrashing around, trying to pull away from Garima and Nita so I can go over and help untie Zwe. "What are you—" Nita starts, then, following my gaze, tightens her grip on my hand. "No, you can't go there. If it comes to it, we have to run."

"I'm not leaving without him!" I cry. "You all go! I'm not leaving!"

The fire has entered the room by this point, all the wooden furniture in here acting as oversized tinder. Heat pricks every ounce of my exposed skin, and my body screams for a large body of water to dive into.

"We're going to die!" Nita is still going at it, but she's slowed down from exhaustion. Noticing it too, Leila takes the shears from her without a word, and continues on, white knuckles gripping the dark green plastic handles.

"We are *not* going to die," Leila says, her red, splotchy face marked with tears and sweat. "I—"

Without any warning, Zwe kicks the shears out of Leila's hands.

"What the—" she starts, but can't finish because Zwe pushes both of them with enough force that their backs slam onto the floor.

While we're all stunned, he bends over, scrambles for the shears, and tosses them into the flames.

"What the fuck," I whisper, refusing to believe what I just saw with my own eyes. "What did you just do? Why did you do that!" I scream, wanting to slap him.

"Go," he orders.

"No!" I say. Then, because I'm so angry I don't know what else to do: "Fuck you."

But he doesn't even flinch.

At this point, I can feel all of their eyes on me, but I can't stop shaking my head at Zwe.

There's movement beside me, and I turn to see Leila helping Nita up. "We have to go." Leila's voice is the quietest I've ever heard it. She catches my eye for only a second before assessing the burning room. "We have to go now, it's our last chance."

"You guys go," I repeat. "I'm staying."

"No, you're not," she and Zwe both say at the same time.

Anger overtakes the rest of my emotions. "You don't get to tell me what to do," I reply.

"Leila, knock her out again if you have to. Get her out of—" Zwe orders.

"Screw you!" I yell.

"Poe, we have to go! Now!" Leila says, then nods at her cousins. Faith and Garima start moving, but I dig in my heels. "Poe!" Leila repeats.

Zwe's hands are curled into fists. "Listen to her!" he pleads. "You're going to die!"

"Then I'll die!" I cry. "I don't want to do any of it without you anyway!"

Zwe looks like he'd knock me unconscious himself if I were close enough. He's going to yell at me to leave until his dying breath, and I'm going to refuse until mine. Unstoppable force, immovable object.

Right as he opens his mouth to beg once more, an alarm screeches over the sound of flames and wind and rain. It's so sharp and loud that it feels like it's drilling itself into my skull.

Wetness. Rainwater being splashed at me from all directions.

But it's not rainwater. And it's not coming from all directions.

It's only coming from *one* direction: up.

I look to the ceiling, where the sprinkler system is pumping water down onto us.

A drenched Andrea comes over, looking as weary as the rest of us. "You all are so dramatic," she says with a reprimanding shake of her head when the alarm dies out. "I told you all I needed was some peace and quiet. Not that any of you delivered on the 'quiet' part. And this goes without saying, but you guys need to chip in to buy me a new laptop."

We stare at her, mouths agape, water still showering down on us. It's cold, but I don't even care.

"You little nerd!" Nita is the first to snap out of the trance, leaping over and throwing her arms around Andrea. Leila pounces from the other side.

Garima and Faith go to join them, but upon realizing they're still propping me up, stop themselves right before accidentally letting go.

"It's okay." I laugh. "Can you help me sit down?" With a lot of care, they help me down to the floor. Then, in a distinctly unromantic manner, I crawl over to Zwe. "Hi, fancy meeting you here," I say, looking up at him from the floor.

"Do you mind freeing me before you jump straight into flirting with me?" He motions at the garden shears on the floor, which hadn't actually made it into the flames and are still intact.

"I can try," I say, picking up where Nita left off. To be fair to her, she *had* gone through most of the rope. A couple more minutes, and Zwe would've been free.

"Do you want me to—" Zwe reaches down for the shears, and I whack his hand away.

"You're the damsel in distress here," I say as I saw through the last strand of rope. "So sit back up, shut up, and look pretty."

"Aye aye, ma'am." After a few seconds of intense sawing, the brown jute snaps in half, and the coil of rope falls to his bare feet. "My hero!" Zwe exclaims.

"I expect a hefty monetary reward," I say. I try to drop the shears, but it's more like they fall out of my limp, noodle-esque hands.

"How about a hug?" Before I can ask what he means, he's bending over, scooping me up, and putting me back down on his lap. I wrap my arms around his neck, although on account of their frail and shaky state, they're not doing much to keep me upright. "Don't worry, I got you," he says, and lifts his shoulder to indicate that he's not letting go of the arm behind my back.

I wrinkle my nose. "You smell."

"Yeah, because *you* smell like freshly washed laundry right now."

"But you—" I lean in, my nose grazing the stubble on his jaw as I take a deep inhale. "—you really smell." I move back, and I can see him prepping to return whatever insult I'm about to hit over to his side of the court. Instead, I cup his chin in one hand, letting my thumb trace every millimeter of his jaw. A thrill whisks through me at the fact that I get to do this now. Finally. "You smell like home."

His jaw works under my touch, and his Adam's apple bobs as he swallows. "Do you still mean everything you said back there?"

This takes *me* by surprise. "What? About . . ."

"Yeah." He whispers it, like he's bracing himself for what comes next.

"Why wouldn't I?" I ask.

He shrugs. "Maybe it was just adrenaline. Maybe you thought we were dying and you didn't want to hurt my feelings—"

I snort a laugh. "You think I told you I loved you because I didn't know how to let you down gently?"

"Maybe," he says. Then, cautiously, discreetly, "Do you?"

And in an instant, he looks so soft and vulnerable and just like a kid again, the same one who let me use his library book allowance to borrow *Betty and Veronica Digest* No. 135.

I run my fingers up and down the nape of his neck. "I meant every word. I am so grateful for everything that *Give Me a Reason* has given me, but none of it would've meant anything if I'd lost you in the process, and I can't believe I came so close to doing just that with this second book. They're just books. *You*—" I move forward, resting my forehead against his, inhaling once again the same scent that I would smell when he leaned over to remove my laptop and put a blanket on me whenever I fell asleep on the couch. "You mean everything to me. None of it would be worth it if I didn't have you in my life. But I've wanted this life and this career ever since I was a kid, and it just felt scary, you know? Like suddenly I had everything I'd ever wanted, and *you* were so proud of me and I was scared that I was going to let you down and also that I was going to let myself down. I'm terrified that I've only ever had one good book in me."

Zwe shakes his head. "That's not—"

I press a finger to his lips. "But that's okay." Lines form across his forehead. He tries to speak again, but I get ahead of him. "I'm okay if I don't write any more international bestsellers for the rest of my life. I'm okay if none of my other books get turned into movies. Look, will it suck if my next book *doesn't* hit any of the bestseller lists? Yes, of course, and I'll cry to you about it, and I'll feel like a failure and like no one will ever want to publish another one of my books ever again. But you know what? Then I'll get over it.

"Because you were right. I didn't used to care about writing international bestsellers, I just wanted to write. I remember when I dreamt about getting to a point where I could spend my whole day writing. That's all I wanted to do—write. I need to get back to that. Because as much as I love writing books, and I *do* want to keep writing for as long as they'll let me, at the end of the day, they're just books. This is just a job. I'll still be a writer even if my publisher drops me and no other publisher signs me. I can live with losing a job. But over the last forty-eight hours, I was petrified that I would lose *you,* and that I'd never see my family again, that the last time we saw them was the *last* time we saw them—and suddenly it didn't matter at all that I didn't know what my next book was going to be about. I couldn't live with losing you."

We're both crying now, holding each other like two people who were moments away from tipping over the edge of the world. "You'll always be my favorite author," he tells me.

I nod. "That's all I want," I say. "*You* are all I want. I've been so busy worrying about never writing another *great* book that I'm not even enjoying the rewards of this one. I mean, my book bought us our home. It bought my parents *their* new home. It bought me a fancy last-minute holiday with my best friend, which, 'armed intruders and nearly being burned to death' hiccup aside, is pretty darn cool."

"It is," Zwe agrees. "You're the coolest person I know." Then, "Ask me again," he says hoarsely.

I'm about to ask *Ask you what*, but when his gaze drops to my lips, I don't need to. I never want to reset again, because I see it now, how every single thing we've been through over the past two decades had to happen for us to arrive here.

"Can I kiss you?" I ask. I feel myself smiling so wide that my cheeks hurt, and I'm scared I'm smiling *too* big to be able to kiss him.

"Always," he says.

In another very unromantic moment, the kiss starts off awkward. For one, we're both too impatient for it and our teeth bash into one another, causing us to pull back with muffled *Ow*s.

"That was such a shit first kiss," I laugh.

"Doesn't count," he says, shaking his head.

"You're right." I school my features into the most no-nonsense expression I can manage. "I need to start gathering material for a romance novel, so you're going to have to be serious about this."

"Okay, then tell me. How do you like to be kissed?"

My mouth opens but no sound comes out. A burning knot that had been too tangled for too long inside of me begins to unsnarl, a knot that had been braiding hope and desire and fear. "How about I show you instead?" I say.

I plant my lips on top of his responding smirk, and even though bursts of *Holy shit, you're kissing Zwe* spark through my brain, they quickly settle, turning into *Holy shit, why haven't you been kissing Zwe this whole time?* Because I now know how I like to be kissed: like I am and always will be more than enough, like he would die of hunger if he'd had to go one more second without kissing me, like if it were up to him, kissing me would be all he ever did. Because that's exactly how he's kissing me, tongues and lips searching for *more, more, more,* making up for lost time even though we know we've got the rest of our lives. My spine arches up, his curves down, the heat between our bodies captured in a closed-loop circuit.

In the back of my mind, I'm faintly cognizant that the context of all of this—the ashes around us and traces of smoke still lingering in the air, the roaring wind, in the far distance, the ocean waves bellowing as they crash again and again into the shore—while dramatic, isn't exactly the most romantic of settings. Not to mention, Leila and her cousins are still here.

But also, I don't care. We've waited *so* long for this that, frankly, I'd keep doing this even if we were front and center onstage in a packed circus tent. It's that relief of coming home after a long, long journey, every muscle in my body relaxing, settling back into the only place in this world I've ever truly belonged.

"I love you," I say at last when we come up for air.

"I love you so fucking much." His voice is wet and still a bit shaky. "So, so much you have no idea."

And for several delicious moments, it's just us, the way I always want it to be. Him bracing my upper body, one of my hands tangled in his hair, the other cupping his face. Both of us grinning like we're kids who've just agreed to keep *the* best secret of our lives to ourselves—which, I suppose in some ways, this is. Or at least, that's how love *feels,* right? You're giddy with glee because you're convinced you're the first people in the history of humankind to feel this way, to the point where you might positively burst.

A loud, loaded clearing of the throat pops our cocoon of obliviousness.

"Don't get me wrong, we are very happy for you—" Leila makes a circular motion with both hands, and all of her cousins nod enthusiastically.

"You two are *so* cute!" Faith says.

"But, well, we've been talking and . . ." Leila looks at the women, who sheepishly drop their gazes to the ground. "I've asked them to leave. Obviously you're allowed to do whatever you decide to do, but I wasn't lying when I told you earlier that all of this was my idea. Please, please let my cousins leave." Her eyes are shining, and it's not just water that's running down her face.

I turn to Zwe, whose shoulders move with an imperceptible shrug. "What do you think?" he asks.

"I don't know," I answer honestly. "On the one hand, we nearly died." A dry laugh escapes out of me as the absurdity of that sentence hits. "But they *did* come back. They were willing to risk their lives to save us. Even if they *were* the ones who tied us up in the first place."

"Yeah, we're *really* sorry about that," Nita says, grimacing. "But like I said, we were terrified you'd escape and tell the police about us and describe my face, and—" She stops herself, takes a deep breath, shakes her head. "But that's no excuse. We're sorry. You have to believe us, hurting people was never part of the original plan. We're *so* sorry."

The thing is, I'm less concerned about them hurting me. When I look down at Zwe's bloody knuckles, a new fit of anger flares through me. I *want* to say that them coming back to save us negates their initial actions, but then I'm transported back to that horrible moment where we couldn't undo Zwe's rope and I was silently begging the universe to let me switch places with him. It feels like I'm trying to shove forgiveness through a too-narrow doorway—even if I *wanted* to, it just doesn't fit. They hurt the person I loved more than anything in the world.

"What about you?" I ask Zwe. "What do *you* think?"

He looks at me, at them, then back at me. "I don't think I could forgive anyone who tried to hurt you," he tells me.

"Me neither." It's anger that's only proportionate to the amount of love that I feel for Zwe. The kind of anger that, if I let it take root, would make me want to hurt *them*. Make me want to . . . get revenge. "They did it for love," I say quietly.

"What?" Zwe asks, confused, but I'm looking directly at Leila. She nods slowly. "They hurt my family," she says, just as softly, like we're taking first steps onto ice that we have no clue is or isn't strong enough to hold the weight of our collective anger and regret.

Because *I'm* sorry, too. She might've taken it one step too far, but she made some good points earlier about how we weren't—or specifically, *I* wasn't—much different from any of the other rich, entitled guests who came here. I saw those expansion plans earlier and my first thought was, *Hey, maybe there'll be even more for us to do next year and we can make this an annual trip.* When she'd lied that her family had chosen to relocate up to the mountains, I had simply accepted it, even though Zwe and I both have parents who couldn't feasibly live in an apartment building without an elevator or in a house with steep stairs. The shame is enough to make me want to throw up.

"We *could* let everyone else go and turn you in," I tell her. To her credit, she never breaks eye contact, returning my gaze with the solemnity of someone who keeps their word. I know for a fact that she's not going to try to escape, and it would be justice served.

I turn to her cousins, all of whom are teary-eyed, and whom I can tell are holding themselves back from grabbing Leila and making a run for it. "But what would be the point?" I say. "You told us that you were the sole breadwinner for your parents—were you lying about that?"

She shakes her head. "No."

"And knowing your cousins, I'm guessing the second we take you away, they're going to start hatching a plan to break you out of jail." I can't hold back a smirk as I shoot a questioning look at them.

They're all giving me the same conspiratorial smile. "If it helps," Garima says, "we will neither confirm nor deny it in your presence so that you can make the case for plausible deniability later down the line."

That makes me laugh. "The thing is—" I turn back to Leila. "I have spent the last forty-eight hours doing everything in my power to keep the person that *I* love most in the world safe." At this, Zwe gives my arm a squeeze. "I don't know what I'd do if someone kicked my parents out of their home, but I don't think it would be anything 'nice' or even 'sensible.' You guys saved me, and you saved Zwe, and you made sure that nobody was hurt. And at the end of the day, all that was harmed was—" I shrug as I survey the wet, charred mess around us. "A bunch of buildings. Well, that, and a bunch of rich people's wallets." Everyone chuckles at that, including Zwe.

"I would understand if you wanted me to pay for what I did to you guys," Leila says.

I nod. "I know. But I think risking being burned alive to come back and save us wiped the slate clean. We're good." Remembering, I swivel around to Zwe. "Unless you object?"

"I just wanted you safe," he says.

"And I just wanted *you* safe."

"Sooo . . . what now?" Andrea asks.

I grunt as I try to sit up. Zwe helps me to my feet before getting up himself. There's a moment where he has to steady himself by grabbing the chair, but ultimately we're both standing, even if we're slightly wobbly and holding on to each other for balance.

"Now we do what Leila said," I say. "The four of you still escape the way you were planning to. Or if the storm has gotten too bad to go out to sea, then you go join your family and hide out there for a bit. Do you think you'll be able to do that? In the rain?"

They assess the weather situation. "It'll be difficult, but manageable," Nita says as she peers over toward the start of the hiking trails. "And there's four of us, so together, we'll be okay."

"Perfect," I nod. "You should get going soon, though, in case anyone who was on the beach sees that the fire is out and comes up here to check what's happening. The three of us will stay here until the rain lets up. Afterward, we'll—" I pause, unsure where we actually go from here. "Join the others?" I look at Leila. "Where *are* they? What did you guys do with Antonio after you recaptured him?"

"We brought him back to join the rest of the staff," Leila says. She nods down in the direction of the sand. "They're all on the beach. We left them there with their hands tied. I'm sure they've freed each other by now, but there's no way they'd have come running up here with the fire. They're all waiting for help to come, which should arrive by sunrise, if not earlier. All the hotel alarms have been tripped by this point."

"Okay, then, let's go down and join them."

"What will we say?" Leila asks. She fidgets, and I realize she's still a tiny bit concerned that we might expose her.

"That they had left us unconscious and locked in a room before setting the fire. Thankfully we woke up and managed to escape right as the sprinklers went off. Oh—" I snap my fingers. "We can tell Antonio we escaped thanks to his handcuff trick. He'll get a kick out of that."

Zwe returns my grin. "He won't stop talking about that for at least a year, probably more."

"So we have a plan?" I ask, and everyone nods.

The women take turns hugging Leila. "I'll see you all soon," she reassures each of them.

As they're leaving, Nita stops and turns to me.

"Thank you," she says to me and Zwe with a grateful smile. "For protecting Leila. For protecting all of us. You might be rich, but you're not an asshole."

"We owe you one. Anytime you need to burn down a resort, the Chen girls will be on call," Faith says, throwing in a small salute.

"Now there's a card I never thought I'd have in my back pocket," I laugh. "But I'll take it. Now go. Be safe."

SEVENTEEN

"Ms. Poe! Mr. Zwe! Leila!" Antonio practically wails when we're close enough for him to make out who we are. Dropping the giant rock he was holding as a precaution, he sprints across the wet sand at an impressive pace. I'm expecting him to come to a stop when he's near, but instead, he keeps charging forward with outstretched arms. Leila swiftly sidesteps right before Antonio barrels into us and all three of our bodies go down.

"Hey, kid," Zwe laughs. He tries to shake the sand out of his hair, but it's so caked there's not really any point. His grin tells me that he doesn't mind the tackle one bit.

I don't care either that I can already feel sand slipping into crevices in my body where I'd rather there not be any sand. "I'm so happy to see you!" I exclaim, properly hugging Antonio. "Are you okay? How about everyone else? Your grandpa?"

"We're all good! Are *you* okay? I thought you guys were goners!"

"I'm happy to see you, too," Leila calls out. She's hovering above us, arms crossed, one brow cocked and lips pushed to the side in an annoyed manner.

"Are you feeling left out?" Antonio stands up, wiping sand off of his trousers.

"Of being tackled by you?" Leila scoffs, but there's a trace of softness in her voice, and I know she *is* feeling left out.

Antonio does, too, because he fully embraces her, hugging her so tight she emits a soft grunt. "I knew you'd be okay," he tells her without letting go. "You're the toughest person I know, Leils. You know how much I love you."

That melts her exterior, and she smiles into his shoulder. "Ugh, I suppose I love you, too, you doofus. Glad to see you're safe," she says, although I have an inkling she'd made it clear to her cousins that not a single strand on Antonio's head was to be harmed.

They don't immediately let go after they pull apart. Leila ruffles his hair with affection, and Antonio beams. After a satisfying enough reunion, they reach down and help me and Zwe up.

"How'd you two get free?" Antonio asks us.

Zwe and I trade a look. "Well, funny enough," I say with a nonchalant air, "an extremely smart friend of ours once gave us this great tip about how to position your hands when—"

Antonio gasps, his excitement propelling him ahead of me. "When you're being tied up!" he yells, and punches the air. "See, and Grandpa's always accusing me of knowing too little about too much, but wait until he hears about this!" He's moving away when something catches his attention. "Leils—" He points at mine and Zwe's bruised and torn wrists, and then at hers. "How come your hands don't look like they've gone through a shredder? Didn't they tie *you* up?"

Leila stutters an "Well, uh, I—"

"Because she didn't know about the trick," I jump in. "Remember? She left to use the toilet when you were explaining it to us? Only Zwe and I knew to turn our hands, so hers were in the wrong position. Leila had to wait for us to free ourselves before we could undo her rope."

Antonio raises a finger in an *Ah* manner. Behind his back, Leila mouths, *Thank you*.

"We were taking bets on which of you would make it out alive." He waves at us to follow him toward the rest of the group, who are still waiting from a safe distance farther back. "Well, to be honest, we were taking bets on which of you two"—he gestures at me and Zwe—"would make it out alive. We had no doubt Leila would survive."

Leila places a hand on her heart. "Aww, thanks."

"You didn't think I would make it out alive?" Zwe scoffs.

"I thought *you* would," Antonio replies instantly. He darts me a suspicious glance.

"Ye prick of little faith!" I go to hit him on the back, but he glides out of the way.

"Do you think we'll be saved soon?" Zwe asks. He nods back up toward the resort. "We can gather everyone back indoors, or, well, what's left of the indoors. Probably safer than just on the beach."

"Good call," Antonio says.

He and Leila walk ahead of us, talking and laughing and occasionally thwacking each other.

Zwe and I crisscross our arms around the small of each other's backs. "We did it," I say, leaning my head against his bicep. For the first time in days, I let out a full, satisfying exhale. "We're going home soon."

"Do you think you got enough inspiration for your next book?"

"Actually—" I gaze up at him, and even though I've known this face for most of my life, my breath catches. Because it's just hit me that this is mine now. Zwe is mine now. "I do."

He tucks his chin in. "Do tell."

"Well, I haven't figured out the *whole* story yet. But it's going to be a love story between two best friends." A grin overtakes his handsome face, and my love for him grows in an instant. I already know that that's how it's going to be from now on—despite it feeling impossible, every day, I'll love him just that much more. "And the reader's going to be told from the first page that this is a love story between two best friends. They just don't know it yet."

One boat ride and multiple police interviews later, Zwe and I are finally able to check into a hotel and take long, hot showers. We had very momentarily toyed with the idea of taking a sexy shower together, but decided that it would be better if the first time we had sex with each other didn't involve streaks of dirt and blood running across the bathroom floor. So, I shower first, nearly crying with joy when the warm water hits my skin.

Stepping out of the bathroom, a damp Zwe pauses when he sees me sitting on the bed in one of the plush white hotel bathrobes. The knowledge that I'm naked underneath hangs in the cool air-conditioned air. Without so much as a nod, he retrieves the other robe from the wardrobe, wraps it around himself, ties the belt, then removes the towel that was covering his lower body out from under.

"Hi," I say. I'm trying to start some kind of innocuous conversation since I don't really know what we do now, but there's an unending siren inside my brain that keeps announcing *Zwe is naked under the robe, Zwe is naked under the robe, Zwe is naked under the robe.*

"Hi" is all he replies.

I lie down on my stomach, nod at him to join me.

Once he's beside me, I suck in my cheeks as I consider what to say next. "Wanna . . . watch TV?" If this were a scene in my book, I'd immediately make a note on the side that said *Better dialogue.*

"Is this how you always seduce men?" His cheeky smile is made all the more cheeky by his dimples. "No wonder you always have suitors kicking down your door."

I kick his exposed shin, and he laughs, and I don't remove my foot, and now my calf is on top of his and I'm embarrassed at how *scandalous* bare calves suddenly feel, like we're in an Austen novel. "So, no TV? Okay, what would *you* rather do?"

"Don't make me say it," he says. His gaze slowly descends down to my chest, where there's a small gap between my flesh and the robe. I swallow, heat roiling in my stomach.

"What if we're bad at it?" I ask. I'm half joking, which means I'm also half not.

Judging by his short laugh, that's a legitimate fear of his too, or at least, it is now that I've brought it up. "Then we try again tomorrow when we're well rested," he says.

I'm aware that in reality, there are still the occasional footsteps walking in the corridor past our door, and cars still honking away down on the pavement outside our window, but in my mind, there's just us. Which scares me until it doesn't, because that's how it's always been. Just us.

"I love you," I say. When I inch closer, the movement widens that gap between my skin and the fabric. Zwe's jaw muscles flex, and I revel in the knowledge that he's trying to remain a gentleman and not look down, even though I wish he would. What an honor it is to be wanted so thoroughly by the best person you know. "Even if you turn out to be the worst sex I ever have."

"I'd say—" He moves in, too, so that our lips are almost brushing, but not quite, two boats floating *just* out of reach. "That if you telling me I might be *the worst sex you ever have* still isn't enough to kill my erection, then we're off to a pretty good start."

A shiver races down my spine, and I abruptly feel as though I'm about to have sex for the first time. I want to stall with another quip, and I know that Zwe would let me take all the time I need.

Time.

We have spent *so* much time not doing what we wanted, not going for what we wanted—time that we thought we'd have an abundance of until we didn't. He's waited, and so have I, and we both nearly died mid-wait.

So—I cup his jaw and kiss him, and he kisses me back, and I set the tempo, except I can't decide what I want. We start off slow, my tongue teasing his lips, but then the rest of my body wants to move, too. I lower my hand from his face, pushing the robe off of his shoulders, touching the dark hairs on his chest and then his arms and then even lower to the softness of his stomach.

"You are so beautiful," he tells me, right before he nips my earlobe. "Just . . . beautiful."

We undo the loose knots on each other's bathrobes at almost the same time. "I'm going to see you naked," I say with a gasp that's sharper than I intended.

"Poe." Zwe's voice is teasing. "You've seen me naked."

"Not since we went through puberty!"

"What, you think I grew a second penis during puberty?"

I bury a snort into his shoulder. "Great, now I'm imagining

you with two p—" But I don't finish the sentence, because Zwe has moved his fingers down my waist, and now he's rubbing me in a way that makes my eyes roll back. "Softer," I tell him. "It's very sensitive right now." He slows down his pace, lightens the pressure, and my back arches with pleasure.

Removing my robe, I climb on top of him. We stare at each other like this is the first time we're meeting. "Fuck," he exhales. "So beautiful," he repeats, as though the rest of the English language has left him.

"I'm on birth control," I say, knowing that if there's one person on this planet who finds responsible intercourse sexy, it's Zwe Aung Win.

"I know," he says. "You put it on the list the last time I went to the pharmacy."

I feel my face burst into a grin. "I don't think I've ever slept with someone who knew my exact brand of birth control," I say, making us both laugh. I have a vision of us seven years down the line, giddy and shy and hopeful as we talk about beginning to try for kids. *Are you sure?* he'll ask because he always double-checks, and I'll want to laugh because I'll have been sure for a very long time. I'll tell him I was waiting for him to bring it up, and he'll tell me he was waiting for the same with me, and then we'll both end up laughing, just like we are now.

I bend over just enough that I can tangle my fingers in his curls. He looks so gorgeous. *Mine,* a greedy voice in my mind revels. *All mine.* "I love you," I tell him.

"And I love you."

There's some slight shifting, but the moment he pushes into me, my toes curl. It takes a couple of minutes for us to find our rhythm, mainly because we can't decide if we want to make this last for as long as possible, or if we want to give in and let the electric currents between our bodies flow as high as they can. Ultimately, we decide on the latter.

"Fuck, this is amazing," I pant as we pick up the pace. "Who knew you were this good at sex?"

He laughs into my hair. "I'm going to take that as a compliment."

"It is," I hiss, which makes him laugh again.

I want to do this forever, I think.

"I want to do this forever," I say out loud.

"Forever?" Zwe slows down the pace, but not without gripping my ass with both hands. His nails dig into my flesh, and I want to arch even deeper into him. "What about that book you have to write?"

"What book?" I exhale. His chuckle comes low behind my ear. Utilizing the decrease in pace, I lift myself up ever so slightly so I can put one hand between our bodies. Right as I do, Zwe's hand reaches in, too. I meet his eye, and he makes a *Can I?* expression. I want to nod and go along with the moment, but Zwe picks up on my hesitation.

"What's wrong?" he asks, stopping altogether. "Did I—"

"No!" I say hurriedly, almost desperately. "It's just . . . it feels better when *I* do it. No offense."

He lets out a relieved laugh. "Why would I be offended?"

"I dunno, because you're a *man*?" I growl the last word.

He shakes his head. "Come here," he says, and pulls me closer to him. He sits up a few degrees and puts my hand back where it was, albeit now at a better angle. A low hum escapes my lips as I start rubbing my clit. When I look down at Zwe, he looks positively mesmerized. "I want you to come while I'm still inside. I want to feel you come around me."

Already, my body is aching for the friction again. "Good," I whisper. "Because I do, too."

We rock and clutch, his warm, protective hands roaming my back, my ass, my hair. He keeps varying the speed and rhythm of his thrusting so that just as I'm close, my body has to readjust.

"Stop teasing me," I eventually growl, feeling more animal than human.

His wicked chuckle confirms to me that he's doing it on purpose. "Are you going to be a good girl and come for me now?"

My insides are violin-string taut at this point. "Yes," I exhale. I couldn't hold myself back even if I wanted to.

"Perfect," he whispers, although it sounds so disjointed that I don't know if he meant to say it aloud or even knows that he did.

You are, I think.

Afterward, we cuddle facing each other, my face buried in his chest, his arms locked around my back, his chin on top of my head. Two limp, tangled, *happy* bodies.

"Did you know—" he starts.

"Oh, fun fact incoming," I mumble.

"You love my fun facts," Zwe huffs.

I smile into his warm skin. "I do. So tell me. Did I know what?"

He makes a big show of clearing his throat. "Did you know that scientists predict that in several billion years, the Milky Way and Andromeda galaxies will collide?"

"Oh, yeah?" I hope my snorting doesn't offend him, but it's such a subject 180 that I *have to* laugh.

"Yeah, NASA has simulated photos and everything of what it'll look like," he says, not bothered at all by my reaction. "It won't really matter to *us*, though, because humans will all be dead by then."

"Well, that's a . . . nice image." I slide back so I can look at his face, but his eyes remain closed. Still, I reach to brush away some hair that was flattened on his forehead. "This is some top-notch pillow talk."

His eyes open lazily, like he knows he can take his time opening them because I'm not going anywhere, and this is how it's going to be every night and morning from now on.

He rakes one hand into my hair at the crown. "Well, *I* think it's a nice image," he says with an eye roll. "Because this whole time, there's this tidal pull between the two galaxies. Like, *right now*. Right while we're having this conversation, the Milky Way and the Andromeda are moving closer and closer to each other, and at some point in the faraway future, they'll collide and warp into one another, merging into a singular new, bigger galaxy with this bright core that will dominate the night sky."

I consider this. "After billions of years of steadily being pulled together, huh?" He nods. "Are you saying *we're* two galaxies colliding after a billion-year wait?"

"I'm saying—" He returns his hand to the small of my back, the motion tightening his grip on me. I wonder if he's having the same fleeting moments of *What if I wake up and this is all a dream?* as me. "That there were times where it *did* feel like I had been in love with you for a billion years, and that it would be several billion more before I found the courage to tell you," he says.

I positively melt, and if I weren't certain before, I am now: I am a goner. It feels like my heart is going to drill its way out of me to lie at his feet. *Here you go,* it seems to want to say. *You have me. Do whatever the hell you want with me.*

"Well, I for one am glad it only took us two decades and not a billion years. Or even a million." I remember something. "I have to text Soraya."

Zwe gives a dubious laugh. "That's what you're thinking of right now? Soraya?"

"I never told you this, but Soraya's always thought we were going to end up together," I say. There's not a shred of surprise in his reaction. "You . . . knew?"

"The first night I met Soraya," he says, a blush creeping onto his cheeks. "She looked me in the eye and said, 'What are you doing? Get your shit together.'"

"No," I gasp. "What did you say?"

"I told her I didn't know what she was talking about, and she rolled her eyes, muttered, 'Why do men *insist* on standing in the way of their own happiness?' and walked off. To be honest, it . . . was a good question."

I shake my head, laughing. "I can't wait to see her again. She's going to flip when she finds out."

A shadow of concern falls over his face. "Do you think maybe we should not tell anyone for a while? What if we mess it up?" he asks. "What if a year from now, we hate each other and we're not speaking anymore?"

I smile. "Do you know what the most difficult part to write in a book is?"

"What?"

"The middle," I explain. "The start is where everything is new and shiny, and the ending is where it's all wrapped up in a neat bow. But the middle—that's the complicated bit. It's where the good things happen and the bad and where the characters have to figure themselves out. The middle is the messiest bit, but it's also the most fun bit. Because it's where everything *happens*. It's where your characters make mistakes and then they learn how to fix them, and they ultimately become better people for it. But they don't get to the end unless they get through the middle. That's the toughest part, both for the characters and for the author.

"All that is to say—" I raise a finger to let him know that I *do* have a point to make. "That's what's coming up now: the middle. And yeah, it's going to be real shitty sometimes and I'm *positive* we're going to fight and we'll accidentally hurt each other. But we're also going to have *so* many great moments that we're going to walk through our door every day and think—"

"*Look at this beautiful life we've built together?*" Zwe's eyes crinkle and shine at the corners.

Unable to stop myself, I go in for a long, delicious kiss. "Yes," I say after we pull apart. "I wish I could promise you a happy ending, but we won't know that the ending *is* happy until we get there, and we can't get there until we go through the middle. You don't get to achieve the big dream unless you're willing to fall flat on your face in the process. Trust me, I would know."

He plants a kiss on my forehead. "Okay, then. Let's get through the middle together."

"And we'll start with you applying for that PhD."

He stiffens, clears his throat like he's having trouble breathing on account of my having sucked all of the oxygen out of the room. "What are you talking about?" he asks as if he doesn't know precisely what I'm talking about.

"You answered that in your ideal future, you'd be doing a PhD," I say.

"I said that because I thought we were going to die—"

"Exactly!" I jab his chest. "People are the most honest when they think they're going to die. You say *exactly* what you mean because you figure there's nothing to lose."

"It's a pipe dream."

"No it's not, not even close," I tell him. "No more waiting to go after what you want. You're going to do your PhD, and you're going to leave accounting behind and become a teacher. Exactly like you want to."

He exhales a tired puff of air. "The bookstore—"

"Will be fine."

"How?" He begins chewing on his bottom lip. "What will my parents do if sales are slow? What if they can't afford to hire an accountant? How—"

"I'm buying the store."

That stuns him into silence. He surveys me for a long time, like he's waiting for me to take it back and say *Just kidding!* But I don't, because I wasn't. "Why?" he asks, drawing out the word.

"Because I love that place," I tell him, plain and simple. "Because your parents are going to retire soon, and I don't want it either getting shut down or being sold to someone who won't love it nearly as much as I do, or *you* feeling pressured to keep running it when you don't actually want to. It goes without saying that I'm not kicking them out. They can keep running things for as long as they want to, but I don't want them to feel like they have to do *everything*. We'll hire a new accountant, and a couple of part-time staff members who can help with the eventual transition. I'll work with an advisor and propose a fair number that makes sure Auntie and Uncle never have to worry, even during a bad sales month. That place took care of *me* when I was struggling; it would be my *honor* to be the new owner."

"I can't let you do that," Zwe says, but his tone has gotten soft. "My parents won't let you do that."

I dismiss this with a wave. "Please, your parents love me, they'll let me do basically anything I want." He smirks because he knows I'm right. "What Leila said before, it made me reconsider how I want to spend all of this money I now have. I know I deserve to treat myself every once in a while, but I also want to put it toward something . . . good. And selfishly, I can't think of a better way to spend a chunk of it than buying my favorite bookstore in the world. I mean, how many people get to do that?"

"You . . . haven't run this by my parents, have you?"

"Oh, of course not," I say. "I know who you get your stubborn genes from. I'm not going to Auntie and Uncle until I've got a solid, color-coded PowerPoint presentation—"

"A PowerPoint presentation?" Zwe asks, amusement tugging up one thick brow.

"Complete with graphics and charts, obviously."

"Obviously," he replies.

"It's always been our bookstore, our place," I say. "And this way, it always will be."

I don't realize I'm crying until he brushes a thumb across my cheek and I feel the wetness get smudged. "Hey, why are you crying?" he asks.

It sounds so cheesy to put into words.

Because I have everything I've ever wanted, finally.

Because I do. I have Zwe, and we have a home, and now I have (or am going to have, once I wear down Auntie and Uncle) *our* bookstore, and we have our health and our families and I just cannot imagine wanting or needing anything else.

"Just . . . thinking about all of those new releases I'm going to get my hands on in advance," I say with a sniffle.

His face wrinkles as he laughs. "Come here," he says, and pulls me into him. "I love you," he tells me.

"Love you more."

"Not possible." He plants a soft kiss in the middle of my forehead. "You've really thought this all through, haven't you?" I can see the hope building in the way his voice softens, in the new spring of tears in his eyes. It's as though he's thinking, *Do I really get all of this?*

"Nothing has felt more right," I tell him.

"I can't wait to go back to our safe and cozy home tomorrow."

"Me too," I say. And I know it's such a cliché, but when he kisses my cheek, I think, *Actually, I'm already home.*

"Hey, there's . . . something else. In the spirit of confessing things, can I tell you something?"

"What's that?" I murmur into his skin.

"Do you remember that huge fight we had about the sofa? Before we first moved in?"

I pull back, and Zwe's got a sheepish look. "Yeah." I frown. "I remember you were so mad about a stupid sofa."

"And *I* remember you were so annoyed that *I* was annoyed about wanting the expensive sofa and not the cheaper teal one that you picked out. And I made up some bullshit about it being a better investment, but the truth is, I got angry because you said—" He pauses to swallow. "You said that there was no point in buying the more expensive one, because *what will we do when one of us moves.* And I know it wasn't logical because you were with Vik and I was with Julia and we were both happy in our relationships, but the thought of sharing a home, of *building* a home with anyone else . . .

that's what set me off. I was pissed off that here we were, not even fully moved in yet, and you were already talking about moving in with someone else."

"You . . . That's why you were mad? I . . . thought you just really hated teal sofas," I say with a laugh.

"I do hate teal sofas. It makes me feel like I'm in a Barbie Dreamhouse."

"What's wrong with a Barbie Dreamhouse, you misogynist?" I shoot back. "What if *I* wanted our home to look like a Barbie Dreamhouse?"

He gives a heavy sigh. "Don't make me say it."

"I don't know what *it* is—" I tease. "But now you absolutely have to say it."

"If you wanted to live in a Barbie Dreamhouse, then I would live in our Barbie Dreamhouse with you. You're the only person I ever want to pick out a sofa with, teal or otherwise. And you're the only person I want to come home to, Barbie or otherwise."

My heart feels like it's going to collapse under the weight of all this love.

Another round of sex later, I'm drifting off but not fully asleep, and my eyes flutter open at a gentle tug around my neck. Zwe's lifted my necklace so he can trace the phrase on the front. "Sorry," he whispers, running the pendant between his thumb and forefinger. "I just . . . still love seeing this on you. I know it's wrong, but whenever you'd go on dates, a possessive part of me would think, *She's wearing the necklace. That means something.* That no matter where you went, no matter which new guy tried to woo you, a part of me was always connected to you."

"Zwe Aung Win doesn't get jealous," I murmur, dazed and sounding like I'm addressing a room.

I feel the breath of his low chuckle. "Zwe Aung Win does weird, unfathomable things when he's around you."

Sleepily, I reach up to hold the piece of gold between my own fingers, and Zwe laces his in between mine. I smile at the warmth, the familiarity, this sense of *blindfold me in a sea of people and I could still pick out your hands by touch alone.*

I trail a fingertip along every line and curve of the small letters. *Little by little.*

I tell him, "It's the truest thing I know."

All four of our parents had been waiting at Zwe's parents' place hours before our plane touched down in Yangon.

Zwe goes to put the key in the lock, but the door opens before he can even reach over.

"I am going to kill you!" Mom yells, crushing me to her. "I'm glad you're not dead because that means now I get to kill you."

We had had a serious debate over whether to tell them in advance over the phone or in person, but decided on the former before they could read the news.

"I'm okay," I say into my mother's chest. As I inhale her fragrance and melt into her hug, I'm a kid again, leaping over to her at the end of the school day and excited to tell her everything that happened.

"No, you're not, you're grounded."

I pull back and loop my arms around her neck. "You can't ground me, I don't live under your roof anymore."

"Like that'll stop us," Auntie Eindra says. She's got one arm around Zwe. "You're both grounded. And from now on, you have to share your location with us at all times."

"I—" Zwe starts.

"At. All. Times," Auntie says with a glare that means business.

"We love you, too," I say.

Mom and Auntie both give a *harrumph*.

"Okay, we agreed to give you both first hug but now you're just hogging them. Give us our children," Dad says and waves me over. He hugs me, Uncle Arkar hugs Zwe, they tell us they love us and that we're idiots and we tell them we know, on both counts.

They try to guilt-trip us into staying for dinner. "Mother! We've been traveling for over half a day! I don't feel human. I just want to go home and shower," I cry.

"Oh, so you nearly die and you can't even have dinner with your elderly mother?" She gives a dramatic tut.

"We will have dinner every night this week," I say, and plant a kiss on her cheek. "I promise."

On the taxi ride home, I slump sideways onto Zwe's shoulder. Despite the fact that he's exhausted, too, as evidenced by the bags under his eyes and his straggly voice, he remains upright and alert.

"Hey, do you think they know about us?" Zwe asks.

"Oh, absolutely," I say.

"Did you tell them?"

"No," I say. "But when have we ever been able to hide anything from them? I guarantee you they're gossiping about us right this minute."

That gets a tired chuckle out of him. "My mom is the happiest woman on the planet."

"No, she's not." I look up and strain my neck to kiss his jaw. "I am."

He rolls his eyes. "You are so corny."

"But you love me, corn and all."

He gives my thigh a squeeze. "And all."

The four flights of stairs up to ours have never felt more laborious. When we arrive on our floor and are standing in front of our door, butterflies appear in my stomach. I know this has always been our home, but now it's *really* our home. *Our* home.

Zwe goes in first, finagling both suitcases down the hallway. "I'll put yours in your room?" he calls out.

"Mm-hmm," I answer as I turn on the lights. I look around, feeling my heart glow brighter as I take in everything, from our fridge covered with an assortment of magnets, to the whiteboard by the front door, one half dedicated to groceries, the other to games of Hangman, to the framed snapshots of us at fifteen and eighteen and twenty-five and twenty-nine that are peppered on top of various cabinets and shelves. And then there are the little things that I can't see right now but whose mere existence adds to the warmth of this place—kitchen cupboards stocked with our favorite snacks, mismatched plates and glasses that we've accumulated over the years at assorted secondhand markets, the mixed scent of my shampoo and his cologne that's infused itself into our bathroom walls. All the things that, together, form the foundation of a home. Of our home.

I take a seat on our couch, my grin spreading now that I'm looking at this piece of furniture with new eyes as well.

"What?" Zwe asks when he emerges from putting his suitcase in his room. "Why do you have that goofy smile?"

"We're gonna have to fix that, you know."

"What? Did something break?" His head starts swiveling around, trying to locate the fault. "Is something wrong with the fridge? Is there a leak?"

"No, you doofus," I laugh. I pat the seat beside me for him to come join. As he warily sits down, I lift my chin down the hall where our rooms are. "I mean the two bedrooms situation. One of them is going to be *our* bedroom now."

A shy but irrepressible joy unravels across Zwe's features. "I like the sound of that," he says. He takes my hand and kisses the back of it, and already a warmth is spreading through my body. I'm going in to kiss him on the lips when he starts looking around the apartment again, as though taking a mental inventory stock. "Mmhmm," he murmurs occasionally, his head bobbing in a slight nod.

"What?" I ask.

"Oh, just—" He flashes me a wicked grin. "—making note of every spot in our home where I'm going to fuck you until we forget our names."

A laugh whisks out of me at that. "Are you just going to have dirty thoughts all the time now?"

"Hey, when you have a girlfriend this hot—" Without warning, he fully leans over, and I let out a small yelp as I'm forced onto my back.

"Yes?" I prompt.

But he doesn't answer. Instead, his eyes dip down my figure, down to the sliver of stomach where my shirt has rolled up. When they come back up and latch onto mine, he licks his lips like he's going to devour me, and I respond with a small whimper of need.

"I want to taste you," he says, one hand reaching down for the waistband of my sweatpants but not actually doing anything.

"Yes," I say. "Please," I add, to clarify the urgency of this moment, and he laughs as he removes my trousers.

I vaguely recall telling him on the flight that I feel disgusting and announcing dibs on the shower, but Zwe keeps touching, licking, kissing, stroking me, repeating "God, you are so sexy" again and again until I think it myself.

When we're done, we cuddle facing each other, him wrapping his arms around me, one of my legs thrown over his.

"We've never done this," I say. "Cuddled on this couch, I mean."

"No," he says. "I . . . wanted to, though."

"I did, too," I admit through a smile.

He alternates between playing lazily with my hair and my nipples, with the occasional ass squeeze thrown in. "So this is it, huh?" he asks. "You and me?" There seems to be a silent *Finally?* tucked on at the end.

"Yes." I kiss the tip of his nose. "This is it."

"Speaking of love, when do I get to read this romance novel of yours?" he asks.

"Eventually," I say. "Right now, I'm a little busy living out my own love story. And I gotta tell you, it's a real good one."

EPILOGUE

18 MONTHS LATER

"Ms. Poe! Mr. Zwe!" Instead of waiting for us to step onto the pier, Antonio takes the initiative of jumping into the boat, consequently rocking the whole thing and causing me and Zwe to fall back down onto the bench seats. "Oh my god, I'm sorry, are you okay? Leila will murder me if I've injured our guests of honor."

As he says it, I hear Leila's gasp, followed by "Antonio, you're literally a child!" She crouches down and waves into the boat. "I'm sorry, it's been like trying to rein in a toddler during the countdown to Christmas. *Are* you two okay?"

"We're good," I laugh as Antonio simultaneously takes me and Zwe in one arm each and gives us a tight squeeze. "We're happy to see you all, too."

"I'm sorry I couldn't pick you up at the airport," Antonio says. He throws a very unsubtle glance at Leila. "I was given *chores* to do."

"Chores?" Leila scoffs. "You mean your *job*? You're the grounds supervisor, Antonio. Your job is to supervise the grounds. How are you going to do that, on the day before our grand opening, might I add, if you're busy stuffing your face with ice cream at the airport? We still haven't finished decorating the reception walkway, or assembled the tent for the beach, or—"

In one whirl, Antonio's facing her, and grabs both of her shoulders. "Leils, I know you've taught me that it's not right to tell a woman to calm down so I'm not going to do that, but you need to breathe. We've talked about this. You're going to give yourself an aneurysm. You've gotta go smoke a joint or something. It's still not too late to add a shrooms section to the garden."

At that, Zwe and I snort. "Never change, kid," Zwe says, patting him on the back. "And it's okay that you couldn't pick us up. Leila's right, you're a big-shot supervisor now. Although—" He pulls back to scan Antonio up and down in an exaggerated manner. "Your boss lets his supervisors walk around in shorts and a tank top?"

"Thank you!" Leila throws up her hands while Antonio rolls his eyes, the two of them clearly having had this exact conversation before.

"It gets hot! I'm outside *supervising the grounds* all day!" Antonio argues. "Why are you complaining? I ditched the one I was wearing this morning because you asked. This is one of my good ones!"

"You want me to thank you for *not* wearing a tank top that says FREE KE$HA? With a dollar sign *S*?" Leila asks.

Antonio raises a fist. "You're welcome, thank you for noticing."

Leila gestures at him. "If *this* is what our management team looks like, what will the guests think?"

Straining his neck, he makes a show of peering behind me

and Zwe, and then around at the boat. "One problem with that argument—there are no guests!"

"The grand opening is tomorrow—"

"So I have until tomorrow to get dressed—"

"Would it kill you to be dressed today—"

"Do you want me to get up early and do my job or—"

Zwe's piercing finger whistle makes all three of us clamp our palms over our ears. "Okay, children!" he announces. "Antonio, no tank top and shorts tomorrow," he orders, and although the ends of his mouth droop, Antonio gives a small salute. "And Leila—" He turns to her with that small, amused smile, which is easily one of my top-five Zwe smiles. "The kid is right. You need to smoke a joint."

Antonio bursts into laughter. "Don't be a dick!" I say, smacking Zwe on the arm. "Remember you're talking to the new head of operations now. Forgive her for wanting to make sure tomorrow goes smoothly."

Leila puts her hands together in a grateful gesture. "Thank you, Poe. See, this is why I hate working with men." Darting a glance in Antonio's direction, she adds, "Boys, even."

We start heading for shore, and by the time we reach the end of the pier, Leila and Antonio have finished taking us through the plans for tomorrow night's party.

"By the way," I interrupt. "How's your new boss?"

"Why don't you ask him yourself?" Leila nods behind us.

Dressed in blue jeans and a slim-fit white shirt with the sleeves rolled up, six feet of "tall, dark, handsome" personified is jogging across the sand toward us.

"Poe! You made it!" Tyler Tun yells right as he envelops me in a hug. When we part, I must still have traces of an expression that reads *Oh my god, Tyler Tun smells amazing* lingering on my face because Zwe subtly rolls his eyes at me. "How was the journey? I know it's a bit of a hassle, to say the least, so thank you for coming."

"Are you kidding? Free first-class tickets to heaven on earth?" I throw back my head and, for the first time since I arrived, breathe in the air. It smells of coconuts and salt water and sand and cozy cold nights and sleepy warm afternoons. "We wouldn't have missed it for the world. Besides, that's one of the perks of being self-employed. We gave ourselves the time off." I know it's been over a year, but I still feel a giddy thrill at being a "we" in this sense. "This is my boyfriend, Zwe," I say, gesturing at Zwe.

"Nice to meet you." Tyler pushes his sunglasses up and extends his hand. "Poe talks about you all the time. You're doing a PhD in . . . I want to say math? Oxford, right?"

Zwe shakes his hand. "Yes. Well, statistics."

"How are you two liking England?"

"The weather is much nicer in Southeast Asia, obviously," I say through a grimace, and they return similar *Well, obviously* expressions. "But it's been a good change of scenery. I've been using 'writing retreat' as a general excuse to explore different parts of the country."

"Speaking of writing—" Tyler's face explodes into a grin. "Did you see the latest script? I think this might be it."

"I saw it arrived in my inbox yesterday," I say. "But we've made a deal to not do anything work-related while we're here, so I'll read it when we get home."

"I really need to take a few lessons from you regarding work boundaries. Do me a favor and please don't tell my wife how good you are at setting them," Tyler says. He looks up, squints, and pulls his sunglasses back down. "Shit, sorry, I just realized I've been making my guests stand in the sun while we talk. Are you okay walking back to the reception area, or should I call for a buggy?"

"Walking is fine," Zwe says, and I nod in agreement. "In fact, I'd say it's welcome after all of that time spent sitting on planes and boats."

"*Your guests,* huh?" I raise my brows at Tyler. "It sounds so natural coming from you. Who would've thought Tyler Tun would've pivoted from acting to hotel management?"

"Not me," he laughs. "Or my wife, for that matter. When I told Khin that this place was possibly up for sale at a ridiculously low price, the first thing she asked was if this was my midlife crisis."

"I would have had the exact same reaction," I admit.

"To be honest, who's to say it isn't?" Tyler shakes his head at himself. "I guess that's the problem with retiring early. I know, I know, champagne problems. But I was trying to figure out what the next chapter of my life would be, and the way you described this place, Poe, it's like . . . like . . ."

"Like I have a way with words?" I offer.

I love Zwe more than anything in the world, but when Tyler shoots me that movie-star grin, my knees go a little shaky and I know it's not just because of this heat. "That," he agrees. "And when I saw it for myself, I just couldn't leave it in the state it was in. To be honest, though, the staff was what sold me in the end." He throws that traffic-stopping grin over in Leila and Antonio's direction, and they both blush.

Staff members drop by the reception area while we're there, including Sandra and Antonio's grandfather. I can't believe how quickly Tyler managed to redo the whole place. It looks similar to what it was before, but also *not,* like a distant cousin of the original resort. The basic architecture is still standing, but all the expensive marble and fountains are gone. It's homier and cozier, like a giant mansion that was built not for show, but to house an equally giant family. The biggest new installment here is a massive mural of the island painted directly on the wall behind the row of reception desks.

"My aunt painted that," Leila says when she catches me staring at it.

"No way," I gasp. "Your aunt painted *that*?"

"Yeah, she's an artist. She used to teach art classes on the mainland," Leila says. "She really missed the island, though. When Tyler said he wanted to commission an artist to paint this wall, I knew she'd be the person for the job. In fact, he loved it so much that he commissioned her to paint individual pieces to be hung in each room. She got to move back home *and* make more than enough money to live comfortably through her paintings alone. They're even talking about maybe doing an exhibition with the pieces for sale so guests can take home a one-of-a-kind locally produced memento."

"That's so cool," I tell her, still mesmerized by the island on the wall. Various layers of paint and textures make up the land, the shades of brown and green getting darker in the mountains and hills to provide a striking contrast to the pastel, nearly translucent blues and greens on the shores. "It's gorgeous," I murmur.

"It's home," Leila says. I turn, and I swear I catch a light sheen in her eyes before she blinks it away. I'm not expecting it when she puts a hand on my shoulder. "Thank you for convincing Tyler to buy this place. He's been the *best* boss any of us could have hoped for. He kept paying all of our salaries even while everything was being renovated and none of us were actually here. I got to take a nice break and spend time with my family without worrying about my next paycheck."

I know I'm beaming. I'm so happy for her that I could burst. I look around, realizing that this is my first time back in this room since I almost, you know, *died* in it.

"I'm happy to be back. And that you're still here," I tell her. "How's the rest of your family? How do they feel about the new ownership?"

"They love it," Leila says, grinning like she's been waiting for me to ask. "Tyler's given them full access to the whole island. He's also even given my grandparents a job."

"A job? I thought they were retired."

"Retired and bored." Leila shakes her head in a *Don't get me started* manner, but her grin doesn't falter. "So now they're going to host cooking classes as a new resort activity. Guests can trek up to the village and learn how to cook traditional dishes using ingredients that are found on the island. It's entirely up to my grandparents how many classes they want to host and what they want to make, as long as they give us a few weeks' heads-up so we can inform the guests. My grandma was thrilled. She offered to do it for free because she loves to cook and talk anyway, but Tyler refused."

"I'm so happy for them," I say. "It sounds like your grandparents are actually excited about the resort now."

"I hope so," Tyler's voice comes from behind me. "They're our lead on-site project consultants. Have you guys tried Leila's grandma's rice salad? It's—" He makes a chef's kiss gesture with one hand.

"I was telling Leila that it's so cool you employed her grandparents," I say.

"Well, I want our guests to have a good time, and I realized, who better to ensure that than the people who know this island? Why would I hire some marketing firm to come up with a clichéd activities brochure for us when the people who know the most fun activities on the island are the ones who live here? Besides, I want good people on my team, and anyone that Leila vouches for—" He gives her a nod. "—is a good person in my book."

"You've hired other local staff?" I ask.

Tyler nods, then gestures at Leila. "One of Leila's uncles is a marine biologist, and lucky for us, he was thinking of moving back here."

"The only thing holding him back was a lack of income," Leila explains.

"Now he's designing tours that will introduce guests to the sea life around here without disrupting the local ecosystem. It's *amazing*," Tyler says, eyes widening with delight. Beside him, Leila beams with pride. "I can sign you up for one of the tours while you're here, if you want."

"That would be incredible," I say. Remembering something, "And the helipad?" I ask.

"Dead, deceased, good riddance," Leila confirms. "But they'd already done a bit of damage with the trees there so we're not quite sure what to do with it. Tyler's been having meetings with a group of local and external conservationists to figure out what the best plan is moving forward."

"You seem really happy," I say.

She nods. "I am. It's almost like . . ." She stops with a twinkle in her voice.

"Like what?" I ask.

"Like someone went and wrote us a perfect happy ending," she says on a wink.

"Got our key cards," Zwe's voice says, and I feel the weight of his palm on the small of my back. "What?" he asks when I turn to him with a massive smile that I *know* is bordering on cheesy.

"Nothing," I say. *I fell in love with you here,* I'm about to say, but that's not true.

Here is where I realized how *much* I loved him, and what I would be willing to sacrifice to keep him safe, to which the answer was *everything*. But I didn't fall in love with him here. I fell in love with him on the creaky paint-chipped swings in our school's playground, during late-night university application essay-writing sessions in our parents' living rooms, over chicken dan pauk that he prepared while I was working on my novels.

"What?" he repeats. He twists his lips, like he knows there's something teetering on mine.

"I love you," I say simply.

He cocks a suspicious brow. "Is that it?"

"What do you mean 'is that it'? That used to mean something," I say, rolling my eyes.

"That's where you're wrong, darling. It didn't mean something—" His face softens, and he plants a kiss on my forehead. "—it meant *everything*. Still does."

"Aaawww," Leila squeals, and stops herself by slapping her mouth with a hand. She shoots Tyler an apologetic look. "Sorry, boss. I'll be professional, I promise."

Tyler rolls his eyes. "It's fine. Remember, I'm a cool boss," he says, and Leila snorts. A staff member calls out Tyler's name from near the entrance, and he raises a finger at them. "Sorry, gotta run," he says, walking backward so he can still address us. "I'll see you all at dinner tonight!"

Once he's gone, Leila turns around, her mouth opening with a small *Oh* as she remembers something. "Poe, how's the new book going? Are we getting something soon?"

Zwe's touch, still around my waist, gives me the smallest squeeze. A *You okay?* squeeze.

And I am.

"Actually, this second one might take a while," I answer honestly. "Maybe the end of next year at the earliest. I'm trying not to rush it, though."

"Well, yeah, you've already got so much other stuff going on. I mean, moving *continents* alongside working on a whole-ass movie of your first book?" Leila purses her lips like there's nothing more she needs to add.

And she's right. I *am* doing so much.

When we had gotten settled back home, the next book I finished was, as I wanted it to be, a romance novel. It was a love story that was clearly written by an author who had recently and unashamedly fallen heels over head in love, one that screamed about the transcendent joy of meeting someone who sees and understands you in a way that makes you go, *Oh, so that was why it never worked out with anyone else*; it was *not*, as I wanted it to be, a hit with my agent or my editor. We went through two rounds of substantial edits before I made the call that we'd all been dancing around for months and shelved it. As predicted, there was a *lot* of crying and self-doubt and bouts of "What if I never publish another book? Who am I if I'm not a writer?" crises. For months, I couldn't stomach the thought of even opening a new Word document because every time, I'd think, *What is the point?*

Maybe I'm not cut out to be a romance writer, I told Zwe over dinner one day.

Maybe, he mused.

So you think I'm not a good romance writer? How dare you,

I replied, both surprised and offended at his response, although when he smirked, I knew I'd walked right into a trap.

My instinct, as always, was to dive headfirst into yet another new draft—except this time, I didn't. Instead, I told both my agent and editor that I was going to be taking a few months off (a decision that, despite my unfounded fears, they totally rallied behind), and I let myself enjoy the wonderful, privileged post-bestseller life that I'd worked so hard to achieve but had barely appreciated.

"Does it bother you that you're not a literary darling anymore?" Zwe asked one night as we were settling into the couch to watch the latest episode of *The Bear*.

"A little, but I'll deal with it," I said truthfully. I booped the tip of his nose. "As long as I'll always be *your* darling." And he rolled his eyes and told me I was cheesy, but he couldn't stop grinning for the rest of the day.

With my writing on pause, I went to cooking classes and hosted dinner parties at our place for our friends and for Zwe's cousins and parents, I read books for pleasure, we spent lazy rainy evenings cuddling outside on our balcony. I (finally) finished building the Taj Mahal Lego set, and started volunteering twice a week at an animal shelter (Zwe doesn't know it yet, but we're going to be adopting a dog within the next year; Soraya and I have already decided that it'll be named "Dazzle"). I baked Zwe a three-tier carrot cake with chai spice frosting when he got into his PhD program, and we had cake for breakfast for a consecutive week. I flew out to Bangkok and spent two device-free weeks with my parents, although I did sneak in a work event and acted as Pim Charoensuk's conversation partner for the launch of her gorgeous book, which had my blurb at the top of the cover.

Last summer, I carved out a three-week trip to the UK, and Soraya introduced her son to Cool Aunt Poe and I babysat him so she and Alex could have proper out-of-the-house date nights. As it worked out, mine and Zwe's place in Oxford is a three-minute walk from theirs now, and we have a double date night every Saturday. (The three of them will be arriving at the resort the day after tomorrow, their first foreign family holiday.)

About a month after we'd settled in Oxford, while I was flossing my teeth (of all things), I marched into our bedroom and told Zwe that I had a new idea for a book—another love story, about a woman who is eternally twenty-nine. Given that being one age forever doesn't exactly lend itself to long-term relationships, the woman applies her decades of wisdom to her job, which is counseling men who are in their late twenties/early thirties and need help figuring out how they can become better boyfriends and make the switch from dating around to committing to a life partner. When she starts falling for her newest client, however, she has no idea how to guide *herself* through the process. It's (tentatively) titled *The Agency of Open Hearts*.

Zwe, of course, was the first person to read a draft of the first five chapters. "Will they still end up together in the end?" he asked afterward.

"Of course they do," I said.

"How does that work, though?" he asked. We were in bed, propped up on our elbows, facing each other. He brushed some hair out of my face, and I turned and kissed his palm. "You know, since she stays twenty-nine forever."

"Because she realizes that she'd rather go through that eventual heartbreak than never find out what kind of life they'd have together. And they end up having the best, most beautiful life, and as she's holding his hand during his last breaths, they agree that they'd do it all over again," I said, and Zwe smiled, and it set off that warm feeling in my chest.

I'm nearly done with the very rough first draft, and I have a good feeling about this one.

Despite the unending queue of employees who keep coming up to her for approval or her opinion on one thing or another, Leila personally shows us to our room.

"Oh my god, you didn't!" I exclaim as we pull up outside the beachfront suite, the same one that I'd booked a year prior.

"You didn't fully get to enjoy it during your last stay," she says with a cheeky wink. "It's the best one in the whole resort."

After she leaves, I plop down on the bed. Zwe joins me, and we lie like that in silence for a while, holding hands.

"It's weird to be back, right?" he asks.

"Yes," I say. "But I love what they've done with the place."

He laughs. "I do, too."

"I love you," I say. I flip onto my stomach, leaning my chin on my elbow as I take him in. All this time, and I still feel like I can't look at him for too long or else I might get drunk on it all and do something stupid, like—"Marry me."

Zwe's eyelids flip open. "What?" he asks after a long silence, even though I know he heard me.

For a second, my stomach drops, and the urge to backtrack surges to the front of my brain. But I've been wanting to do this for nearly a year now, and nothing has ever felt more right, the kind of right that settles deep down in your bones, than the idea of spending the rest of our lives together.

"You're my best friend." I brush my thumb against his cheek, and he leans in to kiss my palm, and when that one tiny act still sends shivers down my spine, I know I don't want to take this back. "And to be honest, I've felt married to you for a long time, but I want to make it official. I want to get in front of a room of all of our friends and family and tell them just how much I love you and just how long I'll love you, which is with everything I have for the rest of my life. Zwe Aung Win, will you marry me?"

He doesn't try to blink away the tears in his eyes. His mouth pulls into a grin, opens—and a low, drawn-out "Fuuuck" comes out.

"Huh?" comes out of mine.

With a groan, he pulls himself up and leaves the bed. "I love you," he calls out, his back turned to me as he shuffles through our pile of bags. "But sometimes I also hate you."

"Uhhh—" I'm unsure what I want to say right now. What *do* you say when your proposal is met with a *Fuck*?

His figure is blocking me from seeing what he's doing in front of his backpack. "This"—I practically spring upright when he turns around—"was going to be a surprise for tonight. You literally couldn't wait, what"—he checks his watch—"eight hours?"

There's a maroon velvet ring box in his palm. He returns to me, only opening it when he's sitting down beside me again, and the second he does, the dam breaks and I burst into tears. "How long have you had that?" I ask.

"Since our second date," he answers.

"No, you didn't," I scoff, unbelieving.

But he gives a single thoughtful nod, and I know he has. "Got it the week we returned to Yangon from, well"—he chuckles, looking around at the room—"here. I figured that if I'm still getting regularly distracted by how hot you look even while I'm being chased down by armed women, getting tied up, and nearly dying in a fire, then you must be the woman for me."

My laugh comes out in a wet snort. "Thank you for calling me hot."

"Thank you for *being* hot." He lifts the box a couple of inches higher. I notice that his hand is shaking, and it makes this whole moment even sweeter. "It's always been you, Poe. You're the only person who's ever made me think that forever isn't nearly enough time. I want to be your cheerleader, your best friend, your first reader, your tea and coffee maker, your personal accountant, whatever you want, every day for the rest of our lives."

"That's a long time," I point out with a sniffle. "Will you still think I'm hot even when I'm, like, eighty?"

"When we're eighty—" He removes the ring from the box. "—you will be the hottest woman in that nursing home. And I'll wake up next to you every morning, and I'll think, *Look at this hot woman I get to call my wife.* Poe Myat Sabei, will *you* marry *me*?"

"Only if you agree to marry me," I say. "Remember, I asked you first."

He rolls his eyes. "Can you please put me out of my misery? Yes, I'll marry you. Of course I'll marry you. Who else would I ever want to marry?"

"Yes, of course, yes." My voice comes out in a straggly whisper, which is incongruous with the fireworks going off inside my chest. "There's nothing I want more than to be your hot wife in a nursing home."

We're both laughing as he slips the ring on my finger.

A perfect fit.

I take his face with both hands and kiss him then, knowing that no matter how hard I try, I will never write a story as utterly perfect as ours.

ACKNOWLEDGMENTS

This is my third time writing these, and I still get emotional over it. I hope I always will—I never take this for granted, and I never want to.

Hayley Steed signed me as a young, hungry writer when she herself was a young, hungry agent, and for that I am forever grateful. Hayley, thank you for always letting me try out something new and different; it is easy to stay creative and excited about writing when I have an agent who lets me write basically anything I want to write. Mina, thank you for organizing everything and for sending me exciting books to read ahead of publication and for all the other hundred ways that you keep things running. Thank you to the whole team at Janklow & Nesbit UK.

I once said that if I didn't have Alexa Allen-Batifoulier and Claire Cheek as my editors, I would be so jealous of anyone who did, and I wholeheartedly stand by it (thank you especially for yelling at me to include Only One Bed). Thank you, Saida Azizova, who stepped in and up and whose friendship was an unexpected but brilliant surprise in this book's journey. I am grateful to everyone at Renegade who gives their all to every single one of my books, especially Mia Oakley, Corinna Zifko, Stephanie Evans, Sasha Duszynska Lewis, Isabel Camara, Megan Schaffer, Kyla Dean, Dominic Smith, Sinead White, Georgina Cutler-Ross, Kerri Hood, Jess Harvey, Natasha Weninger-Kong, Meg Shepherd, Sara Mahon, Sasha Egonu, Amanda Jones, Rosie Stevens, Chris Vale, and Jonathan Gant. At St. Martin's Press, thank you Sara LaCotti, Marissa Sangiacomo, Lisa Davis, Chloe Nosan, Chrisinda Lynch, Anne Marie Tallberg, Olga Grlic, and everybody else who brought this book to life. Vi-An Nguyen and Debs Lim, thank you for the magical covers.

It was always easy for me to write a friends-to-lovers story, because I'm the kind of person who starts crying whenever I think too hard about how much I love my friends. Thank you for buying my books and sharing them with people and being my unofficial, unpaid publicists.

Three books in and my family remains my top cheerleaders. I love you, I love you, I love you.

KHS, I am so lucky that the coolest person I know is also my best friend. I hope you enjoyed your little cameo in this one.

Gus and Missy, you will never read this because you are dogs, but I love you two the most, forever, in every lifetime. I'm sorry I keep dragging you around the world, but thanks for always being down for a new adventure.

Corey, somehow nothing seems impossible once I hear you tell me that I've got this. Life's so fun with you.

And S, everything I wrote about how magical and perfect it is to hang out with your best friend on an island in the middle of nowhere is an ode to our love. It was easy to make Poe someone who bravely follows and accomplishes all of her dreams, because all I had to do was look at you. This book is one hundred and fifty percent for you. Trio 4ever <3.

ABOUT THE AUTHOR

Josh Sullivan

Pyae Moe Thet War is the author of the essay collection *You've Changed,* and the novel *I Did Something Bad*. She lives in London with her human partner and their two perfect dogs.